Having had her first book published earlier this year after successfully securing a contract, she decided she wanted to try her hand at another and see if she really did have a flair for it or she had just been lucky. Now with her second release on its way, she has decided this really is for her and is well on her way to hopefully her third.

To all my dog-loving female relatives and girlfriends. If love hasn't found its way to you yet, I hope it's on its way.

Angela Scholes

JUST AN ORDINARY DAY

AUSTIN MACAULEY PUBLISHERS™

LONDON · CAMBRIDGE · NEW YORK · SHARJAH

A CIP catalogue record for this title is available from the British Library.

ISBN 9781528928601 (Paperback)
ISBN 9781528965552 (ePub e-book)

www.austinmacauley.com

First Published (2019)
Austin Macauley Publishers Ltd
25 Canada Square
Canary Wharf
London
E14 5LQ

Only now, after getting a puppy Cockapoo, do I understand the love between a human and a dog. So, to you, Kim; I'm sure Harry was your third child, who on one occasion even dared to steal a can of bitter and get drunk on a visit to your parents' house. Also to you, Karen; when I first heard you talking about Archie, who I thought was an elderly relative, I found out he was your elderly rescue dog.

C1

"Okay, Ruby, you crazy dog, let's go." Having decided after the breakup between her and Matt the house felt a bit quiet and empty, Sarah had taken herself off to the local dogs' home, and instantly fallen in love with Ruby.

It was fate; after three years of living together, Matt had decided that actually he was too young still to settle down, and rather than drag it out, he should move out and get his own place, and literally the day he had told her, was the day he left – clearly a plan he already had in action. What a shame she hadn't seen it coming. The couple of weeks that had followed, Sarah had felt heartbroken; on her days off, sometimes not even bothering to shower or dress. She'd thought Matt was the one; that they were happy. She hadn't noticed until after he'd left that physically and emotionally he'd been leaving for some time, and when she'd finally stopped crying long enough to think about it, she couldn't remember the last time they'd had sex, and making love had stopped long before that. He had still made her laugh, but then so did her friends; and although at times they had still socialised together, it was because they had still been an item and jointly invited to places, not because they'd made plans of their own.

But it had still been a massive shock and so, after a good talking-to from her best friend Amanda, Sarah decided she was right: life wasn't over – it was just beginning, and she should move on, get out and have fun, and be grateful it had happened now and not in another three years. And so, she had gotten Ruby.

Ruby was a cocker poo, crazy as the day, was long and just what Sarah needed. She'd been bought as a puppy by an elderly gentleman who was still young at heart but unfortunately, although the mind was willing, the body was not so great, and Ruby had proved to be just too much for him. So, Ruby had ended up in the local dogs' home, with the assurance that a good home would be found for her. *And along came me*, thought Sarah. Single, sad, man-loathing, and needing a companion, or at least someone she could talk at who would at least appear to be listening and who wouldn't interrupt her.

And now, six months later, they were doing great except it was Monday morning and it was raining. Sarah felt tired having not slept well for no reason that she could think of and now was already running late, with Ruby still needing a walk before she left for work.

"Okay come on, we can do this quick walk before I go to work and I promise you I'll take you for the best walk ever later when I get home, even if it's still raining."

All wrapped up, hat, scarf and gloves, Ruby on her lead and finally picking up the keys, the rain had eased and was now just a light drizzle. But still, the sky was full, and the day was dark with no signs of actually getting any lighter. And it wouldn't now as it was nearly the end of October. Although it may change and become dry and frosty, it would still, for the next few weeks, continue to be those short, dark, tiring days. Hot pot, red wine, candles and a cuddly-dog-on-the-couch weather; what more could a girl ask for?

And so, they were off and with as many times as Sarah told Ruby not to pull, she still persisted, and Sarah was sure that one of these days she was going to end up on her back or wrapped around a lamppost.

Down the road and over the crossing, through the park gates and finally off the lead; Ruby just ran back and to, crazy and full of fun. Still only three years old, she had immense energy to burn. Sarah still had to admit She had been a fantastic tonic; on days when she could have still felt sorry for herself and had a pyjama day, it was certainly not an option now. "Well Ruby, we'll have ten minutes with the ball on the rope then that's it until later."

Work was only a short distance away, but the traffic was always heavy, and until the breakup Matt had dropped Sarah off each morning and then picked her up each evening; but now Sarah used the local bus service, which was fine, just a little more restricting – running a few minutes late would almost certainly mean missing the bus and the next one would most definitely make her late. So, mornings in general and especially now when she had Ruby seemed just a little more hectic. The rain had now eased, and it actually looked like it might brighten up, which would be good, as then although it would be dark and cold it would still make the walk later much more pleasant. *Oh no! NO! PLEASE NO! Not now... don't look over there*, "Ruby, Ruby, Ruuuby," too late, she had seen it. "Ruby come back, come back now!" But no, she was off. There's something completely senseless about a cockapoo – once they've got something in their heads, nothing is going to stop them. Yelling her head off for Ruby to stop and comeback, and running as fast as she could, Sarah could only think that when she did catch up with her, she was going to kill her. *Stupid dog chasing a crazy cat, that thought it would be clever to cross her path.* "OH, NO, NO, NOO, not the park gates, Ruby... STOP," but Ruby being Ruby, hadn't stopped. "Oh my god no, *NOOO!*" But yes, smack! Ruby had run straight into the path of an oncoming car and was now lying flat out in the middle of the road.

The traffic had ground to a halt, the brazen cat long gone, but poor Ruby wasn't moving. The driver now having jumped out of his car, and Sarah now somewhere in her distraught state could hear a voice yelling at her, "Jesus woman why haven't you got that mutt on a lead?" Sarah could feel her mind processing the ridiculous remark. Could he just not see what had happened? And then before she could stop herself, she was yelling right back at him.

"Excuse me, you arrogant sod, I would have thought with a flash car like that it would at least come with a brake pedal! No don't tell me that was an optional extra you never thought you'd need." Crouching down and trying to assess how badly hurt Ruby was, Sarah could feel the impact of the situation kick in and with that came the steady stream of tears starting to roll down her cheeks.

"Hey," said the voice, "look I'm really sorry. Let's lift her into my car and head off straight to the vet's."

It seemed the best and only plan. So gathering her up into his arms, he slid Ruby onto the back seat of his car.

"I'm Sam and again I'm sorry; tell me where your local vets are and let's get her there as soon as possible."

"Sarah," she'd said in return, "my name is Sarah and the vet's is about five minutes down the road from here."

And had given him the address, the tears had stopped, at least for now and although there were no visible signs of injury, poor Ruby was just lying there still and almost lifeless in his car.

"I need to phone work," said Sarah, thinking out loud.

"Have you got your mobile on you," came the voice from the driver's seat, "or do you need to use mine?"

"I have left it at home," replied Sarah, "I was only planning to be out for a short while. I didn't really think I would be needing it."

"Here," said Sam, "use mine. It's the least I can do."

A quick conversation putting them in the picture sorted that out with no added pressure which was a good thing as Sarah felt she had all she could handle going on at that moment. She had been with the company where she worked for many years, and was never known to be unreliable or sick, so all they had said was just how they were sorry to hear her news, and that they hoped Ruby would be okay. Telling her to take care and keep them posted.

The traffic was very heavy, and they were getting nowhere fast, so Sam, using his Bluetooth, rang ahead to the vet's giving them a brief description of what had happened. Now at least when they did get there, they would know and understand it was an emergency.

Finally, after what seemed like an endless journey they had arrived, and had both jumped out of the car. With Sam carefully scooping Ruby into his arms and carrying her inside, the receptionist recognised them straight away from the earlier telephone call and ushered them straight through into a treatment room assuring them a vet would be with them immediately.

C2

After the initial assessment they had been then asked to take a seat in the waiting room, and although only about twenty minutes had passed, it had felt like hours. Ruby had been the best thing that had happened to Sarah since Matt had left; in fact, Sarah was even happier now than when she and Matt had been together. Only realising recently how good she was feeling and how mundane life with Matt had become. Sam was sitting quietly next to her in the waiting room. Sarah had told him once they had arrived and managed to get Ruby into the treatment room, that there was no need for him to stay. But he was insistent that he wasn't going anywhere, and that until he knew how Ruby was, he wouldn't be of any use to anyone anywhere else anyway. "Okay and thank you," Sarah had found herself saying, "and I'm sorry your day has started with all this. We were playing with her ball on a rope to burn off some of her endless energy before I went to work, when she saw a cat. She's crazy about chasing cats and finds it so much more fun than fetching a ball and we were actually in the park but the cat ran, she ran, and then there was you and here we are now and I'm sure you did your best to stop and that you're not really an arrogant sod." Sam just sat quiet but was looking straight at her as if taking in every word she was saying, maybe struggling a bit at the speed she was babbling at him and until now Sarah hadn't even noticed what he looked like. The whole situation had been such a blur that she wondered if she would have even recognised him again if he'd have just driven off and left her to it. But now she was looking at him, and although still on the brink of tears and talking at him like a fast-flowing brook, she was also fully aware her heart had just missed a beat and that she was now staring.

14

Opening his mouth and about to speak, Sarah could see what kind and beautiful eyes he had – the darkest of blue looking almost navy, framed with thick lashes the colour of ebony – his hair although short, was probably due to be cut as it seemed to have a slight wave that would aim to be unruly.

But whatever Sam had been about to say was halted by the door of the treatment room opening, and John the vet, a middle-aged pleasant man, appearing in the doorway. Sarah had brought Ruby here for her check-up when she'd first gotten her from the dogs' home and it had been John who had attended to them then, saying what a fine and healthy dog she had been and hoped Sarah enjoyed spending many hours in the outdoors because he was more than sure Ruby would, and too right he'd been. She was full of life and exactly what Sarah had needed and she just couldn't imagine life without her now John gestured for them to step back inside the treatment room but as they stood up Sam held back, not really knowing where his place was in all of this. Although he had insisted on staying, he now was clearly unsure of what he should do next. "You've waited this long with me," Sarah found herself saying, "you might as well come in or I'll only have to tell you when I come out." And so, they both went into the treatment room while John told them the news of what he found.

"The good news is it appears there are no internal injuries to either head or body and the bad news is that Ruby has a hairline fracture to her front left leg. So I recommend that we keep her here for 24 hours just to be on the safe side." Once again, the tears started rolling down Sarah's cheeks.

"Oh, my poor Ruby," and suddenly she found herself being held close and comforted by the person who'd helped create the situation in the first place.

"I don't think when either of us got out of bed this morning we envisioned this coming," Sam was saying and then turning to John he began asking him that if Sarah wouldn't mind then could he also be kept in the picture and when Ruby was well enough to go home, could the bill be sent to him. Sarah was sure she was still in the room, yet the situation seemed to have been taken completely out of her hands. She didn't even know what Sam's second name was, let alone his job or position was, but he definitely had an air about him that clearly made those around him pay attention. "I will drive you home," Sam was saying, "Ruby is comfortable for the moment and you can call in a few hours." John reminding her that Sam was right that Ruby would be fine, said she had been sedated and that would give her time to get over the shock. He was sure the hairline fracture would heal with no long-term effects and keeping her there for the 24 hours was just precautionary and her leg would just need strapping to give it some support and stop her running for a few weeks.

"Okay," nodded Sarah looking at the two men who between them had clearly decided what was best. *I'm sure it's my dog and I'm supposed to be the one doing the talking,* she thought to herself, *but maybe Sam is right.*

C 3

Outside the vet's, Sam pressed the fob to his car and then proceeded to open the passenger door for Sarah. *Wow long time since that has happened to her* she thought getting into the car, and once inside the car himself, Sam turned to look at Sarah. "So," he said, "not really the way to get introduced to one another or start the day, but again I'm sorry. If you give me your address, I will drive you home. Is there somebody there that can stay with you?"

"I live alone but I will be fine. Thanks Sam, it has been good of you to spare the time. You were merely going about your day, till you bumped into us... literally."

"Sarah," he said with a smile, "but I don't like to think of you on your own after what has happened this morning. Will you take the rest of the day off?"

"Yes, just in case anything happens and I need to rush back."

"And you drive?"

"Yes, I drive but I don't have a car at the moment as I only work just a few miles away and I can get the bus or cycle, depending on the weather. A car seemed an unnecessary expense after the breakup of my relationship."

"Oh, I see," said Sam, "well, I need to go into the office for a couple of hours now, then I will come back and take you to lunch. It will break up your day and I feel it is the least I can do."

"It's fine, I'm fine," she started to protest, "don't worry, I'm sure you are a very busy man. I will call a friend if I feel the need."

"No Sarah please. It's ten-thirty now. I will come back at two, by then you should have had an update. Is that good with you?"

Within minutes they had arrived at Sarah's address and before she knew it, she was saying,

"Thank you, and Okay two o'clock it is." Then stepping out of his car, she lifted her hand in a small wave as she watched him drive off down the street. Standing there for a moment and just watching as his car started to disappear. It was a very nice five series BMW, and she hadn't, until that moment even known what she was traveling in, graphite grey with black leather interior. He couldn't have had it long because it still smelt of its newness and the leather smell still lingered inside. A man clearly doing well for himself and she couldn't help wondering how he really felt about the fact that a soggy wet mutt had been lying all over his back seat. Horrified, she could imagine, and a small smile crossed her face.

C4

By 2 pm Sarah had called work again and everything was fine with them, and she had also spoken to John at the veterinary surgery and Ruby was also fine, just as he had said: no long lasting damage, just a hairline fracture that would soon heal with no long lasting effects, just a bit of shock. He assured her again that Ruby was young, strong and full of life and soon this would all be behind her. So now Sarah was just waiting for Sam. She didn't really know why he was taking her out for lunch, only she suspected he was riddled with guilt for almost killing her dog, when out of the three of them he was the last to blame, it definitely wasn't his fault at all. *Well,* she thought, *you never can tell when you get up in a morning how a day will turn out and over the last few months there have definitely been a few of those.* Pacing up and down the lounge carpet one more time whilst looking for his car, she was sure she would soon be a making at track in it, it wasn't as if it had exactly been very plush to start with. *Suddenly she could hear herself having a conversation in her own head Oh my god, he's here, right well you knew he would come so why are you surprised? You've had a clothes crisis, checked yourself in the mirror twenty times, been peering out of the window for the last ten minutes and been for a final pee, actually you've probably been more times than your own dog does on an early morning walk. Okay, enough, stop, the poor guy probably just feels genuinely sorry for you. Nobody thought today was going to turn out like this. He was only trying to go to work and now just because you've actually taken a look at him and your heart has skipped a beat, your legs have gone to jelly, and your knickers are suddenly damp, which doesn't mean he is ever going to feel the same. He's probably going to take you to lunch and apologise again, give you his email address to forward the bill and save himself feeling any more guilt and hope tomorrow is a better day. So, get out, get a grip and just enjoy it for what it is.*

C5

After a very large deep breath and one more quick look in the mirror Sarah closed the front door behind her and went out to Sam's car. "Hello again, I'm glad you didn't change your mind," said Sam.

"Why would I have done that? And anyway, I didn't have your number," replied Sarah, feeling a little taken aback.

"Well in case that had been an option, I'm glad you didn't because it's good to see you again. Are you Okay with where I have chosen? Or if there is somewhere you would like to go; you only have to say."

"No, anywhere is good with me, Sam. I'm sure you're more in tune with where to go than I am."

"Okay," he said smiling, "that's good. But first, I'm sure you've phoned the vet's – how is Ruby?"

"John says she's absolutely fine and any time after lunch tomorrow she can come home. So that's good. I'll will go to work early so that I can finish early and go and collect her then."

"But you don't have a car."

"No but I can get a taxi; it will be fine."

"No, I will take you and we will collect her together."

"I'm grateful for your help Sam but trust me, truly I will be fine."

"You don't need to be grateful Sarah; you just need to tell me what time."

No wonder he drives a posh car, thought Sarah, *because he definitely must be a boss – born to lead, not born to follow. Do as I say, not as I do. No,* she thought, *I'm not going to get out of this lightly.*

"I'm normally a nine till five girl, so I'll do eight four and skip the lunch and finish at three."

"Great and your work's address is?"

"Will that be all you need Sam? Because I'm starting to think maybe you want my passport number or my national insurance number in case I change the plan?"

"I'm sure whatever his name was, has given you good reason to be cautious but believe me Sarah, I only have your best interests at heart."

There we go again just keep your eyes on the road, and don't look at me like you have no idea what you're causing to happen.

"Okay Sam if you insist and you're sure."

"I do, and I am," smiled Sam. "And a quiet country pub a few miles out is what I have chosen, I hope this is good with you. It's family-run and has a very welcoming, relaxing atmosphere."

Smiling back, Sarah simply replied, "I'm in your hands it seems Sam and my afternoon is yours. I'm happy you have invited me."

"And I'm happy you agreed to come."

What a lovely afternoon it had been, in fact lovely wasn't quite the right word to describe it. It had been wonderful from the minute she had gotten into the car. Sam had been the perfect gentlemen and the pub had been just as he said: very friendly, with a real fire burning which was warm and inviting on a miserable chilly day, and the food, homemade and simple, had been delicious but best of it all had been the company. Sarah couldn't remember the last time she had enjoyed herself so much. He was witty and charming and listened more than he talked. She simply couldn't remember thinking back when Matt had ever listened to her or certainly not in a very long time. His name was Sam Whitaker and he was thirty-two years old, not married and had no children. *How could this be possible*, she wondered. He lived on the opposite side of town not far from her, but in a much classier area. He owned a local accountancy business and had four siblings, of which the youngest still lived at home with their parents. When he had asked about her, she had told him her name was Sarah Forester, that she was twenty-seven and was an only child. Her mum had sadly passed away some years ago, leaving just Sarah and her dad, though now he had a lady friend and they did seem very happy and she was equally happy for him. There had been no doubt in her mind about the love he had and had shared with her mother they had been a team and like most couples had their arguments but had never stopped being in love with each other and so after the great sadness and loss of her mum, she was glad her dad had been lucky enough to have a second chance at happiness. Sarah worked as a PA at the local Mercedes car dealership which was a bit ironic really that she didn't actually own a car. Her car sharing with Matt had meant when he went, the car went with him and somehow getting another had seemed an unnecessary expense putting her under way too much financial pressure that she felt she could well live without. They chatted about food and drink, holidays, and how each other would spend their free time and by the time lunch was over, she felt like she had known him for years and not hours, and to add to it all there was no doubt about it that he was drop-dead gorgeous. He was quite tall, Sarah thought about maybe 5'10" with a body that obviously got a regular work out. There was just absolutely nothing you could not like or fancy about him. Remembering again earlier in the conversation he had said that he was single. *How could that be right?* She thought to herself. Those dark blue eyes drawing her in each and every time he spoke or looked at her, it was just a mystery. They had to be queuing at the door. Sarah herself was 5 ft. four, size eight, with naturally brown curly hair, though at times she did like to blow-dry it straight, but that wasn't often these days since she had gotten Ruby and became a dog-walking park girl. Blow-drying her hair had slipped off the agenda for most occasions. With quite large green eyes and full lips, she would have said her eyes were her best feature but who knows, she supposed, that depended on the looker. It was nearly 6 pm when Sam dropped Sarah back off at her house and after thanking him again he said that the pleasure had been equally his and he would see her the following day at 3 pm. *Something to look forward to even if it was for all the wrong reasons*, she thought once back inside the comfort of her own home. The trauma of the day should have left Sarah feeling exhausted, yet somehow, she felt restless and unable to settle. The house although to most other people would feel like a box, felt large and lonely without Ruby. There had been nobody to greet her when she came in the door and now in the quiet, she couldn't wait for tomorrow. Making some coffee and switching on the television, Sarah sat with her knees drawn up under her chin feeling a chill sweep over her. But the heating was on and the house was warm, when suddenly a wave of emotion came from nowhere, tears rolling down her cheeks, she sat and thought about her faithful four-legged friend who lay in the vet's surgery. For a few minutes Sarah stayed on the couch, legs drawn up with arms around herself, quietly sobbing and wondering if her poor Ruby was okay. Was she frightened or in pain? Yet the sensible side of her knew she was in safe hands and being well looked after, and if nothing changed, she would be home tomorrow with the trauma of today left behind her. She would be fine. Wiping away the tears with a handful of tissues from the box on the small side-table, it was going to be a long night. She supposed she could do a few jobs around the house as it would help pass the time but there wasn't really anything that needed to be done. Sarah kept it all very clean and tidy and living alone she found it easy. It had been Matt who had been the untidy one; leaving a trail from room to room, clothes, shoes, a glass here, and a mug there, it was actually something she had found she had missed after he had left, though goodness knows why, because it had done her head in at the time.

She could curl up on the couch with a book, she loved a lazy hour with a good book. It was definitely one of her favourite pastimes. But somehow, she just wasn't in the mood. Yes, it was definitely heading to be a long night. It had only been a week since the clocks had gone back and now almost bonfire night, the nights went dark so early, and the house seemed so quiet that when she did hear the occasional fire work go off, Sarah couldn't help but jump, and then again wonder how poor Ruby was coping without her. This was to be their first bonfire night together and although there had previously been the odd banger go off so far, Ruby had seemed fine and not in the least bit fazed, but there was no real way of knowing yet.

Sarah stayed sitting on the settee not really watching TV, not really doing or thinking anything mind a million miles away but nowhere in particular. She nearly shot off the couch when her mobile pinged with a message. *God no, not the vet's,* were Sarah's first thoughts, but it wasn't the vet's it was Sam.

'Are you alright Sarah? X'

'Yes, I'm fine thank you, finding the house a little quiet but I'm OK. X'

'Do you need me to come over? X'

'No,' replied Sarah 'I'm fine honestly, you've been great. I am going to have an early night, I'm sure I am tired anyway. X'

'Okay but if you change your mind, I can drive over to your place, after all I was the one who knocked your dog over. X'

'Thanks Sam but I'll be fine, you have been more than kind and generous over a matter that wasn't even your fault. X'

'OK Sarah, goodnight, but don't hesitate to call. X'

'Thank you, Sam, and if I need to, I will. X'

C6

The problem when you go to bed at nine is that you're awake at one, and then three, then five, and then finally you're knackered at seven, when you should already be up. Luckily with hair that stays curly, quick shower, and make up done, then grab a coffee and out the door. All done in no time at all, especially when you don't have to include an early morning walk into the routine, but how lonely it felt even in a rush without Ruby there.

Walking to the bus stop, Sarah at least couldn't help but think how much better the winter sun made everything look and feel, although it was the beginning of November. The sky was bright, the leaves had now mostly fallen, and a very heavy dew lay on the ground. The winter shrubbery was heavenly laden with berries, bright orange, red and yellow, a sign they would say from many an elderly person, of a hard winter to follow with nature preparing food for its wildlife. It was only twenty minutes or so to work by bus, and usually a great time to either just sit and listen to other commuters chatting or to be lost in her own thoughts, but today Sarah found herself unable to listen to the other commuters and was having far too many of her own thoughts. She couldn't wait to see Sam again, yes, she was desperate to see Ruby and to be assured she was well and ready to return home, but she really couldn't wait to see Sam either. The thought kept on going through her mind at the same time as she was telling herself that she was being ridiculous. *Think about it*, she was telling herself, *the man knocks over your dog, but it wasn't his fault, takes you out for lunch, out of guilt, and you cannot get him out of your mind. Yes, ridiculous because when Ruby comes home, he'll kiss your cheek, say goodbye, drive off down the road and put the whole blasted episode behind him. So wipe him from your mind as he is just being kind. That look wasn't for you; he just has beautiful eyes and he took you to lunch because firstly, he felt bad and secondly, he needed feeding himself. When he takes you to pick up Ruby, he'll pay the bill just like he said he would, take you both home, wish you both well, then get in his car, drive off and think he cannot wait till Friday and to get this week over with.* Suddenly, Sarah felt herself jerk forwards and realised in her daydreaming state that the bus was actually at her stop. Jumping up she made her way down the stair case and off the bus back into the cool sun filled winter air, laughing to herself as she did, *that will teach her day dreaming. It could have started the morning with a right disaster.* Once inside her office, Sarah found she was still mentally miles away from devising a plan in her head. Finally, she had it sorted or so she told herself, she would let him pick her up, take her for Ruby, and then take them home. She wouldn't let him pay the bill although she really couldn't afford it, but it wasn't his fault and he had already been very kind and generous. God this had all gotten very messy, but hopefully by tonight Ruby would be home safe and well, if not quite a hundred percent and Mr whatever his second name was, could drive away and move on.

The day flew by. There wasn't a minute to spare. Being off the day before meant playing catch-up all day long, particularly as it had been a Monday, the day which was spent mostly putting the weekend's work in order before a new week even began. So the weekend work and Monday needed sorting before Sarah could even begin to deal with Tuesday and before it all got any worse. Grabbing a quick coffee and a biscuit, Sarah heard her phone bleep from within a drawer of her desk. Usually she would have turned it to silent, but under the circumstances she had decided as it rarely went off in work time anyway, she would on this occasion leave the sound on. There was always the chance that John the vet would want to speak to her if the situation had changed and Ruby's condition altered. Grabbing open the drawer and pressing the phone to see the screen, Sarah saw it was a text from Sam:

'Hi Sarah, I'm hoping, as I haven't heard from you, all is good with Ruby, and that you to are OK? See you at 3 pm as planned, Sam x'

Why does the man who nearly killed my dog give me butterflies in my stomach? Surely this is not normal. Sarah thought whist busy quickly texting him back.

'Hi Sam, sorry I should have texted you, yes all is fine thanks again, and yes see you at 3 pm, Sarah. X'

Sarah had phoned the vet's first thing, and everything was as John had predicted: Ruby was fine, there had been no further issues with her, it was still just a hairline fracture and she had had a comfortable night. She would be ready to leave at 3 pm when they got there if nothing changed in the meantime, and that was highly unlikely. John had gone on to say as he had previously, she was a fit and healthy, young and energetic dog, who would undoubtedly recover with, no after-effects of the accident at all. So at least it had all not ended too badly after all.

The day continued to fly by and It was 3 pm before Sarah had even had time to think about it and gathering her things together two things crossed her mind: firstly, she was so excited to be getting Ruby back home, the last twenty-four hours had been awful without her; but secondly, she couldn't help but feel excited about seeing Sam again either.

She tried again to reason with herself that it was silly to have any feelings like this, that once he dropped her off at home that would be the end of it, he would be gone. But still she couldn't help this feeling of butterflies, anticipation and something that she knew she'd definitely never felt with Matt.

There he was, there outside the door in the parking bay, waiting for her, and she felt her heart miss a beat, a huge smile crossed her face and her legs turned to jelly.

Saying goodbye and taking a deep breath, Sarah headed out to Sam's car aware that he was watching her as she approached, but also glad to see he was smiling like he was genuinely glad to see her too. Opening the car's door and sliding into the seat, Sarah turned to face him, again to thank him for picking her up, telling him she really was grateful, and that it meant a lot. But the words were almost lost on her lips when she realised he was already studying her with a smile which reached his eyes, whilst replying, "No need to thank me Sarah, I've told you it's the least I can do."

Sam pulled out of the parking bay and headed off down the road towards the vet's. It would only take about ten minutes at this time of day and Sarah new that neither would it take long once they arrived there. And it didn't take long to get there, in fact Sarah almost felt disappointed that the journey had ended so soon. They'd chatted all the way there, and it had been an easy, comfortable chat. What a lovely day it was in comparison with the day before, how busy they had both been at work and how fast the day had flown, with Sam saying just before they pulled up that although he didn't really know her and Ruby, he was really glad Ruby was going to be alright and he was also very glad to see Sarah today too.

Once they'd pulled up and parked outside the vet's, both Sarah and Sam got out of the car, and just for a moment again Sam wondered was it his place to just be taking it for granted and heading towards the door with her, but the silent glance that passed between the two of them seemed to be an agreement that they would do this together. And so together they announced their arrival at reception and took a seat in the waiting room. It wasn't long before John the vet appeared and gestured for them to come into his treatment room. Once again Sam followed Sarah; no words spoken again, just part of their silent agreement.

Ruby wasn't in the room. John explained she was fine and that one of the veterinary nurses would bring her through as soon as he'd gone through a couple of things with them. In herself Ruby was fine and seemed to be showing no signs of any trauma from the accident, which was all good. Sam could feel his relief as he listened to John's words, it may not have been his fault, but he had sure as hell felt the guilty party in all of this. Her leg is strapped and will need to stay like that for some weeks to come, he continued to say and although she will appear that she was still bouncing with energy, there were to be no walks for two weeks, and then only walks on the lead for the month after. The idea was to control the speed and pressure she would be putting on the leg until it had a chance to heal fully. Ruby had been given two injections, an anti-inflammatory and a painkiller and they were told she may be just a little drowsy and not quite herself but that would also help stop her from getting over excited when she saw Sarah and was going home. John said he'd like to see her back again in two weeks just to check on how everything was going and that she remained well, and to ensure the leg was healing well already. Finally, they were told to go to reception and book the appointment while Ruby was brought through to them. Sam and Sarah couldn't thank John enough, it really did leave you to wonder who did Ruby belong to.

The appointment was made for their late-night. Sam insisting that way they could both go to work, and he could collect Sarah from work, then drive over to her house and collect Ruby. He also insisted as he had done all along that he was going to, and did pay the bill. And then out she came, leg strapped up, but other than that she looked like the happy dog she always was. Sarah rushed forward, the lump in her throat barely allowing her to swallow. And it was all the veterinary nurse could do to stop Ruby wanting to jump up; clearly both dog and owner were delighted to see each other. Both excited and relieved to be going home.

C7

The journey home didn't take long. Ruby sitting in the foot well between Sarah's legs was no longer the poor, shocked dog, who had lay lifeless on the back seat. In fact, just getting her to lie on the back seat itself now would have been a minor miracle. Sam was busy asking how she thought she would cope having to walk Ruby on her lead, being as even that was another two weeks away from no walking at all. Sarah laughed. "Well I suppose it remains to be seen. She can probably walk nearly as fast as she can run, so I guess I'll just get dragged from pillar to post," she joked.

"I think I should come with you for the first few weeks," he began saying and Sarah could feel herself staring, lost for words...

"Sam, stop this now, it was just an accident. You don't have to feel guilty for the rest of my dog's life," she smiled, "You can see that she is fine, and this is just a short-term thing, we wouldn't have been getting out as much now its winter anyway. I'm grateful for your help and you've been more than generous paying the vet's bill, you really don't need to do anymore."

"Okay, we'll see Sarah," was his reply, followed by, "when we get her home, I'll pop back out and get us a takeaway. I assume you've not stopped for any lunch, and I can't image you feel like cooking?"

"So, you're going to get us both a takeaway and we're having it together at my house?"

"That's what I was thinking; is that okay with you?"

"Erm, yes... why not."

"What's your favourite?"

"Chinese I think actually, Sam."

31

"Fine, that suits me, so which dish?"

"Not sure, I like a few."

"Okay then shall we have a bit of a mix? A few starters and maybe duck and pancakes and just share a main course?"

Sarah could feel herself struggling to speak. It wasn't that she was uncomfortable with the idea, it just sounded like a bizarre situation.

"It sounds like a great idea to me Sam, so I'm going to let you choose at least just this once," Sarah added jokingly.

With a heart-melting smile looking straight at her, Sam simply replied, "Thank you Sarah, I will remember that."

Pulling up outside what she would describe as her small, comfy, happy home, Sarah couldn't help wonder what Sam's house or place must be like. He was so immaculate. Today he had come straight from the office and was wearing the trousers to a dark navy suit, the jacket hanging in the back of the car, the over coat that he had slipped on to go inside the vet's lay on the back seat. A white shirt that, although it had been worn all day, still looked clean and fresh, a tie obviously discarded at **some** earlier hour and expensive looking leather tan coloured shoes which merely added to his very stylish finished look. This all seemed to excite her senses and kept playing games going endlessly around in her mind. There was something dangerous about being in the company of this man, and now she found herself wondering if his house was a reflection of himself: immaculate, very modern with all the latest gadgets; whilst she was eclectic with many bits and pieces she had purchased along the way from antique shops and various days out. Thinking about it now for a brief moment, Sarah thought what would he think when he saw her home; he'd probably look at it like it was tired and cluttered and she started to wonder if then she'd been a bit hasty in agreeing to share a takeaway and maybe she should of let him just go home.

"I'll come inside with you first for a short while if that's ok with you," Sam was saying bringing her back to the moment, "It's a bit early for the takeaway yet and I think we should make sure Ruby is settled first."

Ruby was undoubtedly eager to be home scrambling her way towards the front door, but the medication was making her a little unsteady. That and the strap on her leg making her hobble and wobble on the other three. And Once inside the door, she just seemed to head straight for her basket, climbed inside and lay there with doleful eyes. Grateful to be home, too tired to be bothered about anything else or why this new person on the scene was now in their house.

"Tea or coffee?"

"Tea please, Sarah, no sugar."

"Sweet enough?" she couldn't help herself saying it, rolling of her tongue before she could stop herself.

"Thanks," came the reply, "I'm glad you think so."

They both smiled at the simple banter, and Sarah went on to make the tea. The next half an hour passed with great ease. Sam complementing her on what a nice home she had and how relaxing it felt; admiring her taste in personal touches all around, giving it a feeling of love and comfort.

Sarah looked at Sam. She felt a little self-conscious at his complementary remark and asked, "Are you just being kind again Sam? I bet yours is modern and spacious with no clutter, clean lines like your posh car."

"It may well be Sarah, but that's due to the fact I've not yet met the right woman, and in my opinion, the finishing touches are usually best left to a good woman."

A small silence flared with Sarah desperate to ask, *So why haven't you; if your telling me your single I'm struggling to believe that one!*

But deciding that firstly, it was none of her business and secondly, maybe this was all getting a bit deep and although she would love to know, maybe just now wasn't the time. So, breaking the silence she simply said,

"You know Sam you don't have to have tea with me. I'm sure you're a busy man and you really have already done enough."

"No, I don't Sarah, but I want to, so I think it's about time I nipped out and picked that take away up."

Sam had been gone for about twenty-five minutes when he returned and in that time, Sarah had coaxed Ruby into eating a few pieces of chicken and drinking a little drop of water. She'd laid the table, cutlery, wine glasses, water glasses and a jug of water, salt and pepper, serviettes, and the plates were now warming in the microwave. Had she been on a date she would have gone around and lit endless candles but under the circumstances that seemed highly inappropriate. The last thing she wanted him to think was that she was actually making a hit on him, even if it was a very tempting idea.

And as it turned out, tea was delicious, and Sam's company was even better still but that was just how they seemed to get along, there were no awkward silences no difficult moments they just seemed to be at ease with each other almost like they had known each other for years not days, thought Sarah. And then with the meal finished and the evening rolling by, Sam had decided it had been time for him to leave. He'd been gone now for about twenty minutes and in that time all Sarah had managed to do was daydream about him. This, it occurred to her, was becoming a regular occurrence and not something she was sure was a good thing for her. After all it wasn't that long ago she was picking herself back up after the upset of Matt leaving her and, had she not told herself she wasn't interested in men for at least the time being. *So Sarah have a serious word with yourself,* she could hear the sensible voice in her head saying, *leave well alone you're doing just fine on your own, well you and your crazy dog that is and it will soon be back to just you two.* Maybe it was just the effects of the alcohol, Sam had drunk half a glass of wine, whilst Sarah had two large ones and although she felt a little tipsy, she had also felt it had relaxed her and for the first time in ages she had been able to be herself in male company. She hadn't socialised much at all since Matt had left, other than the odd half-hour for a coffee or an early tea with a girlfriend, but the majority of her time she spent at home with Ruby and that was where she felt most content, not yet feeling ready for wine bars and questionnaires potentially leading to a date. That was something at the moment, she felt she wasn't quite ready for yet.

Sam was now in his car and had started his journey home, and although he didn't live far and at this time of day with very little traffic on the road it wouldn't take very long at all, but it still gave him time to think about Sarah and the evening. He'd of course only had half a glass of wine being very much aware he was driving, and he couldn't help think it would have been nice to have had more relax and chat because realistically he already knew there was something more going on there something was definitely starting, he felt it every time she was anywhere near him and he had already gone out of his way to find ways to stay in her company. Smiling to himself he thought about Sarah he knew already he enjoyed her company, but after she'd drank two glasses of wine and babbled on about various things and talked to him as if she'd known him forever, he'd liked her even more and they'd laughed and joked throughout the whole meal. After they had finished eating and had a coffee, Sam had decided it was probably a good time to be leaving as it had by then been nine-thirty and a long day. That and the temptation to kiss her as he got ever more drawn in by her laughter and chatter was getting harder to resist with every passing minute. "I'll pick you up in the morning," he had said, "that way you can stay home with Ruby till the very last minute."

"No," had been the answer, "that won't be necessary, you have done enough, I am very grateful, but I will be fine. I can get my dad to pop round. I know I don't see him often but he will be happy to help. I'm sure should I need him too. He will check that Ruby's alright at lunch time for the first couple of days, but I'm sure she will be fine, she's used to being left all day."

"Then at least let me take you to the vet's in a fortnight, you did originally agree to that anyway when we were there."

"Okay Sam that would be great, I will be glad of that as it would have been a tedious bus ride or a taxi. So yes, thank you Sam, I'm still counting on you for that." And going over to Ruby's basket before he left, Sam knelt down and gave her a little tickle under her chin and stroked the top of her head. Ruby in return had wagged her tail and tried to lick his hand whilst her large, dark doleful eyes were again staring into his, "See you soon girl," he'd said, "take it easy."

At the door Sam had hovered.

"You alright?" Sarah found herself saying.

"I am," He had said in return, "I just wanted to say how I've really enjoyed the evening, though I'm sorry about how it came to happen." And with that he had bent his head, gently kissing her cheek, turned and left.

C8

It had been a long two weeks, or so it felt, thought Sarah. Long dreary days, lots of rain and going dark, before it actually ever seemed to get light. But more so because she actually couldn't wait to see Sam again. He had sent her the odd text message to see how Ruby was and to see if there was anything he could do, but Sarah had been adamant that things were fine and there was nothing to be done that wasn't already being done. She would have loved to be sharing his company and although she could have used Ruby as a great excuse, it would have been for all the wrong reasons and so it was best left. What all this had done though was make her realise now that the breakup between her and Matt had been for the best. But it had left her feeling vulnerable and she wasn't yet looking for a new man in her life. No, she was actually enjoying being herself and pleasing herself without any complications. And so, as the second week came to an end, she told herself if he does keep to his word and if he does take her and Ruby for her check-up, which would be a great help, then she must keep her head straight. He was doing her a favour and she was grateful and after that he would be gone. No need to ever call her again; she needed to stop thinking about him.

Sam had given up texting Sarah. He couldn't quite work out what her problem was. Did she just actually not really like him or was he overstepping the mark and taking control of a situation that wasn't his to control, even if he had created it? Either way, his head was mashed. What had started out as such a normal day those two weeks before had meant he'd nearly killed some woman's dog and now he couldn't get this woman out of his mind. And he'd thought from the moment she'd called him an arrogant sod, that they had a chemistry between them and then actually got on very well. Especially considering such difficult circumstances, definitely not the best way to meet, but aside from that the chemistry he'd felt he was sure she must also have felt was there. It was alive and very real, from sitting at the vet's, desperate for Ruby to be all right, to going out for lunch, and then sharing a takeaway, they'd got on great, chatted, laughed and had great conversations. So, what was her problem? Why was she so adamant and abrupt when he texted her to see if there was anything he could do? Well now he needed to check if she was still happy for him to take them back to the vet's for Ruby's check-up and he would see from there if her attitude was still the same. He could take a hint and would wish them well and say goodbye.

'Hi Sarah, just checking we're still good for me to take you and Ruby to the vet's tomorrow evening, Sam x.'

'Hi Sam, yes that is still good with us, thank you again, see you tomorrow as planned, Sarah x.'

Sarah stood in her lounge, phone in her hand re-reading her text, thinking well that was short and sweet. Whilst Sam stood in his office, phone in his hand thinking no changes there then. It was now the night before bonfire night, and again a Monday. The air was thick, and the smell of smoke was hanging in the dampness like a blanket waiting to cover everything. Sarah had lay on the couch, listening to the fireworks going off at the weekend. Saturday night had been particularly noisy, with still many more banging and lighting the sky on Sunday. Surprisingly, for a crazy dog, Ruby hadn't really bothered, which had been a great relief for Sarah, for the last thing she needed was a crazy three-legged dog bouncing all around the place out of control. That night Sarah just couldn't catch her sleep, and by the time morning came she could honestly say she couldn't remember the last time she'd slept so badly. In fact, she would go so far as to say she hadn't actually really slept at all. Her mind had been everywhere. She'd needed to be up and out early, she had wanted to look great or at least her best, but now with so little sleep, she was sure she would look a wreck. She was desperate for Ruby to be given the all clear, yet she knew she didn't want to say goodbye to Sam. Crazy, she knew, because actually she didn't really know a lot about him, other than the normal things like his name, his job, good looking… *mmm very good looking* was a better description and that he'd been both kind and considerate in a situation where he really needn't have bothered. She wished the circumstances could have been different and they'd met maybe in a bar and she could have got to know him better. On the other hand, she thought she was better off on her own, free to please herself, not have to worry about another person – just herself and Ruby, nobody to let her down, leave her feeling rejected and hurt, like she had been with Matt. Yes, get today over and get back to normal, stop thinking what if, and get on with what is she told herself.

C9

Sam picked up Sarah as arranged she had watched his car arrive and quickly gone out to greet him not wanting to keep him waiting or maybe more eager to see him then she was willing to let herself believe. She could smell his aftershave as she got into his car; the smile on his face as he said hello whilst looking at her making her heart skip a beat. He then drove them back to her house whilst they collected Ruby before carrying on to the vet's for her check-up. And just as John predicted, Ruby was doing just fine; her leg was healing nicely and from today she could go on short walks for the next few weeks, though she had to stay on her lead so as not to overdo it, that way ensuring no further damage would be done. Sam again insisted paying the vet's bill, also insisting when they were to return in five weeks for Ruby's final check-up that they should make an appointment the same as today for the after-office hours and he would bring them. Sarah tried to tell him that he had really done enough and that they would be fine, but again Sam would have none of it saying that until Ruby was given the all-clear from the accident, he would pay the bills and take them to the vet's himself. And as many times as Sarah tried to object without any success, she found she was quietly relieved inside that for the time being, at least, it wasn't goodbye.

"So," said Sam, as they got back into the car, the sound of his voice penetrated through her thoughts, "are you going to start with just one walk a day for a week or two and if so, will it be morning or evening?"

Sarah hadn't really thought that far ahead until now and felt herself drop into a ponder. "I'm not sure," she said, "maybe just once in the evening. Then I can see if it gives her any discomfort later on."

"Okay," said Sam, "I think that sounds like a good idea. So I will leave you to do your own thing in the morning, but I will pick you up each evening from work, as it will make it easier for you to get home and I will walk Ruby with you so that you're not alone and if she's pulling, I can hold the lead. We don't want any setbacks with her leg, or you dragged off your feet."

Sarah could feel her mouth drop wide open, yet not a single sound was coming out, which really was a minor miracle for her. Speechless!

"Good," said Sam smiling at her, "I'm liking the silence. I'm taking it you've nothing to say because we are in an agreement."

"Erm…" said Sarah starting to find her voice

"Too late," said Sam, "think we just got it sorted."

Sarah couldn't believe her ears. Her first thought was that she was delighted, her second, damn cheek of the man making decisions for her. And although she thought maybe she should argue, she also knew she really didn't want to, because she was happy with his suggestion and she doubted it would get her anywhere anyway. Sam had clearly made up his mind and he was sticking with it, so there it was for the next few weeks – she would have an evening dog-walking companion. *Well,* she thought, *don't get to giddy about it, after a couple of nights in the dark, wind and rain he may well and truly decide that she was more than capable, and driving straight home after a day's work was far more appealing.*

"You took that well," came the sound of Sam's voice breaking her thoughts yet again,

"Rather got the impression you were telling me, Sam rather than asking me, so there seemed no point in arguing about it."

"I was more putting what I thought was a good positive suggestion forward and hoping you were happy with it."

"Okay we'll give it a go. How can I refuse when you're more than happy going out of your way to help, but I think

41

this outing has been enough for today, so no need for a walk tonight."

"No, I quite agree, so from tomorrow I will pick you up from work and then we will take Ruby for a short walk."

"Okay good that sounds like a plan." Sam pulled the car up outside Sarah's house, got out, walked round the other side and opened the passenger the door, then put out his hand for Sarah to pass the lead, taking no chances of Ruby jumping out and doing a runner down the street. Just as Sam had predicted, Ruby did jump out of the car, and anyone watching would have had no idea that this dog had been in an accident only two weeks ago. She was full of energy and was bouncing around the pavement. *Fate,* thought Sam, not something he had ever really given any consideration to before, but there seemed no other explanation for the recent event and now he thought, four weeks to slowly get to know each other, interesting times ahead, he hoped, for he already knew there was something very much more about Sarah Forester that he wanted to get to know. Sarah now stepped out of the car and put her hand out to take the lead back from Sam.

"Thanks, Sam," she said as he placed it in her hand, "well then, I will see you tomorrow."

"You will Sarah, I'll be outside your work when you finish." Sarah could feel she was just staring at him. The whole situation just didn't seem real. Yet as crazy as it was, the upset had now turned into excitement and she was already looking forward to tomorrow. Sam made no attempt to follow her to the door, he just simply said, "Well if you're both okay, I will leave you here."

"No, that's great you go on your way," she replied, with maybe a little more excitement in her voice then she'd hoped to give away. *So,* she thought, *four weeks let's see how that goes,* as she opened the front door and she and Ruby went inside, listening as she did to the sound of Sam's car pull away from the curb and the sound of the engine fade into the distance. It was after all bonfire night and he probably had somewhere he needed to be, with someone he wanted to be with, and it definitely wasn't a dog-walking-night anyway.

No, she and Ruby needed to be inside. With the TV turned up loud and the noise of the fireworks masked far into the distance. Ruby settled into her basket as soon after they returned home. It was Sarah who couldn't settle. She couldn't help wondering where Sam was and more so, who he was with. How could someone she barely knew make such an impact on her? Finally deciding it was stupid, and the only thing for it was an early night. If she could catch her sleep at least the night would pass before her imagination started conjuring up crazy ideas again. PJs on, teeth cleaned, just about to climb into bed and ping, a message:

'Hi, is Ruby OK? X'

'Hello, yes Sam she is fine thank you and has been settled in her basket since just after we got home x'

Again, another ping

'Are you alright Sarah? X'

'Yes, just going to bed as the TV is a bit rubbish tonight x'

Again, another ping

'Have you got time for a quick coffee? I will be passing your house in a few minutes? X'

'Everything is fine Sam; you don't need to worry! X'

'I'm not worrying Sarah, I just wanted to see you. x'

Sarah felt her heart race almost like it might have burst right outside of her chest. Her sensible head said *say sorry I'm actually in bed*, but her wanton heart said,

'Okay, but you'll have to take me as you find me. x'

'That's great Sarah, see you in a few minutes. x'

Sarah couldn't believe that she had actually just sent that message but being as she had, she bounced off the bed and literally ran to the bathroom and grabbed her make-up, re-applying just a touch to her face, eyes and lips as she didn't want to look like she had just put it all on. Yet, neither did she want him to see her when she had just taken it all off. *She must be absolutely crazy*, she thought. She had just gotten down the stairs when the doorbell rang, and there he was, *I wonder if he ever looks anything other than perfect*, Sarah thought whilst opening the door wide and ushering him to come in out of the cold. "Don't tell me you were just driving down this way," said Sarah as she headed into the kitchen.

"No, well yes," said Sam, "I've come from my parent's house. They live sort of this side of town. They always have a gathering for bonfire night. It's their wedding anniversary, so they BBQ if possible and set off some fireworks, good family fun."

"So, Sam why aren't you still there now?" Sarah couldn't stop herself from asking,

"I couldn't get you out of my mind. Wondered how Ruby was. Her leg, the fireworks, I needed to know you were both okay."

"Oh," said Sarah, "well as you can see, we're absolutely fine." Ruby now noticing that they had a visitor as they came into the kitchen, began wagging her tail, clearly glad to see Sam again, whilst Sarah was eternally grateful that she didn't have a tail to wag for although she may have been keeping very calm on the outside, pretending her visitor had wasted his time, that wasn't by any means how she was feeling on the inside. "So," she said, "Ruby has been in her basket all night. I think that the medication John had gave her has done its job and has relaxed her enough as I don't think she has even noticed what's happening outside. Anyway, coffee, wasn't it?

"Please Sarah, with no s…"

"No sugars, I know, I remember, you're already sweet enough." she joked

Just then a big bang went off and Sarah nearly leapt into Sam's arms, it taking her completely unaware steadying herself, she carried on making the coffee laughing the moment off while thinking to herself, *well, maybe I wouldn't have been able to sleep after all.*

"So," teased Sarah, "tell me, you've been to see mummy and daddy for a bonfire?"

"I've been to one of our annual gatherings Sarah, as we are a close family and I am one of five children. Three siblings older than myself and with their own families, one younger and then of course myself, neither of us have children or are married, but the others are and having so, it can be quite a family event."

"How lucky you are," Sarah found herself saying, "and do you all live close enough to all attend these gatherings?"

Sam laughed out loud at his obvious interpretation of what Sarah imagined, saying, "Yes we do and most of the time we actually do all manage it. We make the effort because it can be the only times we actually do get to catch up with each other as we all have busy lives." Sam took a deep breath before continuing, "There's Megan, Michael, Stephen, myself and Olivia. Megan is the eldest as she is 37 years old and is married to Paul who is 39. They have 3 children: Harry 11, Jake 7 and Eva who is 3. Meg works part time as an estates agent and Paul is a bank manager; they have been married for 14 years. Then there is Michael, he is married to Liz who's a full-time mum to their two little treasures," laughed Sam, "Harriet 4 and James 2. They are actually a handful trust me, Michael and Liz are both 34 years old and I think have been married for about 8 years. Now Stephen and Sophie as I can remember because its only 3 years, are both 32 years old and they are expecting their first baby at Christmas and they are both school teachers. I too am 32 years old as I am Stephen's twin, although we are not identical. And then there's Olivia, who has now started dating Tom. As you know, I am an accountant, and Olivia is a nurse at the local hospital, where she met Tom who is a doctor; he's 29. And last but not least, my parents are both retired but fit and full of life. My dad was an engineer for a big chemical company and my mum was a language teacher. They have a good life, but family comes first. So, Sarah there you have it; everything I told you before and much more, so your turn now."

Sarah felt like she was held in a trance, or maybe under some form of hypnosis. She could feel Sam staring at her – looking straight into her eyes, her mouth felt dry and the words, not that she had a clue what she was about to say, had all but got lost somewhere, as Sam continued looking straight at her. "Well, my life's not like yours," she finally managed. "I told you I'm an only child. I'm not married, haven't been married and nor do I have any children. My mum passed away some years before and I love my dad; we are and will always be there for each other. He has a lady friend now and so they keep busy and he's happy." They both now fell quiet each taking in what the other had said, just watching each other The air between them now becoming thick, the silence surrounding them in the kitchen becoming very loud, when suddenly another extremely loud firework banged in the not so far away distance, bringing reality back into the kitchen.

"Have you got a jacket Sarah? Let's step outside and see what's going on." Ruby appears to be sleeping through the whole event which is such a blessing. Like a moth to the flame, Sarah grabbed her coat from under the stairs and the two of them stepped outside into the cool night air. Staring up into the sky where the dark winter night was brought to life with vibrant colours and explosions, the smell of smoke clinging to the damp air, they could hear voices in the distance and laughter; people enjoying the most of good times. Sarah shivered. She wasn't sure whether it was the cold air or the presence of Sam standing so close, and she didn't really want to try and guess which, because really the answer to that she already knew. She could smell his aftershave: heady, woody, spices drawing her senses, drawing her in as his arm came around her gently pulling her close to his side where she found herself leaning in towards him, inhaling his scent and being comforted by the warmth of his body; thoughts whizzing around in her head *why did this have to feel so good?* "It's been a tough few days and you were having an early night until I interrupted it, sorry Sarah I can tell you're tired, I shouldn't have disturbed you."

"It's fine, Sam; I'm glad you're here. Your thoughtfulness means a lot as it's not something I'm particularly used to. Not having a big family like yours, I'm used to just looking out for myself with the odd outburst from my friend Amanda, as she called earlier for a progress report. She has a new man in her life, so she's gone out to celebrate bonfire night somewhere tonight."

"So, what did she want a progress report on Sarah, Ruby or you and I?" Sarah couldn't help but laugh, really laugh out loud at the same time as blushing the same colour as a seasonal toffee apple. "She's just a crazy romantic," said Sarah, "she's always trying to set me up on a date. She didn't really have much time for Matt and when I got Ruby she said, 'Great now you can fill your days in the park instead of watching junk TV and maybe you'll find yourself a hunky single dog owner.' So not quite what she had in mind, though now she truly is like a dog with a bone," she laughed. "But don't worry Sam, it's Amanda with the vivid imagination, not me, so you're quite safe."

"Shame Sarah, I quite liked Amanda's big imagination." There it was again: another of those heart stopping moments leaving the air still and the tension high, neither wanting to say a word, not wanting to spoil the moment but what was the moment? Had he only called out of guilt, and had she only let him in because she felt it was rude not to? But no, she knew there was an underlying chemistry between the two of them and with every meeting it was getting stronger. "I should go," said Sam, breaking the silent tension, "I'm sure you'll be wanting to get to your bed."

"Only if you want to," Sarah found herself replying, whilst thinking at the same time, *did I really just say that*? But yes, she did but did she mean it? Yes, of course she did. There was something about him that made her want to laugh, cry, chat and want to throw her arms around him and never let go, and all at the same time. It was the most exciting, scariest feeling she'd ever felt in her life; but could he feel it? Did he feel the same? She didn't dare ask for the fear that he didn't, and her heart would most definitely fill with disappointment and may even be broken this time. This was absolutely crazy. In fact, this was ridiculous. She barely knew him. He was a temporary accessory to her life for him no them both having bad luck on a rainy Monday morning. Yet, crazy as it was, she could never wait to see him again, and if this was the hand of fate, she was now most definitely a believer.

"What about I say we go out on Saturday night, Sarah?"

"Wow that sounds good, what have you in mind?"

"How about we go somewhere nice where we can have dinner and enjoy each other's company?"

"I am liking that idea Sam thank you, Saturday it is."

"Okay, I'm going to head off home then on that thought and I will see you tomorrow after work."

"There really is no need. The bus stops right outside work and if there are many fireworks or the weather is bad, I won't be walking Ruby, she can manage in the garden till the weekend."

"I'll see you outside work tomorrow," he replied. "You can make your own mind up about the rest."

"Okay you win this time and thanks."

"Good night then Sarah, till tomorrow."

Sam hovered for a minute in the doorway. He really wanted to kiss her good night, but something told him to wait, don't rush her, something about her was telling him she was worth the wait.

C10

The rest of the week flew by. Sam picked Sarah up each evening, just as he said he would, but the weather was awful, so she decided Ruby could manage in the garden. It wasn't a big garden, but it wasn't a big house either. But for now, both suited her just fine. So, each night Sam just dropped her off outside and went on his way. He never hinted at going in for a coffee and she never asked him to, but they chatted constantly between her work and home, and it was as if they'd both decided to wait and see what Saturday night would bring. And so, finally it had arrived – Saturday night or almost. Sam had told her he would pick her up at 7 pm. The only question she had asked was how dressed up she needed to be. So, he'd told her he was taking her into town to the new gin and steak bar and with that she'd decided a little black dress and heels were in order. It was 6:45 pm and he would almost certainly be here within minutes now. Sarah couldn't remember the last time she had been so dressed up and taken so long to get ready to go anywhere. Now standing in front of the mirror she had to admit she felt good and was sure that actually she looked… pretty good too. Although it was only November, she had gone with the opinion that everyone was starting to get into party mode and a little sheer black shoestring-strapped shift dress was in order. Stockings, extremely high black stilettos and a black collarless biker jacket with her shimmering gold pashmina scarf, this adding just a little colour and glam to her other than that all black outfit and she may need the pashmina if it was a little chilly in the restaurant or bar, her look had been completed with smoky eyes, red lips and nails and she had decided to blow dry her hair as opposed to wearing its usual curly self. But after blow-drying, she had then curled the ends to give it a softer, more feminine look. She wore her favourite perfume, Armani Si, and finished the look with large dangly earrings and her Swarovski bracelet, bought for her by Amanda last Christmas. Purse, phone and lipstick in the black clutch bag; she was ready. Now all she had to deal with were the butterflies in her stomach, which she couldn't decide were the nerves, excitement or both, at the thought of a date with Sam.

Sam had toyed with the idea of collecting Sarah in a taxi but after some thought had decided no, he would drive. He wanted this date to go well. He didn't know why but he couldn't remember ever feeling so anxious about a date before. There was definitely something about her and he wanted to know more. He wanted to see her laugh, chat and really enjoy herself with only him as her company for the evening on a real date, not in a situation that had thrown them together. So, he had decided he must drive. He didn't want her thinking: *What now? What next?* When they both knew they lived in opposite directions to the restaurant, he didn't want her thinking he was taking her out and expecting to get in the same taxi home and stay the night with her. That wasn't what he was about. He was sure she was going to look stunning she already was in his eyes he'd already realised, so he himself had gone out and bought new black slim-fit Armani jeans and a silver-grey Ralph Lauren shirt that had a very delicate pattern in the fabric, and choosing to wear his overcoat for getting to and from the restaurant or Sarah's house. He did have to wonder: had he gone slightly overboard with the aftershave? But hoped not. That one last spray may have been enough to anaesthetise, not magnetise he'd thought afterwards, so he'd driven half of the way there with the window open, hoping to blow a bit of its strength away. *For god's sake, man* he was telling himself, *it's not like you haven't been on a date before, so get a grip. You're behaving like a teenage virgin that's been allowed up close to a beautiful woman.* But that was it. That's what he thought. She wasn't like anyone else he had ever dated. She had no idea how attractive and funny she was. That under her sheer independence he could see she was quite sensitive and probably a little fragile after her last relationship. No, there was something very special about Sarah and before he'd even arrived at her house to pick her up, Sam knew one date with her was never going to be enough.

C11

Having paced up and down in front of the lounge window for the last ten minutes, Sarah felt both relief and butterflies flow through her at the same time as she saw Sam's car draw up outside. *Ridiculous really*, she was telling herself, it wasn't really like a first date, they'd by now spent hours in each other's company and so far, it had all gone extremely well. But this was a date. He had asked to take her out. The other occasions they had spent time together were due to circumstances; this was a choice. He had asked to take her out on a proper date and without the slightest hesitation she had accepted because every day she looked forward to seeing him. *Dangerous* she thought, *you're supposed to be off men, even handsome ones with a good personality. Don't go falling for him. You have only just taken the plasters off your wounded heart.*

Sarah opened the front door to go out to Sam's car, but Sam was already standing there. Greeting her with, "For saying yes to tonight," and handed her a beautiful bunch of fresh flowers. Sarah could feel the colour rising in her cheeks. It had felt like such a long time since a date had arrived with flowers, and any other occasions had been accountable on one hand anyway. She couldn't help but smile a smile so wide he must have surely seen her heart miss a beat. Stepping back into the house, she placed the flowers into a few inches of water in the kitchen sink, assuring him she would put them in a vase as soon as she got home. Still unable to wipe the smile from her face again saying, "Thank you, Sam, they're beautiful."

"You're beautiful, Sarah and you look absolutely stunning." And before temptation became too much and with the desperate urge to kiss her getting stronger by the minute, he managed to say, "Okay, then, shall we go?" As opposed to taking her in his arms and kissing her with all the passion he could feel rising within him. Now almost at the restaurant, they were back to their easy chatter, again like they had known each other for years. Sam parked the car and they got out and headed the short distance towards the entrance of the restaurant where Sarah felt Sam put his hand on the small of her back as he opened the door for her to go in. It felt a cross between electricity and fire shooting through her, sparking each and every one of her nerve endings. Did he know what he had done to her? Did he possibly feel anything of this himself?

Greeted at the door they were shown to their table immediately, and then as in every other occasion in each other's company, the evening flowed with ease. The food was delicious they had both enjoyed both a starter and a main course and by the time they had gotten to dessert they were so relaxed and both unsure to whether or not either really wanted one they agreed to share, so ordering one chocolate caramel sundae and asking for two spoons which had sent them both off into fits of laughter joking they were now like a pair of teenagers although Sarah had a couple of glasses of wine, Sam stuck to his original decision, which was having one small glass of wine with his meal and then staying on water. The restaurant itself was extremely busy. Couples, families and friends also enjoying the good food washed down by many drinks and lots of chat and laughter in the warm, cosy ambience that filled the air; but they were actually lost in their own little world. The night had gone exactly how Sam had wanted it to. And it wouldn't have mattered if they had been the only people there, because they certainly hadn't needed anyone else's company anyway. The drive back to Sarah's house seemed to take no time at all and before she knew it, it was time to say goodnight. Sam had been the perfect date: polite, attentive, humorous, but most of all, charming. She'd wanted to pay half the bill, but Sam had said most definitely not, saying that he had asked her on a date and the bill was his. Hesitating slightly, Sarah was unsure of whether to invite Sam in for coffee. Half of her wanted to, and never wanted the night to end but the other half wasn't so sure. She already knew she was crazy about him, but she was also a little scared of the things she felt and didn't want it to end up in a situation that she would regret getting hurt. Something that happened too fast could end up before it really began. After all, who knew once Ruby was completely well again maybe he would just disappear off the scene and just how would she feel then?

Still unsure, she found herself saying, "I should go. Are you okay? Or would you like to come in for a coffee?"

"No, no I'm fine, thanks," Sam was saying, "but what I would like to do is come around tomorrow and we will take Ruby to the park together for a little walk whilst it's Sunday."

"Yes, that sounds good to me. What kind of time did you have in mind?" After a minute's thought Sam decided to say, "One pm, if that's good with you?"

"Thanks Sam that would be lovely and thank you again for tonight. I can't remember the last time I enjoyed myself so much."

"It was my pleasure Sarah, I feel exactly the same," and with that he lent forward and kissed her gently on her lips. But what started off as a gentle kiss, soon became a passionate embrace that seemed to go on forever. It only ended with the realisation that they both actually needed to draw breath.

"I think you better go Sarah, before I change my mind about that coffee."

Sarah almost wished he would, but neither pushed the conversation any further. So, after a short silence Sarah thanked him one last time, stepped out of the car and headed up the path and inside the house, thinking to herself *at least tomorrow is only hours away* because she could hardly wait to see him again.

C12

Sarah lay in her bed but sleep completely eluded her. Little did she knew that a few miles down the road it was the same for Sam.

The night played over and over in her head. So, at ease with each other and unlike Matt, Sam hadn't just talked, he'd listened. Really listened. She'd talked about her growing-up years and fun things she liked to do: ride a bike, strawberry picking, Christmas markets and long walks now with Ruby in mostly any weather. And as much as it was cosy to be by the fire in winter, curled on the settee watching a good girl film, it was great to be outside enjoying the fresh air and chatting with people. Sam it turned out had very similar interests, though maybe at different levels. He liked walks and bike riding and was in a good social circle of male friends who tried to meet up every month. He had, however said maybe a Christmas market together could be fun, and Sarah had to admit the very thought had filled her head and heart with hope that there was to be another date or even a few.

Sam felt like a restless spirit when he got home. The urge to have taken her up on going in for a coffee had taken all his will power to say no. Thank Christ that kiss had happened in the car. Standing up, she would have surely felt the strength of his erection pushing against the fabric of his jeans, and secondly, if he had gone in, who knows what would have followed or not. He had wanted to know so much more about her and even more so now, but he didn't want to rush it or her. He wanted to spend quality time getting to know her, getting to know each other and so if this was going to be the case he was sure he was going to be taking many a cold shower because whatever it was she had about her, he was sure it was definitely what he needed. Sarah had gone and checked on Ruby again, spending a few minutes fussing her. Then she went and got back into bed. Finally, in the quiet, the wine making her sleepy and at last she couldn't keep her eyes open any longer. Sam, on the other hand, unfortunately was still having no such luck.

C13

When morning finally came, Sarah woke up feeling like she had drunk two bottles instead of two glasses. Wasn't going on a date supposed to be fun and exciting? So why did she feel anxious? What was the problem? The problem she knew was herself. She wanted it to be casual, friendly, nothing serious. Yet she knew in her head it already wasn't. There wasn't a thing she disliked about him. Even Ruby wasn't holding a grudge and wagged her tail, genuinely always pleased to see him. Glancing at the clock on the bedroom wall she couldn't believe it was 10 am. How had she managed to sleep till that time? It was unheard of, and poor Ruby must be cross-legged by now, and Sam was coming at 1 pm! *Right get up, get in the shower. No let Ruby out first. Make some coffee then get in the shower. What if he's early and catches you looking like this? Stop!* She said to herself, *he won't be that early.* Her mind was everywhere but her body still hadn't gotten her out of bed. Not a great start to a plan. Downstairs Sarah opened the back door and let Ruby out. Poor dog must have been cross legged she was that desperate to get out even with her dodgy leg, but she was so good. The house felt cold. The central heating had come on as normal earlier and then had gone off as normal earlier as well, but Sarah, in her state of dreamland, had missed that and now she needed it back on before she caught her death, or at least before she started to shiver. Outside, a frost lay on the ground; shimmering on the pathway as if it had been sprinkled with fairy dust. The low winter sun bringing a little warmth to the cold and frosty air and adding a gloss finish to the white silvery surface that lay across the leaves of the winter shrubbery. And slowly as the sun began to work its magic, small drops of water were forming at the edges of the leaves one by one starting to fall like lonely teardrops. Oh, there was the robin, such a familiar sight in her little garden these days and such a joy to see. It was funny how these days the simplest of things could make her smile, after feeling, only months before, on the edge of despair. Sarah realised now it had all really worked out for the best, her and Matt would never had lasted forever, and she really did feel now ready to move on.

Sam had been up for hours. There really hadn't been any point in him staying in bed any longer. He wasn't sure he had been to sleep at all, though he supposed he must have dosed at some point. His mind was everywhere. But it all had to do with Kate. He thought of ringing her, but he changed his mind; he had composed a long text message but pressed delete. He thought of telling Sarah about Kate which should be the easy answer but then he thought if that would scare her off. Would she think that she needed to back off and let him and Kate decide if they still did really want each other? Even though he was sure they didn't. And what if it did scare her off after her own break up? No, he decided, he didn't want to take that risk; now was not the time to tell Sarah about Kate. And so, it went round and round in his head: phone Kate and put her in the picture; tell Sarah about Kate. Neither idea was boding well with him and now, by mid-morning, he had decided on absolutely nothing other than the fact that he had the headache from hell.

At 12.30 pm Sam got in his car and set off to Sarah's house. It wouldn't take long to get there, and he was sure the roads would be relatively quiet as it was a Sunday anyway. The frost had now disappeared, and the sun was shining – highlighting all the vibrant colours of autumn; giving the day a really good feeling – perfect for a walk in the park. He was wondering if he could dare ask her out for tea or if that would scare her off. Two nights on the run maybe would appear to be coming on a little too heavy, he would wait and play it by the ear. He decided to start off with the walk and see how the afternoon developed. The traffic was actually heavier than he had thought, which surprised him, but it was all flowing well.

The winter sun seemed to have encouraged people out to the shops or a visit to the garden centres, but in no time at all, may be just over the ten minutes, he was there outside Sarah's house. Pulling up, he couldn't help feeling a little nervous. *What is it about her?* he said to himself. Was it that he found her physically attractive or that he just wanted to chat to her all day long or was it maybe both? She had so much personality, something so many of his previous dates had been missing and after getting off to such a dodgy start, he didn't want to mess it up.

Sarah saw Sam's car pull up why wouldn't she, it seemed her new routine these days was pacing the lounge carpet whilst peering out of the window all whilst fighting of the butterflies summersaulting in her stomach, she grabbed her coat and scarf. It had been too warm in the house to have put them on already, even though she knew from previous occasions that it wasn't Sam's style to be late. She could feel the butterflies again in her stomach just like all the other previous occasions when they'd been together. she really needed to get them under control but There really was something about this man.

Ruby was definitely feeling it too as well as getting back to her usual self and realising that she was going for a walk, she was jumping up and down and dashing back and too to the front door. *Well that's a good sign* thought Sarah, *at least it wasn't hard to tell that she is definitely back to her old self. Just don't let her get too boisterous and start wanting to run free.* John the vet had said that only walks on the lead for the next few weeks. Sam was just about to knock on the door when Sarah opened it, complete with the maniac dog now on the lead and raring to go. He reached out his hand and took the lead from Sarah, so that she could get out of the front door and lock up. But the electricity that passed through them as their hands touched brought both of them to a still and their eyes were suddenly locked in each other's. It felt like it lasted forever, but in reality, was probably no more than seconds before both jumped back with Sam saying, "Okay, I've got the lead," and Sarah replying, "Great, I'll lock the door." It was a lovely afternoon. There was something about fresh air and sunshine that lifted people's spirits. And once they got going off down the street towards the park, they both realised there were many other dog walkers, all out enjoying the same; all saying hello and passing pleasantries, and to all who did, they must have looked like any ordinary, happy couple walking their dog.

Sam had kept hold of the lead. It seemed logical as Ruby did want to pull, the effects of the injury clearly long gone. So, Sarah quite happily just walked along next to Sam as they chatted away about simple stuff such as the weather, how nice it was to be out for a walk in the sunshine and of course how they had both enjoyed the evening before. After about an hour since they'd first left Sarah's house, she decided that it was long enough, and they should start heading back. Sam had to agree; Ruby definitely wasn't pulling anymore and to him it was a sign in itself that their walk had been long enough. They headed back towards the park gates and once through them started the short walk back down to Sarah's house. As the walk neared to the end, the conversation between the two of them just seemed to dry up and a little tension seemed to be building. Sarah wondered if Sam needed to be somewhere else and was getting eager to be on his way. Whilst Sam was working out whether he dare push his luck and ask her out for tea. When they finally reached Sarah's house the last few steps had felt like a mile, she turned and thanked him, "It was really good of you, Sam, to give up some of your Sunday to go for a walk with us. I'm sorry if we've stopped you or held you up from somewhere you need to be," she was saying.

"No Sarah you haven't. This is where I wanted to be and I'm actually sorry it couldn't have gone on for longer." Sarah could feel herself breaking into a smile and so Sam took that as his opening. "I actually was wondering; do you fancy a pub tea?"

Confidence coming from somewhere unknown, the voice from inside her suddenly said, "No. Actually Sam I don't. Thank you, I feel a bit bad for leaving Ruby for so long last night while there were still some fireworks going off and I

60

feel the same may happen again tonight. So no, sorry I'm not prepared to leave Ruby alone again tonight even if she doesn't seem too fazed by them."

Rambling on before he could get a word in, which she noticed at one point where he did try to open his mouth like he might actually try...

"I made a chicken casserole. It's big enough for two. But if you don't fancy it then I can have it over two nights, which is not a problem," she continued. Now Sam was the one who stood wearing the big smile and just simply replied, "Think you just got yourself a dinner date."

C14

The smell coming from inside the house, as they opened the front door, was delicious. Just what you would want to come into after a winter walk and Sam couldn't help feeling grateful for that awful Monday morning that had brought them together, even though he still felt terrible about poor Ruby. "Tea, coffee, wine?" Sarah was asking as she took off her boots, coat and scarf. "Really don't want to rush the casserole," she stammered, "another hour or so would be best if you're okay with the wait."

"My night is yours Sarah, but I'm driving so no wine."

"You could get a cab?"

Was she really suggesting that? A few glasses of wine? Mmmm... who knows what the night could bring? Were the following thoughts running through her mind?

"I could, actually. That's a good idea. But first, I'd have to know what you were planning to watch on TV."

"Pardon?" she replied in a slightly more irritated tone than she had actually meant.

"I'm just teasing you Sarah, because you told me you like comfort food, wine and junk TV on a winter's night when we were talking in the park."

"Oh right," said Sarah, slightly pink cheeked at the realisation that he'd been playing with her.

"And I thought you were both a grown up and a gentleman," she retaliated smiling. "Wouldn't that have meant you'd have suffered any of my choices for good company and good homemade food?" she teased back in return.

"Absolutely and I hope I prove to be both. So, I will take you up on that offer and suggestion, as I'm sure both will turn out to be excellent and waiting is not a problem. I will take a cab later. Your choice is my choice. Do your worst – let's have some fun."

"Red or white?"

"Red? I think, please."

"Okay, here we go. Two glasses and I will let you open and pour while I find us something delightful to watch." She smirked at him, because now she also wanted to play and somehow the banter that flowed between them was flirty and a little bit sexy, and both of them seemed to be finding this game great fun.

"There we go… *Pretty Woman*."

"We don't need to watch *Pretty Woman* Sarah, there's already one in the room."

Sarah could feel the heat rising in her cheeks again. In fact, this time it wasn't heat – it was like an inferno had started in her face. Was he making a pass at her? Or was she over exaggerating on what she thought was happening?

"Not your style?" she laughed. "Don't worry, I'm only teasing you. I'm sure there must be something here or on we both will like. Tell me your favourite and let's see," she said hoping he wasn't completely aware of what was happening to her. But as she stepped closer, she was more than aware that he too was feeling the heat. She could see it in his eyes; feel it in his presence that whatever was starting to go on between them was definitely getting bigger by the minute.

The space between them suddenly became non-existent. Sam had closed the gap in what felt like a single footstep placing his wine glass down on the side table. Sarah was sure she knew what was going to follow and all she could think was how she hoped she was right.

And she was. As soon as he'd done the same with her wine glass, he turned back to her, took her in his arms and kissed her with a passion that took her breath away. And all Sarah could do was wrap her arms around his neck and cling on to him, for the depth and the power of the kiss made her feel that if she didn't hold on, she would simply drop to the floor as she could feel her legs turning into jelly. Sam's lips gently left hers but only to trace down her neck. His arms remained tightly wrapped around her, one hand in her hair whilst the other seemed to have found its way under her blouse and was tracing its way up and down her spine with his fingertips. She could feel herself bending inwards towards him. She could hear her own breathing getting heavy and erratic but more so, she could feel his erection big and hard, pressing against her flat stomach, between the layers of each other's clothing. Suddenly reality was brought back into the room with the sound of a mobile phone ringing. Pulling apart, Sam reached into his pocket for his phone and Sarah smoothed down her hair and blouse. The ringing had stopped by the time Sam had gotten to it, but Sarah could see by the look on his face that whomever it had been, had most definitely ended their moment.

Looking up, whilst putting his phone back in his pocket, Sam said, "So pretty woman it is then. Let's give it a go."

He had actually said he liked it when it went off and was glad he had watched it as his mum and sisters had always raved about it. After the film had finished, Sarah put some part baked bread in the oven and minutes later they sat and had delicious chicken casserole, warm crusty bread and in her case, another glass of wine. But Sam, although had just finished his glass of wine, decided to go on water and despite making general chatty conversation, he had not been quite the same since whoever had tried to call him earlier. He hadn't said who it was but why should he? And Sarah hadn't asked, curious as she was; how could she? When the meal was over, he had offered to help wash up but Sarah had insisted that he was a guest and there was no need and it would take her no time at all later once he had gone So he had patted and stroked Ruby for a few minutes and then kissed Sarah on the cheek, thanked her again and left. Something had changed – whoever that was on the other end of the phone had completely changed their evening from having a couple of glasses of wine and ordering a cab, to drinking water and driving himself home. An uneasy feeling had formed itself in the pit of Sarah's stomach and she couldn't help thinking that if there was yet unspoken baggage in his background that unless he came clean about, she would soon need to step away. Her heart had only just mended, and she didn't want to end up feeling that way again or possibly even worse. The very thought was unthinkable.

Sam couldn't even be bothered with the radio on the short drive home. His head was full of mixed-up and jumbled-up emotions. His afternoon with Sarah had been great, and the evening would have been even better if his mobile hadn't interrupted the moment. It had been Kate. She must be back in the country; he had known that she was due soon but not the exact date. Somehow, he'd not gotten back to her for the final details, assuming she would be picked up and would go and spend time with her family first anyway. After all, they weren't actually an item anymore. She had just asked while she was back if they could meet, but she hadn't actually said why.

C15

By the time morning came Sam realised, after another poor night's sleep, that yet again he had another headache. God they were becoming a team. The no sleep bad head duo. They didn't seem to go anywhere without each other but that, of course, was his own fault and the way it was probably going to stay until he met up with Kate, laid the past to rest, and then told Sarah. Then he decided that he would ask her out properly, as his girlfriend. This was what he wanted, so it was time to get it sorted before another incident happened like the night before and it all went badly wrong. *Funny how things change,* he thought. He'd thought that he and Kate would last forever as they liked the same things; both were career minded; his family had liked her and vice versa, they had sailed along beautifully until Kate's new job opportunity. She'd become so much more ambitious and that was fine, as he had realised now: he liked his job, he had his own business and it was doing very well, but he was also a very family-oriented man. He supposed coming from a large family had been the reason for that. As siblings they may have had their fights growing up, but they were tiffs not real fights and were all now still close, all for one and one for all. So, the thought of moving for a high-flying job thousands of miles away had never entered his head. It would make it more than a little difficult to pop to Mum and Dad's on a Sunday morning for a fry-up and a chat.

But Kate had grown out of that feeling and had wanted to fly high; she had been doing extremely well for herself and he'd been very happy for her. But it had been deeply upsetting when she had first left; leaving him feeling very sad and lonely. But his family had been there for him. The very reason that had kept him there and was still the most important thing to him. So, he knew he'd always made the right choice; it had just been hard at first. And now, she was back. He'd not actually bothered to find out why or ask what were her reasons she was here having not yet actually spoken to her yet and somehow since he'd met Sarah, he didn't even find himself thinking about Kate anymore or who they used to be. His mind seemed to be constantly on only Sarah and the way he was starting to feel about her. Was it just a visit or was she staying? God, he could feel his headache getting worse. Maybe it was he should just have got a dog.

C16

Sam made his way into the office. Maybe as the day went on, he thought, his head might clear and if not then the fresh air later when they walked Ruby would surely do him some good that very thought of later made him realise that part of the day couldn't come soon enough he couldn't wait to see Sarah Sitting at his desk on his third coffee, Sam's phone vibrated whilst on silent lay on his desk top. Picking it up and looking at it he read:

'Hi Sam, Hope you're OK. Don't worry about picking me up tonight, Ruby seems a bit lethargic today, maybe it was a little much for her yesterday, so I won't be walking her tonight. Maybe see you tomorrow. Sarah x'

He felt gutted reading Sarah's text and he couldn't help wondering whether that was true or was she just avoiding him. He thought about texting her back saying, '*I will come and pick you up anyway, or let's have a takeaway; let's carry on where we left off, I know there is more to this.*' But instead, he simply wrote, "Okay Sarah if you're sure but ring or text me if anything changes or you change your mind. Sam x."

The day dragged on and on. His headache was becoming just a dull ache, but his mind was restless, and the worst of the day was, he had nothing to look forward to at the end of it.

When Sarah had arrived at work, she didn't know how she had felt really. Ruby was fine and if she was given the chance then she would have happily spent the afternoon in the park, but Sarah wasn't comfortable with the speed with which her feelings were building for Sam. And so, she had decided it was for the best to use Ruby as her excuse and to take a step back while there was also still that nagging feeling that had to do with his phone call. It could have been anyone about anything. She was probably just still a little insecure in herself. But somehow it continued to play on her mind. Taking off her coat and grabbing a quick coffee, Sarah sat at her desk, switched on her computer and started ploughing her way through her never-ending list of emails. She loved her job and had been there for quite some years. Now the PA to the managing director, she had started off just as a receptionist, what seemed like many moons ago. He was a nice man, Martin, middle aged, with a family growing up and a wife also with a good job; so he was a very on-the-go kind of a guy who also understood there was life outside of work. Yet, he expected nothing less than your best whilst you were there, which had really been a blessing when Sarah had needed little or no time to think, as thinking had only made her feel worse in the early days after the breakup with Matt. And as if channelling into her thoughts there came his voice:

"Good morning Sarah."

"Good morning Martin."

"Do you think you could spare me five minutes now for a quick word?"

"Of course, I will just get a pen and some paper."

"You won't need to make any notes Sarah, he said as it's not that kind of word." A little flutter of anxiety landed harshly in the pit of her stomach. Oh god… had she done something wrong? This would be all she needed right now.

"Have a seat," he said, as she followed him into his office, "And don't look so worried; you've done nothing wrong. It's just something that had been drawn to my attention."

Taking a seat and sitting opposite Martin, Sarah waited tentatively for what was about to come.

"It has been drawn to my attention over the last few days Sarah, that you have been run ragged through obviously the important accident with your dog… erm Ruby? How is Ruby anyway?"

"She is doing fine, thank you, Martin."

"Good, well I was wondering why we haven't sorted you out a company car? You are, after all, my PA. It would have little impact on your wages, and I'm sure, although I know you live not too far away, that it would make it much more convenient for you getting to the vet's, shopping and visiting etc. So, what do you say?"

Sarah sat there astounded. She wasn't sure what she thought he was going to say, but it definitely wasn't that.

"I've had one of that lads pop you an A-Class on the forecourt. Here's the key. Take a look; go for a drive. The decision is yours, but I think it would definitely make your life easier. I don't know why I hadn't thought about it earlier, well, actually I didn't – it was Marion. When I was telling her about your dog, she pointed out that you probably didn't have a car now that you and Matt weren't together, as you shared before. And you must be finding it all terribly hard work. You still haven't said a word Sarah, are you okay?" asked Martin

"Yes sorry, I'm fine. Thank you. I'm just shocked and relieved. I don't know what I thought you were going to say but this never entered my head. Thank you and Marion for thinking about me."

"You are a very valuable employee, Sarah. We need to look after you, as you look after us. So, go take a ride and let me know. It's up to you at the end of the day."

Sarah thanked Martin again and went outside to see the car. Paul, one of the salesmen, was standing by the car with the key. "Here you go lucky lady, seems she's all yours." Smiling back at Paul, Sarah took the key and got into the car. It felt very nice. In fact, it felt great and she couldn't control the smile that beamed all over her face. Life was definitely on the turn around and she was loving it. Having taken the silver sports edition around the block once or twice Sarah pulled back onto the forecourt and parked the car. She loved it, there was no doubt about it and so went inside to tell Martin.

"Good," he said, "I'm glad to have been able to help."

Back at her desk Sarah couldn't stop smiling. This weekend she would go visit her dad not that he lived that far away really or that she didn't already visit but she was just already filling her head with places to go and maybe she thought even a visit to the garden centre. The only negative was that now she wouldn't need Sam to take her to the vet's.

There would be no need for him to pick her up from work; not that there had been anyway, but he'd insisted, and she had to admit she had been more than happy for him to do that.

C17

A bit later on, sat at her desk Sarah decided that she should phone Sam and tell him about Martin, her boss, giving her a company car. She didn't want him thinking that she was ungrateful, and it would be good to hear his voice and have a chat. So, when lunchtime arrived, she took herself outside and decided to sit in the car. Then she could have a chat to Sam in private, bring him up to speed and just see what he had to say. Having a few deep breaths, she gathered herself together and finally managed to ring his phone. Only to hear disappointingly it rang straight through to his answering machine, and there was that feeling again, *who was he with*? She hadn't really been prepared for that she had been excited and apprehensive wanting first to tell him her good news yet not wanting to tell him because unless he wanted to and she knew she wanted to see him again from now on there was really no need and so she felt her heart sink, but after a moment's hesitation, managed to babble some form of garbled message.

"Hi, Sam, it's me… erm me being Sarah. I was hoping for a chat, but you must be busy. Sorry for disturbing you. Anyway… erm my boss today called me into his office and basically gave me a company car so as of today I have my own wheels. So, I just wanted to tell you, so you don't need to make your plans around me anymore and to thank you for all you have done. You have been great and also so supportive. Anyway, hope you're well. Take care."

Sarah finally pressed 'send' on her phone. She felt like she'd just babbled out her own version of war and peace and not even made a good job of it, but it was done. Not how or what she wanted, but he'd only been acting kind to her anyway because of Ruby, so best to let go now before it got messy. *We're on the up* she told herself. She needed laughter, not tears; to have fun not frustration; to be genuinely happy for a change. And with that, she went back inside to get on with the day.

Sam's morning had resulted in not a minute to himself – he had been out to see a client and had taken or dealt with endless phone calls. And now finally at 3 pm in the afternoon he had a minute to himself. He needed a sandwich and he needed five minutes of fresh air in peace. With that thought in mind, he decided on a quick trip to the local supermarket and maybe send Sarah a text and see how things were with her. That's when he saw her missed call and listened to her message. He remembered his phone vibrating now but wasn't able to take the call at the time and then had just been so busy that he had let it temporarily slip his mind. Now he was gutted. Company car – that was no good to him. How was that going to work in his favour? He had a good mind to go down there and see her boss and ask him what he was playing at. Tell him that everything was going along very nicely (apart from the rocky start) and now look what he had gone and done! Suddenly, the sandwich just didn't seem very appetising anymore. In fact, he wasn't sure if he was even hungry anymore. Well, he wasn't giving up. This was not the end and by 4 pm he had sent a text:

'Hi Sarah, great news about your car, you're obviously a very well thought of member of staff and your boss understands and appreciates you greatly. I wasn't working around you I was enjoying your company, so maybe now Miss Posh Wheels, you'd like to pick me up some time and I will pay for tea at where ever you choose to drive us, Sam x'

When Sarah's phone buzzed, and when she read the message, she could hardly believe it. She was so excited and relieved that he too must not want whatever was stating between them to end. What's more, she then had to make herself sit back and let what she deemed a reasonable length of time pass by before she replied to him not wanting to appear as eager, no she would play it cool even if that was proving near impossible. She was so excited. Finally, thirty-five minutes later she calmly or not so calmly for anyone who may have been able to actually see her gave in and sent a reply texting back:

'Sounds like a pretty good idea to me. Think you may be getting yourself a date. Sarah x'

Two minutes later:

'Not sure about the maybe Sarah. How you fixed Saturday?' X

Wow! No name just a kiss now laughed Sarah sat at her desk. He was seriously flirting with her, and she was seriously loving every minute of it.

'Saturday it is then. Are we doing lunch or going out to dinner? X'

Sam had to think about that. What he would really like to be doing with Sarah would hopefully come in time. So, he went for the option of lunch as he thought they could also maybe go for a drive out somewhere. And if they were lucky with the weather being good, it could be a lovely time of the year to wrap up and get out and about.

'Lunch I think and obviously depending on how Ruby is, I will leave it with you to where we go. Whatever we do suits me Sarah as it will be good to see you. X'

Sarah could hardly contain her excitement. She couldn't remember the last time ever feeling like this. She couldn't wait for Saturday. God why was it only Tuesday now? Where would they go? What would she wear? Should she get her hair done? Buy something new?

"Sarah… Sarah, are you alright?"

"Oh, Martin I'm sorry yes… yes, I'm fine thank you. Was there something I could help you with? I just slipped into my own little world for a minute. Sorry."

"I could see that, and it looked very much like you liked it there actually," laughed Martin. "So, I'm hoping things are looking good for you?"

"They are actually, thank you Martin."

"Good, now Sarah I'm going out this afternoon so if you could just deal with any calls and tell them that I will call them back tomorrow first thing. It's open day at the local college and Marion thinks we should both attend. You'd think being this is our 3rd child and we'd know the drill by now, but as she says, and rightly so, 'They are all equal but individual,' so here we go again."

"No problem, Martin. I hope you have a good afternoon."

"I'd say the same to you Sarah, but It looks like yours is already good," he chuckled.

And with that, he left the building. Sarah still felt ready to burst like a bubble, so she decided to send Amanda a quick text before she really needed to do at least a little work. Never had she been so distracted.

'Hope you're okay? Got a date with Sam on Saturday!! Love Sarah x.'

'Spill and spare nothing and yes I'm fine, love Amanda x.'

'Later, I must do some work or at least try. Sarah x.'

'Okay, but you don't get out of it that easy, I want it all, Amanda x.'

C18

Although at first it seemed like it would take forever to get to Saturday but before Sarah knew, it had arrived. Days full of excitement and anticipation had left her wondering where they should go. Should they take Ruby? What should she wear? And so, it went on. But it was the middle of November now – the days were short, and the sunshine limited; so opening up her options, she decided that until she got up on Saturday morning no plan was set in stone. But on Friday night, having finished work, and driven home, Sarah had taken a bath, put a ding dinner in the microwave and poured herself a glass of wine when she then, decided to send Sam a text as they hadn't exchanged any further messages since the original plan had been set. Both were maybe a little worried that the other might change their mind. And so, one more sleep and it would be here, *her date with Sam it felt almost as exciting as when she was a child waiting for Santa,* Sarah thought. And actually it was, in a grown-up crazy-about-the-guy kind of way.

'Hi Sam, hope you're still good for tomorrow, how about I pick you up at 11:30 am. The Christmas craft fair opens at The Hollies tomorrow, so thought maybe we could take Ruby for a walk round the forest, then you and I go to the craft fair then lunch, what do you think? If it's not for you, we can do something else. Don't feel pressured or if you have changed your mind and got something else planned, don't worry it's fine. Sarah x'

'Hello Sarah, that sounds great, looking forward to seeing you, 11:30 is perfect as are you. See you in the morning. Sam xx'

Sarah lay on the sofa reading yet again Sam's reply, "God, Ruby, can you believe it? I've got a date with Sexy Sam. But don't ever tell him I said that otherwise your treats will vanish forever even though I love you." Ruby also lay on the sofa and looked back at her, those beautiful doleful eyes no longer looking sad like after the accident; now more full of mischief as she was getting stronger by the day and although she still wasn't supposed to walk far. Given the chance, she'd to be off with the accident long forgotten; so at least on that part all seemed to have ended well and it had meant she had met Sam; something that other than for that terrible morning would not have happened. When Sarah woke up the next morning Sam had later sent one more text, still a little nervous that he may still want to change his mind she took a deep breath before reading it, but when she did it simply read,

'Think this will be a great help, see you in the morning, and yes it would, how can you pick somebody up if your head was so in the clouds you forgot to ask where they live.'

That was what Sarah had woken up to. Although when she'd first seen his name on her phone her heart had missed a beat in case he was cancelling, now she couldn't stop smiling. Now with both her and Ruby in the car the day had begun, and they were on their way to pick up Sam, it was as he had said, ten minutes in the car with not much traffic, they actually really didn't live that far apart at all. Pulling up outside, it seemed that Sam lived in an apartment in a very nice area on the outskirts of town. There was nothing wrong with the area she lived in and she loved her house, but this definitely had a desired postcode and she felt sure his apartment would match up to the same standards, if not maybe higher.

Having just picked up her phone to send him a text, Sarah realised there was no need to bother, as like on the occasions she had been waiting for him, he must have been watching out of the window, waiting. There he was coming towards the car, and she couldn't help feeling unbelievably lucky at the sight of him.

"Hello again," he said as he got into the car and threw his coat onto the back seat. "I'm glad to see you. And that Ruby was well enough to join us. Oh, and nice wheels."

"Hello again to you," replied Sarah, smiling at the way he made her feel. "Yes she seems perfectly fine, so it seemed a good opportunity to take her out somewhere different, even if she has to still stay on her lead, ready she said and pulled off clearly quite comfortable behind the wheel of her new car, whilst Sam relaxed back in the passenger seat very happy to be chauffeur driven by his beautiful date.

Twenty-five minutes later they pulled up on a car park. It was in fact the car park to the small national trust forest not that far away from where either of them lived. It had taken no time at all to get there. The journey had been an easy ride – not too much traffic and they'd chatted all the way. Now with their coats on, Sarah opened the back of the car, put Ruby's lead on and allowed her to jump out. Sam held out his hand to take the lead a now regular occurrence and Sarah handed it over to him. He was much stronger than her and it seemed far more sensible, but what wasn't a regular occurrence was that as she locked the car and turned to join them, he took her hand with his other free one, simply said, "Ready?" and absolutely took her breath away.

For a moment her mind was a fog and her legs like jelly. Gosh if he could make her feel like this on a cold November's day in a forest, what could he do to her in the bedroom?

"Sorry, Sam, say again? I missed what you said."

"I said it's great to be outside in the fresh air when you've been in an office all week."

"Oh yes, it is definitely," replied Sarah

"Are you alright?" came his next reply. "You look a little flushed."

"No, no I'm fine, thanks. I was just a little warm from being in the car," she said whilst thinking, *and now you're playing with me, coz you felt my hand tremble in yours and you saw my cheeks blush at your touch. It's like the first stages of foreplay with your clothes on*. They meandered the circular pathway of the forest now hand in hand, keeping the walk very simple which was posted to be 2 miles long, definitely enough distance for Ruby. Sarah had collected a bag full of pinecones along the way, saying she wanted to spray some silver, white and gold and add some seasonal fragrance and put them in a large dish on her dining room table, giving it a simple but Christmas feel. And now she comfortably slipped her hand back in and out of Sam's as if it were the norm.

Next stop was to be the Hollies, just a few minutes further down the road and they were soon there and parked again. This time, leaving Ruby in the car. She had water and the window was slightly open; and she was completely exhausted after her walk. Here there was a seasonal craft fair and it was all very busy; adults and children all enjoying the festive feel in the cool winter sun and before they knew it, Sam and Sarah had eaten chestnuts, bratwurst sausages, sampled stolen, and gingerbread men and washed them all down with a mulled wine and were now having a coffee. Sam had bought Sarah a chunky knit bob hat to keep her head warm for their winter walks he had said and a festive candle, for when she was watching her next Christmas movie, which he hoped would include him.

"I don't think I need any lunch now Sam, do you?"

"No, not at the moment. So what's your plans for the rest of the day?"

"I haven't really got any, as I didn't know how long we would be out. So, nothing."

"Me neither," said Sam, "so how about we watch some Christmas movies at your house and then either go out for tea or have a takeaway? I will get a cab home later, so we can share a bottle of wine."

It was a plan, a great plan she thought and soon put into action. In no time at all it had been decided that tea would be a takeaway. Sarah had wine in already and the film would be Home Alone – light and funny. *What a great day this was turning out to be,* both quietly thought as they made their way back to the car and started the journey back to Sarah's house. Somewhere during the film, having had a large glass of red each and after hours in the fresh air, both had fallen asleep on the sofa and when Sam stirred, he realised Sarah was snuggled against him and his arms were wrapped around her. Sensing his presence, Sarah opened her eyes to see Sam looking straight down at her. Not a word was spoken before his lips came down onto hers; an arm tightening around her; the other hand gently lifting her chin, drawing her ever-closer still. Sarah could feel herself drawn into the kiss; her arms moving without what seemed a single signal from her brain, reaching up as she shifted herself onto her knees and her arms slid around his neck. She wanted this kiss. She wanted to feel his touch. His arms were scooping her up closer to him. The kiss becoming deeper, the need becoming greater; on and on the kiss seemed to go, each drowning in each other, clinging to each other and wanting more. Sam's hands gently moving up Sarah's back and down again, gently pressing his fingers into the fabric, making it an unbearable barrier that came between them as he pulled her closer still into him. Finally, in a hoarse tone whispering in her ear, "Let me make love to you Sarah."

"Yes," was her reply.

And slipping her hand into his, she stood up from the sofa. Sam understanding exactly what she meant. Her hand still in his, guiding him towards the stairs. She wanted him more than she had ever wanted anything or anyone in her entire life. And with that, she also knew that she must relax and trust him. Once at the top and entering her bedroom she hesitated. "No lights," she whispered, suddenly a little shy and self-conscious of how her body might not live up to his expectations.

"I want to see you, Sarah. You are the most beautiful woman I have ever met. I want to see you, all of you; touch you; taste you. Don't hide from me. I want to see what turns you on. I want to see, as well as feel your body respond to min."

Sarah wasn't sure whether she felt better or worse for his openness, but she knew she wanted him, needed him and trusted him. So, reaching across she switched the bedside lamp on, lighting up the room but in a soft alluring light. Then she moved to the window to draw the curtain, but not fully, allowing the light from the full moon also to shine into the room. Now standing back in front of him, she simply stood, smiled and said, "Happy now? I'm yours."

Sam was more than happy and gathered Sarah into his arms, kissing her gently at first. His lips then traveling to the side of her neck, nipping at her ear lobe and sending uncontrollable shudders down her spine. She could feel her nipples peaking hard under the fabric of her top, wanting desperately to be free to the touch off his hands. Slowly, Sam did exactly what she wanted; almost like he was reading her mind or most definitely her body language. His hands slipping under the fabric, gently lifting it away from her body. Next, her bra; then her jeans, till all she was left in was a skimpy pair of delicately lace-edged briefs. God she was beautiful. And slipping out of his own clothes completely, he gently lowered Sarah onto the bed where now he lay down next to her… it was time to explore. He could sense her shyness as his eyes lingered over her body.

Bringing his attention back to her face he smiled then gently whispered, "I know already that I will never get tired of looking at you – you're so beautiful."

Smiling back at him, Sam felt Sarah relax in his arms and gently lean into him for a kiss. A gentle kiss so warm and reassuring that it soon turned into a flamed passion and need – both of them wanting to explore each other's bodies, both desperate to hold each other close. Never had a need been so deep or urgent for either of them. Gently touching the side of her cheek, thumb tracing its way down towards her neck he simply said, "I don't want to rush this Sarah. I want to be holding and touching you all night." Confidence returning, Sarah simply slipped her arms around Sam's neck and pulled him close, kissed him hard, full on the lips; letting him know she wanted the same.

It was well into the early hours before sleep finally came upon them. Sam had done exactly as he'd said – taken his time, until he couldn't wait any longer. He'd kissed and touched her. He'd made her climax again and again until she begged him to stop. How could this man make her feel this way? This good, how could she have felt so bold with him? Never before had she felt this confident in the bedroom. She herself had been eager to do all the same things to him. She had kissed and touched him all over; tasted him and it really was a question of who had enjoyed it the most. In the end he had dragged her back up saying if she didn't stop, the night would be over far too soon and then he had gone on to make love to her. She had clung to him like her life depended on it. Finally, they'd cum together in an explosion of complete and utter earth-shattering satisfaction.

Now as the hours had slipped away, curled up together in each other's arms, Sarah was aware of the dawn light coming through that same gap in the curtains as the night before now replacing the moon that had now itself gone to sleep. It looked like it was going to be a bright and sunny day; the sky blue, with any clouds sparse and riding high. Undoubtedly, it would be cold but that was fine with Sarah, she liked to just wrap up, get out and get on with it, that was one of the first things she had learnt about being a dog walker, good days were great, but as for the others, you just had to get on with it anyway.

First thing's first though: What would this morning bring? What would happen now? Next, she could feel her mind ticking into action. Should she sneak out of bed, fix her hair and make-up or should she stay, would he feel her move? As if sensing her awake and her mind going into overdrive, Sam moved closer to her under the sheets whilst at the same time saying, "Good morning. You're beautiful as you are, so don't dare think about going anywhere." Sarah felt the smile cross her face at about the same time Sam's lips found hers and before she even had time to think about it, he was making love to her again.

After lying in each other's arms for some time after, Sam finally spoke, "I'm getting up now and going home so I can take a shower and change. That will give you one hour to do the same. Then I will come back to pick you up to take you to my parent's house for breakfast. Then later we will walk Ruby together."

"No, Sam," Sarah started to protest. "I can't possibly turn up at your parent's house; and how do you know I haven't got plans anyway?"

"So, have you?" He asked.

"No," she said, "but I still can't come to your parent's house with you. It's Sunday morning and they don't know me at all, I can't just turn up with you like that."

"One hour Sarah, and I will be back."

True to his word, one hour later Sam was back, showered and wearing fresh clothes. He looked so handsome and the subtle smell of his aftershave woody and clean made it impossible for Sarah not to go straight into his arms for a desperately needed kiss.

"Good morning again, beautiful," came his greeting words and Sarah couldn't believe how lucky she was standing there simply dressed in jeans and wearing ankle boots and a soft knit pale pink jumper. Yet Sam had to pinch himself at how fantastic she looked – he was already crazy about her.

"Ready?" he said.

"No," she laughed, "but I guess that's not going to make any difference."

"No," replied Sam. "They're waiting for us. I've already phoned and invited us for breakfast."

"Sam, why? You could have gone and just seen me later. I would have been fine. I'm sure they don't really want a stranger turning up on a Sunday morning, and not even just turning up, but coming for breakfast."

"I go most Sundays, so it's normal."

"Oh, so you take a guest most Sundays then!?" Sarah asked, raising one of her eyebrows.

"No, of course not," he laughed, "but I want to take you. So please come with me and have breakfast at my parent's house. You do this for me and then I will do something for you. Anything." For a moment then, both were quiet. Sam waiting, hoping for the answer he wanted to hear, while Sarah smirked and quietly thought, *I'm going to keep boxed away in a corner of my mind for a rainy day.*

"Ok, if you really want me to come to your parents for breakfast, then I will," she finally replied.

Hell now she was nervous; she could feel her stomach churning, had she really just agreed to this, she might be crazy about Sam and have spent the most amazing night with him but she hadn't really known him very long, which wasn't helping either in this come-for-breakfast-meet-the-parents scenario. Sam on the other hand was not feeling those same emotions as Sarah was but sensing hers reached out and gently squeezed her hand.

"I'm really glad you're coming with me. They will love you Sarah, and I'm sure you will get along famously with them both." And so finally when she couldn't put it off any longer, she got her coat and off they went.

In fairness later, Sarah was clueless as to why she had been even the slightest bit worried. Audrey and Harry had been the most perfect hosts, welcoming her as if she had been a regular on a Sunday. Audrey had cooked a delicious full English breakfast and the four of them had sat around the table eating and chattering away about the week they'd all had, work and life in general. Three hours it seemed had passed when Sam finally said, "I think it's time we were getting going. It's after 1 pm and we still need to walk Ruby." *We still need to walk Ruby,* Sarah smiled to herself whilst rising from the table and offering to help Audrey wash up.

"No need for that Sarah," said Audrey. "Harry and I will have this done in no time."

"Well, thank you for breakfast. It has been lovely to meet you both."

"I hope it won't be too long before we see you again."

Everyone hugged each other goodbye and Sam and Sarah got in the car and started the short drive back.

"I'm so glad you talked me into coming with you," she said. "I really have had a lovely time."

"I'm so glad you did. So have I. So, let's go and walk Ruby."

The day was just disappearing so fast. They had woken early but had stayed in bed, making love; they just couldn't

84

get enough of each other. He had gone home but come back to pick her up at 10 am and now it was already past one in the afternoon. She couldn't remember the last time she had felt so happy. By the time they got to the park it was cold and although it had been a bright and sunny start, the clouds were now gathering, and it felt like rain could be in the air. They walked hand in hand whilst Sam yet again had hold of Ruby's lead. It was all starting to feel like the most natural thing in the world.

"How about we head back?" Sam was suddenly saying. "I think it may pour down soon."

"I think that may well be a good idea."

Then he said, "We could have a coffee and watch a film and then go out for an early tea. What do you say?"

"Sam I would love to go out with you but not tonight; I'm so tired. I can do coffee and watch a film. Then you're welcome to stay for a stir fry, but I can't get ready and go out. You've worn me out and not that I'm in the slightest way complaining, but I would just end up falling asleep with my head in my dinner."

Sam couldn't help but laugh at Sarah. She was both beautiful and funny, and apart from still feeling guilty at times over Ruby, he was so glad they had met.

"Well, OK. If that's good with you, that's good with me." So they had done just that: headed on back to Sarah's before the weather had time to change, had a coffee, and watched a film curled up on the sofa, later having tea, which Sam helped to prepare which had worked well and felt good; the two of them working together laughing and joking preparing and sharing their evening meal. Some hours later Sam then left for home at about 8 pm as it was, after all, work for the both of them the next day and he knew he had a very busy week ahead of him. And now Sarah had a car she was independent, so unless he asked to see her now, he had no excuse. So before he had left, he had simply asked if she was free on Wednesday night because he really wanted this to continue. So did she and the answer was yes.

Sarah slept like a baby that night having taken a glass of wine up whilst she had a bath. She'd been in bed by 10 pm and was sure had been asleep by five past ten, although her bed just didn't feel the same tonight she'd thought; she already knew she was missing Sam lying next to her.

The following day, work was busy and apart from one early morning text, that simply said 'Good morning, have a good day', her phone had remained quiet, she had text him back saying the same and had felt like texting him many times during the day but had decided against it as she needed to keep her feet on the ground, not end up in a mess like last time.

When Sarah got home that night, she took Ruby out for a short walk. It was a very damp night and even Ruby didn't seem keen to stay out or maybe she also was missing the extra company. Back home she popped a ready-made meal into the microwave and decided to send Sam a text message:

'Hello are you OK? How's your day been? X'

'Long and tiring,' came back the reply, 'Are you making coffee? X'

'You coming around? X'

'If you're making coffee? X'

'I'm making coffee x'

'I'm on my way x'

Some hours later whilst lying in Sarah's bed, Sam joked that he still hadn't had his coffee and no he hadn't. From the minute he pulled up and she'd opened the door, they hadn't been able to keep their hands off one another. And so, they had only made it from the front door to the bedroom. The lighting hadn't even been talked about this time. Both were hungry to undress one another, both wanting to please; it just seemed natural to want to touch and taste, hands caressing each other's bodies; lips that just couldn't tire of the need of endless kisses.

Slipping out of the bed, Sam felt Sarah reach out for him and leant back in to gently kiss her on the cheek as he whispered, "I must go. It's 6 am and I need to be in work by 8. I will call you later, beautiful."

Smiling and peering through half opened eyes, Sarah gently reached up to kiss him back and replied with a simple, "Okay."

True to his word, Sam called her later on that day and every day that followed. Along with dog walking, dates and nights in, all became things they did together, the weeks now slipped on by and they were well into the December. They didn't see each other every night but it was definitely becoming more they did than less they didn't. On the nights, they did see each other. Sam nearly always stayed over either leaving very early the next morning or now having spare stuff at Sarah's, that then allowing him to shower there and then head straight to the office. Sarah had now been to Sam's apartment but had never stayed over. It wasn't something that had actually seriously been talked about, it just wasn't practical. It was a beautiful place, but a little sparse and manly for Sarah. She was really the kind of girl who loved cushions, throws and candles whilst Sam's place was very minimalistic but that could just be lacking a woman's touch and the biggest issue was you couldn't just open a door in an upstairs apartment and let a dog out. So it was just always easier for them to be at Sarah's house and without talking about it, it seemed to suit them both. Men needed so much less stuff when staying out at night anyway.

They'd been out again on another one of their Sunday outings, and this time bought a real Christmas tree. Sarah couldn't help thinking that when she looked at it all dressed in traditional colours with hundreds of warm white lights on it, how beautiful it looked and how happy she felt. That night whilst having a Sunday roast and a bottle of red wine together, Sam decided he needed to talk to her about Christmas. She had met his parents a couple of times now and he felt serious enough about her that he'd decided that he would like her to spend the Christmas holidays with him. But his usual plans were to spend it with his family, so now he wanted to know what she would be doing, and would she consider going to his parent's for at least Christmas day.

"I've been thinking Sarah; we need to sort out what our plans are for Christmas. When do you see your dad?"

"My dad invites me over every Christmas day. As I told you, there is only him. Although, he is very happy with Nancy and she does have a big family."

"So, is that set-in stone or could we visit them, say boxing day? We could take them out and then Christmas day you can come to my parents with me. Not everyone stays for dinner. Those who don't, usually just visit in the morning before going on to see other family. I'm sure we could even go Christmas Eve. There's always visitors and food and laughter, so what do you say? Because I really would love to spend it with you, but I'll go along with whatever you decide."

"Okay, Sam, I will speak to my dad," she said, smiling from ear to ear. "Nothing has actually been mentioned yet so I'm sure like you said if we offered to take them out boxing day, if that's OK with you, then yes, if that's what you'd like, then that's good with me as well because all I want to do is Christmas with you."

Sam couldn't help but get up from the table, take Sarah in his arms and kiss her with all the love and affection he felt, nobody had ever made him feel this way. And he knew he was falling deeper and deeper in love with her every day.

The weather had turned in the last few days and winter was well and truly now upon them. The forecast was snow and more than just a little flurry. It was now only 5 days to Christmas and festive cheer was everywhere. Sarah couldn't help but think how lucky she was that Ruby had recovered so well from her ordeal, but she also couldn't help but think as bad as it had all been, her life was so much better since the accident did happen and she'd met Sam. They'd taken her back to the vet's for her final check-up and there was definitely no need to go back again. As far as John the vet was concerned, Ruby was absolutely fine. The walks were to be controlled until the New Year and then she could be allowed off the lead to run wild again. The Christmas plans were all now in place and life was just getting better by the day. Sarah couldn't remember ever feeling this happy or excited about

Christmas even as a child: Christmas eve was to be for themselves; Christmas day with Sam's parents and family – they would go there late morning and stay over till boxing day, have breakfast then leave, make their way over to her dad's and take him and Nancy out for lunch. Ruby would also go to Sam's parents as that wasn't an issue and they would keep her with them until Sam and Sarah collected her after their visit to her dad's. *Life,* Sarah had to say to herself, *was great.* In fact, fabulous. Even if the weather was becoming treacherous. She couldn't help but smile and think how lucky she was and how happy she felt; what a turnaround from the beginning of the year.

She had come into work early today, not because it was going to be a busy day, as the car trade was quiet at this time of year and with only three more working days left out of the five till Christmas the staff were more just turning-up as opposed to actually doing any work, but when she had got up that morning there was already snow on the ground and the sky had looked full of it. Sam had been out with his cycle friends the night before, a few drinks and a trip to the local Indian. And Although Sarah had suggested he come back to her house, he'd said he wouldn't like to wake her or worse still, her not be able to sleep waiting up for him. Boys were boys and although he had work, he could go in late. One of his mates had been trying to convince him to stay at a hotel near the Indian, as he lived out of town, so it then became apparent that the more sensible option was for him and his mate, Dan, to share a taxi, and both go back to Sam's as it was a two-bedroom apartment anyway.

But as it was Sarah didn't sleep anyway, or at least not very well. Rarely was she alone in her bed these days, and although she should have enjoyed the time to herself, she didn't and had simply spent most of the night tossing and turning whist forever checking the time wishing for it to be morning then she could just get up. So eventually she had decided to get up early and get ready for work. The sky had been heavy the clouds low and all merged as one with heavy snowfalls promised for later that day and looking at it Sarah really hadn't fancied driving in it. She had always been quite a confident driver however, she had never really driven in bad weather before, so the thought that she could just catch a bus and get Sam to pick her up after work was much more appealing. So she decided to text him that,

'Good morning, handsome, hope your night out was good and that your head isn't too sore this morning. Going to get the bus to work this morning as I don't fancy the drive with the weather forecast, so can you pick me up please? No worries if you're busy. I can catch a bus again back home xx'

It wasn't long before the reply came,

'Good morning, beautiful, head still on my shoulders if a little delicate. Yes, it was a good night and no problem. See you outside at the usual time xx.'

By 10 am that morning Sarah was glad she'd caught the bus; the snow was falling fast and heavy now. Sam would be picking her up and she wouldn't, thank goodness, have to face the drive home. Work was quiet, and everyone was in the Christmas Spirit: just drinking coffee, eating mince pies and waiting for the end of the working day. By lunchtime, the snow was setting thick on the ground and it was plain to see there was to be no let-up anytime soon. Sarah's mobile buzzed and pulling it out of her pocket she expected to see a message from Sam but in this case, it wasn't Sam – it was her good friend, Amanda.

'Hey what you up to? I'm getting out of work in the next hour due to the weather, are you driving? Do you fancy seeing if you can get out and we will go for drinks and a catch-up? Xx'

Busy reading Amanda's message, Sarah hadn't realised that Martin had come out of his office and was standing right in front of her desk and a little startled quickly looked up.

"Oh, sorry Martin, my friend Amanda just messaged about the weather as she's getting off early."

"An excellent idea. There's nothing much going on around here, so I think you should have the afternoon off as it's not like you never work over. Make the most of it."

"Well if you're sure Martin, that would be great," Sarah happily replied.

"Yes fine, you get on your way."

Sarah messaged Amanda back and they decided to meet for lunch. Town was busy when she got there, in fact, it was packed. Shoppers everywhere rushing about, buying everything they needed and probably lots they didn't, she imagined just so they could then get home and not have to come back out in the weather. Sarah and Amanda met at one of the popular wine bars in the centre of town. They decided they needed a liquid, lunch and a catch-up. By that, Sarah knew, what Amanda had actually meant was every little detail of her and Sam. Sarah laughed as the waiter brought the bottle of Prosecco and once he had poured them both a glass and moved away, she started, "Well then, do tell. How is it all going with your new dog walking companion?"

"It's going great, thank you, Amanda, just great. I can't tell you how happy I feel. He is the perfect gentleman, good company, interesting and listens. Makes me feel very special."

"So, has he said he loves you?"

"No but we're getting along just fine," Sarah laughed

"And in the bedroom?" Amanda continued

"We're getting on more than fine, thank you, Amanda."

"Glad to hear it," came the reply, "after Mr Selfish, oh what was his name… Matt."

Laughing, Sarah said, "Trust me, Sam is nothing like Matt. Sam is everything a girl could want, and more."

Another bottle of Prosecco later and thankfully a pizza, Sarah had finally answered all of Amanda's questions and lunch was coming to an end. The snow now lay thick on the ground, but luckily had stopped, or at least for the time being, and outside was now painted a truly picturesque Christmassy scene. It was getting on for three in the afternoon now and Amanda now needed to be heading off to meet Nick, and Sarah was going to Sam's office to meet him. It wasn't far, though between the snow and the effect of the alcohol which was now she could feel starting to kick in, far too many bubbles consumed at lunch time and the very unsuitable footwear she was wearing, she did have to concede that it may turn out to be quite a challenge.

"Sarah you look frozen," Sam greeted her when she arrived; getting up from behind his desk and crossing the room to pull her into his arms, kissing her passionately and holding her close.

"I missed you last night," he said.

"I missed you too," she replied. "The electric blanket just doesn't compare."

"Oh, I bet it doesn't," he smirked at her and gently kissed her lips again. "Just give me 5 minutes to finish then we will go home," he said.

Go home, she repeated in her head. How good did that sound? The two of them to go home to one house. And true to his word, 5 minutes later they were leaving for home, that of course being Sarah's house. The traffic was heavy and slow and the roads extremely hazardous, but Sam was careful and took his time, and Sarah was so glad she hasn't driven.

"Have you warmed up now?" said Sam. He'd turned the heated seats on, and the car heater was on high and she had finally stopped shivering.

"Yes, thanks. I am fine now. I should have thought more about the footwear before leaving for work this morning."

"Probably," said Sam and laughed then suggested, "should we build a snowman before it gets too dark when we get home?"

"What! Are you serious?" she heard herself saying.

"I was, but not if you don't want to, that's fine," he said. "I just thought it might be fun."

Looking sideways at him she replied, "Why not, you big kid. Yes, it would be good fun."

And so, that was what they did. The snowfall had been plentiful way more than enough to make a great snowman. They rolled a large amount of snow into the centre of the garden and then another large amount, this one for his head. They gave him a carrot for his nose, a colourful stripy knitted scarf of Sarah's wrapped around his neck and a hat that had been left long ago by her dad now plonked strategically on his head. They had gotten a packet of giant chocolate buttons out of the fridge and placed some kebab sticks for eyes; then gave him arms using more kebab sticks with gloves hanging off them poked into the snow on either side of his large ice white body; now more giant buttons again down the front of him. Then finally standing back and looking at him, they both smiled, then laughed out loud; both amazed and bemused by their achievement. But it was freezing outside, and they were both now desperate to get inside and get warm.

Sarah couldn't stop laughing now, the thought of them two gown ups playing out in the snow as soon as they'd got home from work, they were like two daft school kids behaving like they'd never seen snow before but what great fun it had turned out to be. In fact, she couldn't remember the last time she'd felt like this if ever and more confident too than she could ever remember and was now giving Sam a sexy little smile. As suddenly she said, with the words popping out of her mouth before she even knew herself where they were coming from, "Let's go get warm. Let's take a bath together." Sam saw the cheeky little twinkle in her eyes didn't need asking twice the smile he gave her in return more than met his eyes as he reached out a hand and took one of hers in his saying anything you like to get up close and naked with you.

It didn't take long before Sarah was resting her head back against Sam's chest in the deep, bubbly hot water they had raced inside of the house and up the stairs throwing of their clothes some at least along the way, both desperate to get warm but more so both desperate to get close to each other. The water still running as they stepped into the bath the argument over who got the taps ending with the solution of no one. Which was now how Sarah had come to have her back against Sam's chest cocooned by the deep hot water, the top half of her body moulded against him whist her nipples appeared and disappeared causing a definite stirring in Sam beneath the water whilst her legs lay free yet encased by his, surrounded by bubbles, Sam's arms wrapped around her as they shared a large glass of red wine, and from there it had been to bed where Sam had made love to her. Then they had made love to each other as if they had been starved of each other forever.

When they woke up the next morning everywhere was still covered in snow, but it had now frozen and was not now by any means of the imagination quite so pretty. The roads were clear but the slush that had been pushed up to the edges of the curbs and pavements was now various shades of grey, dirty and frozen. The picturesque scene from the day before no longer anywhere to be seen, other than their snowman who still stood proud and still looked magnificent in the back garden. Both now up and ready for work, they stood in the dining room area of the through lounge room holding mugs of tea; still bemused at their own achievement they laughed about what a masterpiece they had created and joked he had come to life in the small dark hours and now exhausted, once again stood still .

Sam drove Sarah to work as the roads now clear of snow were very icy and hazardous, she was definitely happier to be a passenger than driving herself in fact just the thought of it, her driving in such conditions terrified her if she was honest. The sky now again looked dark and full with the promise of more snow on the way, it was certainly going to cause further chaos to both shoppers and drivers and according to the met office it was set to continue for at least another day, but they weren't guaranteeing a white Christmas. Sam had taken Ruby on a quick ten-minute walk before work, while Sarah was still getting ready, and if the sky was anything to go by, then that would be her lot for the day, other than out into the garden. Pulling up outside of her work Sam turned in his seat lent over and gently kissed her before saying, "Okay have a good day and I will see you here later unless anything changes."

"Great," said Sarah leaning in for just one more quick goodbye kiss. No matter how many times she kissed him, it would never be enough she thought, "See you later. Oh, and I enjoyed last night, maybe if it snows again today, we will have to build him a friend later."

"And I thought you were referring to what came after," winked Sam as he kissed her forehead and touched her lips with his finger. "Let's see what happens later then, shall we, lady?"

Closing the car door and hearing the engine pull away, Sarah smiled to herself as she felt the ache in the pit of her stomach at the anticipation of later. In work it was another slow day with little to do but pass the time and aim at keeping busy. Sarah decided that although it was short notice, she would speak to Martin about taking the Christmas Eve as a holiday. That would mean today was her last day until January 2nd and as it was a quiet time, made even more so by the bad weather, she thought Martin probably wouldn't have an issue with it. And she was right. He also suggested that as he was going into town to pick up his wife's present and he would drop her off, that way so she could do any last-minute bits to save going out over the weekend and then make her way to meet Sam and save him fighting through the traffic; the roads were bad now and looking to get worse. Sarah got her coat and bag saying her goodbyes and good wishes to those who were still there as she did so and followed Martin out to his car, grateful for his generous attitude, work was quiet, and the weather was definitely getting worse. A blizzard had started and the temperature had dropped yet again further.

It was actually already freezing out there. Martin had dropped her off right in the centre of town as he had been going to the jewellers nearby and Sarah decided it was a great opportunity to grab a last few surprises for Sam. She thought long and hard about what to buy him and decided on a watch, just because she loves spending time with him. She had bought that last week and while she was so excited to be spending Christmas with him, Sarah had decided a couple more wrap-ups would do no harm. Maybe a new scarf and gloves while the weather had turned so awful, and a few toiletries. They could stay at her house, which was always a good idea and she must also pick up something for Audrey and Harry. So off she went almost singing Christmas carols out loud; Christmas couldn't get any better. Yes, Christmas was wonderful; made so by her relationship with Sam.

A good hour or more later, her shopping was done, and although she was still feeling full of festive cheer, she had now had enough of shopping and needed to at least grab a coffee, if not lunch. Sarah tried to call Sam to let him know where she was, but it went straight to his voicemail, so she decided to give the office a call, but only to be told that he was currently in with a client. So, as a last resort, she decided to send him a text:

'I'm in town, Martin gave me the afternoon off. I know you're busy now but if you're free for lunch that would be great if not then don't worry, I'll grab something and get a cab home so please let me know. Love Sarah xx'

After sitting in a coffee shop for half an hour, Sarah decided that Sam must be truly tied up with a client as she had heard nothing from him, so it was best that she just got a cab home and then see him later she was sure he would ring her or realise where she was when she picked up her text.

Sam, on the other hand, had no idea of Sarah's plans; he was now out of the office, having lunch and had earlier switched his phone onto silent as he didn't think anyone would be needing him that urgently and decided it would be less of a distraction and would be for the best. After him and Kate had split up, he had buried his head in the sand but fortunately Kate hadn't, so she had arrived at his office unannounced earlier with a definite plan to see him. Told him they needed to talk, talk today in fact and insisted on lunch. Lunch had, it turned, been lovely, and despite it not being planned, it had worked out well; it had given them time to talk about the past and also about their future. Now, coming out of the restaurant both still chatting and laughing about some trivial thing they stood facing each other on the pavement, Sam took both of her hands in his and squeezed them gently, "I'm so glad you called in today, Kate, this all means so much to me."

"Me too," said Kate, smiling up at him, her hands still held tightly in his. "It would have been unfair to move back home engaged to be married without coming to see you first and telling you my news myself. I'll always love you Sam, but we both know that neither of us have been in love with each other for a very long time now. You've met Sarah now, who I can see you're clearly crazy about. Actually, I'd even say madly in love with even if you haven't told her yourself yet."

"No, you're right, I haven't. But maybe it's time I did," said Sam. "Thank you again for today. I hope that next time we meet it could maybe be the four of us."

"I'd like that, Sam," said Kate. "I really would."

The two of them drew closer and shared a hug; kissed each other on the cheek and drew apart.

"Have a fabulous Christmas, Sam."

"You too, Kate," and leaning across, Sam gently kissed her on the cheek one last time before letting her go. Kate just smiled and walked away.

Sarah couldn't stop the tears from rolling down her cheeks. It was all she could do so as not to break into a heart-breaking sob in the middle of the coffee shop; it was like living a bad dream. One minute you're having a coffee, hoping your boyfriend will text you to meet you for lunch, the next you're watching him come out of a posh restaurant, stand on the pavement and kiss a very attractive, elegant 'other woman'. What the hell had ever made her think he was any different? He wasn't different; they were all the same. And now her heart was broken… again. In fact, this time it wasn't broken, it was destroyed because what she realised now was, unlike whatever she had felt for Matt, she was absolutely one hundred percent sure she was in love with Sam.

Wiping the tears away and gathering her bags, looking back out again across the street she could see that they were long gone, and now so must she go and get a cab home. Sam and whoever she was, at least had disappeared before she had a total melt down. How could she have been so stupid?

When Sam got back into the office, he was greeted with the news from his receptionist that Sarah had called earlier but left no message. He didn't know whether it was because he'd been out with Kate for lunch or because he'd not yet got around to telling Sarah about her, but somehow, the fact that he had missed her call left him with an uneasy feeling. Then, checking his mobile he saw that he had another missed call and also had missed her message. Now he really did feel uneasy. He knew he had nothing to hide and that when he sat Sarah down and explained to her about Kate, told her the whole story, she would understand. But most importantly, before, after, or even during that conversation, he knew that he had to tell her that he loved her. Really loved her. She meant everything to him.

Sam tried calling Sarah to find out where she was. She heard her mobile ring, saw his name appear on its screen but she couldn't answer it. Firstly, she had nothing to say. Secondly, she couldn't stop crying, and thirdly, even if it was his fault that she was so upset, she didn't want him to hear her in such a state. Next came a text:

'Hi Sarah. Sorry I missed you, was out to lunch. Call me when you get this message, love Sam xx'

Sarah could barely read the message through her tears. There was no way she was going to call him she could barely think let alone speak. So sometime later she sent a text:

'Hi Sam. No worries, I've started with a terrible cold. Stay at your place tonight, don't want you catching it. Sarah x'

This uneasy feeling was now rising in Sam like a tidal wave. She didn't have a cold this morning, granted they can just come on quite suddenly, but she didn't even have a sniffle. He tried to ring her again, but still she didn't answer. He thought about going around. It wouldn't matter if she was asleep because he had a key. If she genuinely wasn't well, he wanted to be there for her, and if there was something else, he wanted to sort it out. Was he being paranoid? He really hadn't done anything wrong, but there was something he needed to do; he needed to tell her about Kate, tell her who she was, who she'd been to him, but wasn't anymore. Kate had moved on and met someone new. She was happy, and Sam was happy for her. All he wanted was Sarah.

He texted her again,

'Shall I come over if you're not well? Love Sam xx'

She didn't reply, she thought about it for a little while then decided if she left it, then he would think she was asleep and leave it at that.

But when morning came, she still hadn't made a firm decision about what she wanted to do. Part of her wanted to call Sam and have it out with him; the other part of her was too scared to face what she thought she had seen. No, she knew what she had seen, she just couldn't get her head around it and decided it was easier not to get into it and so, avoid the humiliation and heartbreak with a simple text message:

'Hi, hope you're okay. I'm still not good at all and think that maybe on reflection this has all been a bit fast, so you have a good time at your parent's this Christmas but please send my apologies. I think I just need some quiet time alone, but there is nothing to stop you from having a good time. Sarah x'

What the hell was all that about? Sam immediately tried to call her but again she didn't answer. So, he got in his car and drove straight round there, finding at first that although he had a key he couldn't open the door because of the safety chain, but then she did at least come and let him come in.

"What the hell is going on, Sarah?" Sam demanded as he stormed in through the front door.

"I told you Sam, I'm not well."

Glancing at her, he had to admit, he had never seen her look so out of sorts, and she did sound very sniffly, but she also looked tired almost like she had been crying forever. It was either one hell of a cold or she was hiding something from him.

"I'll be fine in a few days," she was saying, "but for now I feel rough and I just want to be on my own."

"You're sure it's just a cold and there is nothing you're not telling me?" asked Sam.

"No Sam, I just need my bed and some peace and quiet."

"I'm not happy about this, Sarah. If you're not well then fine, we don't have to go anywhere, but to want to be on your own? I should be here looking after you."

"I'm fine Sam, not well, but apart from that I'm fine. So please, let's just leave it here for now. I need my bed and my own space. It's Christmas, go and have a good time."

"And Ruby, he was now saying, "what about her walks. Surely I can at least help you with those."

"No Sam," was her answer to that, "everything is fine," Sam now just felt despair and glanced over to Ruby who was wagging her tail, she at least was glad to see him, though not about to leave Sarah's side she too was clearly worried about her beloved owner.

Sam could see there was no moving her, even though deep down he also knew that something bigger was going on. But in the end, he decided that for today, he would leave it, but this wasn't over, and he would get to the bottom of it sooner or later. Leaving Sarah's house and getting in his car, Sam was devastated. He couldn't get his head around the change in her attitude, all in less than one day. Turning the key and starting the engine, he couldn't help thinking how this had turned from the best to worst Christmas ever. Little did Sarah know how after his lunch date with Kate he had spent the rest of the afternoon, and how devastated he now felt; how could he have got it all so wrong.

Sarah couldn't stop crying. Why did he have to turn up? How could he do that? Be so nice? So concerned? Be so perfect? If only she hadn't seen him with her own eyes, wrapped around a gorgeous blonde stood on the pavement in broad day light in the middle of town. Now she felt worse than ever. Grabbing more tissues and a glass of water she went back to bed where she hugged her dog and cried herself to sleep.

Sarah didn't sleep well, but who would. So, she was glad to get up on Saturday morning. Though, once up, she wasn't sure what she was going to do with her day.

The sky was heavy, dark and looked full of rain and although she neither felt up to it, nor wanted to go to the park, but Ruby seemed to have other ideas. And Sarah had to stop and remind herself, that this was the very reason for which she had gotten Ruby in the first place, that she had needed to get out more, so now she needed to go get dressed and get outside. So after showering and getting warm clothes on, Sarah and Ruby went to the park. It was now the day before Christmas Eve. The traffic was heavy, and the last-minute Christmas chaos was in the air, but for Sarah, now it would most definitely be a quiet one. Just her and Ruby, but that was fine. She was fine; or at least nowhere she hadn't been before. And on boxing day she could still take her dad and Nancy out there. Just wouldn't be Sam as well.

Ruby had a great time in the park. *Poor thing,* Sarah felt as if she had neglected her the past 24 hours, but Ruby wasn't holding a grudge. Fresh air and freedom made her very forgiving so at least no harm was done there.

Getting back home and giving Ruby a rub down, Sarah put the kettle on and two slices of bread into the toaster, she didn't particularly feel hungry; in fact, she had no appetite at all but she knew she needed to eat something, she thought she should probably call or text Sam. Maybe she should tell him what she'd seen; maybe she had over reacted. Now that she'd had time to calm down, she wondered should she have given him a chance to explain. There, after all, may have been a very genuine explanation. But as she thought about it, the rain started; only fine light drizzle at first, almost too hard to see, but as the minutes passed, its damage started to show. and Once again her tears started as she watched the rain hit their snowman and gently it started to help him slip away, leaving tears rolling down Sarah's cheeks and the feeling of despair washing over her again.

It was a while after, Sarah realised that the kettle had long gone off the boil, the bread had almost become almost cardboard in the toaster, and their snowman had become half of his former self, with his chocolate button eyes running down his face; his cap slipped to one side, and his carrot nose gone, dropped to the ground, he was a mess just like she was.

Audrey rang Sam to check if the arrangements were still all the same. He didn't know what to say to her; he hoped so, but he wasn't so sure. Audrey then went on to say how they'd heard from Kate; her news about coming home, new man, plans to get married all sounds very exciting she continued saying. Sam said he too had heard from her, actually he had seen her they'd gone out to lunch and he was fine with it all, that they'd had a good long chat cleared the air and all was good with them. "Yes," he told his mother, "he was very happy for them and had wished them both well." Audrey was pleased about that she had always liked and thought a great deal about Kate but having now met Sarah and seen her and their son together she had no doubt about who was better suited for him and his future and would make him happiest, so the news that Sam also clearly felt the same way had made her very happy, there had in Audrey's eyes always been the risk he would never truly move on until he had seen her again.

"They are calling around here tomorrow for a coffee," replied Audrey.

"Good," said Sam. "I'm glad it's all worked out well chatting for a few more minutes before." Then making his excuses and bringing the call to an end. He didn't think his mother had suspected anything was wrong and so didn't want to get into it at this point hoping his suspicions were wrong and Sarah just really did have a cold.

And so the next day as planned, they had, Kate and Charlie, the new man, called in on Audrey and Harry. They had both always liked Kate and had also been upset when she and Sam had split up. But agreed now having met Sarah, they could see that Sarah was so much more the girl for Sam. *All's well that ends well*, thought Audrey except she had picked up on something in the telephone conversation with Sam the night before that something wasn't right between Sam and Sarah, and it was worrying her.

Audrey and Harry sat round the kitchen table having coffee with Kate and Charlie. The situation was almost bizarre in the fact that they once truly believed that Kate would be their daughter-in-law, but they were glad that she was happy. Although it was the first-time meeting her new man, they had warmed to Charlie instantly who arrived with a Christmas bouquet for Audrey and a bottle of good whiskey for Harry. The conversation was easy, and Kate openly said that she had been to see Sam, as she didn't want her news coming from anywhere or anyone else, that once they had meant the world to one another, but sometimes people's personalities grow at different paces and it just becomes impossible for them to stay together, but luckily everyone seemed happy.

"Is Sam spending his usual Christmas day at home?" Kate asked Audrey in general conversation, "I bet he will be bringing Sarah with him, he seems crazy about her."

"Yes, that's the plan," replied Audrey, "Though unfortunately, Sarah seems to have come down with a dreadful cold and she's decided for at least a day or two she would be best spending it alone at home. We're hoping she's well enough to join us. Sam seems down and very out of sorts about it. Can't quite get the whole story but then again maybe I'm looking for something that's not there," laughed Audrey.

"Probably," piped up Harry, "you are good at that dear. Always worrying about something that doesn't actually exist. Too much time on her hands; think we need more grandchildren," he laughed.

Everyone had more coffee and another hour passed before it was time for Kate and Charlie to leave. All giving each other a hug and wishing each other a Merry Christmas promising to stay in touch and catch up again in the New Year, they were just heading to the door, when Kate stopped and looked at a photo on the radiator cabinet.

"Who is that with Sam in the photo?" she asked.

"Oh," replied Audrey looking at the photo, "That's Sarah with her dog. It was taken only the other week when Sam brought her round. It was in our garden."

"Nice photo, she looks very happy and that's a lovely dog."

"Yes," said Audrey, "Sarah's lovely and so is her crazy dog. Both seemed crazy about Sam."

"Does she live local; did you say Audrey?"

"Erm yes, just twenty minutes away. She lives on Alexandra Road, next to Alexandra Park. Do you think you know her Kate?"

"No Audrey, I was just curious or nosey or both," Kate laughed. "I'm glad he's happy."

"And we're glad you are happy too," said Audrey. "Aren't we, Harry?"

"We are dear. We are indeed," answered Harry whist in agreement yet always happy to please his wife.

When Kate and Charlie said their last goodbyes and got into their car, Charlie spoke almost immediately, "So what was all that about on the way out?"

"The other day when I called on Sam at his office, remember? Then we went out for lunch, had a good chat to clear the air, everything was great and hugged goodbye. Then as I turned to go, I turned back and kissed him on the cheek. I was so relieved, Charlie, that he was happy, I didn't want to be the one that had not only caused the break-up but also be the one that has also found love and happiness first afterwards. Anyway, I never thought another thing about it until just now but it all adds up! She, sorry I mean Sarah, may well be ill. But, as I got into my car and pulled away, I remember there was a girl crying on the pavement, obviously waiting for a cab. I looked at her and couldn't help but think how sad to be so upset this close to Christmas. Don't you see? It was Sarah! She must have been coming to see Sam and then saw us!"

"Well why wouldn't she have just asked him about it?" asked Charlie, looking most confused.

"For goodness sake Charlie! She is obviously devastated and is just saying that she's got a cold while she gets her act together. She probably wants to ask him but is too scared of the answer, especially so close to Christmas. We're not like you men, Charlie. She's probably absolutely heartbroken; emotions everywhere unlike you men that would just go bury your heads in YouTube."

"Thank you for that, Kate," Charlie laughed. "So what's the plan?"

"Find her house and tell her who I am, who I was and why we were together."

"Would it not just be easier to phone Sam?"

"Yes, Charlie, of course it would, but if I do this, she will know for sure and the rest will sort itself out."

"Okay Kate, you know best. Let's go then."

"I'm a woman Charlie we're not always right but we're never wrong!!!"

Twenty minutes later they were curb crawling down Alexandra Road with not a clue as to where Sarah lived, but as luck would have it, there she was returning from the park along with her crazy dog. Kate and Charlie just sat in the car for a few minutes. Then Kate decided she alone would knock on Sarah's door and see if she was the reason for the cold, and maybe help it to go away.

Sarah heard the bell and for a moment, felt reluctant to go to the door. She didn't want to see Sam and wasn't expecting any visitors, but after all, Sam still had a key so why would he ring the bell? Finally, but still reluctantly, she went to the door where for a moment the two women just stood looking at each other.

"You must be Sarah?" said Kate.

"I am," came the reply, "and I recognise you, but I don't know where from and have no idea who you are."

"I know," said Kate. "Can I please come in?"

Feeling very uncertain and an absolute wreck, Sarah still couldn't help but feel that she had no real option other than to say yes and allow the slim, glamorous blonde into her home. Stepping back, she thought best to just get whatever it was, over and done with.

"I think I owe you an explanation," said Kate. "I think you saw something that looked like something it wasn't."

"I remember now, I saw you with Sam. The two of you were on the pavement if that's what you're referring to," said Sarah.

"It is, and we were so here goes…"

Kate explained to Sarah that she was Sam's ex. She explained about the job and the split; explained how she had messaged him to tell him that she was coming home but not the details. She told Sarah that he'd probably not mentioned her due to the fact that he wouldn't have wanted to scare her off by talking about an ex returning onto the scene. She went on to tell her about her engagement and that she had visited Sam's office to tell him, so that he heard it from her personally. She explained that he in return had talked about her Sarah, including how crazy he was about her and that they were spending Christmas together. She then told Sarah how she had also been to see Audrey and Harry, which is when she noticed the photo and managed to piece it all together, remembering a young woman crying while waiting for a cab after she'd left Sam.

It all made so much sense now. How crazy and mixed up everything had gotten. That's why he had seemed so concerned, because he genuinely didn't have anything to feel guilty about. But she had been too scared to ask him, avoiding what might have been the truth and then being left upset and alone at Christmas.

"I'm so sorry," Kate said. "Would you like me to phone Sam and explain what has happened?"

"No, it will be okay. It's just as much my fault for jumping to conclusions."

"Okay, but here's my number just in case you change your mind. I'm so sorry and I hope that you get this sorted very soon and have a happy Christmas."

"Thank you for coming and explaining everything. It was very good of you and I hope both of you have a lovely Christmas too."

With that Kate left and Sarah sat back down on the couch, tears streaming down her face. Why hadn't she just asked him? How silly she felt now and annoyed with herself for not trusting him as really she knew she should, for judging him because of the way she'd had been let down before by Matt.

Pulling herself together, she got her mobile and pressed for his name. Desperate to hear his voice, scared of what he may now say, *What have I done? What if this is it now and he's changed his mind?* Finally, she pressed cancel, taking it back to the menu and sitting staring at her phone.

Ten minutes later, she had decided that a text was all she could bring herself to do now. 3:30 pm on Christmas eve and she didn't know if she was starting to feel better or worse, better because she now knew the truth, worse because she now didn't know how Sam felt anymore after the way she had treated him over the last few days. Eventually hands shaking her heart pounding with her mind everywhere and not really sure what she should say, she pressed send. The message simply read:

'Sorry, I got it all wrong. Please can we talk Sarah x'

Now she sat there clutching her phone wondering how long it would be before he replied or if he would even reply at all, but she didn't have to wait long before the simplest of replies came back,

'OK x'

Although she had said she would leave it to Sarah, Kate had decided to phone Sam, filling him in on the situation. She didn't want to interfere, but this was Christmas Eve and clearly neither were happy without the other, she had found happiness and she wanted the same for Sam so if it took a little help in the form of a quick phone call that was least she thought she could do and she was feeling very bad about the whole situation and feeling it was to some degree partly her fault.

OK? thought Sarah.

So, Then? What now? Not really knowing how to respond, her heart feeling heavy and feeling there was little more she could do, she simply replied with 'Thanks x'.

She stayed seated on the couch, brooding. She now didn't have a clue about what was going on, and neither was there anything she could do about it, until only a few minutes later she heard a key in the door, the door open and in walked Sam. Despite looking tired and strained, he still looked gorgeous. As he stood there, as he said you never asked for the key back so I thought there was always hope, then simply stood looking straight at her waiting for her reaction then deciding to cross the room towards her looking her in the eyes before saying, "Don't you know I love you Sarah?" Sarah was off the settee in his arms and sobbing faster than he could have even wondered what her response could ever be, "I'm so sorry

Sarah, I should have told you about Kate long ago. It was Kate who messaged that night we were watching a film, but I didn't know why she was coming home then and I didn't want to tell you about her and risk scaring you off, because I already knew back then that I was falling in love with you."

"I should have just asked you, Sam. I know you're not that type of guy and I should have known better. There would, I knew, always have been an explanation, but I was just scared because I love you too, so much!"

Taking a step back but only enough so he could see her clearly whilst holding her tightly and looking again straight into her eyes his gaze now holding her still, Sam said, "Then you'll marry me, Sarah."

Sarah gasped, and burst into the biggest ever smile and once again tears as they rolled down her cheeks and she was starting to wonder if for one reason or another she would ever be able to stop.

"Really? You're asking me to marry you?"

"Yes, I am. I love you and I want to spend the rest of my life with you."

"Then the answer is yes. Most definitely yes! I feel exactly the same."

And so, the Christmas plan was back on track, but now so much better, with great plans ahead and exciting times. Christmas Eve was spent together, wrapping presents, watching junk TV, eating take-away and making love into the early hours. But much later, when they woke up wrapped in each other's arms, the first of many Christmas mornings to come, Sarah couldn't help but feel that nauseous feeling again that had been coming and going all week and quickly went to the bathroom. *That shouldn't be happening she was fine now* she had thought. She walked back into the bedroom still not feeling at her best, a little lightheaded and still a little queasy, Sam was sitting up, watching her as she entered the bedroom, a smile came wide across his face reaching all the way to his eyes smiling at her.

"What are you smiling at?" she asked. "I think I need to stop eating those take-aways or maybe stop drinking red wine, something isn't agreeing with me."

"Maybe," said Sam, "you been eating takeaways all week?"

"Erm no Sam actually I've hardly eaten if you want the truth, okay," she laughed.

"So you've been drinking red wine all week?"

"Erm no to that as well again," she laughed, "last time I had an alcoholic drink was with you Sam."

"But you've felt like this all week, and I thought it was just because you were upset over us?"

"Yep that's the one, doctor."

"Okay then, I'm thinking there could maybe be a little unexpected third person in this relationship then?"

Sarah stood looking extremely puzzled at Sam who was still smiling at her, when suddenly the penny dropped, "Oh my god! What if I'm…"

"Yes," said Sam, "What if you're pregnant? Well then I'll be an extremely happy man and you are definitely never fobbing me off to sleep anywhere else again, because soon we will be married and living full time under the same roof."

"So, you wouldn't be unhappy about it?" asked Sarah.

"No Sarah, I'd be delighted. But what about you? How do you feel?"

"Like I'm so happy that I just want to lie in your arms and cry."

"Well you can be in my arms anytime, but the tears can only be for joy. I don't want you to ever be sad."

"I'm not Sam, I'm happy, very happy. And I'm madly in love with you. That's why I want to cry because I can't believe I'm so lucky."

"Oh Sarah, you are so beautiful. Now get back in this bed and let's see if I can help get rid of that nausea."

Epilogue

It seemed like only yesterday that it was Christmas Eve, yet it was actually now the beginning of March. So much seemed to have happened or to have been planned in that short stretch of time. On Christmas morning Sam had produced a beautiful solitaire engagement ring, which was how he'd spent his afternoon after Sarah had said she wasn't well and was staying home that day. The wedding was all booked for Easter, which was now only weeks away. Everybody was excited, it was almost the biggest topic of conversation, but only almost, because the pregnancy test had proved positive and so there would be another baby in the family soon. Another grandchild for Audrey and Harry which there seemed would never be enough of, and a first for Sarah's dad who had been so excited at the news he'd cried as well, and it seemed to have brought them closer with more regular visits to each other. Sam had put his apartment on the market, and now never left Sarah's bed for a single night. Once that was sold, they agreed that they would put Sarah's house up for sale and look for their new home together, but they were fine at Sarah's for now – it was now their home anyway. Hers, Sam's and one still crazy but loveable cockapoo that had, of course, first brought them together. Life was looking pretty much fantastic, and Sarah couldn't help but smile to herself at the thought of being loved by this man, and how much she loved him in return. Yes, in the months that had passed since their first encounter, their lives had come a long way from what had started out as just an ordinary day.

The Wedding Dilemma

The Wedding Dilemma

MARIAH ANKENMAN

Entangled Publishing, LLC
10940 S Parker Rd
Suite 327
Parker, CO 80134
rights@entangledpublishing.com

Amara is an imprint of Entangled Publishing, LLC.

Edited by Stacy Abrams and Wendy Chen
Cover design by Bree Archer
Cover photography by The Killion Group Images

Manufactured in the United States of America

First Edition May 2021

To all the artists out there.

Life would be very dark and lonely without the beauty art brings into it. Keep creating, keep shining, keep spreading joy.

Content Warning

The Wedding Dilemma is a fun, red-hot rom-com with a happy ending, but there are a few elements that might be triggering to some readers. Images of peril in a burning building, death of a parent in a character's back story, and open-door sex are within the novel. For readers who may be sensitive to these elements, please take note.

Chapter One

"Ma'am, the fire department is on the way. Remain calm and stay on the line with me."

Tamsen Hayes clutched the cell phone tight to her ear, wincing as the movement pulled her sensitive skin.

"Thank you," she spoke into the phone, trying her best to remain as still as possible. Every slight movement caused the plaster paste that had hardened to a cement-like substance on her body to pull and tug at the skin and fine hairs covering her chest and stomach. She stared down at the offensively bright white cast covering the front of her from just below her clavicle all the way down to her belly button.

How dare it look so innocent when it was literally baking her skin as she stared? She'd forgotten how hot casting made the skin…among other things she forgot. Thank goodness she'd only done a front casting and hadn't wrapped the damn thing all the way around her torso.

At least the 911 operator didn't laugh when she explained her predicament. This stranger on the other end of the call was her lifeline right now, because Tamsen was about five seconds away from a major freak out. How could she have forgotten to put the oil on her skin before starting? She'd learned all the nuances of plaster casting in Art 101 her freshman year of undergrad. She'd never forgotten the oil before.

It puts the lotion on the skin or else it gets the hose again.

The inside joke she and her classmates used to chant so they remembered to lubricate their subjects for safety's sake had flown right out of her head.

Must be all the stress she'd been under lately. Tamsen had what her dad liked to call "scattered artist brain" on the best of days, but over the past few weeks, her focus had been stretched even thinner. Her father was about to get married, she was up for the day shift manager position at work, and she needed to complete a showcase of pieces to present to one of the city's premier art galleries.

Hephaestus was one of the most popular art galleries in the Santa Fe street art district of Denver. The ten hours a week she worked there learning about the art world more than made up for the crappy pay.

At least this internship was paid. Winston, the owner of the gallery, loved supporting up-and-coming artists and had promised her once she got enough presentable pieces, he'd host a show for her. He even already approved her theme, The Human Form. An exhibit could be her big break into the art world—if she didn't first break her ribs trying to get out of this failed body-casting piece.

She wondered if George Segal ever had setbacks like this.

"Is the front door unlocked?" the operator asked, his voice calm and steady, the complete opposite to how Tamsen felt at the moment.

She turned her head to glance at her front door, swearing as the slight shift of movement caused her skin to pull again against the hardened cast stuck to her chest. "Shit, that hurts!"

"Ma'am?" The operator's voice rose an octave. "Are you

all right?"

"I'm fine." As fine as one could be in her situation. Luckily, she hadn't locked her front door. No way could she get up and move the twenty feet to unlock the deadbolt. The emergency personnel would have had to break down her door, and since she didn't have the money to fix it, she was glad she'd ignored her father's "always lock your door even if you're home" advice today.

"The door is unlocked, so they can just come right in. I can't really…it hurts too much to move." One of the reasons she called 911. After ten minutes of trying to pry the thing off with her putty knife, tossing water on it to soften it, and smacking it with her fists—which did nothing to the cast but left painful red marks on her knuckles—the plaster had hardened to the point that even a tiny movement shot bolts of pain all along her chest. She couldn't get off the couch to drive to the ER. She wished her roommate, Cora, was home. Cora was a NICU nurse and would probably know what to do, but her roomie was at work. At the hospital—how was that for irony? She'd been too embarrassed to call anyone else for help. Besides, what could her friends or her dad do that she hadn't already tried?

"Okay," the operator said, his voice back down to a calming tone. "Don't worry, the firefighters will announce who they are, so just tell them they're allowed to enter. They should be there any—"

A sharp knock on the door took her attention away from what the man on the phone was saying. Then a voice shouted from the other side: "Hello? Ms. Hayes? Denver Fire Department."

"Oh, they're here." She let out a deep sigh of relief before shouting, "Yes, come in. The door's unlocked." Finally, this would all be over soon. Every moment this stupid white brick of a failed art project sat stuck to her chest, she felt it getting tighter and tighter. Might be a figment of her panicked imagination, but she wanted it off all the same.

She thanked the operator and ended the call as her front door opened and three of the biggest men she'd ever seen filed into her tiny apartment. They each wore those tan firefighter pants things with the neon stripes around the ankles, but they didn't have the matching coats on. No, these men had deliciously tight gray T-shirts hugging their every muscle like a second skin. Even the big red suspenders connected to their pants were sexy.

Only a firefighter could make suspenders sexy.

They swallowed up all the available space, looking like one of those calendars the department sold every year as a fundraiser. Big, strong. And sexy. Maybe it was the tight-fitting T-shirts that read Denver County Fire Department. Or maybe it was the fact that they were here to set her free.

One of them, the tallest one standing in the back, had a large case in his hand that looked like some kind of medical kit. The guy next to him was a bit shorter and had sandy blond hair, but it was the firefighter in front, the one who opened the door, who drew her attention.

He stepped forward. "Ms. Hayes?"

Hello, handsome! The firefighter knelt in front of her. She nodded, because she couldn't form words at the moment. She stared into the most beautiful brown eyes she'd ever seen, so pale they almost looked golden. His brown hair was short and slightly mussed. Not in an unkempt way, but in that charming roguish way men managed to pull off. He had a long blade of a nose and a sharply cut jawline, but his lips were curved in the most charming smile. A smile that made her heart race while at the same time putting her nerves at ease. It would be just her luck to have the sexiest firefighter in all of Colorado see her at her most embarrassing moment.

Fan-freaking-tastic.

"I'm Kincaid. How are you doing?"

"I've been better," she said, finally regaining her composure and finding her voice.

Kincaid let out a small laugh, the sound enveloping her like a warm, cozy blanket. Wow. If firefighting ever fell through, the guy could make a fortune with his own ASMR channel.

"Why don't you tell us what happened?"

Did she have to? She really, really didn't want to admit to her own foolishness. Especially not in front of her personal fantasy come to life. Scratch that. If this were her fantasy, she and Kincaid would be on a private beach with cold drinks in their hands and nothing but the warmth of the sun on their skin.

"Um," she began, knowing she had to give them the facts so they could help her. That was why she called, after all. "I'm working on a project for a possible upcoming art installation. It's a show entitled The Human Form. I'm doing a bunch of paintings, sculpture, and mixed media art pieces on the various parts of the human body and how each one represents a stage of human development and emotions. It's really a fascinating…" She trailed off, noticing the other two men still standing just beyond her open doorway duck their heads together and murmur something. Probably talking about the weirdo art lady who got herself stuck in a ridiculous plaster cast.

"Sorry." She shrugged then winced when the movement caused her skin to pull against the plaster. "I tend to ramble when I get stressed."

Kincaid nodded. "Completely understandable. So you were making a…"

"Molding," she answered when he gestured to the cast on her chest. "I was doing a plaster cast, and then I was going to make a molding from the cast. I've done it before, but this time I...I guess I've just been a little scattered or something, because I forgot to put oil on my skin before I put the plaster on and, um, now it's stuck."

"Ward," Kincaid said, turning his head to his fellow firefighters.

The man holding the case came forward, kneeling beside Kincaid and placing the large plastic case on the floor between them. Kincaid reached out, placing one large, warm hand behind her neck and his other on her lower back.

"Okay," he said, his voice as calming as the 911 operator's had been. "I'm just going to help you lay back on the couch so we can get a better idea of what we're dealing with here."

Goose bumps broke out all along her skin, which was weird because the moment Kincaid touched her, it felt like her body lit on fire...

Hmmm, good thing she had three sexy firefighters in her house.

"There you go," Kincaid said as he gently helped position her flat on her back on her couch. "Now I'm just going to take a look."

She winced when his hands moved to ever so slightly wiggle the plaster stuck to her body.

"Sorry." He gave her an apologetic smile. "Okay, this thing is stuck on there pretty solidly. We have a cast saw, but I don't want to use it if the plaster is stuck to your skin. We need to loosen the cast first."

"Soak it?" Ward asked.

"I tried that," she answered before Kincaid could respond. "I tried getting it wet, prying it off, breaking it apart with my fists, but nothing has worked."

Kincaid sat back on his heels. The other firefighter came over, closing her front door before joining his buddies. The three men crouched down around her couch. Tamsen didn't think she'd ever been surrounded by this much testosterone.

It was a bit intimidating, but in a good way. She wanted to paint each and every one of these muscle-bound heroes. Preferably in the buff.

For artistic reasons, of course. It would go great with the theme of her show.

"We need something to loosen the adhesive from the skin," said the firefighter whose name she hadn't discovered yet, the blond one.

He was just as built and good looking as the other two. Tamsen had always had a thing for blonds, but as handsome as he and all the firefighters were, she found her gaze coming back to Kincaid. Something about him just…called to her muse. Oh, the things she could sculpt staring at this man.

Kincaid nodded in agreement. "Good idea, O'Neil."

He turned his gaze back to her, those golden eyes capturing her, stealing the very breath from her body. Or maybe that was the tightening of the cast. She really needed to get this thing off.

"Do you have any lubricant we can use?"

Tamsen's face flamed. Logically, she knew Kincaid meant grease or oil, but her lust-crazed hormones that had been sent into a frenzy the moment she laid eyes on her sexy firefighter hero, heard the word *lube*, and went to a very naughty place.

"Yeah." The word squeaked out of her. She cleared her throat and tried again. "Yes. I have the oil I was *supposed* to use on my skin before applying the bandages. It's on the counter over there." She indicated with a nudge of her chin, too worried her hands would be shaking from embarrassed lust if she lifted her fingers to point. "I already tried to pour oil down the cast. But I wrapped it in a way that there isn't any place for the oil to slip into."

Because even though she was a scatterbrain, she was a very thorough scatterbrain.

"Hmmmm." Kincaid rubbed his chin in thought, and

Tamsen had to clench her thighs together to relieve some of the tension that deep, delicious sound created in her body.

"We could drill some holes in it?" Ward suggested. "Pour the oil in that way?"

Drill holes? Into the cast that was completely adhered to her skin? Her very puncturable skin? That sounded like the worst idea ever.

"It'll be okay, Ms. Hayes," Kincaid said, grabbing her hand and squeezing.

She glanced down to see her fingers shaking. Who could blame her? That Ward guy had suggested taking a power tool to her chest. Anyone would freak over that idea.

"It's Tamsen," she said, because if these guys were going to drill into her, they better use her first name.

Kincaid smiled. "Hi, Tamsen, I'm Parker Kincaid."

Kincaid? Why did that name sound familiar? She had no idea, but damned if that smile didn't ease some of the panic rising in her throat. Right until Ward opened the case by his feet and pulled out a small handheld drill. She sucked in a sharp breath, heart pounding so hard she hoped it would break the cast right off. Unfortunately, it didn't.

"Tamsen."

Parker's deep voice brought her out of her fog of panic. She glanced up to see his steady gaze on her.

"Everything is going to be fine. I promise."

Easy for him to say. He wasn't the one about to have a deadly instrument used in high school shop classes drilling into a very vulnerable part of his body.

"Squeeze my hand," he commanded.

Worried any movement would increase her pain, she tentatively gave his hand a small squeeze. No pain. His presence must have calmed the pain receptors in her brain or something. Ward turned on the drill, pumping the trigger a few times while he inspected it, the high-pitched whirring sound catching her off-guard. Panicking, she sucked in a sharp breath, gripping Parker's hand tightly, positive she was crushing the poor man's fingers, but he just smiled. As if this was a completely normal thing. Who knew? For him it might be. She bet first responders got all kinds of strange calls.

"Now," Parker continued, "breathe with me. Ward is going to go extra slow, and if you ever feel uncomfortable or scared, just squeeze my hand and I'll tell him to stop, okay?"

She nodded, afraid if she opened her mouth, nothing but sobs would escape. Parker gave a subtle tip of his chin, and Ward placed the drill against the cast on her chest, directly in the middle, right below her breastbone, then slowly pressed the trigger. The bit whirled around and around at a snail's pace, tiny chunks of white plaster spinning around the bit and flying off in all directions.

"Good, Ward," Parker said, his eyes on his buddy but his hand firmly clasped to hers. "Now ease off a bit. Let's take a look."

Ward removed the drill, and the two men glanced into the fresh hole.

"Tamsen." Parker glanced at her. "I'm going to stick my finger in and see how close we are, okay?"

Good grief, could the man stop saying inadvertently dirty things? Her mind was having a heyday between freaking out and horning up.

She shut her eyes tight, muttering, "Okay."

"All right, just another half inch or so," she heard Parker say. Then the drill was back, the slow hum of the power tool wreaking havoc on her nerves.

"Good," Parker said. "That's good, stop there."

Then she felt a slight pressure, the tug and snap of a few fine hairs and then the rough pad of a finger against her breastbone. Her eyes snapped open, focusing on Parker's smiling face.

"There we are. See, Tamsen? No problem at all."

She let out a shuddering sigh of relief. Ward drilled two more holes, slowly, with Parker stopping to check each one a few times. Then O'Neil, who had grabbed her oil from the kitchen, poured the liquid into each of the holes. Parker encouraged her to wiggle slightly to move the oil around in the cast. Then he grabbed a small saw, no bigger than her palm, turned it on, and started to cut away pieces of the cast.

She almost cried with relief as each chunk came off, allowing her skin to breathe. Tamsen promised herself she would never be this forgetful ever again. No matter how much crap was going on in her life.

As the firefighters pulled off the plaster piece by piece, a thought suddenly hit her. She wasn't wearing *anything* under this cast. She was three pieces of plaster away from Parker and the rest of this team seeing her boobs!

"Um, Parker?"

Not glancing up from the saw that was inches away from her flesh, Parker answered her, "Don't worry, Tamsen, we're almost done."

Yes. That's what she was worried about.

"About that." She cleared her throat, glancing at the other two men before lowering her voice. "I, um, I don't have anything on. Under the, um, plaster."

Parker paused, saw stopping, his gaze coming up to meet hers as the implication of her words sunk in. Though she might have imagined it, she thought she saw a hint of heat fill those golden eyes, but it was gone in an instant.

"O'Neil, grab a towel or blanket for Ms. Hayes."

The firefighter glanced around then grabbed the kitchen towel hanging from the handle of her oven.

"This okay?" O'Neil asked.

"That's great," Parker responded.

O'Neil hurried back over and handed the dishtowel to

Parker, who then placed it over the last bits of plaster covering her chest.

"Okay," Parker said once the towel was firmly in place. "Just a few more pieces and you're all set, okay?"

Tamsen nodded, anxious to have this whole embarrassing ordeal over with. As Parker finished sawing and pulled the last pieces free, she clutched the towel close to her chest. They all averted their eyes as she protected her modesty, except Parker, who had to watch what he was doing as he removed the plaster. He removed the last piece covering her breasts, clearly getting a peek of the girls, but he made no indication or comment. A professional to the core.

She was sure as firefighters, they'd seen far worse than a woman's boobs covered in bits of plaster, but these were *her* boobs. And as much as she might want Parker, in particular, to see them, this wasn't the situation she had in mind.

And sadly, after this mortifying fiasco, there was no way she could face the man ever again. Even if he was her hero and the hottest man she'd even seen. She'd just have to thank him, say good-bye, and save the thought of him for a lonely night.

After all, it wasn't like she would ever see him again.

Chapter Two

Parker grabbed another champagne flute from a passing waiter. He'd give his right arm for a beer, but his mother said beer was too crass for her engagement party, and since he needed something to take the edge off, champagne it was. The shit tasted terrible. Seriously, why did people celebrate with this bitter bubble water when they could grab a nice, cold beer that also cost a hell of a lot less?

The Brown Palace Club was filled to the brim with friends of his mother's, members of the charity organizations she worked on, and, he assumed, people who knew the groom-to-be. He recognized less than half of them. He didn't run in his mother's circles too much these days, and he preferred it that way, but this was a special occasion, so he donned his custom Indochino suit and dragged up all the knowledge of high society that had been drilled into him his entire life to paste a pleasant smile on his face.

For his mother.

Money tended to bring out the worst in people. Like the last two assholes who'd dated his mother.

"Hey, Parker." Finn Jamison, a fellow firefighter at Station 42, slid up to his side. "How's it going?" Finn's wife ran a wedding planning company with her two best friends, Mile High Happiness. It was why his blue-collar buddy was here among Denver's richest and snobbiest.

Parker shrugged. "I'm in this stuffy-ass suit drinking shitty champagne, trying to smile politely to a bunch of people I don't know, who are only here to get their picture in some society rag, when what I really want is to catch the Avalanche game at home, in my boxers, while drinking a beer."

Finn laughed. "Wow. Tell me how you really feel, man."

He was being an ass. He knew. But it was hard to put on a happy face when his mother announced her engagement to a man she'd been dating for only six months, whom Parker had never even met. It all stank like the time the barber shop on Broadway burned down. Burning hair was the worst, and so was his mother naively going full steam into another relationship with a man she barely knew. He loved his mother, and he knew she was a grown adult and all, but the woman trusted people far too much. She didn't have the best taste in men, either.

Case in point, his dickwad of a sperm donor.

"I'm just here to make my mother happy."

Which was the truth. Because as wary as he was about this Thomas guy and as much as he lacked faith in his mother's choice of men, Parker loved his mom. He'd do anything for her. Including looking into any man who tried to snake his way into her life...and checkbook. His mom could trust people all she wanted. Parker was here to make sure she didn't get taken advantage of.

It's what any good son would do.

"She looks pretty happy," Finn answered.

Parker followed his friend's gaze to see his mother with her—he still couldn't think it without tensing—fiancé, laughing at something the guy said with a dreamy, lovesick smile on her face. Yeah, she seemed happy, but he'd met Thomas only once. Today. An hour ago, when he first arrived and his mother introduced them. He and his mom were close, but they didn't really talk relationship-type stuff because he preferred to fly solo, and hearing about his mom's love life was just above "running into a burning building without his bunk gear" on the list of things he wanted to do.

Thomas did seem like an okay guy. But that didn't mean Parker wasn't going to look into the man. Just because the old guy made his mom smile didn't mean Thomas wasn't working an angle.

"Pru says the wedding prep is going well. Your mom and Thomas seem to agree on most everything, and that, my wife informs me, is the sign of a long hauler."

Parker had suggested Finn's wife's company to his mom when she told him about her engagement. His mom could have hired the most expensive planners in the state, but she loved supporting small businesses when she could. And the moment she met Finn and Pru's twins, his mother had fallen in love. Not that he blamed her. It was hard not to cater to every whim of Simon and Sasha Jamison. Those two were tiny kegs of adorable dynamite. The second they turned on the charm, *boom,* suddenly you were giving them all the cookies in your lunch box.

Finn turned to face him. "I heard about the call you got last week. The woman stuck in some kind of cast?"

He and Finn were currently on different rotations, but everyone at the station was pretty tight. You had to be. When you ran into burning buildings for a living, it was important that you trusted the men and women who had your back.

"Plaster," he said.

"Huh?"

"It was a plaster cast," he answered. "She's an artist. Was

doing some kind of art project thing but forgot to use oil before she put the plaster on her skin."

Finn whistled. "Damn. Sounds like that would have been a bitch to get off."

It had been, but they managed. Probably one of the top ten weirdest calls he'd ever responded to, along with the time they had to saw a man out of a restaurant bathroom window when he tried to dine and dash, and the time they had to help remove a fifty-five-pound weight from around a guy's penis when the man inexplicably tried to masturbate with it and instead got his junk stuck.

People were ridiculous.

But not Tamsen.

A smile curled his lips thinking about her. Sure, the woman might be a little flighty, but all creative types were, right? Wasn't that kind of their thing?

"I figured it was some kid who got his cast stuck in something," Finn mused, taking a sip of his drink.

Parker grunted. He'd thought that, too, but it hadn't been a kid. It had been a smoking hottie with the brightest, bluest eyes he'd ever seen. Eyes a man could drown in. And dark, silky black hair just begging for his fingers to run through it. It had been piled on her head in a haphazard bun that looked sexy as hell. Made him wonder how long it was. Would it cover her breasts when she rode a man?

Thinking of her breasts made Parker's body tighten. He adjusted his stance, wishing the fit of his suit pants was a little looser. Damn, when Tamsen had pointed out to him that she had nothing on under the plaster, a fact he should have thought about, his professionalism had dropped for a split second. He hated himself for it, but for just a moment when she mentioned her nudity, his mind had gone to places it had no business going.

Parker had seen a lot in the ten years he'd been a

firefighter. Tamsen wasn't the first rescue he'd performed where bare skin had been a factor. He'd had to remove items of clothing for medical emergencies, pulled people half naked from their beds as fire consumed their homes, but he'd always maintained a strict professional barrier. It was his job to save people, often in their worst, most personal moments. But with Tamsen, he'd felt a spark.

Something he'd never experienced before while on a call.

If he'd met her at a bar or in a coffee shop, it would have taken him less than five minutes to ask for her number, but he'd met her on the job, and her safety had been his responsibility. As much as he wanted to see her again, he wasn't a creep. Asking for her number would have been a supremely predatory move. That shit didn't fly with him. He knew there were assholes who took advantage of their position of power, and those people deserved to be locked in a cell and the key thrown away.

So he and his fellow firefighters had helped Tamsen in the most professional manner possible. They'd offered to take her to the ER for a full checkup, but she'd declined, face bright red with embarrassment, saying she felt fine and promising to call her doctor for an appointment. He hoped she was okay, though follow-up care wasn't his job. As a firefighter, he got called to many emergency situations where they either saved the day or...he tried not to think too much about the other outcomes.

Lucky for all involved, Tamsen's call had been easy—only slightly awkward—and he'd just have to put her in the vault in his mind where he occasionally wondered how his past rescues were doing. If fate was kind, maybe they'd meet again under less strenuous circumstances, but he doubted it. He wasn't that lucky.

"Darling, there you are!"

Parker turned to see his mother gliding over to his side.

He had no idea how she did it, but the woman walked as if she floated on a cloud. Even in the designer heels he was sure were pinching her toes like hell, she sashayed around the room as if she wore nothing but the fluffiest of slippers. But as her son, he knew that infinitesimal tightening around her smile meant her dogs were barking.

"Mother." He leaned over to place a kiss on her cheek as was expected, whispering in her ear, "You should take those ice picks off and slip on some flats."

She arched one perfectly sculpted brow. "Parker Kincaid, my dear friend La'Vell custom made these shoes, and I promised I would show them off to all my friends."

Mimicking his mother's pose, he arched one slightly bushier brow back. "Uh huh, and what's La'Vell's real name?"

He would call her expression a scowl, but his mother would never allow such a gloomy emotion at one of her parties.

"His name is Lloyd and he has true talent, but he didn't feel his name would open many doors. I tried to tell him his skill would speak for itself, but he insisted on a pseudonym. We all know how snooty those fashion people can be to new talent trying to get a foot in the door."

"Good thing he has your feet, then, I suppose."

She smiled, patting him on the cheek. "Exactly, darling. I'm simply helping a friend."

Like she always did. Victoria Kincaid had a soft spot for the underdog. Whether it was a struggling designer trying to make it in the fashion world or a charity that needed funding, his mother was always there to lend a hand or her checkbook. And he loved her generosity, but sometimes it got her taken advantage of. Which was why no matter how much she insisted her fiancé was a good guy, Parker would be withholding his judgment until he'd checked Thomas out. Thoroughly.

"Oh, Finn!" his mother exclaimed as she spotted him standing next to Parker. "I can't tell you how grateful I am for Pru and her company handling all these wedding details. They've been an absolute dream to work with."

Finn inclined his head. "Thank you, Ms. Kincaid. I know she and her business partners appreciate you entrusting them with your special day. They certainly enjoy working with you."

"Oh please, call me Victoria. After all, I've asked Pru if your lovely little ones would be our ring bearer and flower girl so I'm practically their pseudo-grandmother." She sent a pointed look Parker's way. "Since it seems this might be the only way for me to get any grandchildren any time soon."

Finn let out a laugh. Parker didn't see what was so funny. He wasn't even dating anyone and his mother was digging the grandkid knife into his chest.

"But I didn't come over here to talk about my son's disappointing ventures in the world of romance."

Ouch. From his own mother.

"I came over because Thomas's daughter just arrived and I want you to meet her, Parker."

The guy had a daughter? This was exactly what Parker was afraid of. Just how much did they know about him? And why hadn't his mother told him he was getting a new stepsister?

Calm down, dude. Everything isn't always about you.

Yeah, he knew that, but his mother was so tight lipped about her fiancé. In the six months she'd dated Thomas, she hardly ever discussed him with Parker, and he had no idea the guy had a kid. How old was she? What happened to her mother? Were they divorced? Was he a deadbeat dad who left a pregnant girlfriend high and dry?

Probably not that last one, considering the kid was here. Still, Parker had questions. A lot of them. And he sure as hell was going to get some answers.

"If you'll excuse us, Finn," his mother said, taking his arm.

Finn nodded. "Of course, Victoria. I better go call my folks and make sure the kids aren't driving them up the wall."

"Oh, I don't think any grandparent would ever think that about their grandchildren. They're such blessings to those who have them."

Another pointed look sent his way. Finn smothered his laughter with his hand while Parker walked away with his mother, mouthing to his buddy all the ways he was going to get back at him once they were on shift together again.

Why was his mom harping so hard on grandkids anyway? Maybe it was the upcoming wedding tugging on her emotions or all the visits she'd had with Finn's twins over the past few weeks. Whatever it was, he didn't like it. His life was fine the way it was. He didn't need a wife and kids to look after. He had his hands full with his mother at the moment.

Maybe her new stepdaughter could give her grandbabies. If the woman was old enough. She hadn't arrived with her dad, so she was probably an adult, right? Unless her mom dropped her off? Damn, he really needed to find out more about this guy.

They walked across the clubroom floor, his mother smiling and accepting congratulations and well wishes.

Time to put on a happy face while meeting his new stepsister. One big freaking happy blended family. He snorted. *Yeah right.*

"Do you need a tissue, darling?" Mom turned a concerned eye on him. "Are you getting sick?"

"No, Mother. It was only a tickle. I'm fine." Just contemplating all the ways he could protect his mother while beating a hasty retreat from this nightmare.

Her eyes narrowed but softened a moment later when

they reached her fiancé. Parker guessed Thomas was in his early sixties, judging by the dark hair graying at his temples and crow's feet around his eyes. His suit was nice, but nothing special like the sea of bespoke they were swimming in. Parker's suspicions pinged. He wouldn't be the first guy to go after Victoria Kincaid for her bank account.

"Vikki, you're back."

The man's eyes brightened, a smile lighting up his face. He appeared to care for Parker's mom. But looks could be deceiving.

"Yes, dear, and I brought Parker with me."

"Wonderful." Thomas turned to speak to a small woman with long, dark hair falling to her mid back in some kind of intricate braid, currently snagging a champagne flute from a passing waiter. "Pumpkin, I want you to meet Parker."

Something zinged at the base of his spine as Parker stared at the back of the woman in the deep blue dress. It clung to her like a second skin, hitting all the right curves and angles. But that wasn't it. Something about her seemed familiar. The moment she turned to face them all, his jaw dropped as recognition and lust hit him right in the gut.

"Tamsen, this is Victoria's son, Parker." Thomas smiled as he made the introductions. "Parker, my daughter, Tamsen."

Bright blue eyes stared at him. Eyes he remembered all too well, as they'd been haunting his dreams ever since he saw them last. So crystal clear, a person could drown in them. He'd been hoping to get the chance to see them again. To see *her* again. His heart literally skipped a beat before pounding a rapid rhythm in his chest as his body tightened at the sight of her. But then the reality of the situation came crashing down around his head.

He swallowed back the groan of disappointment as he stared at the woman he'd been dreaming about for days. But not like this. Dammit! A professional association they could have gotten past, but this…they were going to be connected forever—or however long his mother's marriage lasted. He couldn't hook up with someone he'd see at every holiday, birthday, family dinner. This was a nightmare.

Still, he couldn't deny the zing of excitement burning low in his belly at seeing her again. But why did it have to be here? Like this? He held in a frustrated sigh.

Fate was a bastard.

Chapter Three

Tamsen had the extreme misfortune to have just taken a very large sip of the delicious champagne the moment she was introduced to her future stepbrother.

She'd hustled over after her shift at 5280 Eats, the restaurant where she worked. It was only a few blocks away on the 16th Street Mall, so she'd walked. But the heat of the June sun beating down on her, even at six in the evening, as she made her way the six blocks caused her throat to dry.

Parched, but already late to her father's engagement party, she'd hurried up to the club room, found her father, and gratefully took a gulp of the heavenly looking drink. She'd been so excited to meet Victoria's son. And nervous. First impressions were key, and she didn't want to do anything to upset her father's happiness with Victoria. She'd only met his fiancée once before, but the woman seemed very nice, if slightly intimidating. The money stuff...with her art gallery job, Tamsen was used to serving rich people, not being related to them. She was terrified she might use the wrong fork at dinner and be shunned or something.

But, of course, her luck lately had been on some kind of weird bender determined to embarrass her at every opportunity, and when she gasped in shock, she choked, sputtered, and gasped like a fish wriggling on a hook just pulled from the lake.

"Tamsen, pumpkin." Her father gently pounded her back with concern. "Are you all right?"

"I'm fine," she squeaked out as the coughing subsided. Her eyes watered, and she blinked them dry. Taking a deep breath, she cleared the last of the congestion from her throat and smiled. "Sorry, went down the wrong tube."

Staring into familiar golden brown eyes, she pushed down her embarrassment and tried her best to ignore the curious gazes from the crowded room.

Way to cause a scene, Tamsen.

"Hi, Parker. Nice to see you again."

Her father's eyes widened in surprise. "You two know each other?"

Much to her undying embarrassment, yes. Could a woman die of humiliation? Because she was batting a thousand with Parker here. The guy probably thought she was the most incompetent person ever. She couldn't even swallow properly.

Okay, the first awkward encounter was all her, she'd claim it. But today was partially on him. It wasn't like she ever expected to see Hottie Firefighter again and certainly not in the context of a future family member.

Crap!

There went her idea to bring cookies over to the firehouse and slip him her number. That had been the fantasy she and her roommate discussed when she told Cora about her super sexy hero rescuer.

"Yes," she answered her dad, her attention never leaving Parker's face. They couldn't. Her gaze was trapped by the honey sweetness of his eyes and the sexy smile curling his lips as he stared at her. Whew! It was hotter in here than outside. "Um, Parker was one of the firefighters who helped me out of my...situation last week."

Her father's curiosity morphed into a grateful smile as he patted Parker on the shoulder.

"Oh, thank you, Parker." He shook his head. "When Tamsen called that night to tell me what happened, I—well, this isn't the first time one of her art projects has gotten her into trouble."

"Dad!"

Her father held up his hands. Parker merely arched one eyebrow in her direction.

Yeah, not going to happen, buddy. She was not rehashing the time she forgot to turn on the vent in the splatter room at school while she was working with spray paint and almost passed out. Or the time she left the adhesive she'd been working with too close to the kiln and it started a fire.

So she was a little accident prone. That's why she worked with paints and not power tools.

"I'm sorry, pumpkin, but you do tend to be a bit scattered when it comes to your projects. Remember the time you mistook the glass of paint thinner for your water and we had to rush you to the emergency—"

"Dad!" Her face burned, heat rising up her chest. What she wouldn't give for the earth to open up and swallow her whole right now. But since Colorado was better known for its wildfires and not earthquakes, she'd have to suffer through the humiliation of her hot future stepbrother learning what a dunce she was.

"Sounds like you might need my number on speed dial." Parker chuckled.

Tamsen held back a delicious shiver at the deep sound. Seriously, it should be illegal for the man to have a voice that sexy, let alone to keep saying double entendres like this.

"My father exaggerates my need for rescue." She eyed her father. "I promise I'm not as big a walking disaster as he makes out. He just likes to worry."

"As do all parents, darling." Victoria smiled. "That's our job, after all. Why, when Parker told me he was applying to the fire academy, I swear I didn't sleep for months."

Yeah, well, running into burning buildings and spilling oil paint all over the carpet in your rental unit were two very different levels of worry. She'd say Victoria had much more reason to fret over Parker than her dad had over her.

Parker rolled his eyes, giving her a small, conspiratorial smile. "How many gray hairs has your dad blamed on you, Tamsen? My mom swears I keep her colorist in business with all the stunts I've pulled over the years."

"Parker Kincaid." Victoria admonished him with a slight frown. "Haven't I taught you never to speak of a woman's appearance unless you are praising it?"

"Oops, now she'll have to book another appointment."

He winked at her then leaned in to kiss his mother on the cheek. Victoria sighed, but a smile curved her lips. Tamsen just bet Parker gave his mother all sorts of trouble with that cheeky attitude, but the older woman also appeared very proud of her son. Who wouldn't be? The guy was a genuine hero.

"The party is lovely, Victoria." Tamsen smiled, trying to get the conversation off her and Parker and back on the future bride and groom where it belonged.

"Thank you, dear. The ladies at Mile High Happiness do a wonderful job. However, they don't plan every festivity for our upcoming nuptials." Her gaze slid to her son. "Parker, darling, Thomas and I would absolutely love it if you and Tamsen would put your heads together and plan a joint shower for us."

What now?

"Isn't there another party planning company you could use?"

Parker's brow furrowed. He didn't look very happy to be planning a party with her. She swallowed back a ball of disappointment. Sure, she didn't want to spend time with a man who made her panties melt—yet was wholly untouchable—but did he have to be so obviously adverse to the idea?

Unless there was some other reason he didn't want to be a part of the festivities... Could Parker not be happy about the upcoming nuptials? Did he have a problem with his mom marrying her dad? She frowned at the thought. What was wrong with her dad? He might not be as well off as most of the people at this party, but he was a good man. Wasn't that all that counted?

"I could, darling, but this isn't like the wedding. We want this party to be intimate, only close family and friends." She pressed a perfectly manicured hand to her chest, directly over her heart. "A personal touch, one filled with love from our own children, would mean the world to us."

Oh, she was good. Tamsen had heard of mom guilt, but never having had a mother, she hadn't experienced it firsthand. Victoria was a masterclass in maternal manipulation.

Parker sighed. "It sounds like you're giving us a choice, but you're not, are you?"

His mother smiled, patting his cheek softly. "You always have a choice, darling, but I know you wouldn't want to disappoint your mother. Besides, it will give you two a chance to get to know each other, to bond."

No, no, no, no! More time with Parker was the last thing she needed. She didn't want to bond with the guy; she wanted to bone him. But since that was out the window with their parents getting married and all, spending time with him would be the worst form of torture.

"Of course, Mother." Parker smiled, but it looked a bit forced to Tamsen. "We'd be happy to plan something."

Nice of him to volunteer her. Not that she would say no to her dad anyway. But how in the hell was she supposed to spend more time around this man without embarrassing herself to death or ripping his clothes off to have her wicked way with him?

Both options ended in disaster.

"Um, yeah." She forced a smile to hide her panic. "We'd love to."

"Isn't that lovely, Thomas?"

Her dad stared at his fiancée like she hung the moon and stars. "It is indeed, dear."

Their conversation was interrupted when a woman with dark hair and glasses wearing a classic LBD approached them.

"Excuse me, Victoria? Thomas?"

Victoria and her dad smiled at the woman, apparently knowing who she was.

"I just have a few things I need to discuss with you if that's all right?"

"Of course," her father said, holding out his arm to Victoria. To her, he said, "Tamsen, this is one of the wedding planners, Lilly Reid. Lilly, this is my daughter, Tamsen, and Victoria's son, Parker."

"It's nice to meet you both." Lilly smiled. "Hope it's okay if I steal the bride and groom for a minute?"

Tamsen nodded, watching them walk away. It was so nice to see the blissful smile on her dad's face. She'd been worried about him ever since she moved out a few years ago. She knew she needed to start her own life, but she'd felt guilty about leaving her father all alone. Now he was getting a wife and Tamsen was getting a...stepbrother?

She supposed so, but did people really count the adult

children of their parent's new spouse as a sibling? They'd see each other at family functions, but it wasn't like they were really going to be brother and sister. Still, the whole thing made all the naughty things she wanted to do to Parker move firmly into the it's-too-complicated box. What if they tried something and it didn't work out?

Dammit.

Parker stood there smiling at her, his devastating grin causing a million butterflies to let loose low in her belly.

Down, hormones.

Life so wasn't fair.

"So, Tamsen, how are you doing?"

Completely mortified and ready to crawl into a cave for the next five decades.

"Great!"

He chuckled at her overly bright response.

Inwardly groaning at her continued stellar impression, she tried to go for mature and sophisticated. "It's great to see you. Though I really didn't expect to ever run into you again, let alone here and in the context of being my future stepbrother and all. Kind of a small world when you think about it. I mean, Denver isn't the biggest city, but who would have thought the guy who helped rescue me would turn out to be the son of my dad's fiancée and…" She trailed off as she noticed Parker's eyes widen. Crap, she'd gone off on a tangent again, hadn't she?

Nerves tended to make her mouth run away with her brain. Most people zoned out after a few of her rambling sentences, but Parker's eyes held a glint of laughter. If she couldn't impress him, at least she amused him. That was something, right?

Clearing her throat, she willed her anxiousness to settle the hell down. "I wanted to thank you again for helping me the other day. I've cast dozens of models, and I still can't believe I forgot to put the oil on."

She gestured to her chest, which thankfully had not suffered any long-term ill effects. Just a few days of her skin color resembling the boiled crab legs they served on Thursday nights and a bit sensitive to touch. Not that anyone was doing any touching lately anyway.

Parker's eyes followed the movement of her hand, the golden depths sparking with heat as his gaze settled over her chest. That was the horrible moment Tamsen remembered that while helping her, Parker had inadvertently seen her breasts.

Oh. My. God. My future stepbrother saw my boobs!

Was this seriously happening to her right now? Maybe she'd mixed some paints and set off a chemical reaction that caused her to hallucinate ridiculous scenarios intent on embarrassing her until she was nothing more than a puddle of goo.

She dug her nails into her palm. *Ouch!* Nope. Sadly, this was real life, and in real life, Parker had seen her boobs.

Fan-freaking-tastic.

Desperate to change the subject to anything else, she nodded toward the center of the room where her dad and Victoria stood talking with Lilly and looking over something on a clipboard the woman held in her hands.

"So, how 'bout this wedding, huh?" Oh great, and now she was a bad standup comedian.

Parker's smile dimmed, the heat in his eyes vanishing. He brought the champagne flute in his hand to his lips, taking a healthy swig before giving an offhanded shrug.

"Feels a little soon to me." His attention shifted to their parents. "They've only been dating six months. Why the rush?"

"Why wait when you're in love?" She smiled, watching her father hold Victoria tight to his side. "My dad's always been a bit of a romantic."

He grunted. Huh, could it be Parker was one of those people who didn't believe in romance? The man was certainly sexy enough to have his pick of women. But sex and love were two very different things. You could believe in one and not the other even if both existed.

"You don't believe in love at first sight?"

His gaze slid back to her, golden eyes sparking with something wicked and oh so naughty as the corner of his mouth ticked up.

"I believe in lust at first sight. But love? That takes time. And to be honest, I'm not all that convinced it even exists."

"Wow, cynical much?"

"Just calling it like I see it."

And he saw what exactly? A very dim view of the world if he didn't believe in love. She understood not believing in love at first sight, but not believing in it at all? Seemed kind of sad and lonely to her.

"Well, my dad has always been a big ol' softie. Romantic to the core." She smiled as she glanced across the crowded room to the man who taught her everything about life, held her when she cried, cheered her when she succeeded, and made her feel more loved than any kid ever in the entire world. "He proposed to my mom after two weeks."

Parker made a disbelieving sound. She turned to see a skeptical expression on his face.

"It's true," she insisted. "He told me when you know you know, and with my mom, he knew. According to Dad, they were ridiculously happily married until the day my mom died."

Parker sucked in a sharp breath. "I'm sorry. I had no idea…"

"It's okay." It wasn't really, but people never really knew what to say or do when the subject of death was brought up.

"It happened when I was three, so I really don't remember much. But Dad stayed single for the next fifteen years. He didn't date anyone until I graduated from high school, and even then, it wasn't much."

Sometimes she wondered if the years of grief and loneliness she witnessed—despite her father's attempts to hide it from her—were worth the years her parents shared together. She enjoyed casual relationships, but to lose yourself so deeply like her father had done with her mother...didn't seem worth it to her. Until he met Victoria, she worried he'd be alone forever.

"Your mom is the only woman I've ever seen him get serious about." She glanced back at her dad and Victoria once more, unable to keep the happy sigh from escaping her lips. "I haven't seen him this happy in ages."

"Huh, I suppose at their age having a long engagement isn't exactly prudent."

Seriously? That's what he got from what she said? Not the romantic love stuff, but that their parents were old and should get married ASAP? They were in their sixties, not eighties. It wasn't like they were knocking on death's door.

"I didn't expect you to be such a love downer, Parker."

He arched one brow, his lips curling once again in that wicked smile that threatened to set her panties on fire.

He took a step closer. "Been thinking about me lately, Tamsen?"

If he only knew. No. He shouldn't know. And she had to stop thinking about them. They were going to be family soon. It was naughty. *Wrong!* She meant wrong, not naughty. Jeez, she really needed to get her hormones under control. Maybe she did need to find the time to sneak in a quick date or two. Or at least a few minutes with her battery-operated boyfriend.

"I...um...what?"

He chuckled, low and deep.

Ooooh, she liked that chuckle. Too much. She wanted to wrap it up and take it home, pull it out in the dark of the night, and press it against her until the only thing she felt was Parker's warm, rumbly voice caressing every inch of her body.

There went her artist brain again. Dreaming up improbable situations that defied the laws of physics.

Whatever. She barely passed physics anyway.

Parker stepped forward. Now mere inches separated them. She could see the dark stubble on his sharp jaw, the flecks of deep green in his golden eyes, the fullness of his bottom lip. Oh, how she wanted to grab a brush and paint that lip, and those eyes, and really everything on the man. Or maybe she should break out her clay and sculpt him. Naked.

Her heart started to pound a furious beat in her chest. Yeah. She'd bet Parker would put Michelangelo's *David* to shame.

"Can I have your number?"

"Huh?" Her brain had short circuited. He was too close, too handsome, too…everything.

"For the party planning. We need to talk in order to plan the party, right? Though, if you want to hire a planner on the DL so we don't have to deal with any of this nonsense, I'm all for it."

She frowned. Warm fuzzies squashed by his comment. She knew Parker wasn't as excited for their parents' upcoming nuptials as she was, but could the guy show an ounce of excitement for his mother? Personally, she loved planning a festive get together. Seeing the smiles on the guests of honor's faces when they saw all the hard work that went in to celebrating them.

"We promised we would plan it. I don't think your mother would approve of you pushing it off onto someone else. Besides, it will make her happy."

He sighed as if the party was a giant burden rather than a fun celebration.

"You're right. Sorry, I'm not really a party-planning guy, but if it makes my mother smile, I'll do it."

Awwww, and the warm fuzzies were back. She supposed she should give the guy a break. He might just be having a hard time with his mom remarrying. She might be excited for her dad because her mom had been gone for so long, but she had no idea what Parker's situation with his own father was like. This wedding thing might be harder on him than it was on her.

She held out her hand. "Give me your phone and I'll put my number in."

He pulled his cell from his pocket and unlocked it so she could put in her contact info. She handed it back and he started typing. A second later, her phone pinged with a text message notification.

"And now you have mine." He smiled, slipping his phone back into his pocket. "It was great to see you again, Tamsen."

He leaned closer, so close she could feel the heat of his breath on her cheek, smell the rich sandalwood scent of his aftershave. A shiver raced up her spine as his lips brushed her ear.

"Though I really wish it had been under less...familial circumstances."

Just as her body screamed, *to hell with it all*, and threatened to jump his bones in the middle of their parents' very crowded and fancy engagement party, he pulled back and gave her a wink.

"See you soon."

Then he turned and headed across the room, allowing her to exhale the biggest breath of pent-up sexual energy in her life. Oh no. This was so bad. She could not have the hots for Parker. Well, she could, and she obviously did, but she couldn't do anything about it.

…Could she?

No. Definitely not.

Ugh, this was so unfair! And now they had to spend time together planning a party for their parents. How? How was she going to keep her hands to herself around all that delicious temptation?

Her stomach pitched and dipped with the knowledge, fluttering with all kinds of naughty anticipation.

She was glad her father was happy, but right now, Tamsen wished he had picked anyone other than Victoria Kincaid to fall in love with.

Chapter Four

"Tamsen, order up!"

Tamsen placed her last table's dirty dishes in the bin by the industrial dishwasher. Normally the busser would handle clearing the tables, but they were a little short staffed today. Lucky for her, her coworkers were awesome, and everyone was willing to pitch in when needed.

She hustled over to where her table's food waited under the warming lamps. "Thanks, Ty."

The chef smiled, gracing those deep, dark dimples that made half the women, and men, in Denver lose their clothes. But Tamsen preferred to avoid any drama due to ill-conceived crushes on the job. She didn't have time in her life for dating right now anyway.

She brought the meals out to her table, who were—thankfully—very pleasant and easy customers. The lunch rush had lulled, and there were a few hours until the dinner crowd came in. After her last table left, she headed to the back to catch up on some side work. Rolling silverware wasn't the most exciting of activities, but at least she got to sit down while doing it. She winced as the pressure finally lifted from her feet.

Though she liked her job just fine, she wished she were in the studio today. The truth was she always wished she were in the studio, or her apartment, or anywhere she could pick up a paintbrush, or charcoal, or lump of clay. If only art paid the bills. She sighed. Someday it would—she knew it. All she had to do was work hard and keep creating. Her big break was just around the corner; she could feel it.

"Hey, Tamsen."

She glanced up to see her coworker Jade stroll in with an armful of dirty dishes and...a half glass of lemonade filled with wadded-up napkins? People were gross and didn't tip nearly enough for the crap servers had to put up with.

"Hi, Jade. How's it going?"

"It'd be better if the campers at table seven would leave and the douches who graced me with a giant mess at table two would have left a fucking tip."

Yup, people sucked.

"Want me to go hurry seven along?" Campers were the worst. They ordered a meal or sometimes just a drink and sat yammering on for far longer than should be humanly possible.

"Naw." Jade waved away her offer. "They've paid and it's quiet out there, so it's not a big deal." Sliding in by Tamsen, a bright sparkle in her dark brown eyes, Jade grabbed a set of silverware and a pile of napkins, rolling along with Tamsen. "Besides, I wanna hear how the party went last night."

"It was great. The appetizers were delicious, the champagne was free."

"Best kind there is."

They clinked forks in agreement before continuing to roll.

"My dad looked really happy, and Victoria is really nice."

If not a little upper crust, but she didn't hold that against the woman. If she didn't mind the socioeconomic gap between her and her future husband, why should Tamsen?

"And I...um...she has a son." Nerves fluttered in her stomach. The totally inappropriate and wickedly naughty dream she'd had last night involving Parker and his "fire hose" rose up in her mind. Heat burned her cheeks, and she ducked her head, hoping her friend was too busy with her side work to notice the blush on Tamsen's face.

"Cool, so you're getting a brother? How old is he?"

"*Step*brother," Tamsen emphasized. The *step* was very important. "And I'm not sure, late twenties, early thirties would be my guess. But I...ah, I do know him."

Jade paused in her rolling, eyes focusing on Tamsen. "You do?"

"Yup. It's Parker." At her friend's blank expression, she explained, "The firefighter who rescued me from my... predicament."

Jade's mouth dropped open in shock. "Hottie Hero!"

She cringed at the nickname her coworkers had given Parker when she told them the story last week. Yeah, she might have mentioned a time or twenty how good-looking he was, but did they have to give him such a silly moniker just to embarrass her?

Duh, you gave them the ammo, Tamsen.

No mercy in the service world.

"Hottie Hero is going to be your brother?"

"*Step*brother." Again, a very important distinction.

Jade's lips rose in a wide grin, laughter escaping as she patted Tamsen on the cheek. "Oh, sweetie, I am so sorry. That sucks so much for you. But on the bright side, now you can introduce him to me."

"You can't hook up with my future stepbrother."

One dark eyebrow rose as Jade crossed her arms over her

chest. "And why not? Is he seeing someone? Married?"

She had no idea. She barely knew the guy. "I don't know, but he's going to be my"—she had to swallow past an uncomfortable lump in her throat—"family, kind of. It'd be weird."

"Weirder than you having the hots for your new brother?"

"*Step!* He's my *future* stepbrother. We're not living together. The only time we'll see each other is at family functions. No creepy incest vibes, and anyway, who said I had the hots for him?"

Jade snorted out a laugh. "You did, the other day when you told me how awkward it was that your nipples got all stiff and happy when he was saving you from the plaster disaster."

She covered her burning face with her hands, muffled mortified words coming out between her fingers. "Oh my god, I am never telling you anything ever again."

"Relax, girl." Jade took pity on her, nudging Tamsen with her hip before returning to her rolling. "I'm just messing with you. Besides, I have another date with Hella Hot."

Wait, Jade was going out with a supervillain?

"Who?"

Jade gave a very un-Jade-like shy smile, answering with a small shrug. "Her real name is Ella. She's the lead Jammer for the Rocky Mountain Rollers."

Right, one of the roller derby teams. Tamsen wasn't really into sports, but she loved supporting her friends. She'd gone to a couple of bouts to see Jade play, and it was brutal yet oddly exhilarating. She had no idea how the women could skate so fast and not fall right on their butts. Well, they did fall, but usually only when someone hit them. She was still iffy on how the game was played, but she knew enough to know the Rocky Mountain Rollers were the rivals of Jade's team, the LODO Maniacs.

"Why, Jade," she teased, fluttering a cloth napkin at her

friend. "Are you telling me you're consorting with the enemy? Is this a case of skate-crossed lovers?"

"Shut up." Jade tossed a napkin at her, but the smile on her face grew. "We're just having fun. Nothing serious."

Famous last words from every romcom Tamsen had ever seen. And she'd seen a lot.

At least one of them was getting some action. The last time she had anything resembling fun in the romance department was...far too long ago for her liking. But dating required time, and between the restaurant, her internship at the gallery, and finding those precious spare moments to work on her own creative projects, she had little to zero energy to hit the dating scene. Plus, every guy she'd started dating tended to get to a point where they wanted...more.

Tamsen wasn't a love hater—like Parker appeared to be—but she wasn't sure she wanted to go for all that happily ever after stuff. After all, she knew better than anyone that no matter how happy you were, life didn't guarantee an ever after, and she wasn't going to risk her heart like that.

The way her dad had.

Her entire life, watching the way he missed her mother with a melancholy heartache he always tried to hide, it kind of put the damper on the whole *true love forever* idea in her mind.

But now he's with Victoria.

True, but two decades of loneliness and misery sounded like hell. No, thank you—she'd stick to fun, temporary times.

Maybe she should download one of those hookup apps. Swipe right for some sexual release. Eh, she'd never really been all that good at sleeping with random strangers. To each their own, but Tamsen liked to know a guy for a bit before she hopped into bed with him.

It was the artist in her. She had to feel that...connection.

Her phone pinged with an incoming text message. Even

though they technically weren't allowed to check their phones at work, their manager didn't care as long as it wasn't in front of the customers. Tamsen reached into the small black apron tied around her waist and pulled out her phone.

"Is hottie stepbrother asking for a date?" Jade baited.

"Stop it, and no. It's Cora asking if we're all still on for pub quiz tonight. She found a potential replacement for Cap Hill Bar."

"I'm in." Jade leaned around the corner to shout into the kitchen area. "Hey, Ty, Niko, you guys up for trivia tonight?"

The cooks shouted their agreement, so Tamsen texted her roomie back a thumbs up. Her trivia team, The Lumbersnacks, had a winning streak to uphold. They used to attend a pub quiz at Cap Hill, and since it closed its doors, they'd been looking for a new spot. None of the bars' quiz times had worked out with everyone's schedule until Cora discovered City Tavern had the same time slot Cap Hill used to.

"I'll take these up to the host stand if you wanna grab the refills for the salt and pepper," she told Jade as she scooped all the rolled silverware they'd finished into a clean plastic tub.

"You got it."

The rest of her shift went smoothly, with a busy enough dinner rush that kept her mind occupied with specials and cocktail orders. No time to dwell on frustrating predicaments of sexy firefighters who were soon to be family members. She cashed out, tipping the kitchen before pocketing a nice hundred and ten in tips for herself. Maybe she could afford a call drink tonight at the bar instead of a well.

After running to her apartment to meet up with Cora and change into their team's trademark plaid button-ups, she headed to City Tavern with her roomie to meet the rest of their team.

The moment she stepped through the doors of the dimly lit bar, she felt a sense of rightness. It was intimate but not too small. A dozen or so tables were scattered about the room, most of them filled with people hunkering down over sheets of paper, arguing over team names.

There looked to be another room off to the right with a pool table and dartboard. Good. The last bar they tried had the dartboard in the main room, and every time she went up to turn the answer sheets in, she had to dodge flying missiles. A decent-sized bar took up most of the left side of the room with a small jukebox tucked in the corner, currently off because trivia started in ten minutes.

"Looks like Jade already snagged a table," Cora said, pointing to a far corner where a group of their friends sat in various colors of plaid shirts.

Tamsen waved, nudging her roomie. "You go sit and I'll grab us the first round."

"You sure?"

"Yeah, you want a beer or rum and coke?"

Cora rolled her neck, and Tamsen cringed at the cracking sound indicating her friend had had a hard day at the hospital.

"Make it the strong stuff. Today was brutal, and I need to unwind."

"You got it."

She made her way to the bar, grateful most of the trivia participants were already seated with their drinks. Nothing was worse than coming off a long shift only to sink back into the chaos of a crowd. Once she snagged the bartender's attention, she ordered a rum and coke for Cora and a sex on the beach for herself. Yeah, she liked froufrou drinks, and she wasn't ashamed. They were tasty.

She paid, tipping very generously because solidarity, and headed back to the table where her friends sat.

As she moved through the small throng of people and

tables, the person in the chair to her right suddenly pushed back to stand. She quickly pivoted to her left to avoid collision but ended up hitting a solid brick wall. The drinks in her hands sloshed, threatening to spill the delicious alcohol meant to help them unwind from a hard day, but years of working in the fast-paced world of serving kicked in. A little shuffle and clever balancing and the liquid righted in the glasses. Only a small drop spilled over the side of her drink and rolled down the glass.

"Impressive, Tamsen."

Uh oh. She knew that deep, rumbly voice. She turned to the brick wall, which turned out not to be a brick wall at all but the very hard chest of one Parker Kincaid.

What the hell is he doing here?

"Parker! What are you doing here?"

He smiled, the sight making her thighs clench together.

"Same thing as you, I imagine. Drinking and pub quiz."

"You do pub quiz?"

"Yup. The crew from the station goes every week." He motioned to a table full of buff-looking men and women. "At least those of us not on shift."

Well, this was just perfect. Here she'd been looking forward to a night out with friends to get her mind off the very man who just happened to be standing right in front of her. What the hell had she done to karma lately for it to be such a bitch to her?

"Oh, that's nice. Yeah, my friends and I go every week, too."

He cocked his head. "Huh, I don't remember seeing you here before."

"Oh, that's because we used to go to Cap Hill, but then it closed down and we've been hitting up all the different bars trying to find the right fit. It's hard because a lot of us work odd schedules, and finding a night that works for all of us is tricky. We've been doing it for over a year now and, not to brag, but we're really good, so we don't break up the team, and my roommate Cora found this place that holds trivia the same night Cap Hill used to, so it works out for everyone and..."

She trailed off when she noticed Parker's wide grin as he stared at her.

"And I rambled again. Sorry. I tend to do that when I get nervous."

Curiosity lit his eyes. "Do I make you nervous, Tamsen?"

"No," she lied through her teeth. "I just feel bad because I've been too busy to text you about getting together to plan our parents' party."

He frowned at the mention of the dual wedding shower they were supposed to plan together. Jeez, what was this guy's issue with weddings? Maybe he was just weirded out by his mom getting married again. She'd admit it felt a bit strange to her, too, because she'd only known her father as a single man, but she was happy for him. Wasn't Parker happy for his mother?

"It's been one day, Tamsen." He pasted that carefree smile back on his face. "I think you're off the hook, etiquette-wise."

"I hope your team is prepared to get their butts kicked tonight," she teased because she really didn't want to talk about their parents, weddings, party planning, or anything that reminded her how off-limits this man was to her.

His tongue came out to graze along his top teeth, and she had to hunch her shoulders, hoping her nipples weren't poking through her top. Good grief! One tiny glimpse of the man's tongue and they were harder than diamonds. Perfect little turkey timers. Ding, ding! She was ready.

"Your team is that good?" he asked.

Dragging her thoughts away from the dirty, dirty

gutter they were rolling around in, she lifted her chin. "The Lumbersnacks held the winning streak at Cap Hill for six months straight."

He rocked back on his heels, shaking his head. "I'm sorry, did you say The Lumbersnacks?"

"Yeah." She pointed to her shirt then indicated the table where all her friends sat. Staring at her and Parker with rapt attention, not even trying to hide their nosiness. That was going to be fun when she got to the table.

"Are you all woodworkers or something?"

She shook her head. "No, we thought we'd capitalize on the hipster culture with a funny pun. What's your team called?"

"Most Extinguished."

She laughed. Of course it was. "I get it, because you're all firefighters."

He tapped the end of her nose with a finger. "You got it."

The simple touch sent a zing of electricity straight through her body all the way down to her good parts. If they ever touched in the way she fantasized, in the ways they did in her dreams, they'd start a fire even he and all the Most Extinguished members couldn't put out.

"Well, I...um...better get over there."

He nodded, winking as she moved to leave. "May the best team win."

"Don't worry, we will."

His laughter followed her all the way back to her table where, judging by the eager expressions on her friends' faces, she was about to suffer the inquisition of The Lumbersnacks.

Oh boy. Tamsen set down Cora's drink and took a healthy gulp of her own as she sat, five sets of curious eyes all on her. She swore she could feel a sixth, and when she turned her head, sure enough, there sat Parker, across the room, his hot gaze trained on her. When he saw her looking, he lifted his own drink and…

Winked.

Her entire core tightened, and she took another drink to cool off the suddenly skyrocketing temperature in her body.

This was going to be a very long night.

Chapter Five

"Hey, isn't that the woman we rescued from the stuck cast call?" Ward asked as Parker took a seat beside him.

Parker's gaze locked on Tamsen, sitting with her friends a few tables away. When she glanced his way, he gave her a flirty wink. Her blush sent a burst of lust straight to his gut. He shifted in his seat, hoping the reaction didn't show on his face.

"Yeah, that's Tamsen."

"That's great, man." Ward slapped him on the shoulder. "Now you can ask her out."

"He can't do that," Díaz protested. "She's a call—that's totally inappropriate."

Ward placed an elbow on the large table they were sharing, leaning in closer to Díaz. "No, she *was* a call, but now she's just a woman in a bar, and we're all off shift. He can go ask for her number, and she's totally free to turn his ugly ass down."

Parker snorted, lifting his beer to his lips. "Thanks, Ward."

"Not everyone can be graced by the beauty gods, my friend."

Now it was Díaz's turn to snort. "I think you need a new mirror, Ward. One that isn't so warped."

Ah, the good old firehouse ribbing. The more everyone insulted you, the more they loved you. Some people might find it strange, but when you worked in a profession where you put your life on the line, you had to have coping mechanisms. And giving each other shit under the guise of affection was Station 42's way. But with Ward and Díaz, it always felt like something...more.

"Whatever, I'm sexy and I know it."

Ward bobbed his eyebrows at Díaz, who brushed him off, but Parker saw the tiny smile at the corner of her lips. Yeah, the woman had it bad, but he wasn't about to tell her that. He liked his balls where they were, thank you very much.

"Technically, Ward is right," O'Neil agreed. "And for a call with no fire, there were definitely some sparks in that apartment."

What? Parker had been a complete professional during Tamsen's emergency. On the outside. But his crewmates knew him; maybe he hadn't hidden his attraction as well as he thought. Hopefully, Tamsen hadn't noticed.

"Yup." Ward nodded. "She totally has the hots for you, dude."

"Hero worship," Díaz argued.

O'Neil nodded in the direction of Tamsen. "You should ask her out."

"I can't." With the party planning hanging over their heads, he wondered how often he would see her and how long it would take for this driving need inside him to see her naked—her long dark hair spread out on his pillow as he pleasured her in every way imaginable—to go away. Because as much as he wanted to ask her out, as much as he'd seen the spark of heat in her eyes that matched the raging fire of need low in his gut every time he so much as thought about the woman, there was one big problem. "Her dad is marrying my mom."

A hushed silence fell over the table. It lasted a full minute until Ward opened his mouth and said with a smartass grin, "*Hot for My Stepsister.* I think I've seen that film."

The table erupted in a chorus of groans. Díaz smacked Ward's chest with the back of her hand.

"Ow!" Ward rubbed the offended area. "What was that for?"

"For having the maturity of a twelve-year-old."

Parker tipped his drink to Díaz, who nodded back.

The MC got on the mic, announcing the start of trivia. Everyone settled down, pencils poised over their answer sheets to write down their guesses to round one questions. Parker's head wasn't in the game. It was twenty feet across the room with a dark-haired beauty who, thanks to his mother, was now completely off-limits.

Or was she?

It wasn't like he was thrilled about his mom marrying Thomas, a guy she'd known for less than a year. A guy who appeared to be on another income tier compared to his mom. He remembered his mom said something about Thomas working at a library. That couldn't pay much. Not that Parker had anything against working-class guys. Hell, *he* was a working-class guy. With a sizable inheritance he rarely touched. But he was wary, and rightly so, about any man who got involved with his mother. It wouldn't be the first time someone wooed Victoria McMillian Kincaid for her money.

There was Charles, who told his mother he was some fancy oil tycoon. Turned out, after Parker had his PI do some digging, dear old Charles had been kicked out of the family and the oil business due to his gambling problem. His mother had been just another mark in a long line since his family cut him off.

Then there was Magnus, who almost got his mother to the alter on promises of love and happily ever afters, before Parker discovered that wasn't even the guy's real name. Magnus, aka Mike, was a long-time con man with warrants in two states.

Fucking bastards.

The moment he found out about the engagement, he'd fired off an email to his PI asking him to look into Thomas Hayes and now was awaiting the findings. Frank was a former detective with enough connections to dig up anything, no matter how deep someone tried to bury it. It's how he discovered the last two guys his mom dated were gold-digging scum bags.

His gaze snagged on Tamsen again, hunched over the table, speaking in hushed whispers with her teammates. She looked up, as if she could feel him watching her. A tentative smile curled her lips, and she gave him a little wave.

He smiled back, his entire body hardening from the simple gesture. The tiny gesture of a few fingers. *Damn.* He was in a sticky situation. There was no way he could sleep with Tamsen while investigating her father. The two might have nothing to do with each other, but from the outside, it looked sketchy as hell.

Maybe if the investigation came back clean... It wasn't like he wanted to break up his mother's relationship. He just wanted to make sure her fiancé wasn't hiding any nefarious intent. It absolutely killed him to see the pain in her eyes every time some jerk tried to take advantage of her, but he would feel worse if he sat back and let it happen when he could do something to protect her.

Which meant no sex with Tamsen.

No matter how badly his body burned for her.

The first four rounds dragged as Parker found his attention divided between trying to help his team and sneaking glances of Tamsen. Never had a woman distracted him as much as she did, and she wasn't even paying him any attention. Maybe it was the fact that he couldn't have her that had him so fascinated.

Yeah, that had to be it. Parker Kincaid did not obsess over women. He liked them, loved them in fact, but he never lost his head over one. He'd seen what losing yourself in someone else could do to a person. The power it gave them. No, thank you.

He wasn't even sure love really existed after years of watching his mother constantly try to please his father's impossible high standards, always falling short. The requests and conversations that eventually turned into arguments and shouting matches. The nights he'd heard his mother sobbing in the kitchen when she thought he was fast asleep in bed. All the work of a man who claimed to love her? If that was love, he wanted no part of it.

By the middle of the game, The Lumbersnacks and Most Extinguished were tied for the lead, with every other team at least a dozen points behind. The MC called a short break before the second half. With eight rounds, the questions only got harder from here on in. Or maybe it just seemed that way because by the second half of the night most people were a few *drinks* in.

Parker jiggled the empty beer bottle in front of him. He was still on his first because his team liked to keep clear heads. Let the other teams drink themselves stupid. They were here to win. First place won a twenty-five-dollar gift certificate to the bar, but he didn't care about the monetary prize. It was all about the bragging rights. Which was why he found it so confusing when every time Tamsen's team scored more points, a small part of him secretly cheered her on.

Ward stood, motioning to everyone at the table. "I'll grab the next round. Díaz, you wanna split some nachos?"

Ward and Díaz had come to trivia fresh off shift, unlike O'Neil and him. Sometimes the hunger took a few hours to hit.

"As long as you're not cooking them, I'll eat them." Díaz smiled up at Ward, a wicked glint in her eyes.

"Oh ha, ha. Don't quit your day job."

Ward headed off to the bar to put in their order while O'Neil stepped outside to take a phone call. Parker turned to Díaz. "Kicking the puppy awfully hard today, D."

She stared after Ward, who stood at the bar, patiently waiting his turn. "Got called to a traffic accident today." Her jaw clenched. "One of the drivers didn't make it."

Shit. Fatalities were the hardest calls. It was a hazard of the job that you never got used to. And another reason he and a lot of his fellow firefighters preferred to keep their status in singledom. Navigating a relationship with such a dangerous career was tough.

Still, some of them managed to have families. Finn had Pru and the twins; Turner and his husband were looking to adopt. Hell, even the chief had four kids of his own, all grown now, but somehow, they all managed the tricky dynamic of being a first responder and having a family life.

"You guys didn't need to come out tonight." Now that he looked back, Ward had been kind of tense since he arrived, and the guy had been drinking soda, not beer. Shit, that should have been a big neon sign indicating something was off.

Díaz shook her head, eyes still trained on Ward. "You know Ward. If I treated him with kid gloves, he'd bite my head off and tell me to shove it up my ass. Better to act like normal and let him process in peace."

That was certainly true. First rule of being a firefighter:

when the shit gets tough, you hold it together until you can break down in private.

"I'm gonna hit the head." He stood. She lifted her drink, which he just now noticed was also soda.

"I'll keep the table from floating away."

He chuckled at her weird sense of humor. He liked Díaz, and everyone he worked with at the station. Which was why it sucked so much whenever any of them had a bad call. When one of them suffered, it felt like they all did. But no one wanted to talk about it, because it didn't take the pain away. Somehow it only seemed to amplify it. So they joked and teased to show they had each other's backs.

Who needed a family when you had the firehouse?

Coming back from the restroom, he passed by the women's bathroom when suddenly the door swung open. Right into his face. Parker skidded to a halt, but it didn't stop the hard oak from slamming right into his forehead.

"Sonofabitch!"

He heard a soft gasp, and the door swung back to reveal a horrified Tamsen.

"Oh my God, Parker. I am so sorry. I didn't know anyone was there. I swear I just nudged it open with my hip. I must have bumped it too hard. I don't like touching door handles because gross...there's like so many germs on those things. Seriously the amount of people who don't wash their hands and then get their grubby bacteria-infested mitts on all the door handles of the world would surprise you. I read this article once that said thousands of microbes are living on—"

"Tamsen, Tamsen." He held up a hand to stop her adorable, but headed into disturbing, ramblings. "It's okay. I'm fine."

She bit her lower lip. Cheeks blushing a dusty rose as she stared up at him, her pupils grew bigger, causing her eyes to darken as the black overtook the bright blue. "Are you sure?

Let me see."

She stepped closer, grasping his head in her hands and tilting him down so she could stare at the wounded area. He happily bent his knees to bring himself closer for inspection. Her warm, soft hands set his body on fire, sending signals straight to his dick to wake up for fun time. He willed the eager appendage to stand down. That wasn't what this was. But he couldn't stop the feeling of absolute enjoyment coursing through him at her touch.

This close, he could smell the aromas of acrylic paint and greasy hamburgers wafting from her skin and clothing. It was an odd combination, but somehow, on Tamsen, it worked. He noticed how blue her eyes were. Not a speck of green or brown in them. Just pure, pale blue, like a summer sky without a cloud in sight. She also had a faint smattering of freckles running across the bridge of her nose. And those lips, full and pink, just begging for him to taste them. He was so close. All he'd have to do was lean in another inch or so and he could—

"I don't see a lump. Just a bit of redness." She sighed happily. "Phew. I've already embarrassed myself enough around you. No need to add giving you a concussion to the mix."

He pulled back, grateful she interrupted his wayward thoughts before he could do something outrageous like act on them.

Yeah, I'm super grateful I'm not kissing this beautiful woman right now.

"You guys are pretty good," he said, leaning back against the wall to put as much space as possible between them in the tight hallway. It didn't help much.

She scoffed, cocking out a hip and placing her hand on it. "Good? We're destroying you."

Oh, so she liked smack talk? "Last time I checked, the

scores were tied."

"Only because we're going easy on the heroes. It's a courtesy that ends now." A wicked smile lit her face. "Little tip, we always crush it in the last half of the game."

"The same way you all crush paper towel logo wear?" He reached out to tug on the tail end of the flannel, knotted at her waist, just above the black leggings that were hugging every dip and curve of her legs and ass. Not that he'd been staring. Much.

"I look adorable and you know it."

He grinned at her sass. "I was going to say hot as hell, but adorable works, too."

Oops. Where had that come from? He knew he wasn't supposed to be flirting with Tamsen, but he couldn't seem to stop himself. Her eyes widened, cheeks flushing red.

Lifting a finger, she pointed it in his face. "Don't try to distract me, Parker. You guys are going down."

"Those sound like betting words."

"Wanna put a wager on the game?"

Yes, he did. But not the kind of wager he should.

"Okay, Mr. Hot Shot Firefighter." Her arms crossed over her chest as her eyes danced with overconfidence. "Name your stakes."

"Sex on the beach."

Her jaw dropped, mouth popping. Heat filled her gaze as her face flushed. Her tongue came out to swipe against her lower lip in a move that he was sure wasn't intentional but had him groaning all the same.

"Colorado doesn't have any beaches," she whispered in a breathy voice.

He leaned in close until their faces were centimeters apart. Arching one eyebrow, he answered, "I meant the drink. It's what you had earlier, right?"

The flush on her cheeks turned bright red, a nervous

laugh escaping her as she shook her head. "Oh right, yes. It was. You meant bet for drinks."

He hadn't. Not really. But he'd have to settle for outrageous flirting and taking extra-long cold showers for the next…however long this weird chemistry thing lasted.

"Loser buys drinks."

She held out her hand. Knowing it was a bad idea to touch her, even her hand, but unable to stop himself, Parker grasped her hand in his and shook. Electric sparks shot through his blood at her touch. It felt like the first time he picked up a hose. Thrilling and right. Weighted.

When her team did indeed crush it in the second half of the game, Parker sent over her drink and watched with pained fascination as she sucked from the straw, wishing like hell Colorado had just one fucking beach.

Chapter Six

"These potatoes are freezing!"

Tamsen held back a sigh, cheeks hurting from the tight, wide smile she'd forced her expression into. This was the fifth complaint this table had made about their food, and she was at the end of her rope.

"I'm so sorry, sir." Sorry she couldn't toss his water in his face. The glass of water he made her replace *twice* because there wasn't enough ice in it. Who the hell counted ice cubes? "But you did order our garlic herb potato salad, which is traditionally served cold."

The man's face soured, his frown morphing into a scowl as he glared. *Whatever, buddy.* If he thought a little scowl would intimidate her, he better think again. She'd been a server for years. She'd been yelled at, spit at, threatened, and once a customer even threw her purse at Tamsen. Nothing fazed her anymore.

"I'm the customer," Sourpuss insisted. "That means I'm always right, and I want my potatoes hot."

If she ever found the person who coined the phrase "the

customer is always right," she was going to drown them in a vat of ranch dressing. Ridiculous. The customers liked to order steak well done and ask for crème brûlée without the caramelization. They were far from always right.

"I can ask the chef to heat them for you if you'd like, sir." She drew her eyebrows together, affecting a sympathetic expression, because as much as she wanted to flip this guy the bird, she needed the tips. Not that she imagined Mr. Sourpuss was going to leave her a very good one. Or one at all. Still, she liked her job, and shoving this guy's face in his cold potatoes until they warmed up from all the hot air he was filled with would probably get her fired.

"Yes, and I expect a discount on our bill for all the trouble we've encountered tonight."

Of course he did.

"I'm a top-rated food site reviewer, you know. I'm sure your manager wouldn't like for the restaurant to get a one-star review because of your incompetence."

Her teeth felt like they would crack as she clenched them hard, drawing up all her years of dealing with assholes to keep the smile on her face as she took the man's plate. Why did customers always blame servers for food issues? She wasn't the cook.

Besides, her manager knew the score; she wouldn't care what this jerk said. Everyone and their brother was a "top-rated food site reviewer" these days. The internet was great, but it also made some people feel far more important than they really were.

Self-entitled jackasses.

"I'll be right back with your *warm* potatoes, sir."

The guy grunted as she turned and headed back to the kitchen. The second she swung through the door, she dropped her smile and swore.

"Asshole!"

"Table seven?" Jade asked.

"You know it." Servers could spot a trouble table a mile away.

Jade grabbed her order from the warming shelf separating the servers from the kitchen staff. "Need any help?"

"Can you help me push the guy off a cliff?"

"Too obvious." Jade winked with a laugh. "Just drop his fork on the floor before you return his food."

She chuckled as her friend headed out to her own tables. As much as Tamsen would love to give the guy what he deserved, she'd never intentionally harm someone's food. They could be the biggest jerk in the world—and he was—but the customers trusted her with their food, and she took that trust seriously. Instead, she'd just call him all the creative four-letter insults she could think of in her head and have Ty heat the guy's freakin' food.

"Hey, Ty—"

"No!" Ty pointed his tongs at her from his spot at the grill.

"You didn't even let me finish."

He shook his head, focusing on his task as he spoke. "It's for table seven, and they've already complained a million times. Just no."

"Exaggerate much?" He wasn't wrong, though. They were the worst, and she hated to ask, but it was the nature of her job. "He just wants his potatoes heated."

Ty's frowning, tight mouth dropped open. A look of abject horror filling his face.

"It's potato salad. It's not supposed to be warm."

"I know, but he wants it warm."

She let out a heavy sigh. It was the last half hour of her shift. The day had been super hectic, which meant the tips were bad, since she'd been running around trying to attend to all her tables...and failing some. She'd never understand where people's sympathy went when they saw a busy restaurant. Why did they always think their order was more important than the twelve other tables she had? She was doing her best, but it never seemed like enough some days.

"Toss it in the microwave." Ty motioned to one of the two microwaves lining the far wall on the server side of the kitchen. "I'm sure the asshole's steak is cold now, too—better to just heat the entire plate."

Not a bad idea. Plus, she'd get the added satisfaction of knowing the guy's steak would dry out a little. Not that his *sophisticated* palette would notice. *Warm potato salad.* Ugh, her stomach turned just thinking about it.

Making her way to the microwave, she popped the door open and set the plate inside. Then she turned to grab her water, downing half of it in three big gulps, while the food was nuked.

Man, she was exhausted. At least this was her last table for the day and—

Crack!

The loud sound coming from behind her startled her. Turning, she stared in horror as the plate inside the microwave sparked, bolts of what looked like miniature lightning arching across the inside.

No…not the plate sparking. It's the—

"Fork!"

She mentally kicked herself. In her exhausted haze, she'd forgotten the guy left his fork on the plate and she tossed it in. The metal fork was currently cooking inside the microwave. She had to get it out before—

"Fire!" Ty shouted.

Oh no! No, no, no!

The sparks had become flames, and the flames were consuming the microwave. Panicking, she tossed her water on it, but she'd drunk so much, the bottle hardly contained anything at all. The flames started to flick out the seams of the microwave door. Smoke billowed from the back of the machine, floating to the ceiling, where it set off the restaurant's fire alarm.

"Shit, shit, shit!" She was going to get in so much trouble for this. She had to do something.

Glancing around, she took a deep breath and cleared the fog of panic from her brain, then spotted the fire extinguisher on the far wall. Racing for it, she pulled it from its stand. She'd never used a fire extinguisher before, but she knew the basics. *Pull the pin, aim, squeeze, sweep.* She repeated the steps to herself, pulling the pin and squeezing with all her strength.

A jet of white foam ripped from the nozzle, spraying in a wild arch. Dammit, she'd forgotten to grab the nozzle first and aim. White bits of foam shot everywhere, until she grabbed the small hose and pointed it at the microwave. She moved it back and forth until every last lick of fire was extinguished.

"Shit, Tamsen," Jade said, appearing by her side once the flames were out. "I know that table was a pain, but I didn't think it was *burn down the restaurant* bad."

"I didn't mean to!"

She winced as she surveyed the results of her carelessness. The microwave was a goner, that was for sure. But it didn't appear that the fire had damaged anything else. She'd have to spend an hour or so cleaning all this mess. There was no way in hell table seven was tipping now.

"Think his potatoes are hot enough?" Ty chuckled.

She didn't know whether to laugh or cry. At least she'd gotten it all under control before anything worse happened.

"Is everyone okay?" Prisha, the manager on duty, asked as she hurried in to survey the scene. "The fire department is on its way."

Dammit! She'd spoken too soon.

"I'm so sorry, Prisha." Tamsen pointed to the ruined

microwave. "I was heating up a customer's order and I accidentally left a fork in there and—"

Prisha sighed, lifting a hand to stop her explanation. Yeah, her coworkers were well versed in Tamsen's many mess ups. Usually, it was something small and laughable, like accidentally wrapping only spoons and knives with no forks or mixing up the salt and sugar on the shelves when restocking. But this…this was bad.

"It's okay, Tamsen." The manager smiled. "Today has been hell; it could have happened to any of us."

Seemed to happen to her far too often.

"At least no one was injured. I'm going to go check on the customers and offer them some vouchers for free meals."

Always a crowd pleaser.

"You wait here for the fire department."

"Do we really need them? I mean, the fire's out."

Prisha nodded. "The alarm went off; you know that means the company called them already. Better for them to check things out and give us the all clear."

Yeah, but the fire department meant firefighters and that meant…well, it didn't necessarily mean Parker would show up. There was more than one firehouse in Denver. He might not even be on shift today anyway. She had no reason to worry that she was going to embarrass herself in front of him again—

"Denver Fire," a deep, familiar voice called from beyond the kitchen door.

She winced, knowing her day had just gone from bad to hell in a handbasket.

"In here," Prisha said, opening the kitchen door. "The fire is out, but it was contained to the microwave over there."

A crew of five huge, muscled men and one smaller, but no less capable-looking woman, crowded into the kitchen area wearing head-to-toe firefighting gear. And at the front of the crew stood none other than Parker.

Fan-freakin'-tastic.

"Tamsen?" His eyes widened.

"Hey, Parker." She gave him a little wave and did her best to smile. "So, um, yeah. I might have pulled another me."

He hurried over to her side, concern filling his eyes. "Are you okay?"

She snorted. Now there was a relative question. "I'm fine, but I'm afraid our microwave is done for."

She motioned to the charred mess, its door slightly melted and twisted from the heat of the flames. He let out a low whistle as he stepped closer, surveying the scene. The foam had started to melt into a liquid, running everywhere.

"Jade, can you help me with the customers?" Prisha asked.

"Sure."

They headed out the kitchen door. Ty and the other cooks had stopped their tasks, knowing all the food was now contaminated. Good thing it was the end of the day—there wouldn't be much revenue lost. In fact, she could have sworn she heard Ty mutter to the prep cook, "Sweet, now we can start cleaning early." At least he found the bright side to this situation.

The firefighters surrounded the microwave, inspecting the damage and the outlet, doing...whatever the heck they were supposed to do in a situation like this, she supposed. She closed her eyes on a shudder. A heavy weight of exhaustion settled over her like a lead blanket, pressing down.

"Hey."

She opened her eyes to see Parker standing in front of her, a soft smile on his face.

"You, okay?"

"Physically? Yes. But I'm not sure I can handle one more embarrassment around you. You must think I'm a total klutz."

He chuckled. "Naw, I heard your coworker. You were just trying to get out of work early for the day. A bit extreme, but hey, whatever works, right?"

She laughed along with his joke, grateful he wasn't berating her for her silly mess up. Silly, but potentially deadly. The sobering thought made her smile dim.

"I promise I'm not a walking disaster most days. I was just so tired. It's been a really busy day, and this table kept making all these demands, and I was trying my best to accommodate the jerk. I mean, who the hell wants warm potato salad? And then I just popped the plate in the microwave, not even thinking about the fork, and I swear I'm not a complete—"

"Tamsen, hey."

He gently gripped her upper arms, staring into her eyes. Those warm brown eyes made her melt as if she'd been dipped in a pool of warm fondue.

"You're not a walking disaster."

He reached up with his hand to brush away some foam that must have landed on her cheek during the fray.

"Says you."

He frowned, eyes turning hard as he spoke. "If someone told you those things, they're the disaster, not you. Everyone makes mistakes; it happens to the best of us. I've got stories of people blowing fingers off with fireworks, burning very sensitive parts of their body while trying to light their farts on fire…"

She laughed, wondering who would think that was a good idea and how the hell they managed to get into a position to accomplish such a feat.

"You're not a disaster, Tamsen."

He smiled again, the sight making her breath catch in her throat.

"Thanks." She let out a sigh of relief. "I needed to hear

that, but I am sorry you all got called out here for nothing."

"Not nothing," one of the firefighters added. "It's our job, even if a badass has already put the fire out. Well done, by the way."

She squinted. The guy looked familiar. He was one of the firefighters who had come to her rescue with the plaster incident. And now, too, she supposed. "Ward, right?"

"You got it, dude." He grinned and gave her a wink.

"Ward!" the female firefighter called out. "Get your ass in gear. We gotta go talk to the manager."

"Yeah, yeah, I'm coming. Where's the fire, Díaz?" He laughed at his own joke. "Oh right, it's already out."

"Hilarious." The woman—Díaz—rolled her eyes, her tone deadpan. "You're a laugh riot."

"You just have no sense of humor."

She ignored him and glanced at Tamsen and Parker. "Kincaid, we're all good here. I'm just going to go over the report with the manager. Ma'am."

Tamsen nodded back to the woman and watched as all the firefighters made their way out the swinging kitchen door into the restaurant. All but one.

"Um, so yeah, thanks for coming to my rescue. Again."

He shrugged. "Seems to me you didn't need any rescuing. Looks like you handled things fairly well."

The destroyed microwave and soggy serving area would disagree with him.

"Well, thank you anyway, and I would really appreciate it if you didn't tell your mother about this." At his confused look, she clarified. "If you tell her, she'll tell my dad, and then he'll get all worried over nothing and it'll be a big thing and I just—"

"Got it," Parker said with a small laugh. "My lips are sealed."

She wished he'd seal his lips over hers.

Oops! Those were the exact naughty thoughts she was trying to avoid around this man. Kind of hard to do when he kept constantly coming to her rescue. Although, like he said, he hadn't rescued her this time. She'd put the flames out—the flames she started—but still, if she kept getting into such compromising situations around him, she was going to have to change her name and move to the south of France. Which would be terrible, considering she couldn't speak French.

"You sure you're all right?"

She nodded. "Tired, embarrassed, and my coworkers are never going to let me live this down, but I'm good. Nothing a hot bath and a good night's rest can't cure."

And maybe some accident-proof insurance for her life. Yeah, where could she buy some of that?

"Well then." He moved in a bit closer until his chest brushed against hers. "I hope you enjoy your bath."

She'd enjoy it a lot more if he were there with her.

No! Naughty brain. Stop thinking those thoughts.

His hand came out to brush more foam off her cheek, only this time he lingered, stroking her skin with the rough pad of his thumb. The contrast of texture made her knees weak and her insides go all gooey. It took every ounce of self-control not to grip his fire jacket and haul him into her so she could kiss him until neither one of them could see straight.

But she didn't.

Because she'd already made one bad choice today. She'd filled her quota.

"Kincaid." Ward popped his head into the kitchen. "Time to roll, dude."

Much to her disappointment, he dropped his hand and stepped away. For the best, really, no matter how much her body screamed to grab him and kiss him.

"See ya round."

"Bye, Parker. Hopefully next time won't be so…

disastrous."

He grinned. "With you, Tamsen, it's always exciting."

Then he followed his crewmate out the door. Warmth filled her chest at his words. *Exciting.* Not a hot mess or accident prone or even a walking disaster. No, Parker thought she was exciting.

How about that.

Chapter Seven

"Dad," Tamsen called out as she entered her father's house. "You home? I brought dinner."

Thomas Hayes popped his head out from the kitchen. "Pumpkin, I was going to cook."

Precisely why she'd brought dinner. Tamsen loved her father. He was a great dad, wonderful person, but a horrible cook. One of the reasons she took the cooking elective offered in her middle school was so they could stop eating frozen pizzas for dinner every night.

"Ty sent me home with some extra orders of tonight's special." Working in a restaurant had its perks. Food always tasted better when someone else made it. As long as that someone wasn't her dad.

"Well, bring it in here. I have something I want to talk to you about."

That sounded ominous. The last time her father wanted to talk to her, it was to tell her about his engagement. An event he was happy about, but worried over how she would take it. She smiled at the memory. So silly. How could he ever think she'd be anything other than overjoyed that he'd found someone who made him happy? She'd been trying to get the stubborn man to date for years, but he'd refused, saying he needed to focus on her first.

Well, now she was out on her own. It was time for her father to see to his own happiness, and she was so glad that was happening. But the way he said they needed to talk…

It had an edge to it. Like he was dreading what he had to tell her.

Oh no!

Did something happen with Victoria? Worry filled her stomach. She hoped not. They both seemed so happy. What could have caused a rift? Her mind immediately jumped to Parker and her totally inappropriate attraction to him.

No. That couldn't be it. First, she and Parker hadn't done anything but some harmless flirting. Besides, how could her father or Victoria know about her silly crush? She was simply projecting. He probably just wanted to talk wedding stuff.

Then why did his voice sound all shaky and nervous just now? Like the time he had to talk to me about body changes and becoming a woman?

Whatever it was, she wasn't going to find out standing in the entryway. Closing and locking the front door, she headed to the kitchen with the takeout. She placed the bag on the old wooden table full of nicks and marks from years of homework, art projects, and meals between her and her dad. She was pretty sure the table was older than she was, but it was solid. Her father had never been one to throw away something that still had use.

She hadn't grown up with the amount of funds her dad's future wife had, but she'd never gone hungry, and she'd always had a roof over her head and clothes on her back. There had been some tough times when his income had to cover everything from the mortgage to food to childcare, but they managed. And besides, Tamsen had always felt secure and loved, and that was way more important than wealth.

"What's up, Dad?" she asked, taking the food out of the bag.

"Mmmmm." Her father sniffed. "That smells delicious. What is it?"

He was stalling. "It's lemon garlic chicken with roasted potatoes and dill carrots."

His nose wrinkled. "Chicken? No steak?"

Removing the top from the takeout container, she slid his dinner over to him before opening her own. "No. Your doctor said you needed lean protein. You're supposed to be cutting back on the red meat."

He grunted. "Now you sound like Vikki."

Good. She was glad his fiancée was also taking an active interest in his health. Tamsen's approval of the woman jumped even higher.

"We both want you around for a lot more years, so stop griping and eat up or I won't give you the chocolate lava cake I snuck in on my way out."

That got her dad digging into his meal. They ate in silence for a while, enjoying the delicious food that the stellar cooks at 5280 Eats produced. Once her dad had gotten mostly through his meal, she pushed her empty plate away—she was always starving after a shift—and leaned forward.

"Okay, Dad. Spill it."

"I'd rather eat it." He lifted a forkful of chicken to his lips.

She groaned at his dad joke but pressed on. "I mean, what did you want to talk to me about?"

"Right, yes." He cleared his throat, pushing his plate to the side as well. "Tamsen, as you know, Vikki and I are getting married in a few months."

Oh, thank goodness. She let out a breath of relief. For

a minute there, she'd been worried she'd have to use her art skills to spray paint "Victoria sucks" on the woman's Lamborghini. If she had a Lamborghini. Honestly, Tamsen had no idea, but she did know if that woman ever hurt her father, there'd be hell to pay.

"And once we get married, that is, I've decided…I mean, Vikki and I have agreed that it's best if we, being a married couple and planning on living together and all, take a new step together as we join our lives by…you see the thing is—"

"Dad, spit it out before the lava cake goes bad." And people said *she* rambled when nervous. Wonder where she could have gotten that from?

"I'm going to sell the house."

Tamsen sat back in shock. Her dad watched her with careful eyes. He was selling the house? The home she grew up in. Where she'd spent every birthday, every Christmas. The place she always felt safe and secure no matter what was going on in her chaotic life.

"Oh."

His hand reached out to cover hers. "Are you okay, pumpkin?"

Was she? Logically, a part of her knew that he would eventually sell the house. The tiny three-bedroom bungalow with one bathroom and one car garage couldn't be what Victoria was used to. She didn't begrudge her father moving on with his new life. But her heart broke the tiniest bit knowing the place she'd always called home would belong to someone else.

Realizing she'd been silent too long, she pasted a bright smile on her face, waving her father's concern away. "Of course I am. I'll admit I'm a little bit sad, but I know Victoria probably has a much nicer home for you two to live in."

"Actually, we're going to buy a new place together. Start off fresh for both of us."

Oh. That sounded…lovely. And it eased a small part of her hurt to know her father's fiancée wasn't expecting him to make all the changes. She wondered if Parker knew his mom was selling her home. Was it Parker's childhood home? Would he feel the same loss she was feeling right now? She really didn't know much about him. Except for the fact that he was a firefighter, a worthy trivia opponent, and made her panties go up in flames with a single glance.

All very important facts.

"You're really not upset about me selling the house?"

Now it was her turn to place a hand on her father's. "Really. I figured you'd sell it someday. I'm happy to know it's because you found someone you love and not because you're retiring to Florida."

He laughed. "With all those bugs and the humidity? Not in this lifetime. You know I get cranky when it's hot out."

She laughed. Her dad was such a snowdog. He'd be as excited as a kid on their birthday with the first snow of every season. Come wintertime, it was hard to drag the man inside. He was like Frosty the Snowman come to life.

She served up the chocolate lava cake. It was one big piece, so she cut it in half and split it with her dad like always, wondering if she'd need to get two pieces to bring over when her dad and Victoria got married. Or if she'd even need to bring him dinner anymore.

Probably not. A bittersweet melancholy filled her. She was happy her dad had someone to love him and keep him company, but it was going to be strange not being the most important woman in her dad's life anymore.

"I also have a favor to ask."

She scooped up a giant bite of the cake and pointed her spoon at him. "Need help packing up? Sure."

"No." Her father shook his head. "I mean, yes, I'll probably ask you to come by and sift through some things when the time comes. See if there's anything you'd like to keep."

Keep? Was he planning on getting rid of a lot of stuff? Her dad? It stood to reason. He was getting a new wife, a new house, practically a new life. Of course he'd want new stuff to go with it. It just wasn't something she was used to from her frugal father.

"Vikki asked if you'd be willing to ask Parker something. Artist to artist."

"Parker is an artist?" She thought he was a firefighter.

Silly, she was an artist and a waitress. Stood to reason Parker could be both an artist and a firefighter. Most artists had day jobs, though she assumed with Parker's family money he didn't need an extra income.

"Does she want us to paint something for the wedding?" More time with Parker, exactly what she didn't need.

Her father shook his head. "No, Parker isn't a visual artist. According to Vikki, he's a musician."

Cool. She loved musicians. She often put on music when she painted. It spoke to her soul and she often found her art reflecting the mood of the playlist.

Of course he'd be a musician, too. She sighed, shoving down her growing sexual frustrations. A hero firefighter, funny, sexy, and he had a creative soul? Why? Why was the universe doing this to her? Why couldn't Parker have one freakin' flaw she could point out to stop making the unattainable man so damn tempting?

It just wasn't fair.

"Or he *was* a musician. He hasn't…" Her dad hesitated. "She said he hasn't played his guitar in years, and she misses it. She desperately wants him to pick it back up. According to Vikki, it always made him smile, and she would love it if he performed at the wedding. As a gift, for her."

"For both of you." Because she knew making his future

wife smile would make her dad happy.

"Yes, both of us." Her dad nodded.

"I can try." Though how she was going to convince him when his own mother couldn't was a mystery to her. "Maybe I can appeal to him. One artist to another."

"Thank you, pumpkin. We really appreciate it. It's very kind of you to help your brother."

"Ew, Dad, no." She pushed her half-eaten cake away. "He's not my brother."

"Okay, I know it's not like you two will bond like real siblings, like me and your uncle Ray, but I'm hoping you can be friends."

Friends. Yes, that's exactly what she wanted to be with a man she was intensely attracted to.

"I'm sure we can. Parker seems like a great guy." A great, hot, sexy, funny, smart, untouchable guy.

"Well, we already know he's hero material."

He motioned to her, referencing the cast incident she wished she could forget. *Parker has seen my boobs!* It would haunt her for years.

"And Vikki thinks the world of him."

As most mothers did with their children. Tamsen thought a lot of him, too.

Mostly naked.

While she painted him.

With her tongue.

Her pulse started to race. Oh boy, she really had to stop thinking of Parker like that. Especially around her dad.

They spent the rest of the evening talking about her dad's job at the library, the new manager position she was up for at the restaurant, and the theme of the gallery showcase she was working on presenting to her boss at the gallery she interned at.

And that brought her right back around to thinking

about Parker.

Hmmmm, she wondered if she could add his human form to her show.

No. Bad. That's a naughty, naughty Tamsen.

She drove back to her apartment, trying to focus on all the plates she was juggling instead of what Parker would look like naked. But as she sat down to work on some sketches, she found all her hands wanted to do was draw the man in question. His strong jawline, his full lips, the tiny crinkle at the corner of his eyes when he smiled, the tilt of his head and slight amusement that curled the corner of his lips when she went off on one of her tangents.

By the time she was ready to hit the sack, she had page after page of Parker staring up at her from her sketchpad.

"Dammit, brain. We. Can. Not. Have. Him."

She flopped down on her bed with a sigh.

No, she couldn't sleep with Parker, but there was nothing saying she couldn't draw him. Maybe even do a small painting? And there was certainly nothing she could do if her subconscious decided to have wild, naked, sexy-time dreams about him. She couldn't control what her brain did when she was sleeping.

Figuring she'd let whatever happen while she slept happen, she got ready for bed and turned out the lights. Tomorrow she'd see about getting in touch with Parker, and somehow, she'd find a way to plan a party for their parents without ripping his clothes off and jumping his bones.

As for tonight...

She smiled, sighing softly as her eyes closed and visions of Parker laying on a chaise lounge with nothing but a silk sheet covering his good bits while she stood across the room capturing his raw beauty with her brush filled her mind.

What happened in dreamland, stayed in dreamland.

Chapter Eight

Parker gave the bathroom sink one more swipe before he declared it clean enough for his standards. Which was a lot cleaner than some of his fellow firefighters would give it. That was why he didn't mind bathroom duty at the station. He'd rather have a spotless area to clean up in after a call. Nothing clung to your body like ash and smoke.

He was halfway through his twenty-four-hour shift, and so far, it'd been a relatively quiet one. They'd gone to a local elementary school for a safety demonstration this morning. Always a good time. What kid didn't love firefighters? He always felt like a superhero around kids. They stared with such wonder and awe, like he and his friends put out fires with sheer willpower instead of gallons of water spewing from hoses.

Honestly, it was a visiting fire crew to his elementary school way back when that first sparked his interest in the job. He could have sworn the men and women who came that day were ten feet tall, all muscles and friendly smiles, regaling the students with stories of running into burning buildings to save people, while teaching them the dangers of fire and how to respect it. He'd never been so excited in all his eight years.

That day he'd run into the house after school and declared his intent to be a firefighter when he grew up. His mother had worried but encouraged him in his dream. His father... that asshole let his only child know how "beneath him" a civil servant job was.

Like his father was one to talk. He was a defense attorney for the rich and shitty. The man spent his days getting billionaires and their kids out of trouble that should have landed them behind bars. But money was power, as his father liked to say. *Jackass.* Thankfully, his dad moved to Napa Valley a few years after the divorce. Parker hadn't seen him in years.

Good fucking riddance.

Tucking the cleaning supplies back under the bathroom sink, he washed his hands, stomach growling with hunger. Hopefully Ward wasn't cooking tonight. That man could burn water. Everyone at the station took turns cooking meals, but when it came to Ward, they usually all agreed to takeout.

"Hey, Kincaid."

Speak of the devil.

Ward popped his head into the bathroom. "You got a visitor."

That was unusual. No one came to see him at the station. "Who?"

The corners of Ward's mouth ticked up in a smartass grin. "Your future sister."

Tamsen. He sucked in a sharp breath, his heart rate kicking up. What was Tamsen doing here?

"*Step*sister. And wipe that shit-eating grin off your face, ass. Unless you're cooking tonight and it means you've already tasted dinner."

Ward flipped him off. "Tanner is cooking tonight."

Oh, thank all the taste buds in creation. Tanner's husband was a fantastic chef who shared tips with his spouse. Suddenly Parker's mouth watered in anticipation of the night's meal. Once he stepped out of the bathroom and into the main living area of the firehouse, his mouth watered for a different reason.

Tamsen stood in the middle of what they called the lounge area. A couch and three recliners faced a five-year-old flat screen someone had donated. She smiled at him as he came into the room. Her long dark hair was pulled back into a ponytail, the end swaying as she moved. She had some kind of long, flowy tunic type shirt on. The dark blue color of her shirt deepened the blue of her eyes, but somehow brightened them at the same time. Her legs were encased in neon purple leggings that ended just above her calf, elongating the short woman's stature in that magical way clothing managed to change people's proportions. And since she sported a pair of pink sandals, he could see the sexy little toe ring on her right foot. The green gem winking at him as it caught the overhead lights.

The sight caused his body to tense. Damn, she was beautiful when she smiled. She was gorgeous no matter what, but when she smiled, it was like a light switch. It brightened up the entire room even if it was the sunniest part of the day.

"Hey, Parker." She gave a little wave with one hand, the other holding a plate covered with foil.

"Tamsen, what are you doing here?" He walked over to her, shoving all the weird feelings she stirred in him to the side and giving her a friendly smile. "Not that I'm not happy to see you, but I wasn't expecting a visit."

"I know I should have texted, but I forgot to plug my phone in last night and realized it was dead on my way to work. But I remember you said you were on shift today when we talked at trivia the other night, so I figured I'd stop by and if you weren't here I'd just leave the..."

She trailed off with a little laugh. Parker just stared at her with a huge grin. He couldn't help it. He found her nervous rambling adorable.

"Cookies!" she declared, lifting the plate in the air.

"Cookies?"

"Yes, I made cookies for you." A blush rose on her cheeks, and her blue eyes widened. "I mean not *just* for you. They're for everyone. As a thank-you. To you and the others who helped me out of...you know. A little token of my appreciation. For everyone."

He took it from her hands, peeling back the silver foil. The rich smell of chocolate chips wafted from the pile of cookies. His stomach growled, reminding him again of his hunger.

"You bake?"

"I learned to cook in middle school after one too many nights of my dad's overcooked mac and cheese. I love him, but that man makes food even a starving dog wouldn't eat."

He snorted. "Sounds like he and Ward could open the world's worst restaurant together."

"I heard that, asshole," Ward said from across the room. He walked over, grabbing the cookies from Parker's hand. "And since I was there to assist in the lovely Tamsen's rescue, I think I'll take these cookies *and* her gratitude."

Ward took a step closer to Tamsen and bobbed his eyebrows. "Unless the lady would like to thank me personally with a romantic dinner for two?"

Parker grabbed the plate back, gently shoving his buddy away from Tamsen. Ward was a shameless flirt, but still, his flirting with Tamsen didn't sit right.

"Cut the crap, Don Juan. Tamsen's too good for an ass like you."

Ward snatched two cookies and lifted one to his mouth.

"Damn." His eyes widened as he swallowed. "These are amazing, Tamsen. Forget dinner, marry me. Please."

Tamsen laughed. "You're a cutie, but I'm not in the market for a husband—or a date."

Parker felt his muscles loosen as Tamsen played along and turned down Ward. Why that put him at ease, he had no idea.

Liar.

"Ward," Díaz called from the kitchen area. "Stop harassing the poor woman and come help set up for dinner."

Ward made a production of rolling his eyes, but he snuck another cookie with a wink and called back, "I'm coming, Díaz. Don't get your bunk gear in a bunch."

He walked off, leaving Parker and Tamsen in relative peace. Most of the crew was only a dozen or so feet away in the kitchen area, so while they couldn't hear their conversation, his friends could still see them. And the nosy punks weren't even pretending disinterest.

Tamsen, however, ignored the stares from his crew and focused on him. "Well, Ward seems to like them, but what do you think?"

He grasped a cookie between his fingers, bringing the sweet-smelling treat up to his lips. Tamsen's teeth came out to worry her bottom lip as she watched him. What he wouldn't give for everyone to leave so he could soothe that tiny sting with his tongue. Instead, he placed the cookie to his lips and took a bite.

Rich, chocolate buttery flavor exploded on his tongue. The morsel nearly melted in his mouth, so soft and sweet, but not overly sugary. He wanted to spend hours savoring this one bite and shove the rest of the plate in his mouth at the same time. Damn. Tamsen's cookies were the best thing he'd ever eaten in his life.

"These are amazing."

She smiled, the small, worried furrow between her brows disappearing. "Thank you. I've spent years perfecting the recipe. Chocolate chip is my dad's favorite."

At the mention of her father, the cookie lost some of its deliciousness. It wasn't that he didn't like the guy. He just didn't trust him. Yet. He'd hold off judgment until he had the full and complete report from his PI. Then, if things were fishy, he'd do whatever he had to in order to protect his mother. The past few times, he'd gone to the scumbags, presented them with the evidence, and threatened to tell his mother if they didn't. Except for Magnus/Mike, who was arrested when "someone" tipped off the authorities.

Parker had been the one to comfort his mother when she cried, heart broken once again. Bastards. No matter how much he liked Tamsen, he wouldn't allow this strange pull he felt toward her to interfere with his duty as a son.

"Thanks for the cookies. You didn't need to come all the way down here to drop them off."

She shrugged. "It's on my way to work, plus I realized we hadn't set a time to get together and discuss party planning. And I thought we could set that up real quick if you had a moment."

He nodded. Unless they got a call, he had a few minutes to chat. He still couldn't believe he was helping plan a wedding shower for his mother. He hated fancy parties, hated planning them even more. "Still seems weird to me."

"Yeah," she agreed with a nod. "Uber weird to be planning your parents' wedding shower, but I suppose if it makes them happy, that's good right?"

"If Mom's happy I'm happy." He grabbed another cookie from the plate.

Tamsen pressed her hands together under her chin, staring at him with big, round eyes. "Awwww, that is the sweetest. And good to hear, too, because your mom has another request of you."

She did? And how did Tamsen know? Were they buddies now, texting back and forth? He highly doubted it, since his mother deplored texting. She said her fingers were too big for the tiny keys, but he suspected it was because she refused to wear her reading glasses.

"My mother's requests are usually demands in disguise, so lay it on me."

Tamsen saw the way his mother had worked it so neither of them could say no to planning this wedding shower without looking like a selfish brat. What his mother wanted, she usually got. Most of the time she only wanted the very best for those around her. If she had any idea her son had the hots for her future husband's daughter, she wouldn't be pushing all this family bonding time on them.

"Your mother mentioned you play guitar and—"

"No."

Tamsen started at the sharp abruptness of his interruption.

A small pang of regret hit his gut. He hadn't meant to come off so rude, but that was the one thing he couldn't give his mother. Anything else. Not music. She knew his music was something he'd shared with his dad. Something he'd given up a long time ago.

The day his father had walked out of his life, disappointment for his only son had come off him in waves, since Parker chose to stay with his mother after the divorce. As if the soul-crushing decision of picking between parents wasn't hard enough on a fourteen-year-old kid.

No. He wouldn't play his music ever again.

"Oh, um…"

Guilt pinching his chest, Parker pushed memories of music away and dredged up a carefree smile. "I'm off shift tomorrow. You free for dinner to discuss party planning?"

She raised an eyebrow at his emotional one-eighty.

"Um, yeah, I'm free." She smiled. "I'm sure we can come up with a really great celebration for my dad and your mom."

Interesting how she never called them "the parents." She always made a distinction, clearly indicating a separation. *Very interesting.*

"Sounds good. Your place or mine?"

Her eyes widened, and Parker realized how that question came out. He hadn't meant to make it sound like a proposition. Not consciously, anyway.

"Um, I thought we might meet at a bar or restaurant or something."

"Kind of a noisy environment to plan a party in."

"Good point." She frowned slightly. "Well then, I guess you can come over to my place for dinner. You bring the wine."

"Deal."

She graced him with a dazzling smile that lit up her entire face. "See you tomorrow, Parker."

"Tomorrow." His stomach filled with anticipation and dread as he waved good-bye, kicking himself as he realized he'd just pushed for alone time with Tamsen mere feet from her bedroom.

What the hell had he been thinking?

Chapter Nine

Tamsen glanced at the clock on the kitchen stove. Five fifty. The exact same number it was when she checked twenty seconds ago.

The minute numbers blinked in and out for a split second, and her heart started to pound.

Five fifty-one.

Okay, this is fine. Nine minutes. I have nine minutes until Parker gets here. It's fine. Everything is fine. Dinner is ready. I have a fresh notebook to jot down ideas for the party. Everything is ready and on track.

She didn't know why she was so nervous—*liar.* But it was just dinner. A planning dinner. It's not like they were going on a date or anything. Just two people who were starting up a friendship, planning a party for their separate parents who were getting married.

It sounded convoluted when she put it that way, but it was better than saying she was meeting with her future stepbrother. Her future *super-hot* stepbrother who had seen her boobs, wasn't too jazzed about this wedding, and had some weird wall of ice go up when she mentioned music. That had been a weird moment. Parker had been so easygoing and carefree before then, but the second she mentioned he play his guitar, he'd turned to stone. She knew how touchy the subject of creativity could be, but Parker had completely shut down at her suggestion. She had to admit, it made her curious as to the reason for his apparent anger at something his mother claimed he once loved.

"Hey Tam." Cora flounced into the kitchen, opening the fridge and grabbing a soda. "How's the freak-out going?"

"I'm not freaking out." But right now, she was very grateful her roommate was home. She wasn't too ashamed to admit she needed the buffer of another person tonight. The thought of her and Parker spending an entire evening in her apartment *alone* sent wicked, naughty thoughts through her mind, and she'd never been very good at denying herself the things she wanted.

"Really?" Cora raised one dark brow. "Then why are the plates in the refrigerator?"

Crap!

Tamsen rushed over to open the fridge, and sure enough, the place settings she thought she'd put on the table were stacked all nice and neat next to the leftover cheese she'd nabbed from the art show at the gallery the other night.

"Fine," she admitted, grabbing the plates and silverware. "I might be a tad nervous, but it's only because I want to make sure everything goes smoothly tonight. I have to get along with Parker. For my dad's sake."

She didn't want to do anything to jeopardize her father's happiness. Goodness knew the man deserved every ounce coming his way and more.

"Uh huh."

She shot a reproachful glance to her doubting roomie. "And what is that supposed to mean?"

"I didn't say anything."

"You implied it with your tone."

Cora held her hands up in surrender. "I didn't mean anything bad. I'm just wondering if you're trying to impress Parker for your dad or for you."

"What's the difference?" Didn't everyone want to make a good impression on people? Especially the people who were going to be a big part of their lives?

"If it's for your dad, it's because you want to welcome him into the family. If it's for you, it's because you want to welcome him into your panties."

"Cora!" Heat burned her cheeks.

"Don't try to bullshit me, Tam. This is the guy you were mooning over for days after he came to your rescue like a knight in shining firefighting gear."

She didn't *moon*. And even if she had, she was an artist. They tended toward the dramatic. All those creative juices made life more...everything.

"He's going to be a part of my family."

Cora shrugged. "A stepsibling you're getting as an adult. It isn't like you two grew up together or have any familial bonding. Do you know how close I am to my stepsiblings? I don't even know their middle names. Couldn't pick them out of a crowd if I tried."

Cora's mom was on her third marriage. Her dad, his fourth. She had a slew of new and ex stepsiblings she hardly spoke to. But Tamsen had always envied anyone with a massive familial atmosphere, even if it did get a little chaotic at times. Blended or otherwise, she imagined it would be nice to have so many people you could count on. For as long as she could remember it had just been Tamsen and her dad, with a few extended family members she saw once every few years. But now that she finally had the chance for a wider family circle, she wasn't as thrilled. Why did it have to be Parker?

"Look," Cora continued. "All I'm saying is if you want this guy, why not go for it?"

"Because if the relationship goes badly, it would affect my dad's marriage."

Cora laughed. "Who said anything about a relationship? I'm just saying you should bang the guy."

"Please do not say anything like that in front of Parker. I'm begging you."

Cora's response was interrupted by a knock on the door.

"Speak of the sexy devil." Cora gave Tamsen a knowing look and strode toward the door.

Tamsen turned back to the stove, opening the oven to check the contents. Her nerves hit the ceiling as she heard Cora's muffled voice speaking to whoever was at the door. As if she didn't know.

"Hello, you must be Parker. I'm Tamsen's roommate, Cora."

The deep, sexy voice she'd been hearing all week in her dreams replied, "Nice to meet you, Cora."

"Oh, Tamsen," Cora called out as she led Parker into the kitchen. "Look who it is."

"Hi, Parker!" She winced. Did she shout that? She sounded loud, too bright. She really needed to take a chill pill. Or twenty. It was only dinner and discussion. Nothing to stress out about. "Welcome."

"Or welcome back, I should say." Cora tilted her head and smiled. "You were already here once, right? When you rescued Tam from the plaster disaster."

"Cora," her voice squeaked a warning, but her friend ignored it.

"Did you hear about the time she used adhesive spray on Styrofoam? Ate right through it. Destroyed her final project in stagecraft design. Then there was the time she mistakenly grabbed temporary tattoo paint instead of regular body paint for the life canvases class. Her poor model looked like Picasso's Weeping Woman for two weeks. She was so pissed. Remember that, Tam?"

"Yes, I do." But Cora wouldn't for long because Tamsen was going to kill her. "And as much fun as this walk down memory lane of Tamsen's finest disasters is, dinner is ready."

Parker smiled. "Art's all about experimentation, right? Not all experiments pan out. What did that hippy-looking painter say? The one with the big hair? There are no mistakes, just happy little accidents."

"Bob Ross." She nodded to Parker. "And thanks, that's a great way to look at my...happy little accidents."

"I didn't know what we were having, but I brought this." He held out a bottle of wine. "Figured red goes with almost everything."

"Thank you." She took the bottle, noticed the brand was one of the wines they served at the restaurant. One of the more expensive labels that also happened to be her favorite.

Cora leaned over to whisper in her ear. "Sexy, sweet, and springs for the good stuff? Makes a woman wonder if he's as good in bed as out of it."

Her face burned, flames of embarrassment racing up her cheeks. She shushed her roomie, praying to everything in the universe Parker hadn't heard her friend's inappropriate comment. The tightening in her core made her wish she hadn't heard it, either, because now her mind was coming up with all sorts of naughty imaginings of what Parker could do in bed.

"Well, I'm out. It was nice to meet you, Parker."

Shock had her jaw dropping as she turned to Cora. "What do you mean out? Where are you going?"

"Jared got us tickets to Comedy Works tonight. Anjelah Johnson is headlining."

Cora and her boyfriend loved standup, but it seemed

awfully convenient that her roomie suddenly had tickets to a show she was sure sold out weeks ago.

"I didn't know you had tickets tonight."

Cora ignored the suspicion in her tone. "His boss had a family emergency and gave them to us." Kissing Tamsen on the cheek, she whispered, "Have fun, Tam."

Parker waved as Cora closed the door, sealing Tamsen in the apartment with a bigger temptation than a 50 percent off sale at her favorite art supply store. He turned back to her, that devastatingly sexy smile on his face turning her stomach into a whirlwind of butterfly wings.

"Something sure smells good."

Grateful for the distraction from her distraction, she grabbed the baking dish from the oven.

"Have a seat. It's all ready."

She brought the hot dish to the table, setting it on the potholder she'd laid out earlier. Though Parker sat in the chair across from her, the round table was so small, his large presence made her feel surrounded. When she sat, she tucked her feet under her chair so she wouldn't be tempted to tangle them up in Parker's. Seriously, how had she never noticed how small her kitchen table was before? She swore she could feel his body heat radiating across the table, wrapping around her like a warm, sexy blanket.

Or maybe that was the casserole.

She scooped out a portion of the chicken fajita casserole for Parker and one for herself. Steam rose from the dish, lifting the scent of spice and cheese into the air. Parker slid a forkful into his mouth and groaned. She squirmed in her seat at the sensual sound.

"Tamsen, this is amazing."

Pride had her beaming. With all her family and friends telling Parker every blight and blunder of her artistic endeavors, she was happy her cooking hadn't caused her any embarrassment.

"Thank you. Cooking relaxes me. It's kind of like art. There's always a recipe to follow so I know I'm doing every step right, but also room for personal interpretation. That's what makes it so magical."

"Cooking or art?"

"Both."

"I can see that." He grabbed the serving spoon. "I'm glad your roommate left."

Her heart rate kicked up. "Really?"

He grinned, scooping out another serving onto his plate. "Yeah, more for us. You want another?"

She shook her head. "I'm good."

Of course he was excited about the prospect of more food and not of alone time with her. She was letting her imagination run wild—the exact thing she specifically told it not to do. Parker was here to help her plan the shower and nothing else.

You hear that, hormones? Chill. The man just wants more food.

"Do you cook?" she asked, grabbing her wineglass and taking a deep sip. Delicious. The light and somewhat spicy flavor of the wine rested on her tongue, a perfect complement to the dinner.

"Not really. My buddy's husband taught me how to make a mean seared chicken and glazed carrots, and I can do most pasta dishes, but I've never fully mastered the art of cooking."

He took a sip of his own wine, and she tried very hard not to notice the sensual way his throat moved when he swallowed or moan when his tongue came out to swipe a small drop of red liquid off his lips. She failed, but dammit she tried.

"Why not?"

He shrugged, leaning back in his chair, apparently satisfied with two helpings.

"Growing up, I never had to make my own meals. We always had staff on hand for those things or went out. We share making meals at the station, so I've had to learn a little in order not to poison my crewmates, but when I'm not at the station, it's just me." He shrugged. "Doesn't seem worth it to make a nice, fancy meal for one."

She supposed that made sense, even if it did sound a little lonely. She didn't really understand it. Having grown up just her and her dad doing everything themselves, the mere thought of a staff to take care of your every need seemed like something out of a fairy tale. She had no idea Parker's family had that kind of money. Suddenly she wondered what her budget-brand dishware and mismatched bathroom towels would look like to him.

"Wow, kinda wish I had a staff to cook for me growing up. Dad did his best, but he worked so hard as it was…I wanted to help out, so I took over meal duty. He was a good sport about it when I started and wasn't that great at it." She laughed, remembering a particularly disastrous lasagna recipe failure.

"But it was always fun experimenting with recipes, switching things out to make something new, something different than what was on the page. I started to have a lot of fun with it, and seeing Dad enjoy what I made, well, that was a joy in itself." For Tamsen, cooking was another form of art. One that fed the soul along with the body.

He frowned, as if the idea of cooking being fun was an alien concept.

"So tell me something about your mom." She needed to know more about the woman if she was going to plan the perfect party. And, secretly, she wanted to know more about Parker, too.

A loving smile lit up his face. "Mom's great. She used to come into my room and sneak me cookies when she got home late from the office. Chocolate chip—just like your dad. Even after a long day of work, she always made sure to check in on me. Her career was as important to her as her family. Always has been."

The light she saw in his eyes when she brought him cookies made much more sense. It was a sweet image, a young boy waiting under the covers for his mom to get home from work with a special treat. She was ashamed to admit she hadn't thought of Victoria as the workaholic type, but it seemed Parker's mother really was a superwoman. Admirable for sure.

"Did she often work late?"

Parker stared at the deep red wine in his glass. "Yeah. She was the CEO of the McMillian property management firm before she retired. Put in hard work and long hours, but she always showed up for my important stuff. Baseball games, school awards, those kinds of things."

Sounded a lot like her dad. "And what did your dad do?"

Parker snorted, downing the last of his wine. "He's a bloodsucker."

That was a bit extreme. She knew some people didn't like their parents, but Parker seemed to downright despise his father.

"A bloodsucker?"

He smiled, but it wasn't a pleasant one. "A lawyer. For the rich and powerful. Defense, mostly. Protecting hedge fund managers who embezzled. Getting teens of prominent people off with a warning when a DUI caused a major wreck. I have no idea what my mother ever saw in him. As far as I can remember, they were always fighting."

"What about?"

"He thought she should quit her job and be his little society wife. She didn't agree with the cases he took." He shrugged. "He took off when I was fourteen. Haven't seen him since, but I hear he's still protecting the pockets of the power shakers."

Okay, then. Sounded like Parker's dad was a real piece of work. At least she had loving stories about her mother from her dad. Unable to stand the tense silence in the room, she poured the rest of the wine into their glasses.

"I'm sorry, Parker."

He grabbed his glass and downed a third of it. "It's not a big deal."

Kinda seemed like it was.

"Mom was always there to take care of me, protect me. And I intend to do the same for her."

That was a bit strange. A parent's job was to protect their child, at least until adulthood, anyway. But a kid protecting their parent? Was she running from the mob or something? Maybe he was worried she'd get taken advantage of in her old age, not that Victoria was old, but scammers did like to target the above-fifty crowd. Some guy tried that crap on her dad a few years ago with a spam call claiming to be from the IRS, but he was smart enough not to fall for it. Was that what Parker was worried about? Someone scamming his mom?

Reaching over, she squeezed his hand reassuringly. "She's a grown woman. I'm pretty sure she can protect herself. Besides, she's got my dad now, and I know he's seems like a big ol' softie—and don't get me wrong, he totally is—but he would never let anything happen to your mom. I promise you that." She laughed, but he didn't join in. The temperature in the room seemed to drop. She had no idea what was going through Parker's mind at the moment, but she would bet it wasn't happy wedding thoughts.

Shifting in her chair, she stood and grabbed their plates. "Let me clear the table, then we can get to brainstorming ideas for the party."

Because that's why he was here. Not for a touchy-feely get-to-know-you session. She did need to know more about

Victoria, but she didn't think asking him about his mom would go to such a morose place. Much like the incident with the music request yesterday, she had to remember she didn't really know that much about Parker.

He placed a hand over hers as she reached for their plates. A spark of awareness shot up her arm, heading straight to her breasts. Her nipples perked up, poking into her bra. Thank goodness she wore the one with the slight padding to cover the reaction. Nothing she could do about the heat on her cheeks, though. She was sure she was blushing, dammit. Why did her body react to this man this way? When was it going to get the memo?

She. Couldn't. Have. Him!

"You cooked, I'll clear."

He smiled, and she nearly melted into a puddle right at the table, worried if she opened her mouth, she'd beg him to forget doing the dishes and do her instead. She nodded and motioned to the dishwasher, unable to take her eyes off his deliciously tight ass as he bent over and placed the dirty dishes inside.

"Mind if I use your restroom before we dive into planning?" he asked once he closed the dishwasher back up.

She quickly adverted his gaze, hoping he hadn't caught her shamefully staring at his backside. "Of course, it's down the hall on the left."

Tamsen grabbed the notebook with the few ideas she'd started to write down for the party and sat at the table going over the notes she'd made. After a few minutes, she glanced up and checked the clock on the stove. Parker had been in the bathroom a while. She hoped she didn't mix up some ingredient in the casserole and give him stomach problems. She didn't have as many cooking disaster stories as she did art project stories, but there had been a few. The salt instead of sugar incident of 2013, last year's baking soda disaster cupcake fail, and the expired milk episode on her father's sixtieth birthday. That one still haunted her.

Wanting to check and make sure everything was okay—at this rate she would need to change her name and move to some remote island to avoid further embarrassing herself in front of this man—Tamsen hurried down the hall to check on Parker.

But he wasn't in the bathroom.

The only bathroom in the apartment was empty, the light off. As she made her way down the hall, she was surprised to see Parker standing in the doorway of her room staring intently at the sketches and easel set up in the corner by the large window. It got the best light in the apartment, so it's where she did most of her drawing and painting.

She cleared her throat loudly, gaining some satisfaction from the small jump in the corded muscles of Parker's back. He turned with a sheepish grin.

"Sorry, I didn't mean to snoop."

She raised one eyebrow.

"Okay, I did. I saw a light on and..." He waved an arm, encompassing her art. "Tamsen, these are amazing."

Her cheeks heated, warmth and pride filling her at his compliment. "Thank you."

"I'm not an art aficionado, but these are...powerful." He stared at the drawings again. "I don't know if that makes sense. It's just the word that pops into my head as I look at them."

"Whatever emotion you feel is the goal," she answered, coming to stand beside him. "That's the beauty of art. It's interpretive. The artist may create one thing, but it truly comes to life in the observed. Whatever it makes you feel, it's right."

"Are these all for that human body project you were talking about?"

"Some of them."

They were all sketches of the human body. Some drawn from life, some from pictures, others she created in her head.

"Life drawing is one of the first things they teach you in art school, but I've always been drawn to the complexity of the human form. How different we all are. How similar. The curves and angles, big and small. Each body catering to the soul inside it. I love capturing that soul on paper. Every subject brings new insight. I…I'd love to draw you sometime."

She sucked in a sharp breath. Her mouth had started to ramble again, running away without her brain. Why had she said that? Yes, she did want to draw Parker, but that didn't mean she had to tell him about it. She certainly wasn't going to tell him about all the naughty dreams she'd been having involving him or the sketches she'd already drawn of him…

The heat of his body enveloped her as he moved in closer. She felt the brush of his lips against her ear. A shiver of pleasure running up her spine as his warm breath tickled the hairs on the back of her neck as he spoke.

"You want to draw me? How about in the buff? That can be arranged."

Chapter Ten

What the hell was he doing flirting with Tamsen? He had no idea, but he couldn't seem to stop himself.

Future stepsister!

And daughter of a possible con man.

Right, the big red flag waving over their heads reminding him what a monumentally ridiculous idea it would be to hook up with Tamsen. The mental reminder caused him to take a step back. And a physical one. This close proximity to Tamsen was messing with his head. He rocked back on his heels, affecting a teasing tone.

"Maybe you could come down and draw the whole crew at Station 42. We could make this year's firefighter calendar real classy and charge a fortune for it."

She blinked, the hazy, lust-filled look in her eyes disappearing as her lips curled up in a smile. "I don't think 'classy' is what people want when it comes to those calendars. Come on, let's get back to party planning."

She shook her head with a laugh and headed out of the bedroom back into the kitchen. Parker gave her bed a fond glance before following.

"Can I get you some coffee or a cup of tea?"

He'd rather have more wine to dull the aching need burning for her inside him. "If you have decaf, coffee sounds great."

"I do. Cream and sugar?"

He shook his head. Years of working the chaotic and exhausting job of a first responder had taught him to take coffee black because most times, that was the only way you could get it. Tamsen moved around the small kitchen, dumping the grounds into her coffeemaker and filling the reservoir with water.

He found himself fascinated by her movements, the swing and sway of her purple blouse that did that weird thing where it hung down farther in the back than the front. Her slim legs were encased in yellow leggings today. They hugged every dip and curve of her body, moving effortlessly with her like a second skin. His mother's snobby society friends might say leggings were not appropriate attire. But Tamsen's clothes were almost an art piece in and of themselves. He knew people tended to stare a lot at good art, and he found his eyes locked on Tamsen whenever they were in the same room.

Once the coffee was done, Tamsen brought it to the table and pulled a red notebook in front of her.

"Okay, let's brainstorm," she said, opening the notebook.

"I still think this is a weird idea."

"Aren't all traditions associated with weddings a little weird? The thing with the garter and the bouquet toss. Throwing rice. Decorating the car with streamers and tin cans. Giant inflatable penises at the bachelorette party."

He recoiled in mock horror. "Please tell me we're not planning my mother's bachelorette party, too. Silly shower games I can handle, but I draw the line at shopping for dick paraphernalia for my own mother."

She reached out to pat his hand. The small touch seared him, sending heat all the way down to his cock. Tamsen didn't seem affected, so he told his dick to cool it and adjusted in his seat, grateful for the table masking his reaction to this woman.

"Poor Parker. How awkward that would be for you. Try being a thirteen-year-old girl explaining to your father that you have to go to the store for tampons."

Yeah, she had him there.

She pulled her hand away and picked up a pen. "Your mom and my dad want a shower as a way to celebrate with their friends together, that's it."

He nodded. "Yeah, that's more like Mom's style."

"First things first, we have to pick a location." She tapped the pen against her lips. "Somewhere nice, but not as fancy as that clubroom place where they had the engagement party. This party will be much more intimate."

"No need to impress the upper-crusts?"

"Exactly. They only want close friends and family invited to this one. Those who truly care."

He could roll with that. Though, with the kind of money his family had, sometimes it was hard to know who cared and who was pretending to get in good graces with the family fortune.

"A nice restaurant?"

She shook her head at his suggestion. "The problem there is most only allow you to rent out a back room, not the full place, and we want something a bit more private."

Her brow furrowed in concentration before her eyes suddenly lit up. She smiled, raising the pen in the air.

"I got it! I can ask Winston if we can use the gallery. As long as there's not a show happening that night, I'm sure he'll say yes. Hephaestus is the perfect location."

An art gallery could be cool, even if it did have a weird-ass name. His mom would probably like it. She loved art. She was on the board of a few artist foundations in the area. Though she couldn't paint herself, she loved attending gallery showings. Then there was the summer of his sophomore year they spent in Paris. She'd taken him to the Louvre five times. Once had been enough for him, but he'd been happy to go as many times as she wanted because of the way joy filled her face whenever she stared at the artwork.

Yeah, an art gallery would be perfect.

"Is that where your art is?" He didn't know if Tamsen sold any of her pieces, but she should. The stuff he'd seen was amazing.

"No, it's where I work."

"Wait, I thought you worked at a restaurant?"

She glanced up from writing things down on the paper. "I do, but I also work at the gallery. And I do some freelance stuff online. Hopefully the show I'm working on gets my foot in the art world door. Then sell some pieces, arrange commission work, shoot, maybe I can even find myself a fancy, rich benefactor and I can kiss the starving artist life good-bye. But until then, it's nose to the grindstone and multiple jobs. Such is the life, right?"

She chuckled, but he didn't feel like laughing at the moment. *Fancy, rich benefactor.* Suspicion rose within. It was obvious Tamsen was a hard worker and managing to get by, but even she admitted it'd be a dream to have someone supporting her. Did her dad think the same way? He knew the guy worked at a library, but he had little idea what the man's financials looked like.

Maybe Thomas Hayes wanted to pad his golden years by marrying into money.

"But," Tamsen continued, "I'm doing what I love, so I guess I can't complain, right?"

Now, that he understood. Parker's dad had been prepping him for the bar exam since kindergarten. His mother hadn't pressed, but he knew she assumed he'd follow her into the family business. His father had scoffed at his childhood dream of becoming a firefighter, but his mother encouraged him. She'd always been in his corner, encouraging his decision to follow his dreams, to enter the fire academy. She never questioned his decision or made him feel inferior for choosing it over the family business. And now, he was doing what he loved, despite the lack of riches or power.

Tamsen was right. Nothing could beat following your dream.

"So what do you think about the gallery? I'll show you around, see what you think?"

What he thought was his head was aching from ping-ponging back and forth between wanting this woman and being suspicious of her father's motives with his mother. If his damn PI would just finish his report, maybe Parker could have some peace of mind.

"Sure. I mean, I think you probably have a better idea of what would make for a great party spot. The last party I planned was O'Neil's birthday at the firehouse, and all it entailed was getting a cake and rigging the fake snake to jump out at him when he opened his present."

She glanced up from the notebook she'd been scribbling down ideas in. "I'm sorry, what? Fake snake?"

"Yeah, O'Neil is a wimp when it comes to snakes. He refuses to be lead on any animal calls involving reptiles. Says they creep him out. The fangs remind him of needles or something. So the crew and I decided it'd be hilarious to rig one of those rubber snakes to jump out at him when he opened his gift. Like those old snake-in-a-can gags."

"Sounds like a very odd birthday gift."

He chuckled. "He got a real one, too, but the gag came

first. It's kind of a thing at the station—we're always doing harmless pranks. I guess you could say it's a form of bonding. Why, don't you guys prank each other at the restaurant?"

"No." She smiled coyly. "But we like to do magic tricks."

Hmmmm, something about the way she said that had his suspicions rising. "Magic tricks, huh?"

"Yeah, would you like to see one?"

The spark of mischief in her eyes told him he should say no, but his curiosity had always gotten the better of him. "Sure. Dazzle me with your mystical ways, oh Mysterio."

She pushed away from the table and headed toward the fridge.

"Don't get too excited. It's not like I'm going to levitate or cut you in half. It's just a coin trick."

There was a jar of loose change on top of the fridge. Tamsen reached in and pulled out a quarter. The movement made her shirt rise, the longer tail end hiking up, giving him a fantastic view of her ass in those leggings. He hardened to the point of pain at the sight. An image of himself holding her hips, watching those firm, round cheeks bounce against him as he took her from behind. He reached for his coffee, wishing it were ice water. He needed something to cool down the raging fire of need inside him.

Tamsen opened the fridge and pulled out a water bottle. For half a second, he panicked, thinking he'd accidently spoken out loud, but then she turned with a smile and headed back to the table, placing both the quarter and water bottle in front of her. He breathed out a sigh of relief. He hadn't muttered any of the inappropriate thoughts in his head—she was just thirsty.

"This is called the teleporting coin trick. I'm going to magically teleport this coin into this bottle of water."

Oh, it was part of the trick. Wait, why did this sound familiar? He wasn't a huge magic fan, but he'd seen a show or two as a kid at some birthday parties. He racked his brain but couldn't put his finger on it.

"I have in my hand a normal, ordinary quarter. Parker, will you please take this coin and confirm it's a legitimate one?"

He grinned. "You take your magic tricks very seriously."

"Shush." She frowned at him. "The theatrics are what make the magic work."

He chuckled. He'd never been so thoroughly charmed by a woman. "Sorry. I'll be good."

"I seriously doubt that," she muttered under her breath. "Now, take the quarter."

He plucked the coin from her, their fingers grazing at the exchange. Pinpricks of electricity shot up his arm at the contact. Judging by the sharp intake of breath from Tamsen, she felt it, too.

He rubbed the coin between his fingers, tapping it on the table but drawing the line at biting it the way people always did in movies because money was disgusting.

"Seems legit to me."

"Thank you."

She held her hand out, and he placed the coin back into her palm, purposefully stroking the tips of his fingers along her skin as he did. One dark eyebrow raised, but she didn't call him out on it. He saw a slight tremor in her hand as she curled her fingers around the coin. Dammit, he really had to stop testing this line they were both dancing on.

"Good. Now can you confirm this is an ordinary bottle of water? Feel free to open it and take a sip if you want."

He grabbed the bottle, flipping it all around, running his fingers along the plastic. No leaks, no false bottom. Seemed normal. It even still had the safety seal. Again, his brain tried to warn him of something, but the danger was just outside his grasp. He twisted off the cap and lifted the bottle to his lips but paused before taking a sip.

"Wait, you're not going to poison me or anything?" he joked.

"I'm an artist. If I was going to kill someone, I'd hack them into pieces, encase those in body casts, and pretend it was an art installation. Probably sell it for a mint, too."

He tipped the bottle down. "It's kind of terrifying how much you've thought of this."

"Naw." She pushed a lock of dark hair behind her ear. "It was a real story. Some artist in the seventies did too much acid and thought his landlord was a giant snake monster trying to devour him. He grabbed an axe and hacked the poor man to death then tried to cover his crime by dunking the body parts in cement. The cops discovered him mid-dunking, and he was sent to prison for thirty to life. But it's a great line to give creepers at the bar when they won't take no for an answer."

He laughed, bringing the bottle to his lips again. Cold, fresh water filled his mouth. He swallowed the sip and passed the bottle back. "I can confirm that's a normal bottle of water."

"Thank you. Now." She held up the coin. "I will put this quarter on the table."

She put the quarter down between them.

"Now I will place the water bottle on top of the quarter." She waved her hand over the bottle. "And say the magic words, presto change-o."

He snorted. "Presto change-o?"

"Shhh!"

He mimed zipping his lips, amused by her dedication to a silly trick.

"Now, look deeply into the bottle and see the quarter in the water's depths. No, no, from the top," she insisted when he stared through the side.

He scooted forward on his chair, leaning over the top

of the water bottle, his eye over the opening. How was he supposed to know if the quarter—

Suddenly a gush of water came shooting out of the bottle, hitting Parker square in the face. He sputtered, the sound of Tamsen's bright laughter filling his ears as he wiped water from his eyes.

"Oh my God, I can't believe you fell for that."

Oh, shit, now he remembered. Ward had shared a video of this a few months ago. Some viral prank. It was funny when he saw it, not so funny when it happened to him. But Tamsen's glee was infectious. He found himself grinning as he subtly reached for the water bottle.

"Touché, but I'm a firefighter, sweetheart. A little water won't make me melt. Of course, you're as sweet as sugar, so…"

Her eyes widened as he rose from his seat, water bottle in hand. She popped up from the table, hands held out in front of her, laughter spilling from her lips as she shook her head.

"Parker, don't even think about it."

"Oh, I'm thinking about it."

She squealed, trying to dodge around him, but he scooped her up with one arm, holding her close to his chest as he tipped the water bottle over her head. She yelped out a half scream half laugh, water pouring down her face.

"I can't believe you did that."

"Turnabout is fair play."

She smiled up at him, tiny droplets of water catching on her dark lashes, rolling down her face. His laughter died as Parker took in their position. Tamsen was pressed up against him, and as much as he tried to control himself, it was turning out to be impossible around this woman. His cock was so hard he was about to bust through his damn zipper. She had to feel it. One subtle shift of her hip, pressing closer, and he knew she did.

"Tamsen," he growled out a warning, but she ignored it, making the tiny motion again. He grabbed her hips, meaning to put some distance between them, but instead he pulled her tighter, ground himself closer.

"Parker," she moaned his name, gaze hazy with lust as she stared up at him. "Kiss me."

Hell, he couldn't fight this anymore.

He dipped his head, lips crashing down on hers. It wasn't a gentle kiss. It was hot and raw and so damn good, it nearly blew his head off. He felt her arms snake around his neck, fingers digging into his hair. Her touch was electric. Every bit of him felt alive in a way he never had before.

She moaned, lips parting slightly, tongue coming out to lightly taste him. He took the invitation, thrusting his tongue against hers, drinking in the uniquely amazing taste that was Tamsen. He wanted her. More than he wanted his next breath. More than he wanted a cold shower after working to put out an enclosed fire. More than anything in this damn world right now.

But as her hands slid down his chest, nimble fingertips slipping under the hem of his shirt, his brain screamed at him.

Future stepsister! Investigating her father!

Shit!

He pulled back, dropping his hands from her and taking a huge step back. Already he missed her warmth, missed her taste.

"Parker?"

He shoved his hands into his pockets to avoid the temptation of reaching out again. "This is a bad idea, Tamsen. Our parents are getting married."

She frowned. "True."

"So this"—he pointed back and forth between them—"wouldn't work out."

She touched her lips as if she could still feel him there—

he sure as hell still felt her—her bright gaze focusing on his face as she appeared to be gathering her thoughts.

"I won't deny the fact that I'm...attracted to you." Her cheeks flushed bright pink. "And I understand this is a...complicated situation. But we can keep it casual. Actually, I prefer that, to be honest, and our parents don't ever have to know. If you don't want to explore this chemistry thing between us, that's fine. I just figured I'd put the offer out there in case..."

Oh, he wanted to. He was desperate to, but there were so many things that could go wrong. His brain and body were in a war, and the more time he spent in this woman's presence, the more his brain lost. Which was why he made his feet move to the front door.

"I should go."

She sighed, hands coming up to cover her bright pink cheeks. "Oh god! I can't believe I actually asked you to—"

A pang of guilt hit him square in the chest at her dejected look. "Tamsen, I don't want to leave, but..."

"Yeah." She waved a hand in the air. "You probably should."

"If things were different..."

"But they aren't."

Nope, and wasn't that a bitch.

"Thanks for dinner, and let me know what your boss at the studio says about the party."

She nodded. "Will do. Bye, Parker."

"Bye, Tamsen."

Parker headed out of the apartment, knowing he'd done the right thing but wishing like hell he hadn't.

Chapter Eleven

"Tam, we're going to be late," Cora shouted through the bedroom door. "Stop primping and let's go already!"

She wasn't primping.

Glancing in the mirror, she applied the final swipe of her cherry berry bombtastic lipstick. It went perfectly with her red checker sundress. She'd spent half an hour curling her hair in order to make it look like soft, just got out of bed, tumbled waves. She usually kept her messy mane up in a bun or ponytail, but tonight she didn't want to look like a disheveled artist. She wanted to look more like the sensual art she created. Her red heels were cute and only a little bit pinchy, but they made her legs look great, so…okay, she was primping.

She couldn't seem to stop herself. Tonight was trivia night, and that meant the possibility of seeing Parker. Last night her dreams had been filled with the memory of their kiss.

She had no idea what possessed her to proposition him like that last night, but the more she thought about it, the more she knew she'd done the right thing. This chemistry thing they had going wasn't dissipating. And the more time they spent together, the worse it would get until it boiled over and exploded, like that time she tried to make a mug cupcake and accidently set the microwave for ten minutes instead of two.

They couldn't risk anything exploding around their parents. They had to nip this thing in the bud. Screw away the sexual tension.

"Tamsen!"

"I'm coming!"

A phrase she'd muttered to herself in the dark last night as she remembered how warm and delicious Parker's lips tasted. Imagined pushing the man to the floor, stripping them both naked, and staying that way until they'd re-created every position in that *The Art of Sexuality* book Cora had gotten her for her birthday last year. Yes, she'd taken a trip to self-pleasure city, but it had either been that or stay up all night wallowing in sexual frustration.

The bedroom door opened, and an exasperated Cora leaned in the room. "Okay, seriously, girl what is… Aren't you a little dressed up for pub quiz?"

"What? It's nice out. I'm just celebrating sundress weather, and technically checker print resembles plaid, so it's still team appropriate."

Cora bit back a smile. "Mmmm hmmmm, and this 'celebration' with full hair and makeup wouldn't have anything to do with the fact that Parker might be at trivia tonight?"

"No." She shifted under her roommate's knowing stare. "Okay, maybe…I just… Shut up."

Cora gasped. "Something happened last night, didn't it?"

"Sadly, no."

"But you wished it had. Tell me everything! No wait,

we need to leave. Tell me on the way." She glanced down at Tamsen's feet. "You really wanna walk in those?"

She looked down at her heels, checking to make sure the cute ankle strap was securely fastened. "It's only four blocks, and they're pretty comfy."

Two blocks later, Cora had all the details of the almost kiss and Tamsen was eating her words. Her toes were pinched, and her arches were killing her.

The second City Tavern came into sight, she was practically weeping with joy. The thought of seducing Parker with her shoes now seemed like a really ridiculous idea. He was the one who had left last night, despite that hardness she'd felt pressed against her and the hungry need she'd glimpsed in his eyes. Why would she think a sexy pair of shoes would be the thing to override his common sense?

Cora opened the front door. But before Tamsen could get inside to a blessed seat to rest her aching toesies, she found herself flailing, arms spinning as something caused her to trip. Once she'd steadied herself, she looked down to see her heel had gotten stuck in the grate on the sidewalk.

Who the hell thought that was a good place to put a grate? Why was it even there?

Cora hurried to her side, letting the door swing closed. "Are you okay?"

"I'm fine." She tried to pull her foot up and failed, the ankle strap digging into her skin. "Maybe."

Another tug. Nothing. The thin, spiky heel was not budging.

"Crap. I think I'm stuck."

"Again?" a deep voice chuckled from behind her. "We have to stop meeting like this."

Double crap!

Tamsen turned her head to gaze over her shoulder and, yup, sure enough, there stood Parker with a few of his buddies.

"Hi, Parker." She tried for a laugh that fell flat.

"Tamsen." He nodded. "Need a little help?"

What she needed was disaster insurance to save her from all the embarrassing situations she kept putting herself in around this man.

"It appears I've gotten my shoe stuck in this grate."

"I can see that." He rubbed a hand over his mouth, smothering his smile.

She'd give him points for trying to hide his laughter. It *would* be a pretty funny situation. If it wasn't happening to her.

He turned to his friends. "Why don't you guys go grab a table? I'll be in in a minute."

"It seems like Parker has this well in hand. I'll leave you to your hero, Tam." Cora gave her a little wave. "See ya inside."

He sure had something in his hand. Currently it was Tamsen's calf as he bent down to inspect the latest disaster she'd gotten herself into. Warmth seeped into her skin and at the same time chills raced up her spine as his rough palm skimmed down her leg to gently grasp her ankle. She bit her lip to hold the moan of pleasure back.

One embarrassment at a time, please.

Parker glanced up. "Think you could take your foot out? It might make it easier to wiggle the heel free."

She could, except...

"I have to unbuckle the ankle strap, and this sidewalk is filthy, and I'm not wearing any pantyhose." Bare feet on the streets of Denver? Yuck, no, thank you.

"Yeah, I noticed."

His eyes blazed with desire and...was he stroking her ankle with his thumb? A zing of pleasure shot straight up between her legs. Now if only they were somewhere a little more private so he could move that stroke a few feet higher and to the center.

No, naughty body. We came to play trivia.

Who was she kidding? She totally came all dolled up tonight to drive Parker wild. Was she playing with fire? Probably.

"Here." He undid the buckle and slipped her foot free of the shoe and placed it on his thigh. "Keep your foot there while I rescue your shoe."

She sighed dramatically, raising her voice an octave. "My hero."

He chuckled and began jiggling her shoe out of the tiny grate hole. She tried her best to focus on watching his task and not on how warm and firm his thigh felt under her bare foot. Right now, she wanted to glide it up his leg.

Good grief, what was this man doing to her?

"All set."

Parker popped her shoe free, turning it in his hand as he inspected it.

"Doesn't seem to be any damage."

Good, because as much as she regretted wearing the shoes tonight, they were her favorite pair, snagged on sale at the outlet mall.

He gently lifted her foot from his leg. She tried not to sigh in disappointment at the loss.

He grinned up at her as he slipped her shoe on like some kind of fairy tale prince. "There you go, Cinderella."

"Thank you."

He stood, and she found herself taking the tiniest step back. Not because he towered over her—which he did—but because she was afraid if she let herself get too close to him, she might thank him in a way that would have more than her shoe coming off.

He'd been pretty hesitant last night about them not crossing that line.

But she couldn't help but think, maybe if they gave in to

this intense chemistry they seemed to have, it would die off. It'd happened to her before. She and a college classmate had nearly combusted anytime they were in art class together, but after months of being sex buddies, their attraction fizzled, though they remained friendly.

Would that work with Parker? Might be a good idea to try. She certainly couldn't keep behaving like a hormone-crazed teen around the guy. Maybe they should bang it out—so to speak. Get past this…whatever it was and transition into being friends.

For the sake of their parents.

"We better get in there before it starts." Parker nodded to the bar. "You all ready to get your butts kicked tonight?"

She laughed. "Excuse me? Who kicked whose butt last time?"

He waved a hand at her logic. "Yeah, but I have a good feeling about tonight. We're going to cream you."

Do not think dirty thoughts. Do not think dirty thoughts. Do not think dirty thoughts.

"I guess we'll have to see." Turning carefully on her freed heel, she made her way into the bar, scanning the room until she saw Cora waving from a table with Jade and the rest of the Lumbersnacks.

"Saved by the stepbrother?" Cora asked with a smile as Tamsen sat down.

"Stuff it. Where's my drink?"

Her roommate slid a sex on the beach over to her. Tamsen ignored the tiny straw and tipped the glass to her lips, taking a healthy sip. Not that she needed the alcohol. Five minutes in Parker's presence and her head felt floatier than the time she and Jade split a pitcher of margaritas at last year's work holiday party.

Trivia started, and Tamsen tried her best to keep her eyes on answers Jade was writing down, but she found her gaze wandering over to Parker's table. A few times, he caught her looking. She put two fingers to her eyes then pointed them at him with a sassy smile—letting him know she was watching him and that he was going down. He shook his head and toasted her with his drink, challenging her declaration. Damn the infuriatingly sexy man. He was distracting her from the game, and he knew it.

When they took their mid-game break, the Lumbersnacks were trailing behind Most Extinguished by five points.

"I'm going to grab another round," she declared, rising from the table.

"Can you grab your attention span while you're at it?" Jade asked, tilting her head toward Parker's table.

Tamsen sighed, because she knew Jade was right. "Leaving now."

She headed to the crowded bar, ignoring her friends' laughter. Catching the bartender's eye, she motioned for another drink.

"Looks like someone is in danger of losing. Do I see a free drink in my future?"

She turned at the deep voice to see a smug, smiling Parker standing behind her.

"Oh please, I'm just trying to protect your poor little feelings before I crush you into the ground."

He took a step forward, his chest pressing against hers. The thin material of her dress did nothing to hide the fact that her nipples were hard, painful points. Damn the sorry excuse for a bra that was built into the dress.

"Trust me. Nothing on me is little."

The evidence of that was currently pressed against her stomach. She swallowed a moan and tried to remind herself they were just engaging in a little harmless flirting. Or were they? For a man who said they shouldn't step over any boundaries, he sure was dancing awfully close to them. Had he been rethinking their kiss, too?

An idea popped into Tamsen's head. One so delicious and wicked, she couldn't stop the proposal from coming out of her mouth.

"How about we up the stakes for the bet?"

One dark eyebrow arched. "What did you have in mind?"

She tapped a finger to her chin, even though she knew exactly what she had in mind. Better to make the man sweat. Waiting always made men sweat, in her experience.

"If I win, you have to pose for me."

"You want to sketch me?" The other eyebrow climbed his forehead, joining the first.

"With props."

He leaned back, eyes wary. "What kind of props?"

An impish grin curled her lips. "Whatever kind I decide. That's the advantage of winning the bet. And if *you* win…" She paused, glancing down to take a moment of bravery before glancing up at him from underneath her lashes. "You can help me redo my body casting. Make sure I get the oil all. Rubbed. In."

His jaw tightened, eyes burning with heat. Oh yeah, he'd been thinking about the almost kiss just as much as she had.

"Playing a dangerous game, Tamsen," his low voice growled.

She shrugged one shoulder. "Didn't take you for a chicken, Parker. But we can bet for safe, simple drinks if you'd prefer—"

"Deal," he said with a devilish smile.

Yes! She tried not to gloat or let her conscience remind her this was potential disaster in the making. There was nothing wrong with a little harmless flirting. And if it led to one night of passion that helped burn off so much pent-up lust, all the better.

"May the best team win." He tipped his chin then turned

and headed back to his table.

Tamsen moved back to the bar, noticing that sometime during her exchange with Parker the bartender had dropped off her drink. She grabbed it and walked on unsteady legs back to her table, determined to win this game.

Or not. She honestly didn't know which outcome she preferred.

Either way, it looked like naked time with Parker would be in the near future for her.

A grin spread across her face. So really, she couldn't lose.

Chapter Twelve

Parker scrubbed shampoo through his hair a second time. He was convinced the *wash, rinse, repeat* instructions on shampoo bottles were written by a firefighter. The smell of smoke clung to everything, clothing, furniture, and especially skin and hair.

They'd gotten called to an apartment building fire. Some dumbass college kids were grilling on their balcony and poured an entire bottle of lighter fluid on the charcoal grill. Thing went up like a flash bomb. The flames caught some kind of gauzy netting strung around the balcony that had been put up to keep bugs out.

It kept the bugs out all right. And lit up like dry tinder.

At least there were no injuries. They were smart enough to call 911 right away and close the patio door. Parker and his crew got there in under five minutes and had the fire out in ten. The balcony was made of some kind of cement material. Not the prettiest, but great for stopping the spread of fire. All in all, they just had some warping to the patio door, a bit of smoke damage, and hopefully a lesson in not being an idiot.

Fully rinsed, he shut off the water and stepped out of the shower. He had been the last in, letting his crewmates take first dibs while he did the equipment check. They took turns sharing duties, and he enjoyed showering last. Gave him a few moments alone to decompress. Even a non-fatality call screwed with your head. Because every first responder knew it could have gone the other way.

Running a towel over his body, Parker reached for his phone to check his messages. He had a new email from his PI. Eager for any news, he opened the message and began to read. Frank had dug into all the public information available on Thomas Hayes and found nothing suspicious. He'd also interviewed past coworkers, which was technically legal, but ethically might be seen as a bit sketchy to some. Thomas had been married before, to Tamsen's mom, which Parker already knew. But she'd died suddenly of a brain aneurysm when Tamsen was three.

Damn. That sucked. He dealt with death often in his job. He knew how precious life was, how it could be taken away at a moment's notice, but it was still hard to deal with the fragility of it all.

He continued reading. Thomas Hayes had been working for the Denver Public Library for the past two and a half decades and was set to retire in a few more years. He had a pension and some retirement saved. Not anywhere close to what Parker's mother had in the bank, but nothing about the guy screamed red flag. And yet…his gut still said something was up. It also called him an asshole for secretly investigating his mother's fiancé while wildly flirting with his daughter.

"The two have nothing to do with each other," he said into the silent air.

His attraction to Tamsen had nothing to do with his desire to know more about her father and his intentions. Besides, he hadn't done anything about it.

Yet.

As much as he hated to admit it, his willpower plummeted around Tamsen, and her apparent eagerness to throw caution to the wind and indulge in...whatever the hell this chemistry thing was between them, was not helping him stay the path.

Replying to the email, he asked his PI to dig deeper. Criminal records, civil complaints, anything that might indicate Thomas wasn't the perfect guy his mother and Tamsen claimed him to be. Was he reaching? Maybe. Creating an issue where there wasn't one? It wasn't like he wanted there to be an issue; this was his *mom*. He wanted her to be happy, but there was no such thing as too thorough when looking out for the person who always looked out for him. And if his guy still didn't find anything after this? He swore to himself he'd back off.

Yeah, some people might say he had trust issues, but he trusted his crew. Kind of a necessity, since you had to trust the people at your back when lives were on the line. But he trusted them with his life. It was trusting people with his heart Parker had a problem with. How did people do that? Put such blind faith in another person? Be so emotionally vulnerable and open. Hand them the power to uplift your soul...or destroy it.

He didn't understand how people did that.

After getting dressed, he headed out into the main living area of the fire station. Turner, Díaz, and O'Neil were sitting at the table playing cards. Ward was in the kitchen, *oh crap,* making dinner. He glanced at the schedule on the wall. Yup, sure enough, tonight was Ward's turn to make the evening meal. He'd have to check his locker to make sure he had enough antacids to survive the night.

As discreetly as possible, he made his way over to the kitchen, stretching his neck to see if he could get a glimpse of what Ward would be subjecting them to tonight.

"It's chowder, asshole," Ward said without turning around.

Busted...

"I didn't say anything."

Now Ward glanced over his shoulder, spearing Parker with a suspicious glare. "You didn't have to." His chin nodded to their crewmates at the table. "I've already had an interrogation. And don't worry, I didn't make it. I'm just reheating it."

"If anyone can fuck up reheating soup, it's you, Ward," Díaz called from her card game.

"Thanks, Díaz. Appreciate the vote of confidence. Do you have to bust my balls when all I'm doing is making a nice meal for everyone?"

Without glancing up from her cards, Díaz shrugged. "From what I hear, your balls could use a little action lately, and I'll save my appreciation once I know the meal goes down and stays there."

Parker laughed, turning it into a cough when Ward sent him a death glare.

"I should put poison in this," Ward grumbled as he turned back to the soup. "Just to spite you dickwads. And my balls are none of your concern, Díaz."

She snorted. "Thank God for that."

Parker shook his head, making eye contact with O'Neil and Turner, the three sharing a silent communication as they always did when Ward and Díaz went at each other. Which was every day.

"You want in?" O'Neil asked when Parker took a seat at the table.

"Five card stud."

His game. "Deal me in."

Fifteen minutes later, the soup was ready and Parker had won three hands. They didn't play for money since they were on the clock. Bragging rights were better than cash anyway, especially anytime he beat Díaz. The woman hated to lose— at anything. But she was a good sport about it, at least with him. If she ever lost to Ward…well, he was just glad Ward sucked at cards because he did not want to see that outcome.

Hell might freeze over.

Ward's chowder was surprisingly good. Really good, in fact.

"This is excellent, man," Turner said as he helped himself to a second bowl.

Parker agreed. This might be the first time one of Ward's dinners didn't have him racing for nausea medication. "Yeah, where'd you get this?"

"I called up 5280 Eats. Tamsen recommended it and sent it over while we were at the call."

"Tamsen? My Tamsen?"

All sounds of eating stopped. Four pairs of eyes focused on him with varying levels of curiosity.

"*Your* Tamsen?" Ward asked, eyebrows high.

"Shut up, you know what I mean."

"No, I don't think we do," Díaz said with a smile. "Enlighten us."

Oh, so now she decided to play nice with Ward. When they could gang up against him. Jackasses. It was just a slip of the tongue.

"You two were looking awful cozy at trivia last night," O'Neil commented.

"We were talking." And flirting, making sexually charged bets, eye fucking each other from across the room. "Nothing more."

"Uh huh." Díaz tilted her head. "That talking have anything to do with the reason we lost last night? Again?"

Yeah, Díaz definitely hated losing. But it hadn't been his fault entirely. The Lumbersnacks were really good. And okay, he might have been a little too distracted by Tamsen to focus completely on the game, but they were a team. They couldn't put all the blame on him for losing a round or two.

"I think our lack of knowledge about eighteenth-century impressionist painters was the reason we lost." He tried to get the focus off him and Tamsen. "Why the hell would they pick such a specific category?"

Turner pointed toward the calendar hanging on the firehouse wall. "It's the sidewalk art festival this week. I bet they were going for a theme or something."

"That explains the category," Ward said with a nod. "But not how the Lumbersnacks—worst name ever, by the way—managed to get every single question right that round. I mean, come on, who knows that much about dead artists?"

"Tamsen." *Shit!* He shouldn't have said that. Now everyone was staring at him again for an explanation. So much for shifting the focus away from him. "What? She's an artist. Ward, O'Neil, you knew that."

"No, we didn't," O'Neil stated.

"You were both on her call with me."

"Eh." Ward gave a small shrug. "We knew she was doing an art project. I thought your girl worked at a restaurant."

"She does, but she's also an artist, and interns at a gallery, and she's not *my* girl."

"Then how do you know so much about her?" Turner asked with a knowing smile.

Were there any people nosier and more infuriating than firefighters? Seriously, they gossiped worse than a bunch of high schoolers in the locker room after prom.

"Look, Tamsen and I are friends, okay? Nothing more." Not yet, anyway. "We're planning a wedding shower for her dad and my mom, so we've hung out a bit. And I'm done talking about this."

Ward opened his mouth, no doubt to say something

obnoxious Parker would have to smack him for, but just then Parker's phone pinged with an incoming text. *Saved by the phone.* He pulled his phone out of his front pocket, heart racing when he saw the sender.

Tamsen.

"Who is it?"

He glanced up at Ward, careful not to reveal anything on his face as he stared at his fellow firefighter, refusing to give him anything. The smug ass smiled, his eyes lighting with mischief.

"It's her, isn't it? Tamsen."

Parker pushed his chair back, standing and taking his empty bowl to the sink as he threw over his shoulder, "I'm not discussing this."

"Ha! It's totally her."

"I'm going to grab some air." And some privacy, because if he didn't step outside, he'd have four necks craning over his shoulder trying to read his conversation. Irritating, but he knew he'd be doing the same thing if the situation were reversed. When you basically lived with your coworkers half the week, they became more like family. Nosy, annoying family.

He stepped out into the warm evening air. It was just after six, but the summer sun still hadn't made its way behind the Front Range yet. The noisy traffic from the Denver city streets filled the air. He sat on the bench by the front of the firehouse door and pulled up Tamsen's text.

Tamsen: *Hey. You free some night this week?*

His thumbs flew across the screen as he texted back.

Parker: *On my 24hr shift now, but I'm free Monday night.*

He waited as the three little dots danced on his screen, curious as to what she wanted to see him for. Could be something about the bet. Maybe she wanted to set a time to cash in on her winnings? Or sex.

He really hoped it was sex.

Tamsen: *Perfect! Come by the gallery after 8. I think it's the perfect spot for the shower.*

His hopes sank. The party. Of course she was talking about the party.

Parker: *Yeah, I can do that.*

Tamsen: *Hephaestus. It's in LODO.*

He leaned back against the bench, surprised at how disappointed he was. Which was ridiculous. She'd been the one to proposition him the other night, and he'd put the brakes on it. But all that flirting at trivia—and his friends were right, it had been flirting—was really testing his resolve. He couldn't ever remember wanting anyone as badly as he wanted Tamsen, but it wasn't just that. He also really liked being around her. She was funny and smart and had this warm quality that just made everyone feel…at home.

Corny, but it was really the only way to describe her.

His phone chimed again.

Tamsen: *Oh and fair warning…I plan to claim my winnings, so be prepared because I have found the absolute BEST prop to paint you with.*

That sounded ominous. After the water bottle trick, he'd learned Tamsen had a wicked sense of humor. He dug it, but who knew what she was going to subject him to?

Parker: *You're not going to make me pose with some*

creepy taxidermy squirrel riding a scooter, are you?

Tamsen: *I wasn't, but now…*

Parker: *No! I draw the line at dead rodents.*

Tamsen: *I don't remember us setting stipulations on the bet.*

Damn. He should have.

Parker: *I'm going to hate this, aren't I?*

She sent back a winking kiss face emoji. Laughter spilled out of him. Even in text this woman could get to him. He was super curious about what prop she found but even more curious if she wanted him to be naked while she painted. He hoped so. Him naked might lead to her naked, and then they could have naked time together.

His favorite kind of time.

Bad idea, future stepsister, investigating her father.

He ignored his conscience. Wishing for something and actually having it happen wasn't the same thing.

Tamsen: *See you Monday at 8.*

Parker: *See ya.*

He held his breath while more dots appeared, wondering what she was going to say, a feeling in his gut telling him it was something big.

Tamsen: *As you saw, most of my subjects are drawn au natural…so plan accordingly.*

Oh shit! She did intend to draw him naked. As much as he knew he shouldn't be excited by that prospect…he was. God, he was so tired of fighting the attraction he had to this woman. After their kiss the other night, it was damn near impossible now. Maybe if they took one night, and were up front about their expectations with each other, they could get it out of their systems and go on as friends. What was the alternative? Lusting after a woman he'd soon be pseudo-related to? That couldn't happen. His mother was a smart woman. She'd see something was up and take him to task for it.

No, better to try and burn this fire out before it got out of control and destroyed everything.

After sending the heart eyes emoji back to her, which received another winking kiss face emoji, he slipped his phone back in his pocket, adjusted his pants, and counted backward from one hundred until he could walk back into the station without a raging hard-on he knew his crew would notice and comment on.

Now all he had to do was make it through the rest of his shift and then...Tamsen.

A little voice in the back of his brain warned him getting involved with her while investigating her father was a bad idea, but he ignored it. What he and Tamsen did had nothing to do with his checking into her dad. They were two separate things. Besides, so far everything with Thomas looked on the up and up. Parker hoped Frank wouldn't find anything else, and he could let this heavy suspicion go. His mother would get a loving husband, he and Tamsen could have their fun, and no one would ever have to know anything about the PI.

Everybody won.

And he'd just ignore the tiny clench in his gut warning him he was headed for a five-alarm fire of epic proportions.

Chapter Thirteen

Tamsen did one last walk through of the gallery. The doors had been locked an hour ago. She'd finished all her closing duties. All the client purchases were packed up and ready to go out in the morning. Winston knew she was staying late to work, as she often did when she had shifts at the gallery. A great perk of her internship.

Another perk was the large back room that included a studio where visiting artists were invited to create masterpieces. The place she intended to use tonight to make a masterpiece of her own.

It was finally Monday night. She swore time had moved at a snail's pace since she texted Parker Saturday afternoon. But here it was. Monday evening and in a few minutes the reason for her constant distraction lately would walk though that front door.

There was clearly chemistry between them. *Tons* of it if that kiss was anything to go by. And if they kept ignoring it, it might explode at the worst possible moment. Like, say, their parents' wedding. The open bar, the romantic atmosphere…

yeah, they needed to work this lust situation out before they made the mistake of sneaking out of the ceremony for a quickie and getting caught. Because with her luck, that would be the exact way the situation would go down.

Better to make a plan, get it all out of their systems now. Or, as Cora put it when they discussed the situation while pairing wine with Girl Scout cookies the other night, *you better put that man under you so you can get over him.* Yup. If she kept acting like a horny teenager anytime she was near Parker, her dad would eventually notice, and that was a conversation she didn't want to have.

Ever.

She pushed back the heavy blackout curtain separating the back studio from the rest of the gallery. Everything was set up for Parker's arrival. The large blue tarpaulin was set out on the floor underneath the massive canvas.

Heat rushed to her cheeks. She'd read about this particular technique a few years ago but never imagined she'd have the guts or opportunity to try it.

A soft knock sounded from the front of the gallery. Her fist clenched around the curtain, pulling it closed tightly. This was it. He was here.

She made her way to the front of the gallery, the bright outdoor security lights of the building illuminating the figure standing just beyond the glass door.

Parker.

Heart racing with anticipation, she hurried to unlock the door.

"Hi." He grinned as he stepped inside. "Hope I'm not late."

She relocked the door and turned to him. "Nope. Right on time."

"Great."

He moved into the gallery, taking in the spacious area,

the paintings hanging on the wall, the sculptures and mixed media installations they had roped off. She stood back, watching him take in each piece. One of the reasons she loved art so much was it tended to reveal more about the person consuming it than the artist themselves. The artist created, but the observer brought it to life.

"Wow." He turned in a circle, taking it all in. "You're right. This place is perfect for the party. My mom will really like it. She digs art."

"And you?"

"I appreciate things that catch my eye."

"Like what?"

His gaze swept the length of her, leaving a physical touch in its wake. She shivered, thighs clenching together as he smiled.

"Oh, you know, beautiful art, beautiful artists."

He winked, and her panties nearly disintegrated.

She cleared her throat, moving to the side of the room where they had a small bar set up for show nights. "We have the bar here for cocktails, and there's tables in the back we can bring out for more food, cake, party favors, and that kind of thing."

As anxious as she was to get behind the curtain and start painting Parker, she had to take a moment to calm down. She was supposed to be the one in control here. He'd stepped inside and in less than five minutes he had her so flustered, she knew she was about two seconds away from doing something embarrassing, like tripping over her own damn feet, crashing into the wall, and setting off the security system. Boy, wouldn't that put a damper on the night she had planned.

No. She could do this. She just had to find her chill. Not a problem.

Parker moved to the bar, leaning over to glance behind it.

The movement gave her a great view of his perfect butt. Her mouth literally dropped open, a tiny droplet of drool falling from the corner of her mouth to slide down her jaw.

Crap! Her chill, where was her chill?

One view of Parker's butt—his clothed butt—and it flew away. If she wanted this night to go as she planned, she needed to move them both behind the black curtain. The sooner the better. The front walls of the gallery had giant windows to let in optimal light—great for viewing artwork, not so great if you were planning on paintings that involved getting naked… and other things.

"Yeah, I think this place will be perfect."

He stood back up—*dang it*—and leaned against the bar. "I still think it's kind of weird to have a wedding shower."

"Lots of people have them."

"Lots of people are weird."

"What's wrong with being a weirdo?" It was a moniker she'd been graced with many a time in her life. She didn't mind. Most people were weird; some were just better at hiding it. Which she never understood. Why hide what made you unique?

He smiled softly. "Absolutely nothing. In fact, I think people who see the world from different angles, who live to the beat of their own drum no matter what anyone else thinks, are some of the bravest people around. You amaze me, Tamsen."

She sucked in a breath as his gaze penetrated hers.

He rubbed his hands together, breaking the moment. "Well, should we move on to the next part of the evening? I'm ready to pose for you, Picasso."

He did it again. That was supposed to be her line. Well, not that exactly, but she was supposed to usher him back to the next part of the evening. How did she keep letting him distract her?

Because he's sexy as sin and I'm too focused on ten minutes from now instead of now.

"I've got everything set up in the back."

She pointed to the black curtains. Parker's eyebrows rose. He glanced from the curtains back to her with a wary expression.

"You're not going to make me put, like, a rubber chicken mask over my head and have me sit in an oversize nest made out of garbage, are you?"

A bark of laughter burst out of her as the absurd image filled her head. Once she had her hilarity under control, she shook her head. "What kind of art are you looking at?"

"I saw a picture of something like that in a coffee shop once. Kinda creeped me out." He lifted his hands. "Then again, what do I know about art?"

"It's not about knowing. It's about feelings." She hoped he'd be feeling a lot. Very soon. "Come on."

She motioned for him to follow her as she moved across the gallery toward the curtains, hitting the main room lights as they went. The front room plunged into darkness, but the lights from the street allowed enough of a glow that they made it to the curtain without stumbling over anything.

"Now," she said turning to face him, one hand on the curtain. "If you've changed your mind and don't want to do this, that's fine."

She would never force anyone to do anything they didn't fully want to do. Artistically or otherwise. But she really hoped he hadn't changed his mind. She was quite certain if she didn't touch Parker in the next five minutes, she was going to die of lust, and honestly, that sounded like a terrible way to go.

"As long as it doesn't involve dead animals or pretending to be an animal, I think I can handle it."

"I promise there's no taxidermy or chicken masks, but

I have to say, those are very specific phobias of yours." She gave him an evil grin. "I might have to use them as blackmail later."

He grunted. "They're not phobias. I just prefer my animals alive and adorable. And I don't believe you'd ever stoop so low as to blackmail anyone."

True, but she did love a good April Fool's joke. Perhaps Parker would be getting one of those squeaking rubber chickens in the mail this year.

She pulled back the curtain, stepping through with Parker close behind her. The room was dim, lit by a small lamp she'd left on in the corner. This painting didn't need a lot of light, but they couldn't stumble around in total darkness.

Parker glanced around, confusion filling his eyes as he turned his head toward her.

"Where's your easel? Don't artists usually use an easel?"

She nodded. "Sometimes, but I don't have one big enough for this canvas."

"What canvas?"

She pointed to the floor. His eyes followed her motion, head tilting before they widened as he took in that the white material on the floor was a canvas.

"Oooookay, are you going to have me lay down and trace my body? Because I did that in first grade with Jenny Mews in art class, and it looked nothing like me."

She laughed. "No. I'm not doing a portrait of you. In fact, this isn't a single subject painting."

"It's not?"

Excitement and nerves mounting, she bit her lip. "Nope. So you know how the show I'm working on is all about the human form?" He nodded, so she continued. "Well, I thought it would be great to add a piece to it. It's a new technique I read about that captures human expression, emotion, movement. It's called Passion Painting."

"What is that?"

She slowly made her way over to the canvas, her spiky heels making a soft crinkling sound as she walked over the blue tarpaulin. Reaching down, she grabbed the small box sitting on a table by the edge of the tarp. Her heart was pounding so hard and fast, she was afraid it might beat right out of her chest. She was pretty sure Parker would be down for her idea, but she wasn't psychic.

Please don't let him say no.

This wasn't just about a cool art technique she wanted to try. That was just a bonus. The real objective for tonight was to get this man out of her system. Piece: Fuck the Lust Away.

Hmmmm, she probably shouldn't title it that if she ever displayed it.

"We're going to need some special supplies for this painting."

Opening the wooden box covered in years of splattered paint, she pulled out the first item they'd need.

"Paintbrushes?" The left side of his mouth quirked up. "Seems like standard supplies for painting."

She nodded. "Yup. These are pretty standard. These, however," she placed the brushes on the table and grabbed the next item, "are a little more special."

One dark eyebrow rose. "Looks like normal paint to me."

Typical non-artist. There were so many different types of paint and none of them were normal. They all suited a special purpose. Worked on different media. "These are non-toxic, organic…body paint."

His eyes widened, lips curling in a devastatingly sexy smile. "Oh, are they now?"

"Yes. Perfectly safe to use on any part of the human body."

His gaze heated as she placed the paints on the table, hand reaching back into the box.

"More special supplies?"

"Just one." She swallowed, hard, pulling out the last item they'd need. An entire strip of them.

"Condoms," he growled.

Tamsen saw his muscles tense; she could practically see the air around him vibrating. When his tongue came out to swipe against his lower lip, she nearly lost it right then and there.

"Aren't you tired of fighting this, Parker?"

"This?"

She waved a hand back and forth between them. "This… heat between us."

"Sweetheart," he said in a low voice. "This isn't heat. This is full-blown fire."

Good, he agreed. So then maybe… "Don't you think we better put it out before it gets…out of control?"

The corner of his mouth curled up in a devilish smile. "You know, I was thinking the same exact thing earlier."

The low rumble of his voice was working on her better than any foreplay she'd ever experienced. Seriously, if she could bottle that sound, she'd make a fortune in the sex toy industry.

"Glad we seem to be on the same page."

His smile dipped. "But our parents—"

"Aren't involved in this. This is between you and me. It's temporary, just scratching an itch so future family dinners won't be…tense. No promises. No problems. They don't have to know about our dalliance."

"Dalliance?"

"Dalliance is a casual romantic or sexual relationship with someone. We both agreed we don't want anything serious, and if we try to ignore this attraction, it's only going to boil over until it explodes, probably at the wrong moment. And we can't risk anything happening that would damage—"

"Tamsen," he interrupted her ramblings with a small chuckle. "I know what the word dalliance means. I've just never heard anyone under the age of sixty use it."

She placed the box on the table, narrowing her eyes. "Ass."

He held up his hands and smiled. "I'm sorry, if I let you say dalliance, can we still do the passion painting? You know I think your nervous rambling is adorable."

He thought she was adorable? Her heart started to sigh. No! Bad heart. It was not involved in this. Fun parts only, no feelings.

"So you know what a passion painting is?"

"I'm beginning to get the idea, but why don't you explain it? Just in case. Slowly and in vivid detail."

Laughter bubbled out of her. All her nerves started to dissipate. He had this way of setting her at ease that no one else did. He made her feel…safe.

"A passion painting is when two, or more, people paint their partner's bodies and leave an expression of their joining on canvas."

"Meaning…"

One look at the knowing smirk on his face and she knew he was going to make her say it. Well, that was fine with her. Tilting her chin up, she gave him her sultriest smile and explained in the basest terms possible.

"I paint you. You paint me." She motioned to the white material on the floor. "And we have sex on top of this canvas."

Chapter Fourteen

It didn't get more vivid than that.

Parker needed something to distract him so he didn't rush over to Tamsen, rip all their clothes off, and sate this need that had been driving them both wild since the day they met.

He wanted her, needed her, but he didn't want to rush this. Didn't want to ruin the effort she'd put into place. He'd been hoping tonight's little painting session would end in sex, but he never imagined it would *start* with it.

Passion painting. He'd never heard of such a thing, but damned if he wasn't intrigued as hell. It sounded messy, raw, hot. With anyone else, he might have scoffed it off as silly, but with Tamsen? It was perfect.

His body kept screaming at him to run to her side, lay her down on the floor, and satisfy them both until they couldn't move. But his brain reminded him that taking things slow was better. Savoring the moment he'd been anxiously waiting for would just extend the pleasure.

"So." He cleared his throat when the word came out

rough and gravelly. "How do we do this thing?"

Her lips quirked up in an impish smile. "And here I thought you knew your way around a woman's body."

He chuckled. "I know how to fuck, sweetheart, believe me. And every woman's body is different. So you just tell me what you like, or don't like, and I promise you'll be melting all over that canvas."

She bit her lip, a needy little moan escaping.

"I meant," he continued, taking a small step forward, "how does the whole painting thing work?"

"Well, first we have to be naked."

He grinned, giving her a wink. "Ladies first."

"Brawn before beauty," she countered.

So she wanted to play it like that, huh? Okay, he agreed anyhow. She was far more beautiful than he was. Than anyone he'd ever laid eyes on, truth be told. Something inside Tamsen glowed, lighting her up from the inside out. Great, now he was becoming a sappy poet, waxing on about the beauty of the woman in front of him. What was she doing to him?

Having her wicked way with him soon, he hoped.

Maintaining eye contact, Parker grabbed the bottom of his T-shirt and lifted it over his head. The sharp intake of breath he heard from Tamsen made his ego soar. He knew he was in good shape, had to be for his job, but appreciation from the woman he was about to sleep with never hurt a man's pride.

"How's this for a canvas for you?" He waved a hand over his chest and stomach.

Eyes focused directly on his abs, Tamsen shook her head.

"Better lose the pants, too."

Letting out a low laugh, his right hand went to the button on his jeans, easing it open. He grasped the zipper and slowly pulled the tab down, prolonging the tension and being careful of his painfully hard erection. Nothing would kill the mood like getting his dick caught in his zipper.

He kicked off his shoes. Thank everything in the world he'd decided to wear his Chelsea boots today—those suckers were easy to shuck on and off. He did not have the time or patience to handle shoelace ties right now. He removed his jeans and boxers in one fluid move, hooking his thumbs in his socks and tossing the entire pile of clothing to the side.

A lot of people didn't think men were self-conscious when it came to their bodies, but that just wasn't true. Parker worked in a very physically demanding job that kept him in shape, but he had his insecurities like everyone else. Especially considering the crew he worked with. He knew he wasn't as buff as O'Neil or as lean as Ward. So it sent a sigh of relief through him when Tamsen gasped, her eyes growing wide as she took him in. Her gaze traveling over every inch of his body.

"Like what you see?"

"Shhhh." She raised a finger to her lips. "I'm capturing a mental image so I can sculpt you later and make a fortune selling art of the perfect man."

His head tipped back as a loud boom of laughter spilled from his lips. "Thanks for the compliment, but I'm far from perfect."

"Close enough."

As much as he was enjoying her ogling him and saying pretty things that boosted his ego far more than it needed, they should get this show on the road before he embarrassed himself and disappointed her.

"Your turn," he said with a low growl.

Tamsen blinked, her eyes coming back into focus as they found his face once again. With a coy smile her hands reached to the tie on the side of her dark green dress. She stepped out of some killer black heels, reducing her height by about three inches. He almost suggested she keep them on, but considering they were about to be rolling around on the floor, he didn't think it would be all that comfortable for her. And he wanted her comfortable and sated by the end of the night.

He watched with rapt attention as her hands untied the knot at her hip, slowly. So damn slowly, he thought he might explode. Was the woman trying to torture him? One look at the mischievous smile on her face and he knew the answer was yes.

Damn, he really liked her.

Once the knot was undone, she eased the material apart, revealing the sexiest set of lacy black undergarments Parker had ever seen. There wasn't anything special about the matching bra and panty set, except they were on Tamsen. Which automatically made them the sexiest thing he'd ever seen.

She opened the dress, shrugging her shoulders and letting the material slip off her body and fall to the floor. Then she reached back to unclasp her bra in that magic way women did. A simple flick of the wrist and tada! Tatas. He wanted to laugh at his own joke, but he was too busy swallowing his own tongue at the sight of Tamsen's small, perfect breasts, the tips of her peaked nipples hard and pointing directly at him, seeking attention. Oh, he'd be giving them all the attention they deserved and then some, very soon.

Next, she slipped her fingers into the waist of her panties, dragging them down her legs in a painfully erotic dance he loved and lamented at the same time. This was the hottest foreplay he'd ever experienced, and they hadn't even touched yet.

They stood in front of each other, feet apart, completely bare to one another, silent and staring, the air thick and charged with sexual tension. His blood raced, heart pounding in his chest. Finally, she reached over to grab two brushes, holding one out toward him. Parker took the last few steps separating them. He reached for the brush, grasping it between his fingers, slowly pulling it from hers.

She sucked in a deep breath as if he'd touched her. Passion Painting was the proper phrase, all right.

She opened two of the paint jars, red and a deep teal color. Dipping her brush in the red, she brought it to his chest and swiped the brush over his nipple and down his stomach. The soft touch of the bristle felt like a charged wire, electrifying his skin. There didn't seem to be any rhyme or reason to her brush stroke, so he reached over and dipped his brush in the teal, repeating her movement. He circled her nipple with the color, swirling the brush around her breast and down to her belly button.

Tamsen tipped her head back and let out a throaty moan. Unable to hold it off any longer, Parker grasped the back of her neck, crushing his lips to hers, tasting the sweetness of her mouth. It was even better than he remembered. Her lips were soft and warm. He drank in the sweetness of them, the absolute decadence, each brush of her mouth against his stoking the fire raging within.

He wanted more, and at the same time, he simply wanted this. Hours of kissing Tamsen. Feeling her melt into him as their mouths learned each other's. She kissed him back, her tongue brushing against his with the same erotic stroke her paintbrush had done to his body.

After a moment, she pulled back, dipping her brush again and once more painting him with a sensual care he never imagined an art instrument could achieve. And so it went, stroke for stroke, color upon color, until their bodies were covered in swipes of vibrancy.

"Now what?" he asked as Tamsen set her brush back on the table with the box and paints.

She lifted the strip of condoms, ripping one off and opening the foil packet. "Now comes the fun part."

His smile grew. "So far, it's all been fun."

"I agree."

He laughed along with her, his laughter turning into a rough inhale when she gripped him in her hand, stroking his length in a way no paint brush could ever achieve. Grasping her hip, he pulled her close, his fingers sliding in between her legs. She let out a loud moan as he rubbed, touching her where he most wanted. When she slipped the condom on him, he thrust two fingers inside her, pulling a sharp cry from her lips.

"The…canvas…" she panted. "We need…to get on the…canvas."

He removed his fingers, scooping her into his arms and placing her in the middle of the stark, white material. It was softer than he expected.

"And now comes the part where we let go and allow the art to work through us. Whatever we leave on this canvas is an expression of pure, raw passion. Just open yourself up to the process and…feel."

She wrapped her legs around him, reaching down to position him at her entrance. One thrust and he was inside her. They moaned in unison at the connection. It took everything he had in him to hold still, not pound away like an animal in heat. Tamsen drove him wild, but he wouldn't ruin this by going too fast. If this was the only moment they had, he was going to make it amazing for her. For them.

Her fingers tangled in his hair, pulling him down to her. Her hips arched, taking him in deeper as her lips sought out his. They found a rhythm, slow at first, but as their passion grew, it became wild. Tamsen rolled him on the canvas, taking the top position, riding him with seductive skill. He was vaguely aware of the marks they were leaving, the impression of the body on the canvas, the colors mixing, but all he could really focus on was Tamsen. How she felt, how she made him feel.

Her lips tore from his as she cried out, her body tightening around him. Grasping her hips, he thrust hard against her, prolonging her release and finding his own. A wave of pure elation crashed over him. Every sense he had heightened to its peak. He could have sworn he saw an aura of color surrounding them. It was probably all the paint, but Parker had never felt such a sense of...fullness after sex before. It should have satisfied him, sated him, but he found himself craving more. In that moment, he knew one night with Tamsen wouldn't be enough to burn out this fire between them.

Not by a long shot.

She collapsed against him. Heavy pants filling the silent air. He sat with his realization, wondering how he could possibly bring up the subject of more when they'd agreed to a one-and-done deal. He waited until their breath had evened out before speaking.

"That was amazing."

She sat up, grinning down at him. "I agree. But this canvas is still awfully blank."

He moved his head side to side, but it was hard to see from his angle. Flat on his back, he could only see a few inches to the side of his face.

"You know what I think?" she asked with a smile.

His thumbs stroked her hips, enjoying the soft feel of her skin, the slickness of the paint as it spread along her skin. "No. What?"

"I don't think this painting is done yet."

He certainly knew he wasn't done with her.

"Oh, really?"

She nodded. "Yup."

He was game for playing along.

"Well, what do you think we should do about that?"

"I think we have more condoms and more paint." Her lips tilted down in a mock pout. "And it would be a shame to be wasteful."

"You're absolutely right." He nodded somberly. "We should do our best to use the resources we have."

Tamsen leaned down, brushing her lips over his as she whispered, "Absolutely."

Hours later, they'd used the last of the condoms and every single drop of paint. He and Tamsen took a quick shower in the loft kept for visiting artists in residence, where they found other creative ways to pleasure each other.

The early morning hours were approaching as they dressed. Tamsen had hung their painting on some weird fishing line–looking contraption in the far back. He had to admit, it looked amazing. He couldn't see any real body parts, but there was a sense of…energy that radiated off the swipes and blends of color. There were also some very clear handprints here and there on the canvas.

Sex paintings…who knew?

"Thank you, Parker. That was fun."

"Fun?" He snorted. That was much more than fun. Amazing, invigorating, once in a lifetime kind of experience. Way more than *fun*.

Her eyes widened. "You don't think it was fun?"

Snagging an arm around her waist, he pulled her close and placed a soft kiss to her lips. "Sweetheart, that was much more than fun. That was fucking amazing."

She blushed. "Oh. Okay, then, what do you say to continuing to have fucking amazing fun? You know, until this whole chemistry thing goes away?"

He pulled back with a start, surprised she seemed to feel the same as he did. "You don't think it's gone?"

She blinked. "No. Do you?"

He stared at her, relief filling him. He'd been worried about her reaction if he suggested changing their deal, but she went and beat him to it.

"No."

Her face morphed into a bright smile. "Good. Then how about we keep this no promises, no problems liaison going? Until we're bored."

When she put it like that, it tasted sour on his tongue. Get bored? Of Tamsen? He didn't know if that was possible. But since neither of them was looking for anything serious, this deal she was proposing sounded like something only a fool would pass up.

And Parker Kincaid was no fool.

"I'm in."

"Great. You've got my number."

"And you've got mine."

She lifted up on her toes, placing a soft, sweet kiss to his lips. "See ya later, Parker."

They walked out the back. After seeing her to her car and making sure she drove off okay, he headed to his own vehicle. Tonight had been nothing like he expected and better than his wildest dreams.

You can't keep having sex with her while investigating her father.

He pushed the dark thought away. His involvement with Tamsen had nothing to do with him looking into her dad.

Besides, they were just having fun. Right?

Chapter Fifteen

Tamsen eased her key into the apartment lock, turning over the mechanical device with as much silence as she could. Cora was a notoriously light sleeper, and she didn't want to disturb her roommate. Okay, she also didn't want her nosy friend waking up and asking a million questions. She was still basking in the glow of tonight. Or this morning, she supposed, considering it was nearing four a.m.

She eased open the front door, breathing a sigh of relief when she heard nothing from the direction of Cora's room. The night had been more of a success than she'd hoped. Dream Parker had nothing on Real Parker. The man had skills, but more importantly, he had instinct. He seemed to anticipate what she wanted, changing position and pace to bring her body to places of pleasure it had never been before. She hadn't had that many orgasms in one night in…ever.

Slipping off her heels, she made her way into the kitchen only to stop short with a screech at a tall, shadowy figure leaning against the kitchen counter. The kitchen light flipped on, and Tamsen's heart slipped out of her throat where it had jumped to and settled back in her chest.

"Cora! You nearly gave me a heart attack. What are you doing up so late?"

Her roommate's eyebrows rose high on her forehead. "Technically, it's early. Very early. So early, in fact, one might question why you are just getting home?"

"I asked you first." Mature? No, but she needed a moment to think of a response that wouldn't have Cora pumping her for details she wasn't sure she wanted to share yet.

Cora waved a hand over the Winnie the Pooh scrubs she had on. "I have a double shift today."

Right. Hospital shifts were as hectic as restaurant shifts. More so because the hospital never closed. Tamsen admired her friend so much, working every day with such fragile lives. Whenever Cora lost a patient, it hit her so hard. Tamsen wondered if Parker felt the same sense of grief and guilt whenever he lost someone in a fire. She bet he did. Every frontline worker had such heavy responsibilities on their shoulders. She had no idea how they managed. All she did was serve food and make pretty things for people to look at.

That wasn't true. Cora had told her time and time again that Tamsen's work was important. The world needed the arts to reflect and escape into when life got hard. Plus, she started a Caring Crochet group that met once a month to make hats, socks, and blankets for the hospitals and homeless shelters in the metro area. It wasn't saving lives, but it was something she could do to help.

"Did you make any coffee?" She should be going to bed, but Tamsen was too wired to sleep. With fresh memories of Parker's amazing body in her mind, her sketchpad was calling her name. She wanted to get down as many of his sharp lines and toned muscles as possible. They made such an interesting contrast to his warm smile and the softness in his eyes.

"I did." Cora raised her cup, taking a sip and moving to

stand in front of the coffeemaker. "And you can have a cup as soon as you tell me what had you staying so late at the gallery."

"I was working."

"On what?"

"A piece for my project."

Cora eyed her over the mug. "With who?"

"Don't you mean whom?"

"Don't grammar police me. Spill."

"There's nothing to spill." She already did that. Spilled the paint all over Parker's delicious naked flesh.

"Taaammmmssseeennnn."

How did her friend do that? Drag out her name so it took seven syllables instead of two?

Knowing Cora wouldn't give up and really needing a cup of the delicious-smelling coffee, she broke. "Okay, fine. I was with Parker, okay? We made a bet at trivia night, and since his team lost, I got to paint him."

And oh boy, had she painted him.

Cora smiled as if she knew the answer all along.

"So being out all night was because you got some."

"I did not *get some*." She got it all and *then some*.

Cora snorted. "Don't lie to me, hun. You have sex hair."

Her hands flew up to her frizzy mane. After the shower, she'd towel dried her hair, and since she didn't have any of her products to tame the half curly half straight nightmare that was her ridiculous hair, it air dried into something that resembled the bedhead of a toddler after a long nap.

Busted.

"What time do you have to leave for work?"

"Fifteen minutes. So start talking."

She held out her hand. "Coffee first."

Cora moved about the kitchen, grabbing an extra mug and filling it with the freshly brewed coffee. Normally,

Tamsen added a little cream and sugar, but she needed the full-octane stuff for this conversation.

She sat at the table where Cora joined her, passing over the mug. Tamsen took a moment to wrap her hands around the warm cup, inhale the rich scent of heavenly coffee. After the first sip went down, she finally felt ready to reveal.

"Parker and I did a Passion Painting."

Cora's head tilted in confusion before light dawned in her eyes. Her mouth dropped open, and she leaned forward in her seat. "Wait, you mean that article thing you showed me? The one where people paint their bodies and..."

"Have sex." She nodded. "Yes."

"Wow." Cora sat back. "How's the painting look?"

"That's really what you want to know? How the painting looks?"

Her roommate shrugged. "Is it a single imprint of two bodies barely moving or a wild swatch of colors mixing with each other in indistinguishable shapes and smears of human appendages?"

She lifted the mug to her lips and mumbled into it before taking a sip, "The second one."

"Yes!" Cora pumped a fist in the air. "I knew he'd be good in bed. You can see it in their eyes. How much they focus. The eyes always give it away."

"Technically we weren't in a bed, but yes, Parker is... amazing."

"Amazing, huh?" Cora smiled as she took a sip of her coffee.

"More than amazing." How did she describe what happened last night? The energy, the intensity, the raw emotion of it all? "We connected on a level I didn't even know existed. The man found erogenous zones I didn't even know I had."

"Wow. So when are you seeing him again?"

"Whenever the mood strikes us."

Cora frowned. "Wait, what? I thought you two connected?"

"We did." She ran her finger around the rim of her mug. "Sexually. We both agreed we weren't looking for any kind of relationship. This is just fun. No strings, no promises, no problems. Just scratching the itch until it's out of our system."

Cora rolled her eyes with a delicate snort. "Famous last words."

"Beg pardon?"

"There's no such thing as no problems when it comes to sex. Sex always causes problems. That's why it's so fun."

"Problems are fun?"

"No, but solving them can be." Cora reached over to place her hand on Tamsen's. "Look, the problems aren't always big. Sometimes it's as simple as finding out you aren't right for someone or discovering you don't like a certain kink. But sometimes, big problems happen. Like one person falling in love and the other…not."

She laughed at the absurdity of what her friend was suggesting. "Oh, sweetie, you don't have to worry about that. I have zero time to add love to my schedule right now. Besides, you know I don't want to fall in love."

"No." Cora raised a brow. "You don't want to risk losing the person you love."

She snorted into her coffee, ignoring her friend's intense eye contact.

"Tam," Cora sighed. "You know I love you, but in all the years I've known you, you have never gotten serious about a guy, and I get it, losing your mom so young…it had to be tough."

Not really. She barely remembered her mother. What sucked was growing up watching her dad. She knew how much he missed her mom. He tried to hide it from her, but she saw the pain. She felt it radiate off him. Waves of pain she feared might drown him. Thank goodness he finally found Victoria to pull him from the depths.

But what if he hadn't?

That's what she feared. Losing herself so much in someone, loving someone so deeply that their loss destroyed her, threatened to end her, too. She would never fall that deeply.

"I don't plan on falling in love with Parker."

"And what if he falls in love with you?"

Now there was a situation that would happen after people landed on Mars. He'd already told her what he thought of love and happily ever after. She highly doubted Parker would ever fall in love, least of all with her.

"Not an issue, trust me. Besides, we can't start any type of real relationship."

"Why not?"

"Hello? Our parents are getting married." There was an entire boatload of reasons a real relationship with Parker would be a bad idea due to that, but the biggest was, "If we start dating and things go badly, can you imagine the awkward family dinners? No, thank you. Not to mention it could seriously affect my dad's relationship with Victoria."

And she would never do anything to jeopardize her father's happiness. Not after all he did for her.

"And what you're doing with Parker now isn't the same thing because…?"

"It's just sex."

Cora gave her a disbelieving look. "Things can go badly with sex."

"But there's no emotions involved. If we were dating, there'd be feelings, but with sex only, it's just fun."

Cora shook her head with a small laugh. "That's the most ridiculous thing you've ever said."

"Hey!"

"Sex doesn't always lead to feelings," her roommate continued. "But it always has the possibility to. And if one of you develops feelings while the other doesn't…all I'm saying is be careful. Have your fun, but keep your wits about you. And at the first sign of something deeper, for either of you, if it's not what you want, cut it off. Right away. For everyone's sake."

Somebody sure was a cautious Cora today.

"Sweetie, I love *you*, but I promise I know what I'm doing. Everything will be fine."

She'd just ignore the slight nosedive her stomach took as she spoke those words and the tiny sense of doom that filled her. Everything would be fine. They were just having fun. Tamsen had had a few flings, and they all ended well. Sure, things with Parker felt…more. He made her feel comfortable; even at her most accident-prone and embarrassed moments, he managed to set her at ease, as if those things weren't a failing, but an asset. And yes, maybe he made her heart flutter. A little. But it was only because she wasn't used to people finding her disasters delightful.

Nothing more.

Cora finished her coffee and headed off to work while Tamsen made her way to her bedroom. She grabbed her sketchpad and charcoal pencil from the small desk by the window and tossed them on the bed. She grabbed her PJs, untying her dress and dropping it to the floor. That's when she remembered she hadn't put her underwear back on. Bra, yes, but her panties had gone missing. Well, not so much missing as she had tucked them into Parker's back pocket while he was still drying off from their shower.

She giggled as she thought of him discovering them later today. What would he do with them? Yes, it had been a bit naughty of her, but the man made her do things she never imagined she ever would. She'd had sex beyond the bedroom before, but no one made her step out of her comfort zone like Parker. A parked car her senior year after the prom was as risky as she'd ever gotten.

Once she had her soft, cotton sleep shorts and tank on, she settled in the middle of her bed with her sketchpad and pencil. An hour later, dozens of papers surrounded her on the bed, each one filled with bits and pieces of Parker. His warm eyes, powerful forearms, the thick muscles of his upper thigh, the sexy curl of his smile, that yummy *V* shape where his hip met his groin. All the imagery made heat coil low in her belly. She should be full up on orgasms considering how many she'd had last night, but apparently all it took was simply remembering Parker, and drawing him, to make her crave another.

Her fingers cramped. Setting down her pencil, she stretched them, doing the hand exercises she'd learned from Jade's last boyfriend who happened to be a physical therapist. Just as she was about to call it and catch a few hours of sleep, her phone chimed. She checked the text and smiled. Speak of the devil.

Jade: *OMG you slept with Parker?!?!!!*

Jade: *Deets. Now!*

She typed back.

Tamsen: *How did you find out?*

Jade: *Cora texted me.*

Oh, course she had. The problem with having close friends was that there were no secrets.

Tamsen: *What are you doing up at...*

She glanced at the time on her phone.

Tamsen: *6 am?*

Jade: *Derby team workout is at six thirty. Now quit stalling. Details, woman!!!*

Tamsen laughed, her thumbs flying across the screen as she typed.

Tamsen: *We made a passion painting and that's all I'm telling you, perv. If you need to get your rocks off watch porn like everyone else.*

Jade: *1: I'm insulted you think I don't watch porn already. 2: Ew, I don't want to know for jolly's I just want to know if it was good.*

Tamsen: *It was…*

Instead of words, she sent Jade two rows of the fire emoji.

Jade: *Hell yeah! Get it girl!*

She laughed when Jade sent back a gif of a dancing cat with exploding champagne behind it.

Jade: *You seeing him again?*

Biting her lip, she debated how much to reveal, but if Cora already texted her, there was no telling what Jade knew. Everything, probably.

Tamsen: *Hopefully. We're keeping it casual.*

Jade: *I'd lock the sexy fireman down if it was me, but you do you.*

So Jade wasn't going to give her the "be careful with your

heart" speech like Cora. At least, not yet. She knew Jade was just waiting for the right moment to get into the talky feely portion of the discussion. Cora was always direct whereas Jade liked to bide her time and pounce when the timing was perfect. She knew her friends were just looking out for her, but she had this. They didn't have to worry.

Jade: *I gotta hit the gym, but I'm on lunch shift. You?*

Tamsen: *Dinner.*

Which was good because she'd need a few hours of sleep to account for the lack of sleep last night. Totally worth it.

Jade: *Then I'll high-five you as I leave.*

Tamsen: *See ya.*

She placed her phone in the charger base on her nightstand and put all the loose paper and sketchpad on the floor to deal with later. She slipped under the covers and settled her head against the pillow with a sigh. Sweet slumber, here she came.
Ding. Ding.
Or not.
Slapping her hand against her phone, she pulled it from the cradle and went to turn it on silent, until she saw the message.

Parker: *Found your underwear in my pocket*

Grinning to herself, she typed back.

Tamsen: *Oh my, is that where they went?*

She sent the kissing wink face emoji.

Parker: *I hope you know these are mine now*

Tamsen: *Have an underwear fetish?*

Parker: *Never used to think so, but you're opening me up to all kinds of new experiences, sweetheart*

She could say the same about him.

Parker: *Are you free tonight?*

He was already ready for another round?

Tamsen: *Got the dinner shift. Won't be off until eleven.*

Parker: *Pick you up after work?*

She usually walked home if it was early enough or drove if she had the night shift. But the idea of Parker picking her up and taking her back here where she had a nice, soft bed…if she wasn't as exhausted as she was, she might consider asking him to drive over here right now. When had a man ever made her crave this much? She couldn't remember.

Tamsen: *Such a gentleman*

Parker: *If I promise to not be a gentleman in your bedroom does that mean I can pick you up after work?*

She barked out a half laugh, half needy moan into the silent bedroom.

Tamsen: *You better!*

Parker: *See you tonight*

Tamsen: *Tonight*

She replaced her phone in the base, rolling over to

snuggle down deep into her bed, a large smile curling her lips as she closed her eyes. She knew Cora and Jade might argue that she was moving too fast with Parker, but this was just sex. Just fun.

But as she drifted off to sleep, a voice inside warned her she was getting in over her head. That her friends were right and fun would lead to feelings and falling. And everyone knew when you fell, things could break.

She'd just have to be sure if that happened, the thing that broke wouldn't be her heart.

Chapter Sixteen

"Parker, darling," his mother called, waving from the table.

Parker nodded to the maître d' who escorted him to where his mother sat. They tried to meet for weekly lunch. Lately her schedule had been a bit more occupied by her fiancé. Parker told his mother he didn't mind extending the offer of lunch to Thomas—spending more time with the man might give him a better read on the guy—but Thomas hadn't been able to attend today's lunch. Which was probably a good thing considering he wanted to talk to his mother about this whole wedding thing anyway.

"Hello, Mother." He bent down to place a kiss on her cheek before taking the seat across from her.

"Coffee?" She motioned to the silver decanter on the table.

"Yes, please."

He needed about a gallon and a half today. It was a good thing he was used to running on little to no sleep because he only caught a few hours before his alarm blared, reminding him of meeting his mother. A secret smile curled his lips as he remembered why he'd stayed up until the pre-dawn hours and with who.

Tamsen.

Just thinking her name had all kinds of memories flooding his brain. Delicious, wild memories that he should probably stop thinking about while with his mom.

He smiled at his mother, noting that there wasn't a menu on the table. Not a surprise, since most of the staff knew they didn't need one. He and his mother had been meeting at Café Altier for lunch for five years now, ever since his mother helped the owner with the start-up money she needed to open. Jeanne Alterier, owner and head chef, always cooked up something special every time they dined.

"How is work going, dear?" His mother took a dainty sip from her cup. "Staying safe?"

He smiled, answering the question she always asked him. "As safe as I can."

"I know, I know." She waved a hand in the air. "And I'm very proud of you for choosing a career that's so selfless, but I'm your mother. I'd be worried if you were sitting at a desk all day. It's just what parents do."

He would die of boredom if he had to work a nine-to-five office gig. He loved the thrill of rushing head-first into danger, the high from saving someone. He supposed that wasn't a very selfless motive. Of course, the lows of his job were worse than others. The people he couldn't save still haunted him some nights.

He didn't consider himself a hero, but his mother probably would have called him that even if he was working as an accountant. She'd always been so supportive and proud of him. Like the time in third grade when he won the spelling bee. She acted like he solved world hunger when he'd really just given the proper spelling for hatchling.

"How'd the event go last night?" he asked his mother.

"Did you receive enough donations?"

He had been invited to another one of his mother's charity events last night. He gladly sent money their way, but he hated going to those stuffy parties. He always felt out of place. Yes, he had his own money, but he wasn't some big CEO or investor. He never had anything to talk about with the people at those parties. It wasn't like he could hang out with his mom all night.

"It was successful. We reached our goal with an extra five thousand on top. I do wish you could have come, dear. Margaret Burns was there."

He barely held back a sneer. Now he was doubly glad he didn't go. His mother had been trying to pair him up with every single daughter of her socialite friends for years now. Some of them were okay, but Margaret Burns was a blue-blooded bully who looked down her nose at anyone she felt was beneath her. And according to Margaret, that meant everyone. She played the sweet face to his mother, but he'd seen the way she treated the service workers at events.

Rule of thumb: never date anyone who was a jerk to servers.

It wasn't like Margaret was interested in him anyway. He'd heard the whispers about what she thought of his chosen profession. Not that he gave a rat's ass. He much preferred the company of the woman he spent last night with to anyone who would have been at the charity event.

"I hear you've been spending time with Tamsen?"

He choked on the sip of coffee he'd just drank. Had he said that out loud? Did someone see them and report back to her? Were last night's activities written all over his face? He glanced down at his hand and arms to see if he'd missed any paint. Nope. Not a sexy paint swipe in sight.

"Parker, dear. Are you all right?"

Clearing his throat, he set his coffee down and smiled.

"Fine, Mother. Sorry, just a small tickle in my throat, I suppose."

She had her worried mom face on, but thankfully she let it go.

"How is Tamsen?"

Or not.

"Why would I know?" Evasion, good move, that didn't seem suspicious at all.

"Aren't you two planning our shower together? I assumed you'd been in contact with her recently."

Oh right, that. Of course his mom was talking about party planning and not...the other thing he was doing with Tamsen.

"It's going well. She suggested we use the art gallery she interns at for the party. I saw it last night." Among other things. "Looks like a great venue."

His mother smiled. "An art gallery? That does sound lovely. According to Thomas, Tamsen is a very talented artist herself."

She was. Tamsen not only had skill, but she also managed to infuse emotion into her art. He hadn't just looked at her drawing and paintings when he snuck a peek of them in her room, he'd felt them. He had no idea how to describe it, but something in his chest resonated as he stared at the dark lines, the bright colors on the canvas. She had a gift, for sure.

He also appreciated her more...experimental art projects.

"Have you seen any of her artwork?"

Seen it, been it, done it.

"I have. She's amazing." At his mother's arched brow, he corrected himself. "Her artwork. She's an amazing artist."

"The creative arts are so important. Art and music nourish the soul. Even if only as a hobby."

Oh no. He knew where his mother was going with this. She could hint around it, get Tamsen to ask for her, but none of it would work. He was not picking his music back up.

Ever.

He was saved from further discussion by the server arriving with their food. Sweet smells of berry and sugar wafted up from the delicious-looking crêpe on his plate. Red slices of strawberry filled the thin pastry, spilling out the sides. A dollop of fresh cream lay on top with an artful drizzle of chocolate sauce. He dug in, lifting a forkful to his mouth and closing his eyes as flavor exploded on his tongue.

"Mmmm," his mother made an appreciative sound as she took her own bite. "Jeanne makes the most divine dishes."

He agreed.

"I wonder if we can hire her to cater the shower?"

"I can talk to Tamsen about it." He still thought this party was ridiculous, but if his mother wanted Jeanne's delicious food there, he was all in for that plan.

"I'm so pleased to hear you two are getting along."

More than she knew.

"Thomas and I did so hope you children would become friends."

"We're adults, Mother. Not children."

And he wouldn't necessarily call them friends. Friends with benefits maybe. But his mother didn't need to know that and neither did Tamsen's father.

"Well, we're just happy to see you both taking to each other so well. Not that I was too worried. With as wonderful as Thomas is, I knew his daughter would be something special, too."

More than she knew. But Parker didn't want to think about him and Tamsen right now. Since she brought up the subject of Thomas, he had more pressing questions.

"Mother, are you sure…" He trailed off, uncertain how to word his question without upsetting her. No one was allowed to hurt his mother, not even him.

"Am I sure of what, darling?"

He waited until she'd taken a bite of her meal to pose his question. Carefully forming it to show his concern.

"Are you sure you're not rushing into this marriage? I mean, how well do you really know this guy? Six months isn't really that long of a time. What if he's just trying to…" At her stern look, he amended the accusation he was about to volley. "I just don't want to see you hurt again."

Placing her fork on the table, his mother reached across to place her hand over his. A warm and loving smile lit her eyes.

"My dear boy, I know how hard it was when your father left and that my taste in men over the years may not have always turned out for the best."

There was the understatement of the century.

"I know you worry, Parker, but you don't have to. That's my job. I'm the parent."

Didn't mean he couldn't worry about her. Family worried. It's what you did for the ones you loved whether they raised you or you raised them. He couldn't help it.

"I just think that maybe you should find out a little more about Thomas. Dig into his past a bit. See if he's keeping anything from you." A task he was already doing, but he wasn't going to tell her that. He was only going to reveal his investigation if the PI turned up something dirty.

"Parker Vincent Kincaid."

Uh oh. He got the full name. Every kid, no matter how old they were, knew when their mother used all their names, it wasn't a good sign.

She sat back in her seat, hands folded together and placed primly on the table. Yup. Full-on lecture mode.

"I am not going to spy on my fiancé. Thomas loves me and I love him. Yes, we may not have known each other long, but when you get to be our age, you don't need time. Or have a lot time to spare fluttering about with longwinded courtships.'"

"Don't say that." Now it was his turn to grasp her hand. "You're going to be around for a long time."

She was barely in her sixties. Sixty was the new forty. She had another thirty years easy.

"No one knows how much time they have left on this earth. That's why when we find something as special as what Thomas and I have, you have to grab hold of it with both hands and dive in. Sometimes you just have to trust people, darling. I know you're the suspicious sort, but I promise if you just give people a chance, they might surprise you."

Yeah, that wasn't his strong suit—a complaint lobbed at him by every former girlfriend. That and his inability to share his feelings. Whatever the hell that meant. He shared. Smiled when he was happy, frowned when he was upset. What more did they want?

"I get that," he said, "but I just don't want you to be distracted by your emotions again."

She frowned, mouth dropping open slightly. "Parker."

He reached over to take her hand, worried he'd upset her, but refusing to drop this so easily. Not when she could get hurt again. "I'm sorry, Mother, but remember Charles and Magnus—"

"Parker Kincaid, that is enough." Her voice was hushed but firm as iron.

He ducked his head, guilt sinking like a stone in his stomach. "I'm sorry, Mother. I didn't mean to upset you."

His mother pulled her hand back, picking up her coffee and taking a small sip before arching one eyebrow at him. He knew it wasn't kind to bring up the former men in her life who'd hurt her, but it killed him to think it might be happening again. He only wanted to protect her like she'd always done for him.

They both let the matter drop, chatting instead about how

various family members were doing, his mother's charities, his work. She told him about her and Thomas' plan to pick out a new home together. His mother was a bit of a real-estate addict, moving homes every five years or so, so the news didn't surprise him. But was Thomas seeking out a new fancy home by marrying his mother?

When they finished lunch, Parker knew he should go home and rest, but he found himself driving through the streets of Denver and parking right in front of 5280 Eats.

He found a spot in the small, crowded lot and headed inside. He had to; if he didn't, they'd tow his car. That was the logic he was going with. Sure, he'd just eaten lunch and Tamsen probably wasn't even working. So why was he here?

An excellent question. One he really didn't have an answer to. But he needed one. And quick. As soon as he stepped through the front door, he bumped right into a soft, familiar body.

"Parker!" Tamsen's wide eyes looked up at him. "What are you doing here?"

He enjoyed one gentle stroke of his thumbs along the soft smoothness of her upper arms as he steadied her before dropping his hands and stepping back.

"I was having lunch with my mom and she had some ideas for the catering. For the party. So I thought I'd swing by to see if you were free for a chat."

A smile spread across her face. "Really? You just thought you'd pop by? Even though there's this newfangled thing called texting?"

Busted.

Leaning down close, he whispered in her ear, "Okay, maybe I just wanted to make sure you...didn't miss any paint."

She shivered, a soft sigh of warm breath hitting his cheek.

"And you thought you could inspect for this missed paint

while I'm working?"

He laughed softly. "Actually, I didn't even think you'd be here." But he'd hoped. "I thought you had the dinner shift?"

She shrugged. "Came in early. One of the servers called in sick, and since I'm trying to nab this manager position, I'm on call for all no shows."

"That's rough."

"Such is the life of the service industry."

"Since you came in early, do you get to leave early?"

She nodded. "Yeah, luckily I found someone to come in tonight, so I don't have to work a double."

"What time do you get off?"

She bit her lips, speaking low so only he could hear. "About half an hour after you pick me up from the end of my shift."

"Good answer," he growled.

He wanted to pull her close and sate himself on those delicious lips he was already missing, but they were in public.

"I get off at six."

"Sounds good."

His phone chimed. Pulling it from his pocket, he read the notification. A new message from his PI.

"Something wrong?" Tamsen asked.

He glanced up, not realizing he was frowning until she reached out and smoothed the wrinkle lines in his forehead with her fingers. Pasting on a smile, he shook his head.

"Nope. I'll see you at six?"

He could tell by her worried expression she didn't believe him, but she let it go with a nod.

"Tamsen, just sat you a table!" a voice from the hostess stand called.

"Oh, gotta go. Bye!"

She rushed off, leaving Parker there, his phone feeling like it weighed a thousand pounds in his grip. What was this heavy, uncomfortable feeling in the pit of his stomach? He told himself this thing with Tamsen had nothing to do with his investigation of her father. So why did he feel a little sick keeping it from her?

Maybe the email had good news. And since when was he hoping for good news? It wasn't like he wanted his mother's heart broken. Again. But he'd hired the PI because he didn't trust Thomas. When had he suddenly started wishing that he could?

He glanced across the restaurant to the charming woman who gave her customers a bright, engaging smile even though he knew she had to be as exhausted as him. And it hit him.

It was her. Tamsen. She made him do something he hadn't done in a long time...hope.

Chapter Seventeen

"Okay, Tamsen, you're good to go."

Prisha nodded to her when Tamsen dropped off her receipts to be counted. She was so glad her manager hadn't held the microwave incident against her. She'd been worried a misstep like that would have cost her any chance at the day-shift manager promotion or, even worse, her entire job, but Prisha didn't blame her. The older woman claimed it could have happened to anyone and then joked about how at least it brought some sexy firefighters to the restaurant.

And speaking of sexy firefighters…

Tamsen nodded to her boss and went to the small break room, where she dropped off her apron and grabbed her purse.

"You out?" Jade asked, coming into the room.

"Yup."

"That's good, because Hottie Hero is here, and he looks awfully excited about something." Jade tapped a finger to her smiling red lips. "I wonder what it could be."

Tamsen chose to remain silent but couldn't keep the

excited smile off her own face. She'd just been with him last night, but her body was already craving another round.

"Bye, Jade." She waved to her friend.

"Have fun tonight!"

Oh, she planned to.

She made her way out into the restaurant to see Parker was in fact just beyond the host stand waiting for her. Her thighs clenched in anticipation, butterflies taking flight in her stomach as all the delicious memories from last night flooded her brain.

"Hi there," he said as she approached him.

"Hi."

He moved to open the front door, motioning with his hand for her to precede him. "Shall we?"

Yes please.

Once outside, she tucked her arm into his and allowed him to steer her toward his car. He opened the passenger door for her, and she slid inside. Parker rounded the car and slipped into the driver's seat.

"I know this is totally cliché, but your place or mine?"

She giggled, unable to keep the glee inside. "Hmm, well, my roommate has the overnight shift, and my place is five minutes away, so—"

"Your place it is." He grinned, starting up the car.

They made it to her place in record time, probably thanks to the hand she'd placed on Parker's thigh and kept slowly inching upward. Each inch earned her a low, sexy growl. She should be exhausted after last night's activities and a full day of work, but she wasn't. Parker sparked something in her. An energy, a high she'd only experienced when creating art.

Technically, we did create art.

She smiled at the memory of their painting. Tonight would be a lot less messy, but she had no doubt it would be just as fun.

Parker pulled into her apartment's parking lot. She navigated him to guest parking, grateful there were spots available, but then was out of the car before he even turned off the engine. No chance for him to play chivalrous knight and open her door. She was aching for him. Chivalry could wait until after her first orgasm.

She grabbed his hand and rushed up the stairs, unable to wait for the elevator. With the way Parker kept sensually stroking the back of her hand with his thumb, she doubted they would be able to keep their hands off each other in such an enclosed space. Since she didn't want to get kicked out of her place for indecent exposure in the elevators, stairs it was.

She was breathing hard by the time they reached her apartment door, but it wasn't from the climb. No. It was all due to the man currently standing behind her, crowding her with his heady presence. His large hands gripped her hips as he pressed the thick ridge of his erection against her ass. She fumbled with her keys, almost dropping them as she attempted to slide them into the lock, distracted by the way Parker's mouth was working magic on her throat.

Finally, she got the damn key in the lock and turned. They practically fell inside. Parker slammed the door behind him, turning them so her back was against the door and lifting. She gladly complied, wrapping her legs around his waist so every intimate inch was pressed together.

"Dammit," he growled between drugging kisses. "We have too many clothes on."

She agreed.

Her hands moved down his broad shoulders, gripping his shirt, but before she could try and tug the thing off, he pulled them away from the door and started to move.

"Parker!" Her arms went back around his neck as she held on.

"Bedroom. Now."

He'd forgotten verbs. She tried not to delight in the knowledge that she'd reduced him to grunting monosyllabic phrases, but...eh, who was she kidding? She loved it.

He moved them into her room, gently laying her down on the bed.

"Naked. Now."

There went those monosyllables again. But she was feeling rather playful tonight. Something about this man just made her so...free. Free to be herself, free to open up. It was a feeling she wasn't all that used to in her relationships. A lot of her past lovers had complained about her constant mishaps and accidents. Not Parker. He didn't think she was a walking disaster, even after witnessing more than a few of them.

He accepted her just as she was.

She had to admit, that acceptance was a high. One she was riding right now. One that gave her the courage to rise to her knees, look him straight in the eye and say, "No."

One eyebrow quirked. His smile dipped a bit, but he didn't seem angry. "Change your mind, sweetheart? That's okay; we don't have to—"

"I didn't change my mind." Sweet guy had the complete wrong idea. "I just want to taste first."

"What do you—"

His question broke off in a very creative swear as she unzipped his pants and reached in to grab the hard shaft of his erection.

"Fuck me, Tamsen."

"Mmmmm," she hummed, enjoying the warm, velvety feel of him in her hand as she stroked him from base to tip. "I intend to."

She leaned forward, glancing up at him through her lashes before saying, "After."

Then she took him in her mouth. He shouted another curse, his hands slipping into her hair, not grabbing or pulling but stroking, massaging her scalp as she worked him. She moaned deep in her throat at the prickly sensations his fingertips created. Who knew the scalp could be such an erogenous zone? Parker swore again at her moan.

"Sweetheart, you gotta stop or I'm not going to last long."

Since she wasn't nearly done with him, she sat back, releasing him. His grin was wicked as he quickly shucked off his clothing and stood at the edge of her bed.

"Now get naked. Please."

So polite. She really should reward such good manners.

With a devilish smile of her own, Tamsen removed her shirt and shimmied out of her work slacks. Her bra and panties soon followed.

"Please tell me you have condoms in here," Parker said, his eyes glazed over with lust as he stared at her.

She tilted her chin. "Bedside table."

Without breaking his focus on her, Parker reached out and pulled the drawer open, his hand shifting around until he encountered something and pulled out a strip of foil packages.

She chuckled as she noticed what he'd grabbed.

"What?" he asked. "What's so…"

She watched as he glanced to the items he held in his hand, his eyebrows raising.

"What are these?"

"They're paint samples from an online supplier I use. They send me new colors in small quantities so I can test them out to see if I want to buy full-size tubes."

He blinked. "Thank God I didn't put one on my dick. I'm guessing these aren't the body paint kind?"

She shook with laughter. "Nope."

She really should find a better spot for those, but her place was so small, all her art supplies were smashed in wherever she could fit them. Reaching into the open drawer, she grabbed a condom and held it up triumphantly.

"I think this was what you were looking for."

He grinned, coming down over her on the bed. "It is indeed."

His lips pressed against her in a soft kiss, but she was too amped for soft. Grabbing the back of his head, she pulled him closer, nipping at his bottom lip. He opened for her and she thrust her tongue against his, tasting the sweetness that was unique to Parker.

His hands cupped her face, thumb stroking her chin as his left hand moved down her body, pausing to pay special attention to her breasts before continuing its journey down her stomach, over her hips, leaving a wake of fiery need along every bit of skin he touched. His mouth devoured her while his hand mapped her every inch, finally coming to rest between her thighs.

She tore her mouth away from his, crying out as he slipped two fingers inside, his thumb working her as he pumped his fingers in and out.

"Parker!" She whimpered, the sensations too strong. "I want you."

"You want me what, sweetheart?"

"I want you inside me, now."

She was on a razor's edge here. Luckily, he seemed to be as desperate as she was. He pulled away, ripping the condom open and rolling it down his length. Then she felt the blunt head of his cock at her entrance.

"Ready?"

She nodded. "Yes please."

He entered her in one thrust that had her crying out from the sheer ecstasy of it. It was even better than she remembered. How could it be *better*? She figured she'd built it up in her mind over the day, exaggerated their night together because of the canvas and uniqueness of their first time. But this second time was even better, and they were in a plain old bed.

How was that possible?

She wrapped her legs around him, arching her hips for a deeper connection. His mouth found hers again, and she lost herself in the very essence that was Parker. He was like a living, breathing expression of art. Beauty and strength, hard edges and soft caresses. All the contradictions that made life beautiful.

All too soon, she felt that low tightening in her core. The wave rising over her. She didn't want this to be over so quickly, but her body wasn't giving her a choice. It was a good thing they had the entire apartment all to themselves tonight. She planned to use every last minute of it to sate her thirst for this man.

"Parker," she cried out. "I'm close."

"Me too, sweetheart."

He quickened his thrusts, going harder, deeper with each one until she screamed, her orgasm rushing over her, enveloping her body with tiny pinpricks of warm electrical sparks. He pressed deeper, crying out his own release, whispering her name like a prayer before collapsing on top of her.

He rolled them so he wasn't crushing her. That chivalry again. A woman could get used to it.

"Shower?" she asked, stroking his hair.

"In a minute," he muttered. "I think you might have killed me, and I need a minute to recover."

She giggled. She might have killed him, but he'd done just the opposite. Tamsen felt invigored, renewed. Being with Parker was unlike anything she'd ever experienced, and she had no idea what to do with that except enjoy the ride.

• • •

"Mmm," Tamsen moaned as the warm arm around her waist squeezed gently.

"Mornin', sweetheart."

Parker's lips caressed her cheek. She turned her head, capturing his soft, full mouth with her own. "Morning," she mumbled between kisses.

"Can I bring you some coffee?"

That got her eyes open. Coffee often did, even just the mention of it.

"You made coffee?"

He grinned down at her. The smile was so bright and happy, it nearly sucked all the air right out of her chest.

"No, but I can figure it out."

"Then by all means." She waved a hand in the air and snuggled further into the cozy blanket.

The mattress bounced as Parker rose. She glanced over her shoulder to sneak a peek, a small moan of disappointment escaping her when he slipped on his boxers.

"I'll make you coffee, but I'm not doing it with my junk out," he said with a chuckle.

"Why not? Cora's probably not home yet; it's just us here."

He winced. "Let's just say it's a preventative measure after a particularly horrifying story Ward told about a guy he knew who made romantic gestures involving making naked breakfast that went south real fast."

"You know, usually those 'I have a friend who knew a guy' stories are made up…" She laughed.

He pointed at her, a smile curling his lips. "No naked coffee making."

"Spoilsport." She stuck her tongue out at him.

"After coffee, we can have more naked time."

Sounded good to her. She blew him a kiss, which he caught because he was adorable like that, and flopped back into bed. She could stay here and wait for him or—a naughty thought entered her mind—she could go out there and ask him to see how sturdy her kitchen table was.

Delicious images filling her brain, Tamsen threw back the covers and tugged her robe on over her naked body. The soft, fuzzy material rubbing against her hypersensitive skin ratcheted up her anticipation.

Leaving her bedroom, she made her way down the hall to the kitchen, but before she could pinch Parker's scrumptious-looking butt, a knock on the door interrupted her. Parker turned from his position at the coffee maker, his eyes widening at the sight of her before he glanced at the door, his brow furrowed in question.

She shrugged. She had no idea who it was. Cora would just use her key. It could be a salesperson; they didn't get many in the building, but sometimes those newspaper people would drop by to try and get her to sign up. Who the hell read the newspaper these days anyway?

Didn't matter. Whoever it was, she was going to tell them to go away.

Politely, because it wasn't their fault they were interrupting morning sexy time.

She moved to the door, opening it slowly to peek out and see who it was.

"Dad! Victoria!" She nearly slammed the door in horrified shock. Nearly, but didn't.

"Pumpkin." Her dad's smile was a mile wide.

"What are you doing here?" Her gaze shifted to Victoria. "Both of you?"

She did her best to keep the door open barely more than a crack, positioning her body in a way so they couldn't see into the kitchen area—where Victoria's nearly naked son was.

Her heart raced, palms sweating as she hoped to everything in the universe that they couldn't see Parker. She wanted to turn around and make sure he wasn't visible, but that would just draw their attention. What the hell was she going to do?

"We were just in the neighborhood," her dad said. "And Victoria wanted to drop by and get your opinion on the wedding colors."

"As an artist, you know these things so much better than I do, dear." Victoria smiled. "I would love your professional opinion."

While she was flattered Victoria considered her worthy of such a task, right now the woman could pick hot pink and pea-soup green and Tamsen would smile and nod, because the only thing her brain could focus on was the half-naked *future stepbrother* in Tamsen's kitchen.

A half-naked future stepbrother who a few moments ago was fully naked because we had sex last night.

Oh no! This was a disaster. She had to get rid of her dad and Victoria before they discovered Parker. If he had clothes on, they might be able to come up with a plausible excuse for him being here so early in the morning. They could say they were party planning. But who the hell planned a party in their underwear?

"Tamsen..." Her dad tilted his head with a small frown. "Aren't you going to invite us in?"

"No!"

She winced at the shocked expression on their faces, turning her outburst into a small groan.

"I would, totally, but...um..."

She searched her mind for a reason her dad and future stepmother couldn't come into her home. A possible excuse that wouldn't seem rude or suspicious.

As she thought, something caught her gaze. Out of the corner of her eye, she could see Parker, army crawling on the ground in all his half-naked glory. Her pulse skyrocketed, and she moved her body even more into the open wedge of the door, doing her best to cover his escape back to the bedroom. She thought she spotted a small smirk on the man's face as he passed.

The punk better not be enjoying this. She was seconds away from a freakin' heart attack!

"Tamsen, pumpkin." Her father's voice held a note of suspicion. "What's going—"

She opened her mouth and blurted out the first thing she could think of. "Cora's sick."

"Cora?" Victoria asked.

"Her roommate," her dad answered, patting his fiancée's hand.

"Oh dear, is there anything we can do? Should we call a doctor?"

"No, no, you don't have to do that. Uh, Cora's a nurse and it's just some stomach bug, so no big deal. She must have eaten something bad at the hospital or picked something up from a patient or visitor. She was up all night blowing chunks, and then it started coming out the back end. She seems better this morning, but I don't want to risk your health, so maybe we can do the color thing another time. I would hate to have you get sick, especially if it was my fault, and you know what they say about people who live in the same spaces—if one gets it, the other will, so I'm sure if it's a viral bug, I'll be kissing the porcelain throne tonight myself, so—"

"We get the idea, pumpkin," her dad interrupted her rambling. "We can come back another time."

They started to turn when Tamsen saw a figure heading down the building's hallway that made her heart freeze.

"No!" Again, she winced as her dad and Victoria stared at her with shock. She really needed to cool it, but how did one stay cool in a situation like this? "Um, the elevator has been on the fritz lately. You better take the stairs."

She pointed down the hallway to the left. As they glanced, she frantically and silently motioned to Cora, who was currently heading down the other end of the hallway. Cora noticed her wave and gave her a puzzled look, but thankfully her friend sensed something was up and turned back, disappearing around the corner.

"But we took the elevator up and it seemed fine."

"Oh, you know how it can be." She tried for a lighthearted chuckle, but it came out as more of a manic cackle. "Working fine one minute, stuck inside for hours the next. Plus, Dad, didn't your doctor say you needed to get more exercise?"

"He did say that, Thomas, darling."

Points to Victoria for agreeing with her.

"Well, all right, I suppose. We can take the stairs, but please give Cora our best and let me know if this bug gets you."

"Yes, dear, I can have some soup delivered or send over my private doctor if you need."

Private doctor? Wow, Parker's family really was rich. She didn't even know those were a thing.

"I'm pretty sure it's something she ate, but just to be safe, you guys better go. Thanks for stopping by—see you later!"

She plastered a smile on her face, watching and waving as her dad and Victoria made their way to the stairwell door and disappeared behind it. Once they were gone, she let out a massive sigh of relief.

"Do I even want to know?" Cora asked once she made her way down the hall and came to stand in front of Tamsen.

"No. No, you do not."

She opened the door for her roommate, who stepped into the apartment a few feet before stopping, her head swiveling to the hallway and back to Tamsen, a knowing grin curling her lips.

"Oh, I get it now."

Tamsen shut the door and came to stand by Cora, seeing what her roommate was staring at. And what her roommate was staring at was Parker, in his boxers, doubled over, trying to hold in laughter.

"It's not funny, Parker! We almost got caught by our parents!"

"It's pretty funny," Cora said, a chuckle escaping her lips.

She shook her head, the laughter bubbling up inside her. Okay, it was a little funny.

"You." She pointed at Parker. "Go get dressed. And you." She pulled Cora in for a hug. "Thank you for helping out, and sorry I told my dad you had explosive diarrhea."

She let go of her friend, turning to grab Parker's arm and hustle them into her bedroom to the cry of her roommate demanding, "You told him what?"

Chapter Eighteen

Two days later, Tamsen was standing in front of Parker's door. After the *almost getting caught by their parents* incident, Cora and Parker teased her playfully all morning until he'd left for his shift at the fire station.

They'd texted back and forth, and it was strange how addicted to this man she was already. It had only been two days and already her body was craving his touch. Starving for it like a chocoholic standing outside the gates of Willy Wonka's factory.

This whole thing was new and shiny. It still had the wow factor. And Parker was good in bed, *really* good. Eventually this burning need for him would dwindle. She'd make sure of it, because she refused to consider the alternative.

Falling for a man who was clearly a commitment-phobe? No. She couldn't do that.

She lifted her hand and knocked, but the door swung open to reveal the object of her thoughts in the flesh. Parker had on a pair of dark blue jeans and a gray T-shirt snug enough to show off the muscle definition of his biceps.

Yummy. Each human body was beautiful in its own way, but Parker's was a masterpiece of sharp lines and hard muscles. Such an interesting contrast to his warm personality and soft smile.

"Hey there."

He grinned in welcome, and she nearly melted into a puddle of goo, like the time she accidently left her wax sculpture in her car on a hundred-degree day. No one should have this much sexual charisma. It wasn't fair. But she was glad she got to be the recipient of it. For now, anyway.

"Hi." She lifted the box in her hand. "I come bearing tasty treats."

His gaze traveled down her body, eyes heating with desire. "You sure did."

Was the AC on? Because she was overheating.

She bumped him with her hip, stepping inside when he shifted to let her by. "Cool it, Casanova. We have food to sample before we can...sample other things."

He shut the door with a chuckle. "If you say so. We're both going to need the calories for what I have planned anyway."

She liked the sound of that.

She moved into his apartment and stopped short. Her jaw dropped slightly as she took in the place. This wasn't an apartment. *She* had an apartment. One that could fit into his living room one and a half times, it appeared. This place was huge. Possibly bigger than the house she grew up in. And fancy. There was a giant flat-screen TV taking up a significant portion of the far wall, a hallway that went off to the left, which she assumed held bedrooms or the passage to Narnia for all she knew.

A large, plush-looking couch and loveseat were placed in the middle of the living room. A few bookshelves lined the opposite wall, and the third wall was taken up by floor-to-ceiling windows, providing an astounding view of the city below. She should have guessed when he told her he lived on the eighteenth floor that his place would be fancy, but she hadn't imagined it would be...this.

"Wow."

'What?"

"Your place is amazing."

He glanced around, shrugging like he didn't see what she did. "Yeah, I guess it's pretty great."

"Pretty great?" She snorted. "Parker, how can you afford to rent a place like this?" She knew firefighters could make a decent living, but nothing that could afford something like this.

"I don't rent it. I own it."

She turned to face him, shock causing her eyes to widen. "You own it?"

How the hell did he manage that? She was still paying off her student loans from art school. She couldn't even buy a season ski pass, let alone an opulent condo on the eighteenth floor.

"I had an inheritance from my grandparents. It was enough to go to a fancy Ivy League school, but I went to the firefighter academy. I used the rest for this place."

She kept forgetting that Parker's family was loaded. He didn't act like a snob. Not that all rich people did, but she worked in the service industry and people with money tended to let you know it. Repeatedly.

"Come on," he said, moving toward the kitchen. "I've got the samples from Café Altier in here."

They were taste-testing appetizers to choose who to cater the wedding shower. She'd heard a lot about Cafe Altier, but it was too pricy for her budget. She, of course, was bringing a selection of Ty's finest bites.

"Holy crap." And speaking of Ty, the chef would flip his lid if he saw the fancy-looking stove in Parker's kitchen. It had two ovens. She didn't know they even had that for personal homes. "Please tell me you cook on that thing."

If he didn't, it would be a crying shame. A waste. If Ty ever found out, he might try to sneak in here, rip the oven from the wall, and carry it home. Heck, *she* wanted to rip it out of the wall and take it home.

Parker grimaced. "I try. My crewmate Tanner's husband is a fantastic cook. He's given me a few lessons. Actually helped me pick out this stove, in fact."

She'd bet. Only someone who knew a lot about cooking would know to buy an item like that. What she wouldn't give to have an entire weekend to test that baby out. The things she could make. Her mouth watered just thinking about it.

She followed him over to a large, round table. It was made of some kind of wood and stained a dark burgundy type color that matched the kitchen cabinets. There was a tray of decorative-looking foods. Breads with fruit and cheeses, pâté, tapenade, all artfully arranged on the tray with a flourish of green garnish surrounding the tiny morsels. They looked almost too pretty to eat. She placed her box on the table, knowing what she brought might not look as fancy, but she'd bet it tasted better. Ty was an amazing cook.

"Hmmmm, I don't know, Parker." She grinned. "Is that food or art? Seems too pretty to eat. I think I might win this one. Again."

A challenge sparked in his eyes. "That was trivia. This is food. Something I have a lot of experience with."

She snorted. Who didn't have experience with food? Everyone ate.

"Hello?" She pointed to herself. "Works in the food industry. I highly doubt you know more about food than me, fire boy."

He grinned, leaning close to whisper in her ear. "Ah, but you forget I grew up tasting the work of world-class chefs.

My palate has been trained since birth to recognize the most delectable of dishes."

She shivered as his lips ran along her cheek. He pressed his mouth to hers, running the tip of his tongue along the seam of her lips until she opened for him. He kept the kiss soft and sensual, but it had her knees quivering all the same.

"I know heaven when I taste it."

He pulled away with a smile. Tamsen sunk into the chair at her side—it was either that or collapse on the floor. The things this man did to her.

"Let's bet on it."

He sat in the chair beside her. "You want to bet on whose chef choice is better?"

"Whose food is better, but yes." Feeling the need for some playful payback, she placed her hand on his thigh and stroked upward as she spoke. "As you said, you've lost twice now. I have to give you some opportunity to reclaim your manhood. Even though I know I'm going to win."

He growled low in his throat as the tips of her fingers lightly stroked him through his jeans.

"My manhood is hardly in jeopardy. How about if I win, we have sex in the living room and if you win, we have sex in the bedroom?"

She laughed. "Sounds like we're having sex either way."

"Exactly. Win-win."

She couldn't argue with that, even if she wanted to.

"Deal."

Parker lamented the loss of Tamsen's talented fingers as she slid them away from his body. But since he knew it was only minutes until they—and every delectable inch of Tamsen's naked flesh—was pressed up against his, he tamped down his disappointment.

"Okay, whatcha got?"

She smiled, opening the large cake box she'd brought in. Mouthwatering smells rose from the box. He peeked inside and nearly swallowed his own tongue.

"Are those pigs in a blanket?"

"Yup." She pulled out the small parchment paper holding four tiny sausages wrapped up in bread baked to golden perfection. "My dad's favorite."

"Mine, too."

"Here, try one."

She held it up to his lips. He accepted the appetizer, nipping her fingers playfully, then closed his eyes to enjoy the savory morsel. The chef managed to add the perfect amount of butter to the roll surrounding the dog. He'd loved pigs in a blanket ever since he went to sleepaway camp in the fourth grade. No fancy meals there, but somehow those tiny sausages wrapped in doughy goodness had been the best thing he'd ever eaten. Maybe because he could eat them with his hands without anyone admonishing him for improper table manners.

That they were Thomas's favorite food, too, was…he didn't know what it was, but the pit was back in his gut. The more time he spent around Tamsen, the worse he felt about this whole PI thing. His mom would be pissed if she found out, and Tamsen would be crushed. But he couldn't stop the investigation now.

Frank's last message said he still had a few things to look into. The longer this took, the more Parker felt like he was doing something wrong. He was only trying to protect his mother. So why did it feel like he was betraying everyone?

"Is something wrong?"

He realized he'd stopped eating and was staring down at the table. Swallowing the last bit of food, which didn't taste as delicious as it had ten seconds ago, he smiled. "Yup. Just realizing I might be losing again. Seems to be a pattern around you."

A blush rose on her cheeks. "Yeah, well it seems only fair considering my pattern around you involves getting myself into the most embarrassing situations possible."

He laughed. "Okay, your turn."

Reaching for the tray, he grabbed one of his favorites, goat cheese and tart apple on a sliced baguette. He held it out like Tamsen had done for him. She took a small bite, her lips brushing against the tips of his fingers as she left half the appetizer in their grip.

"Mmmmmm," she moaned falling back against her chair. "That's amazing."

No, what was amazing was how they were both still sitting at the table with their clothes on. Since she walked in the door, Parker had been damn near aching for her. Her sexy little moans turned him from hard to damn steel.

He stood, grabbing her hand and pulling her up to him. He led her out of the kitchen and down the hall toward his bedroom.

"But we haven't declared a winner. We haven't even tasted all the samples yet."

"I don't care. You win."

She laughed. "Do I win because you think my chef is better or because you want sex?"

"Does it matter?"

Chapter Nineteen

Turned out it didn't matter as Parker hauled her up, tossing her over his shoulder in a fireman's hold.

"Hey!" she squeaked out with a small giggle. The giggle turned into a moan when his palm came up to lightly smack her ass.

He rushed down the hall to his bedroom. Once inside, he tossed her on the bed, and she bounced slightly, sighing as he came above her, his arm bracing above her head on either side. She could get used to this sight.

"Hi," she said, unable to think of anything else.

He grinned like a kid on the first day of summer as he stared down at her. "Hi there."

"So, you admit defeat?"

"I admit that all the food was amazing, but if I don't get the chance to taste you in the next five seconds, I might just die of starvation."

Wow, well, she couldn't have a starving man on her conscience, now could she?

Lifting her head slightly, she nipped at his bottom lip,

soothing the small sting with a soft kiss as she whispered against his mouth, "Feast away."

He growled, the deep sound vibrating around her, making every nerve in her body tingle. His mouth pressed down on hers, pushing her back onto the soft pillow. She wrapped her legs around his waist, arching her hips, seeking a release for the heavy throbbing between her thighs.

Parker pulled away. She reached for him, whimpering because she was starving, too, and the only thing that could sate her hunger was him.

"When I said I wanted to taste you, sweetheart," he grasped both her hands in one of his and raised her arms above her head, staring down at her, "I meant I want to taste. All. Of. You."

A shiver of needy anticipation racked her body. "Then by all means."

His hands moved down her arms slowly. So slowly she thought the wait would kill her. When he reached her shoulders, he moved his palms across her collarbone and down over her breasts. He cupped them in his hands, squeezing gently through her shirt and bra. Her nipples hardened behind the silk, begging for the same attention, but he moved away. She was about to complain until she felt him grip the bottom of her shirt and tug.

Sitting up slightly, she helped him pull off her shirt and bra.

"Beautiful," he murmured a moment before his mouth came down to capture one tight bud between his lips.

Tamsen cried out, a rush of euphoria bursting inside her. She fell back to the bed, Parker following, never breaking the connection of his lips to her skin. He took his time, showing great care and attention to one breast before switching to the other. Her breath came out in short, frantic pants. She thought she might pass out due to the overwhelming sensations overtaking her body.

After many agonizingly bliss-filled minutes, he left her breasts, kissing his way down her stomach and over her hips.

"Parker?"

"I said I wanted to taste it all, Tamsen."

His words vibrated against her as he nuzzled her through her leggings. His fingers slid into the top of the elastic waistband, tugging slightly. Her body was a mass of quivering nerves, she could barely move, let alone sit up to take her pants off. Lucky for her, her sexy firefighter knew just what to do. He gripped the fabric, peeling it down her legs along with her panties and tossing it to the floor.

She felt his gentle touch on the inside of her thighs, then his head bent to her core. The first swipe of his tongue made her cry out, desperate for more.

"Yup, just as I thought," he chuckled. "You, sweetheart, are the most delicious thing here tonight."

She started to say thank you, but her words were lost as Parker proved true to his word and feasted on her, his tongue and fingers doing wickedly naughty things that had her crying out minutes later when the orgasm rushed over her.

She sucked in a deep breath, her soul floating back down to her body. She was pretty sure he'd sent it straight into the stratosphere. Parker moved off the bed, frantically ripping his clothes off and reaching to his bedside drawer, pulling out a small silver packet before returning to her. She wanted to grab the condom from him and roll it on, but he'd sated her too well. Her limbs had turned to jelly, leaving her unable to do anything but smile.

He tore open the foil, pulling out the condom and rolling it down his length. Her eyes widened at the sight, heart racing again, fingers itching to reach out and stroke his impressive erection.

Okay, maybe she had enough energy to do a few things.

"Do you want me, Tamsen?" he asked.

More than she probably should.

"Yes," she whispered, lifting her legs to wrap them around his waist.

He moved down, positioning himself at her entrance. She was still sensitive from her previous orgasm, and when he pushed inside, she cried out as sensations overwhelmed her. Parker paused, glancing down at her with concern.

"Shit, did I hurt you?"

"No." Quite the opposite, in fact. She'd never felt so euphoric in her whole life. "More, Parker," she said, arching her hips up to take him in deeper. "More."

His lips crashed down on hers as he plunged into her, seating himself fully. He set a fast pace, seemingly as desperate as she was. He'd said he wanted to taste all of her, and she felt consumed by him. Her body vibrated, in tune with his as they moved together. It was amazing, but not enough.

She arched up, pushing his shoulder slightly. Parker took the hint and rolled them, leaving her on top. Just where she wanted to be. She came up to her knees, lifting herself and sinking down on his cock. He swore, gripping her hips in his hands, grinding her against him with delicious pressure. She thanked her lucky stars for her yoga classes as she arched her back, placing her hands on his thighs behind her. The angle creating amazing friction. For both of them, if his deep growl was anything to judge by.

His thumb moved across her hips and down to the center of her, rubbing against her with just the right amount of pressure to send her body spinning toward another orgasm. But this time, she wanted him with her. She let go of his legs, moving back over him to capture his mouth. Feasting on *him* this time.

He quickened his thrusts, his grip on her hips tightening. Her body coiled tight, like a spring about to burst. Parker replaced his thumb with the heel of his hand, pressing firmly, and it sent her over the edge into oblivion. She pulled away from his lips, crying out as another orgasm crashed over her.

• • •

Parker roared with triumph. Watching Tamsen in the throes of ecstasy was the most beautiful thing he'd ever seen. The fact that he was the one to help her get there made him feel like a damn superhero. He felt his own body tighten with impending release, and he held her to him, reveling in the wonder that was Tamsen Hayes as he lost himself inside her.

She collapsed on top of him, and he tugged her close, tucking her into his side, her dark hair tickling his chin as she laid her head on his chest.

"Well, I am thoroughly exhausted. You were right about needing the calories." She glanced up at him. "Should we go finish the rest of the samples?"

"In a minute. I don't think I can move just yet."

She gave a soft laugh. He loved her laughs, the soft ones, the loud ones. She had such passion and joy for life, even with all the chaos of working two jobs and creating her art. It never seemed to faze her. He had to admit: he admired her strength a whole hell of a lot.

"Hey, what's that?" Tamsen sat up, pointing to something in the corner of his open closet. "Is that a guitar?"

His gaze followed to where she pointed. The euphoric high he'd been riding since Tamsen had ridden him died when he spotted the object of her query. How had she even seen it? He'd tucked the damn thing back there and covered it with a blanket so he could forget about it. And everything it represented. At some point, the blanket must have fallen off because the bright red and orange Les Paul guitar shined from the corner of the dark closet. A mocking reminder of what happened when he placed his trust in people.

She turned back to face him with a hesitant smile. "So,

um, is that the guitar you don't play anymore?"

Jaw clenched, he avoided looking at her or the cursed instrument, staring instead at the ceiling. "Yeah."

He really should just donate the damn thing, but for some reason he couldn't bring himself to part with it.

"I'm sorry." Her soft voice drifted down to him. "I didn't mean to pry."

Shit. Now he felt like an ass. He hadn't meant to snap. "It was my dad's," he offered as an excuse.

"Oh."

She said that like she understood, but she didn't. He knew she wouldn't dig deeper, but for some reason Parker found himself wanting to open up.

"He gave it to me on my seventh birthday. Told me he was going to teach me to play."

"Did he?"

He nodded. One of the few promises his old man ever kept. "We practiced a couple nights a week. We'd break out the guitars at family gatherings, on Mother's Day, that kind of thing. He even sent me to one of those rock star camps for three summers during middle school. My mother would film every single performance. I think she still has the videos somewhere."

"That sounds nice."

It had been. Then everything went to hell.

"When my dad left us, I asked if we would still play guitar every week." Embarrassment and pain still burned him, remembering the patronizing look in his father's eyes when he asked that question.

Tamsen lay down next to him again, placing a hand on his chest, seeming to sense his need for her touch.

"What did he say?"

He had to unclench his teeth to speak. "He told me I needed to grow up. That since I'd chosen to stay with Mom instead of live with him, I picked my side."

"That's horrible!" she exclaimed. "Children don't pick sides in divorce. Besides I'm sure you weren't even old enough to choose. Don't the courts do that or something?"

Yeah, and the lawyers. The judge asked his preference and he hated having to pick, but his mother had seemed so devastated by his dad leaving. She needed him. He couldn't leave her then and he wouldn't abandon her now.

"So you haven't played at all since?"

He shook his head.

"If it was something you loved…" She hesitated. "Don't you think giving it up gives more power to your father? Music is very healing for the soul. Maybe if you started playing again you could let go of—"

"There's nothing to let go of. I'm fine."

She arched one dark eyebrow at his sharp tone. Shit, now he was just being an ass. He didn't understand why she cared so much about this. He played music once. He didn't anymore. No big deal. It wasn't like he ever dreamed of being a rock star or anything. Sure, he'd loved it. Once. But it wasn't his life or anything.

"I'm sorry, I didn't mean to snap. I just don't…I don't play anymore. It's tainted now."

She stared at him for a moment with a tiny frown before laying her head on his chest.

"Okay. I understand." She kissed his chest, right above his heart. "I shouldn't have brought it up."

He kissed the top of her head. "You didn't know."

But she did now, because he'd shared with her. Shared something he'd never told anyone else. The weird thing was a part of him felt lighter. As if somehow telling Tamsen had lifted some dark spot off his soul he'd been carrying around for years. He trusted her with something he'd never shared with anyone because Parker generally didn't trust people.

But he found himself trusting her.

Chapter Twenty

Parker finished replacing the sheets on his bunk. He had two more hours left on his shift, then he was off for the next forty-eight. He liked his down time as much as the next person, but lately he'd been enjoying it a lot more, and he knew why.

Tamsen.

He still couldn't quite believe he'd shared all the stuff about his dad with her the other night. He never talked about his dad. With anyone. Even his crew at the station knew next to nothing about Parker's old man. But Tamsen...she made him feel comfortable, safe. He could share things with her without fear of judgment.

"Hey, dude."

He turned to see Ward standing in the doorway of the bunk room.

"You off shift soon?"

Parker nodded. "Yeah, few more hours, then I'm out of here."

"And off to see your special lady?" Ward waggled his eyebrows.

"Special lady?" Parker snorted. "Channeling your inner eighty-year-old today, man?"

"No, I'm channeling my inner *I don't want Díaz on my ass for saying 'woman'* today."

He laughed, knowing Ward would eventually say something that would annoy Díaz. It was a day that ended in Y, meaning the probability was high.

"So," Ward continued. "You and Tamsen?"

Parker crossed his arms over his chest, staring at his friend and crewmate. "Tamsen and I what?"

Ward held up his hands. "Don't get pissy, dude. I'm just saying you talk about her a lot, text her a lot, seem happier since you met her."

Did he? He rubbed at the warm spot in his chest. The one that had started as a small spark the first moment he set eyes on her, sitting in her apartment with a thick white plaster cast stuck to her. It had grown, getting warmer with each interaction. Each silly blunder he witnessed. She might think they were disasters, but to him, being around Tamsen was an adventure.

Never boring, that was for sure.

"Hey, O'Neil," Ward called as the man passed by the door. "What's your opinion of Tamsen and Parker?"

O'Neil stopped and glanced between the two men. "Didn't know I was supposed to have an opinion, but I like her. She's nice. A little accident prone, but a cool person. I didn't know you guys were a thing—"

"We're not." At least not openly. But this was the station, and gossip spread faster than a forest fire in the middle of June. "And why the hell are we talking about my love life? Don't you all have better things to—"

A loud siren screeched through the air, cutting off the rest of his tirade. His body tensed, recognizing the call to action. Ward and O'Neil turned and rushed out of the room,

Parker hot on their heels. He followed his crewmates, racing to the bay where the trucks were.

"Office fire on 18th and Larimer," Chief Jeffords shouted as everyone raced over to their bunk gear. "People stuck inside."

Parker jumped into his boots, pulling up the straps on his turnout trousers, before slipping on his turnout jacket. He grabbed his helmet and tank, heart racing with anticipation and a pinch of fear. It was always this way, no matter how many fires he responded to. There was always the thrill of excitement. The rush of adrenaline. The high they each rode from doing a dangerous but necessary job. He felt like a superhero, but he also knew the risks.

Fire was deadly, and it didn't care how much training or caution you used around it. Given the opportunity, it would burn you alive. It was best to approach his job with cautious enthusiasm.

He hopped into the truck with his crew, Turner at the wheel. The sirens blipped on, their loud peal warning drivers of the emergency as they headed out of the station and onto the streets of Denver. The damn one-way streets in the city were always a pain in the ass, but Turner had been driving the rig long enough to know exactly how to get them where they needed to go.

In less than five minutes from when the call came in, the truck was pulling up to the scene. Smoke billowed out of the windows of a tall office building.

"Do we know what floor the fire is on?"

"Third floor," Turner said from his position in the driver's seat. "It's not spreading yet. Ladder 41 is already on the scene. They got most of the people out, but there's still half a dozen in there."

The stations in Denver often worked together on the bigger calls, and from the flames Parker could see flicking out the windows on the third floor, this had the potential to be a very bad call.

"Let's go," Díaz called as she hopped out of the truck.

Parker followed her as they all hustled into the building. The first floor had already been cleared. They hurried over to the stairwell, his muscles protesting a bit as he hauled himself up the stairs at a fast clip. Running with forty-five pounds of gear on wasn't easy, but they trained for this exact situation.

He told his body to suck it up and do its job.

When they reached the third-floor door, he moved to it, glancing down at the bottom. No smoke or flames billowed out from underneath. Satisfied they wouldn't be opening the door to a wall of flames, he carefully moved in, his crewmates following close behind him.

Visibility immediately plummeted as the hazy wall of smoke surrounded them. Parker's heart raced, his gaze scanning his surroundings, clocking every important detail. They were in an open-concept office-type room. Huge with zero walls or doors. Great for spotting people. Also great for fires to spread. Fire needed lots of room to grow, plenty of oxygen, and this room was filled with it.

"There!" Ward shouted, pointing to a group of people huddled underneath a long table at the far side of the room.

Parker raced over, bending down low as he approached the group.

"Denver Fire," he shouted over the roar of the flames and sobs of the scared group. "We're going to get you out of here. Is anyone hurt?"

There were more sobs, a few headshakes, and one woman who nodded.

"I lost my glasses, and there's so much smoke I can't see anything. I forgot everything they taught us and—"

She choked on a cry, her coworker wrapping an arm around her in comfort. People often panicked in emergency situations. No matter how many fire drills someone did, the real thing was far scarier and more disorienting.

"Are you the only ones left? Is anyone else on this floor?"

"June," a younger man in a gray hoodie said, his eyes going wide with terror. "Where's June?"

"She was getting coffee in the kitchen," the first woman said, tears pouring down her face.

"Where?"

She pointed to the back of the room, where Parker saw a small open doorway filled with smoke. What made his heart stop was the orange flames he saw popping out.

"I'm on it," Parker said with determination, then turned to the others. "You got them?"

"We've got them," Turner reassured him. "But you sure you want to go in there?"

But Parker had already stood, booking it across the room, knowing his crewmates were taking the others out to safety. When he reached the kitchen doorway, he ducked low, trying his best to see in the dense, dark smoke.

"June!" he shouted as loud as he could. "June! Denver Fire Department. Can you hear me?"

Heat bombarded his body as he stepped into the room. His suit was fireproof, but the heat still got through. He ignored his body's protest, the innate instinct ingrained in every human that told them to run where there was danger. He didn't run from anything.

Staying low, he scanned the room. His heart leaped in his chest as he spotted a small lump of a figure in the back corner of the small kitchen area. The fire had consumed the cabinets on the wall and was eating away at the ceiling, but his path to the woman was clear.

"June?" He rushed over to her, sending out all the hope he had in the world she was breathing.

"Cough, cough."

Relief loosened his tense body as he saw the woman move, heard her lungs working to expel the gritty smoke from them. Wouldn't work until he got her out of here.

"I'm from the fire department, June. I'm here to help."

He saw her eyes open slightly, relief filling them as she lifted her arms. She was clearly too weak to walk by herself. Too much smoke inhalation. He had to get her out of here.

Scooping her up into his arms, he turned and headed back toward the door. Just as he got there, a loud, smacking *pop* rent the air. Debris tumbled down in front of him as pieces of the ceiling collapsed in the doorway.

"Fuck!"

A large metal beam had fallen right in his path, blocking the exit.

"Kincaid!"

He heard the shouts of his crewmates. They must have come back after getting all the people out.

"O'Neil?"

"Yeah, we're here."

"I found June; she's taken in a lot of smoke and needs to get out of here."

"Can you fit through that space down there?"

Carefully, Parker maneuvered the woman in his arms. He saw O'Neil thorough a small space near the floor, between the beam and the doorway. Big enough to pass a woman in casual business attire through. Not big enough for a firefighter in full bunk gear.

Didn't matter. He had his priorities. Get the victim to safety, worry about himself later.

"I can pass her through."

"Okay."

Gently, he maneuvered June through the small space into the steady arms of his crewmate. Once O'Neil had her in hand, he turned and hustled back toward the stairs.

"Kincaid," Ward shouted as the fire roared around them. "We're gonna get you out of there."

The shattering of glass sounded, meaning the fire was superheating the windows and exploding them. Things were going FUBAR real quick.

"Guys, get the hell out!" He didn't want his friends getting injured or worse, dying, all because his ass was stuck. He'd find a way to escape, but he was not risking them.

"Fuck no, dude," Ward replied.

"We are not leaving you," Díaz agreed.

"It's too dangerous."

"Danger is my middle name." Ward laughed as he inspected the beam, searching for a solution to get Parker out. "Actually, it's Peter, but—"

"For shit's sake, Ward, now is not the time!" Díaz yelled.

A smile curled Parker's lips. Even in a deadly situation with flames all around them, his friends could manage to make him laugh.

"Kincaid." Ward's tone dropped the joviality. "Do you think you can squeeze through if we give you a few more inches?"

He glanced at the small space he'd just passed June through. "Maybe. I'll have to take my tank off."

"Do it," Díaz commanded.

He unstrapped his tank, shoving it through the hole to the other side. His helmet would be a pain to get through, but no way was he taking that off.

"Ready!" he called to them.

"Okay, Díaz, on three."

His vision was obstructed by the beam and all the smoke, but he could just make out his friends positioning themselves to lift the massive ceiling beam. Something physiologically they shouldn't be able to do, but he knew in situations like this, adrenaline could give people superhuman strength. He just hoped this was one of those times.

"One...two...three!"

Parker heard the grunting from Ward and Díaz as they pressed hard against the beam. The large obstruction started to shift, moving slightly. Centimeter by centimeter, they lifted until Parker saw his shot. He dove through, squeezing his body, made thicker by all the gear he had on, with all his might. Once he was fully through, he shouted, "Clear!"

His friends dropped the beam with a shattering crash.

"Let's get the hell out of here," Díaz said.

He nodded his agreement, grabbing his tank, and raced with them toward the stairwell door.

Outside the building was pure chaos. Ladder 41 was busy dragging a hose up their aerial. He heard Turner shout "all clear!" before a heavy stream of water let from the hose and into the third floor where the flames raged.

Ambulances were parked on the street, some tending to people, others driving away with the more serious injuries.

"How's June?" he asked when O'Neil walked up to him.

"She's going to be okay. The EMTs got her on oxygen and took her over to County Health along with a few others."

He breathed out a sigh of relief, the tension in his body draining. Losing a person on a call was an inevitability in his line of work, but that didn't mean it didn't gut him. Haunt him in the dark of the night with what ifs.

Ladder 41 had the fire under control now; it would only take a few more minutes to have it out completely. Parker made his way among the people, offering what help he could, along with his crewmates. Once the scene had been cleared, they all piled back into the truck and headed back to the station.

"Hey, thanks," he muttered to Díaz and Ward once they were all on their way. "For, you know, not leaving me back there."

"Dude," Ward scoffed. "Never leave crew behind. You know that."

He did, but in the heat of the moment—no pun intended— all he'd been able to think about was his friends' safety. Not his own.

"We've always got your back." Díaz nodded. "You can trust us."

He could trust them, and he did. You had to trust your crew when you worked a job as dangerous as they did. Intellectually he knew that, while emotionally...yeah, he knew he still had to work on that area of his life. Trust hadn't come easy to him since his dad left. But lately, lately he was discovering that he did trust some of the people in his life, in different ways. He trusted his crew to have his back, and the other night...

The other night he trusted Tamsen with a part of himself he never thought he'd feel comfortable sharing. He wasn't sure what that meant exactly, but he knew it was significant.

I should probably call off the damn investigation.

He started at the thought, mulling it over in his mind as they navigated the streets of Denver back to the station. He'd hired his PI because he wanted to protect his mother, because he didn't trust her new fiancé. But now...after getting to know Thomas a little and getting to know Tamsen a lot, he was starting to wonder if he could let his guard down. Start trying to believe the best in people.

And if he did that, what would it mean for him and Tamsen? What if he truly opened himself up to her? Could they make a real go of this thing between them? Did he even want to?

He sucked in a sharp breath, shocked to his core when he looked deep inside and realized that, yeah, he kind of did. But the real question was—did she?

Chapter Twenty-One

"Do we have any more cookies?" Cora asked from the kitchen. "I could have sworn we had half a sleeve in here last week."

Tamsen winced. "Yeah, um, I kind of got into the groove last night and forgot to eat dinner then ended up scarfing the entire package. I'm sorry."

It happened a lot when she was working on a project. She'd get so immersed in her work she'd forget to eat for hours. Then she'd be famished and devour everything in sight. Made for great art but terrible heartburn.

Cora sighed, grabbing the box of graham crackers. "A poor substitute, but at least they're sweet."

Her roommate came to join her on the couch where they were bingeing the last season of their favorite comedy show. They each had such hectic work schedules, it was hard to consistently watch anything together. So they picked out favorites to binge when they had spare moments and swore not to watch any episodes without the other under penalty of full rent payment.

"I'm so sad this is the last season," Cora said as she passed over a graham cracker square.

Tamsen accepted the sweet cracker, breaking it in half and bringing a piece to her lips. "Me too, but everything ends eventually."

True in entertainment and life. Endings were just beginnings anyway. Like her dad selling the house. The era of him living in her childhood home was over, but he would be starting a new adventure in a new home with his new wife. And one day, hopefully, she'd be able to leave the restaurant to be an artist full time. It would be sad to end that time with all the friends she'd made at work, but she'd be starting a new journey with her artwork. And with Parker...

Actually, she didn't want that to end.

The thought struck her like a whack to the head. She didn't want things with Parker to end. They'd agreed it was just temporary. No promises, no problems. But Tamsen was discovering she wanted promises. She wanted...*more* with Parker. The sex was phenomenal, but she also liked talking with him, being with him. He was funny and sweet, and he never made her feel awkward or weird.

She could be herself around him and she liked that.

It was a terrifying thought for a woman who lived her entire life determined not to fall as hard as her father had. She didn't want to care about someone so much that losing them would hollow her out. She made sure all her relationships were light and fun. No deep feelings, no deep hurt. It was how she operated. The protection she needed. She poured all her heavy emotions into her art, because art couldn't die and leave you with an empty hole inside you that never healed.

She'd never been tempted to want more from anyone... until now.

Her stomach pinched in terror at the realization.

No. She shook her head, pushing away the uncomfortable

thought. She was getting ahead of herself. She was probably just feeling this connection because she and Parker had been spending a lot of time together lately, that's all. The fantastic sex was messing with her emotions, creating a closeness that wasn't there.

But that wasn't entirely true. She swore she'd felt the pain radiating off him as he shared the story of his father and the guitar. As much as she yearned to hear him play, she understood why it might be too painful for him. She wished she could help him get over that pain. No one should give up their art because of someone else. It was such a healing and lifegiving practice. One that the world often pushed aside as silly or pointless.

Or taken away as punishment like his father had.

She saw the anguish of the small boy inside, being torn apart as his father forced him to choose between parents. Parker had opened up to her. That wasn't some throw-away thing you said to a sex buddy. That was real. He trusted her with a part of him he didn't share easily. It was humbling and a little scary. All she'd wanted to do after was wrap him in her arms and take all his pain away.

Oh crap, I like the guy.

And not just a little like, either. Tamsen was afraid their "just fun" agreement was quickly falling into feelings.

"Hey, Tam. You okay?" Cora asked with a worried expression.

"Huh?" She shook her head. "Oh yeah, just spacing, I guess."

Worrying about falling for her sex buddy, the implication of it, the opportunity for pain and heartbreak and the impact on her father's happiness. No biggie.

Cora stared, but when Tamsen smiled back, her roommate grabbed the remote and hit play. They'd watched two and a half episodes when Cora got a notification on her phone.

"Shit."

"What?"

Cora stood, reading the message on her screen. "There was a fire in one of the office buildings off Eighteenth and Larimer."

"A fire?" Her heart jumped up into her throat.

"Yeah, fifteen people were sent to County Health. Carlos is asking for backup because two nurses called out sick today. Since I have ER training, they called me in."

If her boss was asking her to come in on her day off, Tamsen knew it was bad, but since she heard the word *fire*, the blood had been pounding so loud in her ears she couldn't think properly. Her fingers were flying over her phone, shooting off a text before she'd even realized it.

"What station responded?"

Cora glanced up from her phone, sympathy filling her eyes. "I don't know, but I'm sure even if Parker was at that fire, he's fine."

She knew that. It was his job to save people from burning buildings and other dangerous situations. Didn't mean she wasn't terrified. Her rational brain and her erratic emotions were at odds right now, and the emotions were winning.

"Were any of the burn victims firefighters?"

"Oh, sweetie." Cora frowned. "You know I can't tell you that, even if I knew."

She did. But again, logic out the window.

Tamsen glanced down at her phone. No texts from Parker. Not a surprise. If he was at that fire, it wasn't like he could respond to her. And it wasn't like they were dating or anything. He wasn't supposed to check in with her, and she didn't have the right to demand that of him no matter how worried she was. Even if it was over now, she was sure he'd still be busy. It's 'cause he was busy, right? Not because he was in the back of an ambulance, injured on the very dangerous job he performed.

Her chest tightened. A vice of worry and pain gripped her, stealing her breath as a million horrible scenarios entered her mind. See, this was why she didn't get involved! This fear, this horrible pain, she hated it. But there was nothing she could do about it now. She'd fallen. She cared. She couldn't pretend Parker was nothing to her, and she wanted, no *needed*, to make sure he was okay.

"I have to go," Cora said. "They need me."

"Yes, of course." She grabbed her friend in a tight hug. "Go, help."

Cora needed to tend to the wounded, make sure those people were okay. And Tamsen needed to check on Parker. Make sure he was okay. Tend to anything he needed. Even if he wasn't hurt, she knew a call like this would be hard on him.

She grabbed her purse, following Cora out the door to the parking garage. She shot off a text to Parker as she sat in her car, but her nerves wouldn't permit her to wait. She drove as fast as speed limits allowed to station 42. Parking in the small lot, she got out and rushed into the front of the building.

"Tamsen."

She glanced up to see O'Neil walking toward her. Judging by the slicked-back hair and the fresh clothing, she'd say he just got out of the shower. Cora hadn't said how long ago the fire was, but if the victims had already been transported to the hospital, she imagined it was long enough ago for the men and women of station 42 to be back. And she was right.

"What are you doing here?"

She stepped closer, heart pounding so hard the frantic organ was nearly beating out of her chest. "I heard about the fire."

His eyes softened. "He's okay."

She let out a huge sigh of relief, blinking back tears. The vice easing slightly. She knew only seeing Parker's face, whole and unharmed, would release it entirely.

O'Neil placed a gentle hand on her shoulder. "It's his job, Tamsen. He's good at it. We all are."

She knew that. She also knew she couldn't help the clawing worry twisting up her stomach at the thought of Parker being hurt. How could you be so proud of someone and so terrified for them at the same time?

"Can I see—" She had to choke back a sob, clearing her throat and trying again. "Where is he?"

O'Neil smiled. "It's good to have people who care. Sometimes the calls...people tend to see us as heroes, but it gets to us, too." His smile fell. "We do the job, but we also feel the suffering. Helps to have someone after, just to be there."

She could be there for Parker. Whatever he needed, she could do it. She just needed to see him.

"He's at home," O'Neil said. "His shift was close to ending when we got the call, but he was still here so he jumped on the rig with us. Chief sent him home the second we got back."

"Thank you." She threw her arms around him, needing to give him some comfort, too.

Rushing back outside, she hopped into her car and navigated the one-way streets of downtown Denver to Parker's place. Lucky for her, his building had guest parking, and she was able to find a spot. She locked her car and rushed inside, impatiently waiting for the elevator that seemed to take a decade. O'Neil said Parker hadn't been hurt. Not physically, at least. She wouldn't feel completely at ease until she saw him with her own eyes.

Finally, the elevator came, and she made it to his front door. Lifting her clenched and trembling fist, she knocked. No answer. She knocked again. Still no answer. She was two seconds away from trying her best to jimmy the lock. Didn't matter that she had no idea how to do that, her brain was freaking out with the need to see Parker. Touch him, make sure he was all in one piece.

Just as she lifted her fist to knock again, the door swung open, and her clenched hand slammed right into Parker's surprised face.

"Ow!" He clutched his nose.

"Oh my God, Parker! I am so sorry. I heard about the fire, and I didn't know if you were called in or if you were hurt. Cora got called into work for some burn victims, but they didn't say if they were civilians or first responders. I tried texting you, but you didn't answer, and I know you were busy, but I was worried so I went by the station and O'Neil said that—"

"Tamsen." He chuckled, dropping his hands, a small smile on his lips. "It's okay. I'm fine."

She pressed her hands into her stomach, worry and embarrassment mixing together to make her stomach as sick as the day after a midnight margarita party. "I'm sorry. I didn't mean to punch you in the face. We should put some ice on that."

"That's okay." He pulled her inside, closing and locking the door behind her before leading them to the kitchen area. His voice turning husky as he stared at her with need in his eyes. "You can kiss it better."

For the first time since Cora told her about the fire, her panic subsided. Her brain and body finally relaxed enough for her to take in the situation. The situation being that Parker had clearly taken so long to get to the door because he'd been in the shower. Evident by the towel wrapped around his waist and...nothing else.

She took him in, from the damp, slicked-back hair, down his cut chest and delicious abs, still glistening from the shower. Not a sign of injury or ash anywhere. He was fine. He was safe. And she was so relieved she could kiss someone. And since someone was standing in front of her, that's exactly what she did.

Tamsen ran her hands up Parker's chest, around his shoulders, and up the base of his neck to dig her fingers into the short strands of hair at the back of his head. She pulled him down to her, pouring all her relief and happiness into the kiss. His hands grasped her waist, tugging her closer until she could feel just how flimsy that towel was at hiding his arousal.

"Bedroom," he growled between kisses. "Now."

She shook her head. "Too far. Here."

"As much as I want to bend you over this counter and take you right now, sweetheart. I don't keep the condoms next to the cutlery."

"In my purse," she panted as his hands went to her breasts, cupping and squeezing with just the right amount of pressure to make her eyes cross. "Emergency condom."

This definitely constituted an emergency. If she didn't get Parker inside her in the next thirty seconds, she was going to die.

She reached into her purse and grabbed the strip of three condoms she kept with her. Tossing her purse on the ground, she ripped one of the foil packets off, letting the other two fall to the floor. She was sure they'd use them later, but right now she didn't care. She held it out for him, but Parker shook his head.

"You put it on me. Please."

Well, since he asked so nicely...

Maintaining eye contact, she moved her hand down his chest, lightly skimming her fingers along all that scrumptiously hard muscle. When she got to the towel, she flicked the knot, allowing the terrycloth to open and fall down to rest with the other abandoned items. She gripped his hard length in her hand, stroking him from base to tip. Parker groaned, arching his hips into her touch.

"Sweetheart, you can play later, but right now I need you."

She released him, but only long enough to open the condom and roll the protection over him. She lifted her hands to her skirt, intending to slip it off her hips, but Parker put a hand over hers. Stopping her.

"Leave it on. Please."

She smiled. "Keep begging me for things and I might start to think I have power over you."

His eyes darkened, thumb coming up to brush softly over her lips. "You have no idea, sweetheart. But turnabout is fair play, and I promise you, by the end of the night, you'll be the one begging."

A shiver racked her body. She removed her hands, leaving the skirt in place.

"Now put your hands on the counter."

From polite to demanding. The man sure knew how to do a one-eighty. Body humming with anticipation, she did as he commanded. Turning to face the kitchen counter, she placed her palms on the cool marble surface. For a moment or a millennium, she couldn't tell, she stood like that. Waiting. Every part of her ached for Parker's touch, but it didn't come. What the hell was he doing back there?

Finally, she felt the warmth of his body against her back, the brush of his lips against her ear.

"Why did you come here tonight, Tamsen?"

What? He was asking questions? Now? Why, for crap's sake?

"I...I was worried."

"About me?"

"Of course." Sure, they weren't technically in a relationship, but that didn't mean she didn't care about him. Far more than she should, actually. "I knew even if you hadn't been hurt, you'd be…hurting."

Because he shared with her a little of how hard his job hit him at times. She didn't want him suffering through that alone.

She felt her skirt slowly being pulled up her legs as he gathered the material in his hands.

"Sounds like you care about me, sweetheart."

"I do." Her words turned into a moan when one large palm skimmed up her thigh.

Tamsen cried out when his palm covered her center, pressing against her through her panties.

"And you came to make me feel better?"

His fingers slipped inside the cotton, rubbing her bare flesh, causing her brain to short circuit. All she could do was nod and moan. He kept up the torture until she thought she might pass out.

"Parker! Please!"

His chuckle vibrated against her cheek. "Told you you'd beg."

She'd beg, plead, threaten, anything to get him to get on with it. This slow torture thing was killing her. Thankfully, she didn't have to do any of that. He tugged her panties to the side and then the blunt head of his cock was pressed to her core.

"Ready?"

She loved that he asked, but she was beyond waiting and coming dangerously close to exploding. "Now, Parker!"

He pushed inside, and she almost wept with pleasure. Nothing made her feel as whole, as complete, as having Parker inside her. His hands gripped her hips, protecting them from colliding with the countertop as he set a furious pace. She arched back, meeting him thrust for thrust.

He filled her. Not just physically. Tamsen felt his essences meld into her own. As if for a moment in time they weren't two people, but one. One body, one soul, sharing breath, sharing space in the universe. He surrounded her inside and out. She couldn't tell where he ended and she began. It was such a heavy feeling, and yet she felt as though she was floating among the clouds.

Her heart ached in her chest as this new, unfamiliar emotion overwhelmed her, bringing tears to her eyes. She blinked them back, focusing on the bright burning light Parker was stroking within her. She had no idea what this man was doing to her, but she never wanted it to end. But all things come to an end, and far sooner than she would have liked, she found herself crying out with release. Parker held her tight, following her into bliss just a moment later.

She collapsed against the counter, the marble cooling her overheated skin. Parker's heavy weight pressed against her back, but she didn't care. She loved feeling him. Any of him. All of him. She'd happily take his weight and his burdens if he'd let her. Carry the load. She hadn't intended for this man to mean so much to her, but somehow, at some point, he had.

"I meant it," she whispered. "I do care for you, Parker."

She felt his body tense against hers. Crap. Her mouth had run away without her brain again.

"I don't say that hoping to hear anything back. I know what this is." He never promised her anything, and she wouldn't demand it of him now. That wasn't fair. "But I just wanted to let you know. I care."

He was silent, the only sound the heavy pants of their breathing trying to return to normal. She'd just started to admonish herself for ruining a great thing when his lips pressed against her temple in a soft kiss.

"I care, too," he whispered back.

She had no idea what this meant for them, but for now Parker was safe, they were together, and that was all that mattered.

Chapter Twenty-Two

"Hey, sweetheart."

Tamsen sighed, burrowing deeper into the plush comforter on Parker's bed. His lips grazed her cheek, but when she turned over to snuggle into him, she found the bed empty. Blinking her eyes open, she looked up to see him standing above her. He smiled down at her. That sexy grin ramping up her heart rate, among other areas of her body.

"What are you doing out of bed?"

She preferred him in bed. With her. Naked.

Sadly, he was fully dressed in a loose pair of shorts and a gray T-shirt.

"I'm heading down to the gym. Wanna come?"

The only workout she wanted was a repeat of last night. Sex was far more fun than running to nowhere on a treadmill. Who needed exercise when you could have sexercise?

"I think you've mistaken me for someone who's a morning person. And a workout person." Crooking her finger, she motioned to him. "But come back to bed and I'll forgive you."

He laughed. "Hold that thought. Let me get the daily calisthenics out of the way, then I'll be back up here to show you how fun working out can be."

He placed a knee on the bed, leaning down to cover her mouth with his. After thoroughly kissing her until her toes curled against the soft cotton sheets, he rose, giving her a wink before heading out the bedroom door.

"Make yourself at home. I'll be back up soon," he called over his shoulder.

She heard the front door open and shut. What kind of man turned down morning sex? She sighed. The kind who had a job that demanded he keep in peak shape. Hard to be mad at him when he was only doing what was necessary to make sure he could keep being a hero, pulling people out of burning buildings.

Yesterday's event rose in her mind. The fire. Her worry. The absolute relief that filled her once she saw him unharmed with her own eyes. She'd never known fear like that. Never felt the piercing sting of worrying for a loved one. Her mother died when she was barely more than a toddler. Yes, she missed her, but more the idea of her. She didn't actually remember her mother at all. If she would have lost Parker...

No. She couldn't think of it. Besides, he was fine. She'd made sure to inspect every inch of him. Just to be safe.

Last night had been amazing. Not just the sex, though she was sure they'd set some kind of sex record for most joint orgasms in a single night. She'd admitted to Parker that she cared about him, and he'd returned the sentiment. Were they in a relationship now? Could they be in a relationship?

They were both consenting adults. Navigating a relationship that wouldn't impact their parents' marriage might be tricky. But if there were genuine feelings there, didn't they owe it to themselves to explore it? She knew her father would want her to be happy, same as she wanted for him.

And for the first time in her life, the excitement of the possibility of a future with Parker was overriding her fear of losing him one day. She was still terrified of the possibility, but she finally understood why her dad always said marrying her mother was the best thing he ever did, even after he lost her. Those years they had together were worth more than all the painful ones that followed.

She was getting ahead of herself again. All this needed to be talked out with Parker. The silly man who was currently downstairs pumping iron when he could be pumping her. Oh well, this gave her time to freshen up anyway. She hopped out of bed and headed to the bathroom, deciding against a shower or getting dressed. No sense in either since she planned on sharing a shower with Parker when he got back from his workout. A shower and more.

She grabbed the plush-looking robe hanging on the back of the door and put it on. It swamped her, Parker's scent drifting off the fuzzy terrycloth material. She brought the collar up to her nose and inhaled deeply. Calm settled over her body.

Now that she'd taken care of business and was covered, it was time for coffee. She should probably check her email, too. The manager job at work was being announced today. Day manager wasn't her dream job, but it did come with better pay and a steadier schedule. That would allow her more flexibility to work on her art and hopefully make a bigger dent in her seemingly unending student loan payments.

After starting up the coffee pot, she went on a search for her purse. She found it under the table where she must have flung it after grabbing the condoms. She pulled out her phone only to curse.

"Dammit!"

Dead. And of course her charger was at home.

Phone in hand, she moved around the condo in search of a phone charger. Nothing in the kitchen, living room, or bedroom. She made her way down the hallway, peeking her head into the other rooms. Bathroom, guestroom, bingo! Office. If any place had a charger, this would be it.

The office was decent sized. About the size of her bedroom, but less cramped with stuff. All he had in here was a shelf full of books ranging from comics to non-fiction, some sports equipment in the corner, and a large oak desk set against the far wall. She headed to the desk, pulling the drawers open in her search.

"Crap!"

No cord. But there was a laptop sitting on the desk. She was sure Parker wouldn't mind if she used it to check her email. Patience had never been her strong suit, and she was anxious to hear about the promotion. And he had said to make herself at home.

She pulled out the leather office chair and sat, flipping open the laptop. The screen came to life immediately. She pulled up the Internet browser. The home page opened to his email. She started to move the cursor to the top to log him out when something caught her eye. A subject heading and a name.

Report on Thomas Hayes

Her fingers froze on the track pad. She read it again, but the words didn't change.

Report on Thomas Hayes

Report? On her dad? What did that mean?

Maybe it was another Thomas Hayes. Heart pounding, she moved the cursor back down to click on the email, opening it. Nope, it was definitely about her father. Her eyes scanned the report, stomach clenching with each line she read.

Check everything. I wanna know if he got even so much as a parking ticket.

Dig into his financials, all of them, especially if he has any suspicious insurance policies.

Leave no stone unturned, I want every bit of dirt.

Bile rose in her throat, anger and shame covering every inch of her. Parker had hired some PI to investigate her father: his finances, job history, criminal record, which consisted of a few parking violations and one speeding ticket. Something she could have told him if he asked, but he didn't.

Why?

Suddenly, she felt suffocated. The fluffy, comforting robe she had on now felt like heavy, cold steel covered in thorns. She pushed back from the desk, rushing back to the bedroom, stripping the offending garment from her body as she went. Her clothes were scattered all over Parker's floor. A testament to her foolishness. How could she have slept with a man, cared for this man, when he'd been lying to her the whole time?

He had my father investigated! What about me?

She wasn't sure she wanted to know the answer to that question. Right now, all she wanted to do was get dressed and get out of here before Parker came back.

"Honey, I'm home."

Shit!

The sound of Parker's chuckle and the closing of the door echoed like a doomsday bell in her ears. Quickly, she finished dressing. She reached the hallway, taking a deep breath before lifting her chin high and heading out into the living room to face the lying, sneaky sack of crap.

"Thanks for making coffee." Parker lifted a cup, smiling as she came into the room, but his smile soon dimmed. He placed the mug on the counter and rushed to her. "What's wrong?"

When he reached out to her, she leaped back, practically tripping over her own feet. She couldn't stand his touch right now. Not with the sting of betrayal so fresh.

"Tamsen?"

His brow furrowed, lips turning down as he stared at her, brown eyes filled with concern. Good. His ass better be worried. Her thoughts and emotions were all jumbled up in her head, but she would not break down in front of him. She opened her mouth, but pain choked back the words. Taking a deep breath, she tried again. Her voice came out harsh and scratchy, but she managed to speak the awful truth she'd uncovered.

"Why did you have my father investigated?"

He blinked, silent for a solid minute as her words landed. Recognition finally filled his expression. If she was being hopeful, she'd say there was a tiny bit of guilt in there, too, but she was too heartbroken to have much hope.

"My father, Parker. Why did you have him investigated?"

He crossed his arms over his chest, his voice defensive as he responded, "How do you know about that?"

"Do not answer my question with another question!" Her eyes glossed over, but she blinked back the tears. He didn't deserve her tears. "My phone died so I went looking to see if you had a charger. I saw the computer in your office and thought I could use it to check my email, but it brought up yours and I saw the email from your PI and I—"

She sucked in a shallow breath. Hyperventilating, unable to catch a breath. She could barely control her tears, but not her rambling, and now, not even her breathing.

"Tamsen, breathe."

He placed one large palm on her chest.

"Don't touch me!" she shouted, pulling away. Last night his touch had been the only thing she wanted. It made her feel desired, fulfilled, cared for. Now it was tainted. She glanced up at him, unable to stop the tears this time as they rolled down her cheeks. "How could you, Parker?"

His jaw clenched. He stepped back from her with a pained expression. "I was protecting my mother."

"How?" Protect her from what? He wasn't making sense.

"My mother doesn't have…the best judgment when it comes to the men in her life."

Ouch. Tamsen was offended on behalf of his mother *and* her father.

"My dad treated her like shit, always wanted her to be someone she wasn't, and when she didn't cater to his demands, he left her. Then she started dating these men who told her everything she wanted to hear, but only so they could get access to her bank account. My mom is all about helping people, but sometimes she helps the wrong person."

Umbrage burned in her gut. "And you think my dad is the wrong type of person?"

"No." He ran a hand over his head, tugging at the dark brown strands of hair matted down from his workout. "Men have tried to marry her for her fortune in the past. The last one even got her a month away from the altar before my PI discovered the scam he had planned to take her for half of what she has. I was just making sure your dad… I didn't…I didn't want my mom hurt again."

She got that. She really did, but what she didn't understand was how he could investigate her father without telling anyone. Without telling her. He could have just asked—she would have told him whatever he wanted to know. It wasn't like her dad had any secrets. He wasn't a con man or a secret spy. Her dad was the best man she knew. He took care of her on his own her entire life. He provided for her, read bedtime stories to her. He took a class on menstruation just so he'd have the knowledge to help her when the time came because she didn't have a mom for that kind of stuff.

How could Parker think a man like that would take advantage of anyone? And why the hell didn't he talk to her about his worries? She thought they cared about each other. That they had something real.

Sickness turned her stomach as a thought entered her mind.

"Oh my God, is all this—" She pointed back and forth between them. "Was all this just some way to find out more? Get me in bed, get my defenses down to worm information about my father out of me?"

"How could you even ask that?" He frowned.

Oh, now he was the offended one? No.

"I don't know, Parker. Apparently, I don't know anything about you."

She tried to brush past him, but he grabbed her wrist. Not tightly, and dammit his touch still made her burn. It shouldn't. It should disgust her. But it didn't.

"You know me, Tamsen." He sucked in a sharp breath, his voice soft and censured. "Better than a lot of people."

She glanced up into his golden eyes, taking small solace in the pain she saw there. Good. He *should* feel bad. Because right now her heart felt like it was cracking into a million pieces.

"I thought I did, but now..."

"Seriously?" His eyes hardened. "You go snooping around, find something you don't like, and suddenly I'm the bad guy here?"

She pulled out of his grasp. "I didn't snoop! I told you I was looking for a charger. I opened a browser window and his name popped up right there on the computer screen."

Grabbing her purse, she moved past him, careful not to make any contact with him. If she touched him right now, she'd either kiss him or punch him.

Or both.

She hated that her body still craved him. After what he did, she should hate him.

"Tamsen, please."

She turned at the pleading in his voice.

"I was just trying to protect my mother."

A tiny bit of understanding poked through her cloud of pain and betrayal. She took a small step closer, staring up into the face of a man who just an hour ago she thought she had a real shot at a relationship with.

"You could have asked, Parker. You could have talked to me. I would have told you the truth."

One dark eyebrow rose. "Would you have?"

Her heart broke a little more. Of course he would think she'd lie for her father, not that there was anything to lie about. A sigh escaped her.

"How sad it must be for you to distrust everyone so thoroughly. Not everyone is out to take advantage of people. My dad doesn't give a flying fuck about your mom's money. And I know as his daughter, my word is shit to you—"

"It's not shit, Tamsen, I—"

She held up a hand, stopping whatever he was going to say because she didn't want to hear it. "Some people are good. Some people do love without conditions. My father is one of those people, and if you would have taken the time to get to know him instead of hiring some stranger to dig into his life, you would have seen that."

He had nothing to say to that. Didn't matter, she was done here anyway. Done with this, done with him. She turned to go, but his voice stopped her.

"Tamsen." He hesitated. "You aren't...you won't tell them about this—your dad, my mom? About the..."

She wasn't quite sure if he meant the investigation or their relationship. Check that, *former* relationship. Didn't matter.

"No." The words tore from her throat like glass. "I would never hurt my father like that, or your mother. Because, unlike you, I trust the people in my life to make their own decisions. Good-bye, Parker."

She moved quickly toward the door, wrenching it open and hurrying through.

No promises, no problems.

It was what they agreed on. It was supposed to make this easy, but nothing about this was easy anymore. Because they'd forgotten the biggest P of all. The one that crept up on you, infiltrated every relationship no matter how light and easy you tried to make it. The one universal truth that came up to bite you in the ass when you least expected it.

Pain.

And right now, Tamsen was in more pain than she ever imagined. Her heart felt like it had been dug out of her chest with a dull spoon and stomped on. And she didn't know how she was ever going to feel whole again.

Chapter Twenty-Three

Parker slammed his locker closed. His shift was over, and not for the first time this past week, he wished the chief would let him put in some overtime. But the man was very particular about their twenty-four on, forty-eight off schedule, and overtime was rarely approved. Sucked because Parker could really use the distraction of work to get his mind off the absolute fuck of a mess he'd made with Tamsen.

"Hell, man." Ward grunted, leaning against his own closed locker to his right. "What did the locker ever do to you?"

"Leave him alone," O'Neil said from his other side. "The guy is clearly suffering from being a dumbass."

Parker glared back and forth between his crewmates. "What does that mean?"

O'Neil shrugged, closing his locker so gently it didn't make a sound. "It means you missed pub quiz this week, and not because you were on shift. But someone else was also absent from pub quiz. A certain dark-haired artist who has you spinnin' your wheels lately."

What? He wasn't spinning his wheels. He didn't even know what that meant.

"Since you've been grumpy as shit all shift, I imagine both of your absences weren't from being shacked up together, but due to you both trying to avoid each other. Which means you fucked it up somehow."

"Hey!" He turned to face O'Neil. "Why do you assume I fucked it up? Why couldn't Tamsen have been the offending party?"

"I'll take this one, dude," Ward said from behind him. "Because as accident-prone as she is, the woman is a sweetheart. You, on the other hand, pretend to be this fun-loving guy without a care in the world, but underneath, you're a suspicious bastard."

He whipped around. "Am not."

Ward chuckled. "Are too."

"He's right." O'Neil came around to stand beside Ward. He did not appreciate the way his supposed friends were ganging up on him. "I've worked with you for five years now, and I've never seen you get close to anyone, except Tamsen. Not even us."

He didn't know what to say to that.

"If you don't let people in," O'Neil continued, "you can't get pissed when they decide to leave."

O'Neil's expression darkened. That's when it hit him. His friends were right. If he even had the right to call them friends. He did keep people at arm's length. Sure, he joined in on pub quiz and joked around at the station, but beyond that, he kept things very surface level with...everyone. Everyone except Tamsen. He'd let her in, showed her bits of himself he'd never shared with anyone.

And now she was gone. Because of him. Because he couldn't trust anyone.

Thanks, Dad. Seems you can still fuck up my life without

even being in it.

"Just go apologize, dude." Ward snapped his fingers. "And buy her a present. Women love presents."

"Ward!" Díaz's loud voice called from outside the bunkroom. "Did you leave this charred, encrusted nightmare in the sink?"

"Shiiiiiit." Ward's head tipped back, his eyes rolling to the ceiling.

Parker chuckled. "Yeah, I think I'll take my advice on women from someone who's actually good with them."

"I'm great with women." Ward scowled. "Díaz is not a woman. Well, she is, but she's also a punishment for something I did in a past life, sent here to torture me with her constant disapproval and badgering."

"Wow, didn't realize you believe in reincarnation, Ward. How enlightened," O'Neil said with a small smile.

Ward flipped them both off. "Screw you both."

Parker moved past his friends to the door, more than ready to head home and crash. Maybe he could sleep off this dark ache in his chest that had been haunting him ever since Tamsen stormed out of his place last week.

"See you guys."

They shared a look, like they wanted to say more but didn't. As a fire crew, you got close to the people you worked with, but sharing feelings wasn't really his strong suit. The people he saved needed him to be strong and sure in the face of any crisis, and sometimes it bled over to his personal life. Healthy? Probably not, but it was how he coped.

Parker pushed out of the room to see Díaz leaning against the wall a few feet down. He nodded to her, and she smiled at him before opening her mouth and shouting.

"I swear, Ward if you don't get your ass out here and clean that—"

Ward came storming out of the room, passing a glare to

Díaz as he hurried toward the kitchen. "I'm coming, jeez, Díaz. Don't get your bunk gear in a twist."

"I'm not wearing any bunk gear, but if you don't start cleaning your messes, I'll put itching powder in yours."

She winked at Parker, grinning as she slowly ambled after Ward. Parker shook his head with a laugh. Those two loved to push each other's buttons. Sure, they fought like cats and dogs, but there was playfulness under it.

It reminded him of Tamsen, how she teased him, placing silly bets, her eagerness to explore in the bedroom, or kitchen, or back of an art gallery. Damn, he missed her. This was supposed to be fun and simple. When had it all gotten so complicated?

When you started to care about her and betrayed her trust.

He ignored the annoying voice and headed out of the firehouse to his car. He'd just locked the doors when his phone chimed with a message. Hope rose as he pulled out the phone, but those hopes were dashed when he saw the sender. His mother. He had no idea why he thought it would be Tamsen. She'd made no attempt to contact him over the past week. Just because he was obsessively thinking about her didn't mean she was doing the same.

He read the message. His mother wanted him to come over. But spending time with anyone right now was the last thing he wanted to do. He wanted to crawl into bed and stay there. For a week. But this was his mother. She might need him. So he shot off a text saying he'd be right over.

Ten minutes later, he was pulling up to his mother's house in the Cherry Creek area of Denver. He parked in the driveway at the back of the house and made his way inside, knocking before entering.

"Mother?"

"I'm in the sunroom, darling."

He followed her voice to the side of the house where the

sunroom was located. His mother sat in her favorite chair, reading something on her e-reader. She put the device down as he entered the room, motioning to the chair beside her. A spread of finger sandwiches and fruit was set on the small round table between the two chairs along with a pot of coffee and two cups.

Oh boy. He must be in for it if his mother had her cook whip up conversation food. The last time his mother had a spread like this waiting for him was when she informed him she was engaged. Maybe she called him here to tell him they decided to elope. That would be good. Then he wouldn't have to suffer through an awkward wedding, spending time in the presence of the woman who made him feel things he didn't want to feel.

"This looks lovely, Mother." He bent down to kiss her cheek before taking his spot in the chair next to her. "What's the occasion?" AKA the bomb she was about to drop.

His mother took her time pouring him a cup of coffee and handing it over before answering. "I hear you and Tamsen have had a lovers' quarrel."

He paused with the cup halfway to his mouth, grateful he hadn't taken a sip yet or he would have spewed it all over the sandwiches. Then what would he shove in his mouth to avoid his mother's interrogation?

"I'm sorry?" There were so many things to dissect in what she just said, he didn't know where to start.

"You and Tamsen." Her head tilted to the side slightly. "I've been informed there was some sort of falling out?"

"By who?"

"Thomas. He discussed with me the other day how despondent and upset Tamsen was when she brought him dinner. Poor girl wouldn't tell him a thing, but she clammed right up at the mention of your name. So we assume it was a lovers' spat."

Tamsen hadn't told her dad about the investigation. Of course not. She said she wouldn't, and Parker knew he could trust her. The man who didn't trust anyone knew, without a doubt in his body, he could trust the one woman he'd hurt the most. How was that for irony?

As grateful as he was that she kept quiet, he hated that she was hurting. Hated that it was because of him. Hated this whole mess he'd gotten them into. Still, if she hadn't said anything about them to her father, then how did his mother…

"Just because Tamsen and I had a…" He paused, trying to find the right wording for the implosion of their relationship. "Disagreement doesn't mean we are…we were…we're not…"

"Oh darling, please." She waved a hand in the air, saving him from having to utter the word *lover* to his mother. "You get all moony-eyed any time her name is mentioned, you couldn't keep your eyes off her at the engagement party, and a little birdie at your station said you two have been spending an awful lot of *private* time together."

Who the hell at the station was talking to his mother and why?

"A mother knows when her son is in love."

Parker stiffened in his seat, rearing back as if he'd been hit. "I'm not in…"

His mother waited with a patient expression. The word bounced around in his brain. *Love.* He didn't love Tamsen… did he? She made him laugh, feel happy, cared for. She challenged him, had him opening up and sharing things he never imagined he would. He felt safe around her, safe to be exactly who he was. He didn't feel the need to be the strong protector; he could let out his emotions, trust she wouldn't use them against him.

He hurt without her.

Was this aching, driving need in his chest love?

"Shit."

"There it is." His mother sat back with a smile. "And don't swear, darling."

He nodded, his brain still trying to catch up to the fact that he loved Tamsen. Head over heels, hopelessly in love with Tamsen Hayes. "I screwed up, Mother."

"Most men do, darling, but what did you do specifically?"

He took a deep breath, not looking forward to the disappointment about to come his way, and launched into his explanation. How he hired a PI to dig into Thomas's background, spending time with Tamsen while keeping his investigation a secret—leaving out exactly *how* they spent their time together, some things a son should never share with his mother.

When he got to the end of his explanation, he glanced up at his mother. Her lips were pinched, eyebrows raised and, yup, sure enough there was the disappointment in her eyes, blaring back at him. She placed her coffee cup on the table, shifting in her seat so she faced him. Her hands rested on her crossed knees. They were about to have quite the talk; he was sure of it.

"Parker, I think it's time you and I had a talk."

See.

"I'm going to get back to you hiding something of grave importance from the woman you love, but right now I want to discuss my relationship with Thomas."

Could they not? He really didn't want to. But when he opened his mouth, she held up a hand.

"No, darling. This is the time when you listen. I know relationships are hard. You have to put a lot of faith and trust in someone. You have to be vulnerable. And I realize that's never come easy to you. But I love Thomas. I trust him."

"I know, Mother. But you loved Dad and look what he did. You trusted people before and…" He didn't want to insult his mother. He just wanted her to see. "I was only looking out for you. Trying to protect you."

She shook her head with a soft smile and rose from her seat. "Hold on for one moment."

His mother left the room and came back with a dark folder in her hand. She stopped in front of him, holding it out. Parker hesitated before grabbing the folder.

"What's this?"

"Open it and see."

She retook her seat as he opened the file and started to read.

"A prenup?" He looked up in surprise. It outlined complete protection for his mother. In the event of separation for any reason, Thomas wouldn't get a dime.

"Yes." She gave a slight shake of her head. "And it was all Thomas's idea. I said we didn't need one. I don't believe in going into a marriage already planning for its demise, no matter what statistics say. I believe that love should be jumped into with one's entire being, but Thomas didn't want any doubt as to why he was marrying me. He loves me for me. He doesn't care about my money."

She reached forward, grasping his hand in hers. "Your father and I...our marriage was something we thought we should do. We both came from prominent families, moved in the same circles, got along well enough. It wasn't always terrible with your father, but we didn't support each other, we didn't trust each other, and without trust, there can be no love. I trust Thomas, and he trusts me. I don't regret the mistakes in my past. Life can't exist without pain or we'd never grow."

Then he must be growing a ton, because he'd never been in this much pain in his life. Not when he gave up his music. Not even when his dad left.

"The bad parts of our life only stay with us if we let them. It's time to let go of all that pain and mistrust, darling. And stop sticking your nose in my business. I love you very much, but I am your mother. I know more about the world than you might think."

He was coming to realize that. He was also realizing he'd overstepped his bounds. Tamsen had been right; he should have just asked her about her dad, worked to get to know Thomas more closely. He could have handled this whole situation a lot better if he'd acted with trust instead of fear and suspicion.

He needed to make this right. He needed to apologize. But most importantly, he needed to find some way to show Tamsen he trusted her. That he loved her.

He just hoped it wasn't too late.

Chapter Twenty-Four

"Tamsen," Cora called out from beyond the bedroom door. "Someone is here to see you."

Tamsen put down her brush. She shouldn't be painting right now anyway. The only thing she'd been creating the past week were dark and painful. She bled out on the canvas, and it wasn't pretty. Some people might like that *art is pain* type stuff, but she liked being uplifting with her art, challenging.

The red canvas in front of her slashed with black jagged lines of a woman weeping had been cathartic to get out, but staring at it now…it just made her sad. Not her usual brand. But she hadn't felt like herself since that awful fight with Parker.

After her initial reaction to her discovery, she'd begun to understand he was only trying to protect his mother. She'd do anything to protect her father. Including not revealing what a jackass his future stepson was. She could forgive all that. What she couldn't get past was his lies to her. Everyone had shit from their childhood to get over. But who lived their life so distrustful of other people?

She thought they'd had something together. Sure, it started out all fun and no promises, but it changed. They cared for each other. Or, at least, she thought they had. Maybe she'd been fooling herself. Maybe Parker had said he cared because she did and he didn't want to make it awkward. What the hell did she know? Nothing when it came to that man, it seemed.

She should have stuck to her rule of light and fun. This loss thing sucked. Sure, Parker hadn't died on her, but the hole in her heart was still there. His absence from her life was an ache even if he was still walking around. The pain of knowing they could have had a shot if he'd learn to let go and trust…

She picked up her brush and stabbed another sharp red slash across the chest of the weeping woman before throwing it back down in disgust.

Ugh, she really needed to stop thinking about it. And him.

"Hey, pumpkin."

She swiveled on her stool at the childhood nickname. "Dad? What are you doing here?"

A teeny tiny part of her had been hoping her visitor was Parker, coming to apologize and beg her for another chance. But it had been over a week since she stormed out of his condo. Every day that tiny hope got smaller and smaller.

"I came to talk to you about Parker."

At the mention of the man who wouldn't leave her mind after breaking her heart, she made a low sound deep in her throat.

"And that's my cue. Bye, Mr. Hayes." Cora turned from the open doorway and started down the hall, tossing over her shoulder as she left, "My offer still stands to punch him in the nuts, Tam. Just say the word."

Her awesome friend had been making the tempting offer

all week, ever since she pulled the whole story out of Tamsen after a night of crying and margaritas. As mad as she was at Parker, she didn't want him hurt. She just wished he could see that people actually cared. They could be trusted. Not everyone was playing an angle.

"Oh my." Her father made his way into her bedroom, gaze focused on the canvas behind her. "That's a bit...darker than your usual work."

She felt surrounded in darkness lately. Heartbreak sucked. Screw everyone who said it made for masterpieces. The piece behind her might be full of emotion, but every time she looked at it, all she felt was despair. Art was supposed to be uplifting, healing.

Grabbing the drop cloth by her feet, she tossed it over the canvas. It would smear the still-wet paint, but she didn't care. She'd poured out her sorrow, and she didn't intend to keep the thing around to be reminded. This piece was going straight in the trash the second her dad left.

"Does this new direction in your artwork have anything to do with Parker?"

She tried to relax her clenched jaw. "Why would it?"

Her father gave her a look that said she was full of bull.

"Oh, maybe because every time I've mentioned his name recently, you tense up. Get kind of growly."

"I do not growl!"

"You do, pumpkin. Just a little." He stepped closer, placing a comforting hand on her shoulder. "Or it could be because you had a major fight that ended with you two not speaking to each other anymore?"

Tamsen started, nearly falling off her stool. She glanced up at her father with shock.

"You know? How do you know? What do you know? Oh God, does Victoria know?" She grabbed her father's hand in hers. "Did you two have a fight about it? Is everything okay?

Is the wedding off? Crap, I was afraid of this! You don't need to worry. It was a ridiculous fight about...well, never mind what it was about. It's over now anyway. You don't have to pick sides. I'm fine, Parker's fine, we might not be...friends anymore, but we can be adults about this and—"

"Tamsen." Her father pulled her up into a fierce hug. "It's okay. Vikki and I aren't in an argument. There's no side picking. The wedding is still on. And I can answer all your questions if you'll just sit there and listen. I promise everything is okay."

She didn't see how that was possible, but since she wanted answers, she sat back on her stool and told her mouth now was not the time to ramble.

"Parker came to see me yesterday."

She leaned forward on her seat. "He did? Why? What did he say?"

At her father's amused look, she sat back, miming zipping her lips closed.

"He made a confession."

She sucked in a sharp breath.

"Vikki had him over the day before for a talk. It seems her mother's intuition was correct."

"Correct about what?"

He grabbed the stool on the other side of her easel. Lifting the small wooden articulated drawing figure off, he set it on the floor and brought the stool around to her side. Oh boy, if he was sitting, this was about to be one of *those* conversations. The ones where he told her something she didn't want to hear and she learned some lesson like on those late 1990s TV shows the studios kept making reboots of.

"Vikki suspected there was something more between you and Parker than being friendly."

Oh, they were friendly all right. *Extremely* friendly for a while there. And now...they weren't.

"I thought she was seeing everyone with rose-colored glasses. Kind of how when you're in love, you think everyone else is, too, but she insisted she saw the signs."

Avoiding eye contact, she picked at the dried paint on her hands. "Signs of what?"

"Of a relationship. Between you and Parker."

A heavy sigh filled her chest. The cat was out of the bag. No sense in hiding it anymore. Though having a conversation with her dad about stuff like this was the last thing she wanted to do. She was already mired in anger and misery. Why not let embarrassment and discomfort join in? It was an emotional party no one wanted to be invited to, yet here she was.

"Yes." She finally glanced up to look her dad in the eye. "Parker and I *were* in a relationship, but we're not anymore, and don't worry. I won't let it affect you and Victoria. I will be completely civil at the wedding."

And at Thanksgiving, the holidays, birthdays...oh hell. How was she going to face Parker when even thinking about the man caused her eyes to well and her chest to seize? She didn't do well at hiding emotions. But she'd have to learn. For her dad's sake.

"Oh, pumpkin. I'm not worried about Vikki and me. I'm worried about you."

"I'm fine," she lied.

"Tamsen."

"I am." She would be. Someday. Hopefully soon. "It wasn't even serious anyway, Dad. We were just...having fun."

Probably something she shouldn't admit to her father, but it was better than the alternative: sharing what Parker had done and how he broke her heart.

"So then all this anger and sadness has nothing to do with the end of your relationship and more to do with the PI Parker hired?"

Her head snapped up. How did he know *everything*?

Seriously, did parents have some all-knowing superpower or what?

"How did you know about that?"

"He told me."

A slight breeze could have knocked her over. She blinked, her mouth dropping open, but her brain was unable to form any words. Parker told him?

"When?" See there, that was a question. Okay, it was a word, but her voice went up at the end, so technically it counted as a question.

"Yesterday. He confessed the entire thing. His worry over his mother, hiring a PI, his feelings for you."

Feelings, right. All his feelings for her were in his pants. Otherwise, he wouldn't have let her walk out the other day. He would have apologized at some point in the past week. He would have done *something*, but he hadn't.

He confessed to his mother and to Dad.

Okay, that was one thing. She supposed.

"Dad, I am so sorry." Tears blurred her vision, but she blinked them back. "I didn't know he was doing that until I spotted an email on his computer. I didn't want you to be hurt—"

"So you didn't tell me."

"Yes."

"Just like Parker didn't want his mother hurt, so he checked me out."

"Dad." Anger started to replace the sorrow. "It's not the same thing."

"No, but you were both just looking out for your parents. Both protecting the people you love. I'd say that means your heart and Parker's were in the right place even if the actions weren't."

"But actions matter." She shook her head. "How can you not be upset by this? He paid someone to dig into your life.

He violated your trust."

Bushy graying eyebrows rose as he stared hard. "My trust...or yours?"

"You're the victim here!" Why wasn't he angry? Pissed off? Upset even a little bit?

"That's a little extreme, don't you think? No crime has been committed. Should Parker have asked me about my life instead of paying someone to try and dig up a dirty secret I don't have? Yes. But the boy was only looking out for his mother. She's told me about some men in her past who weren't honorable."

Right. But her father wasn't like that.

"But how could Parker know that?" Her father's words made her realize she'd spoken out loud.

"It still wasn't right."

"No, it wasn't. He sees that now, and he acted like an adult, came and told me everything, and apologized."

Oh goody, her dad got an apology. Guess everything was fine and dandy now. They could all move on and be one big, happy family.

"I'm glad he apologized to you."

His head tilted. "But he didn't to you?"

She scoffed, unsure as to why she was burying her feelings from her dad. She never hid anything from him. Not until she'd met Parker, that was. "Why would he need to apologize to me? You're the one he was investigating."

"Yes." Her father nodded. "And you're the one he was having a relationship with. The one he lied to."

"He didn't lie."

"But he didn't tell you what he was doing. And that hurt."

Damn her dad for always being right and knowing her better than anyone. It was that parental psychic mind vibe thingy. He always knew when she was upset growing up and usually what it was about, too, whether it was a school thing, an art thing, or very rarely, a boy thing.

"This was just supposed to be fun," she whispered softly. "I wasn't supposed to...care about him."

Her dad nodded as if he understood. "The people we care for the most have the power to hurt us the most."

"Well, that sucks."

"It's called love, pumpkin, and yes, it can suck, but it can also be wonderful, amazing, terrifying, and the best thing to ever happen to a person."

Something warm and wet rolled down her cheek, and it took her a minute to realize it was tears. She did love Parker. Somehow, sometime in all their *fun*, she'd fallen for him. She loved his laugh, his smile, his kindness, the way he never backed down from a challenge. Most of all, she loved that he never made her feel bad about being herself. He never once got frustrated with her rambling or told her her dreams of being a full-time artist were unrealistic. But...

"But he doesn't love me."

"How do you know that?"

She sniffled, rubbing her nose with the back of her hand. "He hasn't texted or called. Not once since our fight. And it was a bad one, Dad. I was so angry at him, and he acted like he didn't do anything wrong."

He'd blamed her for snooping, which, okay she had been looking around, but it wasn't like she was looking for something to ruin what they had. That was the very last thing she wanted. And maybe that's what she was truly upset about. Not that Parker investigated her father—which she still thought was a jerk move—but the fact that he didn't understand why it upset her so much. He didn't care how hurt she was.

He didn't trust her.

"People in love often argue, especially when they're hurt and angry. They're all very powerful emotions. What makes it real, makes it last, is if afterward you learn something. Grow from your mistakes and commit to being better."

She supposed that was true and Parker did apologize to her father. But she hadn't heard a peep from him.

"Well, I've learned love sucks. All it does is rip your heart out and make you paint shitty dark emo crap." She winced. "Sorry about swearing."

Her dad gave her a gentle smile. "It's okay, pumpkin. In this case, I'll excuse it, but don't let the loss of something you had stop you from accepting things into your life. I lost your mother, and it almost killed me."

His eyes misted at the mention of her mother. "Dad—"

He held up a hand. "I'm okay. I wasn't for a long time. I put on a brave face, focused all my attention on raising you, thinking I had my one shot at love and I would never get another. And then I met Vikki. She's not a replacement for your mom. No one ever could be. But I love her. What we have is different, but no less powerful."

She didn't want a new love. She wanted Parker. But it seemed he didn't want her. If he did, he would have called her the minute he apologized to her father. His silence spoke volumes.

"Just give Parker a little time."

"Are you reading my mind, Dad?"

He chuckled. "No. But your face is as expressive as your artwork."

Yeah, she'd been told that a time or twenty.

"He'll come around."

"How do you know?"

"It's easier to admit fault to someone you don't love."

She scoffed. "Parker doesn't love me."

Loved having sex with her, yes, cared about her…he said he did. But loved her? No. She doubted that very much. The guy had such high emotional walls around his heart, she doubted anyone could scale them.

"I wouldn't be too sure about that." He shrugged. "But what do I know? I'm just an old romantic with stars in my eyes."

She laughed softly. "Lucky Victoria."

"We're both lucky." He winked, rising from his stool. "And speaking of, I better run off now. We have a dinner date tonight."

She stood and walked into her father's opened arms. Dad hugs were the best. Some of the misery and pain she'd been carrying all week melted away at his tight embrace.

"And, Tamsen," he pulled back slightly to stare down at her, "if Parker is too stubborn to see the treasure right in front of him, that's his loss."

She snorted. "Thanks, Dad."

Between her dad and her friends, she was grateful for the people in her corner. She just wished Parker was there, too.

"I have to go. I'll see you this weekend at the shower, pumpkin."

Her dad kissed her on the forehead and left.

Crap! The shower. She'd totally forgotten. Not *forgotten* forgotten, but it slipped her mind that Parker would be there, too. Would he talk to her? Apologize? Ignore her? She honestly wasn't sure which scenario she most preferred.

Liar.

Okay, so she knew what she wanted.

Him. Just him.

Wasn't that a punch to the gut? She'd finally done it. Gone against her lifelong promise to herself and fallen in love, even knowing the heartbreak that could potentially follow. And look what happened. The second she did, boom! It fell apart. A week ago, she would have chalked this up to her being right. Love just wasn't worth the pain. But now...

Her dad was right. She realized, deep in her soul, she

wouldn't trade her time with Parker for anything. He changed her. For the better. And the disastrous end didn't cancel out all the good they'd shared.

Grabbing a fresh canvas and palette, she shuffled through her paint, picking out the colors that called to her. After an intense few hours of pouring fresh emotion onto canvas, she stood back and admired her new creation. Light blue and purple brushstrokes swirled together on the white canvas, creating an impressionist image of a weeping woman holding a cracked heart in her hands, but this time there was a slight smile on the woman's face and a bravery in her eyes. Because she knew love wouldn't destroy her. The pain was still clear in the colors and lines, but there was also hope and growth radiating off the image.

A soft breath of astonishment left her lips as she glanced at her work. So, this was what people meant when they said pain caused great art. This might be her best piece ever. And yet the one person she wanted to share it with…

A sharp pain dimmed her mood as her mind was once again consumed with thoughts of Parker.

He admitted what he had done to their parents. Apologized to her father. He seemed to be righting his wrongs and yet…he still hadn't spoken to her. She might as well admit it. Parker Kincaid didn't love her. She'd fallen in love with a man who couldn't love her back.

Chapter Twenty-Five

Parker glanced over things one more time. Everyone was here, and everything was ready. So why did it feel like his heart was beating a million miles a minute? He hadn't been this nervous in his entire life. It had to go right, had to. He wasn't sure he'd get another chance, and if he screwed this up…

"Darling." His mother pushed past the dark black curtains separating the back of the art gallery from the front. "Everything is beautiful. Simply perfect. I can't thank you and Tamsen enough for such a wonderful party."

He smiled, kissing his mother's cheek as she came over to his side. "We wanted to make sure it was everything you wanted. Not that I can take much credit. Most of this whole thing was Tamsen's idea."

He swallowed past a lump of worry. "Is she…"

"Yes, darling." She smiled. "She's out there working the room, making sure the food and drinks are circling and everyone is enjoying themselves."

"Good. Good."

"I also noticed her eye wandering from time to time. As if searching for someone who should be out there helping cohost."

"I know." He nodded. He'd come an hour and a half before the party to get some stuff set up then disappeared the second his mother texted that Tamsen was on her way. "But I can't see her until... I don't want to mess this up."

She took his face in her hands and stared into his eyes. "You won't."

He tried to take comfort in his mother's conviction. "And you're sure it's okay? Me doing this at your party? This day is supposed to be about you and Thomas—"

She held her hands up, silencing his protest.

"When Thomas heard your idea, he insisted. Today isn't about the two of us. It's about celebrating love, family, new beginnings. And fresh starts." Her eyes warmed. "I've been waiting for this day for a long time, Parker. I didn't want to push you, but maybe that was a mistake. Perhaps I should have insisted."

Her gaze fell to his side where his Les Paul sat in its stand. He'd pulled it out a few nights after the fight with Tamsen, meaning to throw it down the garbage chute, but instead he'd started playing. In addition to blistering the hell out of his fingertips, playing surfaced a host of emotions he knew he'd been pushing down for years. Tamsen had been right. He never should have given up his music. Yes, it reminded him of his father, and there was pain there, but there was also happiness, joy, and healing.

He was still rusty as hell, but he knew if there was any way for him to get Tamsen back, show her he truly had changed, he'd have to prove it with more than words.

"Thank you, Mom."

He wrapped his arms around her, wondering if he'd ever be too old to gain strength and security from his mother's hug. He hoped not.

"Now," she said, pulling away and pinching him on the chin. "I'm going back out there to make sure everything is ready. Good luck, darling."

He let out a deep breath, flexing his fingers and going over the chords in his head. He was about to make a fool of himself in front of who knew how many people. But it didn't matter. The only thing that mattered was Tamsen. He'd be a fool in front of the entire world if it got her back to him.

Showtime.

• • •

Tamsen smiled and nodded at whatever her father's coworker was saying to her. Honestly, she'd been on autopilot since she arrived an hour before the party to find everything set up and Parker nowhere to be seen.

Where the hell is he?

The champagne was flowing, Ty's hors d'oeuvres were plentiful, the music was at a pleasant decibel, and everyone was having a good time. Except her. Sure, she put on a good face, smiled and laughed when appropriate. After all, she didn't want to ruin the party for her dad and Victoria. But she'd been hoping to see Parker, to talk to him before this whole thing started. See if he felt...anything about what happened, about them.

Face it, he apologized to the wronged party, and he doesn't think that's you.

She bit back a painful sigh, trying to focus on what Mr. Hersner was saying. Something about the weather, she thought. Why did people always talk about the weather? It was there, it happened, look outside. Why the endless need to discuss it as if everyone was an amateur meteorologist?

At least the party would be over in another hour. Then

she could slink back home and drown her disappointment in a tub full of raw cookie dough. Salmonella be damned.

"Attention, everyone!"

Tamsen turned along with the rest of the people in the gallery to face the makeshift small stage that had been set up right in front of the curtain to the back. She'd been happy that Parker, or whoever, had already made sure the area was all set for the small, local college band they hired because she had no desire to go near that back room today.

It was hard enough when she'd worked her gallery shifts this week. She'd had to hold back tears every time she passed though those black curtains. Refraining from cursing when her gaze fell upon the floor where she'd laid out the canvas she and Parker...the one that was rolled up and stashed under her bed because she couldn't stand to look at it, but she couldn't get rid of it, either.

"I want to thank everyone for coming out today to help Victoria and me celebrate our upcoming nuptials." Her father paused while everyone in the room gave a soft round of applause. "Love is a funny thing. We find it, we can lose it, we can find it again, but it often comes to us when we're least expecting it."

Boy, he had that right. They'd specifically promised not to fall in love, but it happened for her anyway. Stupid love.

"Love can make people do some pretty wild things. Like agree to wear a bowtie when you know they make you look like a nerdy professor in a kids' show."

Everyone laughed when her father fussed with the black bowtie around his neck. Victoria kissed his cheek.

"You look absolutely dashing, Thomas."

"Well, it must be true." He glanced out among the crowd. "Because she's always right."

More laughter from the masses. It was all starting to give her a headache to go along with her heartache.

"Now, before we all go back to enjoying this wonderful party, we wanted to thank Tamsen and Parker for bringing this whole thing together in such a beautiful fashion."

She blushed when the attention turned to her, waving awkwardly as the people around praised her. She never liked being the center of attention. Damn Parker for not being here. He could have shouldered some of this. Again, she wondered where the hell he was. It wasn't like him to disappoint his mother. Unless…her breath shuddered at the thought of some fire emergency pulling him away. But, no, surely Victoria would have said something.

"And you all are in for a real treat."

She exhaled as her father brought the attention of the room back to the stage.

"We have a special performance for you tonight."

They did? Who? She didn't remember hiring anyone other than the college kids. Parker must have set something up without talking to her about it. How true to form.

"Friends and family, please welcome to the stage Vikki's son, Parker Kincaid."

Tamsen audibly gasped as the black curtain pulled back and Parker walked through with his guitar strapped to the front of him. What was he doing? Had he been back there the whole time? Was he really going to play? What had changed his mind? Or perhaps—she sucked in a sharp breath—his heart? She had so many questions.

Parker moved to stand next to her father who covered up the mic and whispered something in his ear. Parker's gaze immediately found hers, and her breath stopped. Heart pounding so loud she swore everyone could hear it. She watched as he nodded, eyes still fixed on her. Her dad moved aside while his mother stepped up to say something out of mic range, too. Dang it! What the hell was going on up there? Victoria kissed his cheek then grabbed her dad's hand, and the two of them left the small stage area.

Parker stepped up to the mic, his pallor a bit on the pale side, but his gaze never left her.

"Hi, everyone. Thank you all for coming out to celebrate my mother finding her true love." He cleared his throat. "You know, I always thought that was such a silly notion. True love. I thought it was something people made up to sell movies and diamonds. I never believed it existed until, like Thomas said, it knocked me down when I was least expecting it."

She covered her mouth, holding back a sob. If he was saying what she thought he was saying...

"I never really wanted to fall in love, but it happened, and like most people, I made some mistakes along the way, but I'm trying to own up to them, trying to be better. Because I found someone who makes me want to be the best version of myself I can possibly be. Tamsen, you make me laugh. You're there for me when I need you even without having to say. You taught me that people deserve trust, that taking a leap of faith might be scary, but it's so damn worth it when you're with the right person." His lips curled up in a devilish grin. "You introduced me to new and exciting forms of art."

Heat burned her face, but she couldn't stop the smile on her face.

"So I'm doing something else I'd never thought I'd do. I'm reclaiming another love. I'm going to play a song for you all." His gaze moved around the room to the people gathered there. "And I apologize in advance for it. I'm a little rusty."

A smattering of polite laughter rose a moment before Parker started playing. Tamsen stood stock still, rooted to the spot as she listened to the beautiful song. He didn't sing, simply played the opening chords of a familiar melody. Soon the band behind him joined in, the lead singer taking the mic and softly crooning the sweet love words of the song.

He must have planned this days in advance. So all that

time she thought he was avoiding her, he was really just planning something special. Something that would show her how serious he was. He played his guitar again. For her. No, not for her. He played it to show her that he had changed, that he was opening up.

When the song ended, the crowd roared with claps and cheers. The band accepted their accolades, but Parker placed his guitar on a stand and immediately moved off the stage, through the crowd, his sights set on her. He stopped an arm's length away from her, his gaze wary as he stared at her. Everything in her screamed to grab him and kiss him the way she'd wanted to do for days, but she didn't. He had things to say, and she desperately wanted to hear them.

"Hi."

"Hi yourself," she replied. "You're late."

The corner of his lips ticked up. "Technically, I was here before you. I've just been in the back the whole time."

She nodded. "I wondered who set everything up before I got here."

He took a step closer, until they were inches apart. Everyone had mostly gone back to mingling, but there were a lot of side-eyes focused on them, clearly wanting to get the inside scoop. Having had enough public attention today, she grabbed his hand and headed back behind the black curtain that just minutes ago had haunted her.

Once they were away from prying eyes and ears, she turned to face Parker. It almost hurt to look at his face after she thought she might never have this chance again. This chance to be alone with him. She wanted to say something, but she knew she had to let him start.

"I am so sorry, Tamsen."

That was a good start.

"You played." She couldn't keep the awe out of her voice. He nodded. "You were right. Music is healing, and I forgot that. When my dad left, it was too hard to play without feeling all that pain, so I pushed it aside. I thought if I never acknowledged it, it couldn't hurt me. But the pain was always there. Underneath the surface. Running my life and decisions even if I didn't realize it. I should have reclaimed what I loved for me. I should have trusted myself. My mother. Your father. And you."

He took both of her hands in his. "You were right. I was letting my past color my vision of everyone. I wanted to protect my mother, but she can protect herself, make her own choices. I never should have started that stupid investigation or kept it from you once we…"

"Started having sex?"

"Started falling in love," he corrected.

Oh. Her eyes welled again. Good thing she wore her waterproof mascara today.

"I love you, Tamsen," he said, pulling her closer. "I know we promised to just have fun, but being with you is more than fun. It's everything. And I know I screwed up and I know we have some stuff to work through, but if you could—"

She stopped *his* rambling by throwing her arms around his neck and covering his mouth with hers. Something she'd been dying to do ever since he stepped out from behind the curtains.

A moment later—or maybe an hour, time had no meaning when she was touching Parker—he pulled back with a grin.

"I guess that means you forgive me."

There was that cocky confidence he wore so well. "Oh really? Wanna bet?"

His eyes heated. "Always."

She chuckled. "What are the stakes?"

"If you're right, we go back to my place and you let me worship every inch of you in slow, thorough detail until I convince you otherwise."

She shivered; that sounded amazing. "And if you win?"

"We head back to my place and you let me worship every inch of you in slow, thorough detail."

She threw her head back and laughed. Her heart lighter and freer than it had ever been before.

"I love you, Tamsen," he said softly. "And I want to make all the promises in the world to you."

She placed her forehead against his, brushing her lips against his mouth before speaking. "I love you, too, but…"

She felt him tense beneath her touch. "But what?"

She should feel bad for the slight tremor in his voice, but the man deserved a little payback. Not too much. Grinning, she finished, "But we can't leave the party before it's over. I promised Winston I'd clean up."

Parker laughed. "Okay, I deserved that one. Fine, you win, we'll leave after and head back to my place."

"For the body worship, right?"

He pressed a kiss to her lips. "All night long, sweetheart."

Sounded to her like they both won.

Epilogue

5 months later

Tamsen peeked out from behind the black curtain for the fifth time in the last ten minutes. A soft chuckle sounded from nearby.

"Sure you don't want to go out there yet, sweetheart?"

She shook her head. "It's not time. The show's only been open for half an hour. Usually, I tell the artist to wait at least forty-five minutes. It adds to the air of mystery."

But she'd never been the artist before. She never knew how nerve wracking it was to stand in the back of the gallery, knowing people were just a few steps away looking at your work, judging your work, hopefully buying your work.

Parker's strong, warm arms wrapped around her waist. "It's going to be great."

"Easy for you to say. It's not your soul out there on display for the masses to scorn. Why did I want to do a gallery showing again? Maybe it's not too late to make a career out of the service industry. I've got the day manager job at work.

I could move onto night manager, franchise manager, maybe even buy my own restaurant. I could—"

"Except you don't want to work in restaurants forever," he said, ending her rambling and turning her in his arms so she faced him. "You are an artist. You're meant to create joy, inspire hope, challenge ways of thought. And you're damn good at it."

She smiled. He was right. Working at the restaurant didn't fulfill her the way her art did, the way being with him did. She still couldn't believe how quickly these past five months had flown by. So much had changed. Their parents had gotten married in a beautiful ceremony that left no dry eyes in the venue. She'd moved in with Parker about four months ago. While she missed Cora, she loved that she got to wake up next to the man she loved every day.

Almost every day.

She worried like mad whenever he was on shift, but she knew he was doing important work. Other than her intense anxiety over everyone out there hating her show, things were good.

"Tamsen." Winston poked his head through the curtain. "We're ready for you."

She took a deep breath. "Okay, here goes."

Parker kissed her softly. "It's going to be amazing, sweetheart."

She wished she had his confidence, but she was grateful she had his love and support. She stepped out from behind the curtain, Parker slipping out after her and melding into the mingling crowd. Winston called attention and introduced her, garnering a soft round of applause. And then it was room-circling time.

It did go surprisingly well. Better than she could have hoped for. Her friends were in attendance, including a number of Parker's firefighter buddies. Her dad and Victoria were there with a few friends. Tamsen told Victoria not to make a big deal of this, but she insisted that she knew some art connoisseur who would be absolutely devastated if they weren't on the ground floor on new budding talent.

Everything seemed to be going well, and by the end of the night, every single piece of work had a red sale dot.

"I can't believe it," she said to Parker once they arrived back home. "Every piece sold. Like, every single piece!"

Her cheeks hurt from smiling so much, but she couldn't stop. She'd expected four or five things to sell. Not every. Single. Piece. Even the broken chunks of her chest cast that she'd arranged into a piece called *When Failure Meets Fate*.

"You're amazing, sweetheart. I keep telling you that."

He did, and she usually believed him, but the hallmark of any artist was the self-doubt that came along with creation.

She tossed a smile over her shoulder as they walked down the hallway to their bedroom. The fancy silk dress she wore for tonight's show was nice, but she couldn't wait to get out of it and into some comfy leggings.

She entered the bedroom, smiling at the one piece of work not included in tonight's exhibit. The large passion painting hung on the wall across from the bed.

"I still can't believe you bought that."

He tossed his suit jacket on the chair in the corner. "I wanted to be the first person to have a Tamsen Hayes original."

"I would have just given it to you."

He wagged a finger. "No way. No special treatment just because you love me."

"I do love you." She smiled, stepping closer to him, wrapping her arms around his neck. "You make me happier than I ever thought possible."

He placed his hands on her waist, smiling down at her. "Bet I can make you even happier."

"Oh really? What are the stakes?"

"Same as always."

Since their bets almost always included sex, she nodded.

"Well then, I have to inform you the greatest work of art tonight was you."

She snorted out a laugh. "Cheesy, way too cheesy."

He gave her a mock scowl. "I was going for romantic. Now zip it."

She mimed zipping her lips. Parker nodded, pulling away and moving to his dresser. He shuffled around in the top drawer for a bit before turning and heading back to her, hands behind his back. What had he grabbed out of there? She hoped it was a fun new toy for them to experiment with.

"There's another piece of art tonight, but you didn't make it. It was made a long time ago, and it's been in my family for years. And now I want to give it to you, if you'll have it." He started to go down on one knee, pulling a black box out from behind his back. "If you'll have me."

She gasped. Tears filling her eyes as her heart leaped for joy at what she now knew was coming.

"Tamsen Hayes, you are the most talented, funniest, kindest, most beautiful person I have ever met inside and out, and I want to spend the rest of my life with you. Not just because of who you are, but because of who you make me. You make me want to be the best version of myself. You make me want to try harder, love deeper, and always see the good in those around me. It would make me the happiest person in the universe if you would marry me and let me love you for the rest of our lives."

The beautiful antique ring nestled in the box shined, but nothing could be brighter than her love for this man. She nodded, unable to get the word past her clogged throat.

"That's a yes?"

Finally, she managed to find her voice. "Yes! Yes, of course, I'll marry you."

He stood, lifting her into his arms and spinning them around. Her lips found his, this kiss filled with joy, love, and the salty taste of her happy tears.

"I love you, Tamsen," he said as he laid her on their bed.

"I love you, too."

He grinned. "Hey, do you think we could get a deal if we use the same venue our parents did? Like a family discount or something?"

She smacked his shoulder. "Ew, stop being weird."

He laughed, his chuckles soon turning to moans as she pressed herself against him.

Life had a funny way of bringing people together. She never would have guessed that the handsome firefighter who rescued her all those months ago would turn out to be her stepbrother, turn into her lover, and eventually end up her husband. But, as they said, life was stranger than art. And she, for one, couldn't wait to see the plans life had in store for her and Parker.

As long as they were side by side, with love and trust, she knew life would be beautiful.

Acknowledgments

A huge thanks to my agent Eva Scalzo who always encourages my need to give my side characters a story and said, "the firefighters are getting books right?" All my appreciation to my editor Stacy Abrams, it is an absolute pleasure being one of your authors. Special thanks to Judi, Sunshine, and Wendy for catching all my mistakes and helping to make Parker and Tamsen's story so wonderful! A big thank you to all the staff at Entangled Publishing for all their support and dedication on this book. Smooches and hugs to my kiddos for understanding when mommy needs to work instead of play, and as always, all my love to the guy who reminds me to "try turning it off and back on again" whenever my computer gives me a heart attack. Love ya, babe!

Special Shout out to all my BookTok friends and followers. 2020 was a rough one, but meeting all of you brought me so much joy. Thanks for appreciating my silly, sassy ways.

About the Author

Bestselling author Mariah Ankenman lives in the beautiful Rocky Mountains with her two rambunctious daughters and loving husband who provides ample inspiration for her heart-stopping heroes.

Mariah loves to lose herself in a world of words. Her favorite thing about writing is when she can make someone's day a little brighter with one of her books. To learn more about Mariah and her books, visit her website, www.mariahankenman.com, follow her on social media, or sign up for her newsletter https://bit.ly/31yMv07

Discover more Amara titles...

The Wedding Date Disaster
a novel by Avery Flynn

I can't believe I'm going home to Nebraska for my sister's wedding. I'm gonna need a wingman and a whole lot of vodka for this level of family interaction. At least my bestie agreed he'd help. But instead, his evil twin strolls out of the airport. If you looked up doesn't-deserve-to-be-that-confident, way-too-hot-for-his-own-good billionaire in the dictionary, you'd find Grady Holt. He's awful. Horrible. The worst—even if his butt does look phenomenal in those jeans...

Like a Boss
a novel by Anne Harper

As if it wasn't bad enough that her long-term boyfriend dumped her, Nell Bennett goes viral online for ranting in a restaurant about her perpetually single status. Thankfully a kind and attractive stranger offers to share his table with her...and their sizzling banter leads to a surprising kiss before they part ways. Now her tiny hometown of Arbor Bay is buzzing over their latest Internet celebrity, but Nell's no stranger to attention. Still, even she never expected to show up to work only to discover her brand-new boss is a very familiar face...

Rachel, Out of Office
a novel by Christina Hovland

Single mom Rachel Gibson seriously needs a break, so color her less than thrilled when her ex backs out of taking their twin boys for the summer to his family's lake house. The next two months promise to be jampacked with juggling work, family, and some pesky new feelings for her ex-brother-in-law. Could he be just one more messy complication in the dumpster fire of her life, or is anything possible when she's out of office?

The Burbs and the Bees
a novel by Cathryn Fox

I just inherited an apple orchard — a sentence I never would have imagined saying. The orchard is my chance to prove that I can do more than being a socialite. Also, if I can't tough out one month not only will I lose my self respect, I'll lose my trust fund too. But my hot bee farmer neighbor with the bad attitude and a whole lot of sexy seems hell bent on sending me home. Well screw him.